CAPE REFUGE

Books by Terri Blackstock

Intervention
Double Minds
Soul Restoration
Emerald Windows

Restoration Series
1 | Last Light
2 | Night Light
3 | True Light
4 | Dawn's Light

Cape Refuge Series
1 | Cape Refuge
2 | Southern Storm
3 | River's Edge
4 | Breaker's Reef

Newpointe 911
1 | Private Justice
2 | Shadow of Doubt
3 | Word of Honor
4 | Trial by Fire
5 | Line of Duty

Sun Coast Chronicles
1 | Evidence of Mercy
2 | Justifiable Means
3 | Ulterior Motives
4 | Presumption of Guilt

Second Chances
1 | Never Again Good-bye
2 | When Dreams Cross
3 | Blind Trust
4 | Broken Wings

With Beverly LaHaye
1 | Seasons Under Heaven
2 | Showers in Season
3 | Times and Seasons
4 | Season of Blessing

Novellas
Seaside

Other Books
The Listener
The Gifted
The Heart Reader
of Franklin High
The Gifted Sophomores
Covenant Child
Sweet Delights

CAPE REFUGE

BOOK ONE

Terri Blackstock

ZONDERVAN®

ZONDERVAN.com/
AUTHORTRACKER
follow your favorite authors

ZONDERVAN

Cape Refuge
Copyright © 2002 by Terri Blackstock

This title is also available as a Zondervan ebook.
Visit www.zondervan.com/ebooks.

This title is also available in a Zondervan audio edition.
Visit www.zondervan.fm.

Requests for information should be addressed to:

Zondervan, *Grand Rapids, Michigan 49530*

Library of Congress Cataloging-in-Publication Data

Blackstock, Terri, 1957-
    Cape Refuge / Terri Blackstock.
       p. cm.—(Cape Refuge series ; bk. 1)
    ISBN 978-0-310-23592-7 (softcover)
    1. Bed and breakfast accommodations—Fiction.   2. Children of clergy—Fiction.   3.
Parents—Death—Fiction. 4. Georgia—Fiction.   I. Title.
    PS3552.L34285 C37 2002
    813'.54—dc21
                             2001007242

Published in association with the literary agency of Alive Communications, Inc.,
7680 Goddard Street, Suite 200, Colorado Springs, CO 80920.
www.alivecommunications.com

Interior design: Beth Shagene

Printed in the United States of America

---

12 13 · 48 47 46 45 44 43 42 41 40 39 38 37 36 35 34 33

*This book is lovingly dedicated
to the Nazarene.*

ACKNOWLEDGMENTS

*P*eople often ask me if I base my characters on real people. My answer is usually no. In writing *Cape Refuge,* however, I depart slightly from that policy. Thelma and Wayne Owens are based on two very close friends of mine—Nicki and Dick Benz, who created Buried Treasures Ministry in Jackson, Mississippi. Buried Treasures Ministry got its name when Nicki began visiting the women in the Hinds County Detention Center, and started every meeting by blessing each woman individually, looking into their eyes and telling them that they are God's treasures. These are women who have been treated like trash for much of their lives, and they have treated *themselves* like trash. Many have horrible pasts. Their futures look grim. But the truth of their worth in Jesus Christ brings them to tears. Then they listen to the message that Nicki and the others with Buried Treasures bring to them and their children through Bible studies, parenting classes, a Girl Scout troop, and ongoing ministry when they are released.

But the battle is not easy, and the Enemy fights viciously for them when they are back in the world. In many cases, they are released without enough money to support them for a week, and they return to the boyfriends, families, friends, pimps, and drug dealers who led them down the wrong path. Often, they fall back into their old habits and eventually wind up back in jail.

For this reason, the Lord put the Buried Treasures Home on Nicki and Dick's heart. When it is built, Buried Treasures Home will be a transitional place for women to recover, learn, and begin new lives in Christ for a year or longer. Like Hanover House in this book, it will be a place of refuge. However, the Buried Treasures Home will be a much more structured place where residents can complete their educations, study the Bible extensively, learn to be good parents, develop new careers, and develop the strength in Christ that will enable them to stand against evil when they are on their own. The first home will be in Mississippi, but their dream is to eventually have homes like it all across the country.

Unlike Thelma and Wayne, Nicki and Dick are very much alive, and I have learned much from them about bearing fruit for Christ's kingdom, about loving with Christ's love, and about doing Christ's work.

For more information about this precious ministry, or to contribute to the building of the first Buried Treasures Home, please write to Buried Treasures Home, P. O. Box 497, Clinton, Mississippi 39056–0497.

PREFACE

Cape Refuge is a fictitious island which I set just east of Savannah, Georgia, on the Atlantic Coast. To research it, I spent time on Tybee Island, a lovely little beachside community outside of Savannah. Many of my ideas for life in Cape Refuge came from there.

There's another island just south of Tybee called Little Tybee Island, an uninhabited marshland and wildlife refuge. For this novel, I turned Little Tybee into Cape Refuge, after a few alterations to the terrain and the coastline. I hope the kind people of Georgia's coast will forgive me.

I owe a big thanks to J. R. Roseberry, editor and publisher of the *Tybee News,* for his help in my research.

CAPE REFUGE

1

*T*he air conditioner was broken at City Hall, and the smell of warm salt air drifted through the windows from the beach across the street. Morgan Cleary fanned herself and wished she hadn't dressed up. She might have known that no one else would. The mayor sat in shorts and a T-shirt that advertised his favorite beer. One of the city councilmen wore a Panama hat and flip-flops. Sarah Williford, the newest member of the Cape Refuge City Council, looked as if she'd come in from a day of surfing and hadn't even bothered to stop by the shower. She wore a spandex top that looked like a bathing suit and a pair of cutoff jeans. Her long hair could have used a brush.

The council members sat with relaxed arrogance, rocking back and forth in the executive chairs they'd spent too much money on. Their critics—which included almost everyone in town—thought they should have used that money to fix the potholes in the roads that threaded through the island. But Morgan was glad the council was comfortable. She didn't want them irritable when her parents spoke.

The mayor's nasal drone moved to the next item on the agenda. "I was going to suggest jellyfish warning signs at some of the more popular sites on the beach, but Doc Spencer tells me he ain't seen too many patients from stings in the last week or so—"

"Wait, Fred," Sarah interrupted without the microphone. "Just because they're not stinging this week doesn't mean they won't be stinging next week. My sign shop would give the city a good price on a design for a logo of some kind to put up on *all* the beaches, warning people of possible jellyfish attacks."

"Jellyfish don't attack," the mayor said, his amplified voice giving everyone a start.

"Well, I can see you never got stung by one."

"How you gonna draw a picture of 'em when you can't hardly see 'em?"

Everyone laughed, and Sarah threw back some comment that couldn't be heard over the noise.

Morgan leaned over Jonathan, her husband, and nudged her sister. "Blair, what should we do?" she whispered. "We're coming up on the agenda. Where are Mama and Pop?"

Blair tore her amused eyes from the sight at the front of the room and checked her watch. "Somebody needs to go check on them," she whispered. "Do you believe these people? I'm so proud to have them serving as my elected officials."

"This is a waste of time," Jonathan said. He'd been angry and stewing all day, mostly at Morgan's parents, but also at her. His leather-tanned face was sunburned from the day's fishing, but he was clean and freshly shaven. He hadn't slept much last night, and the fatigue showed in the lines of his face.

"Just wait," she said, stroking his arm. "When Mama and Pop get here, it'll be worth it."

He set his hand over hers—a silent affirmation that he was putting the angry morning behind him—and got to his feet. "I'm going to find them."

"Good idea," Morgan said. "Tell them to hurry."

"They don't need to hurry," Blair whispered. "We've got lots of stuff to cover before they talk about shutting down our bed-and-breakfast. Shoot, there's that stop sign down at Pine and Mimosa. And Goodfellows Grocery has a lightbulb out in their parking lot."

"Now, before we move on," Fred Hutchins, the mayor, said, studying his notes as if broaching a matter of extreme importance, "I'd like to mention that Chief Cade of the Cape Refuge Police Department tells me he has several leads on the person or persons who dumped that pile of gravel in my parking spot."

A chuckle rippled over the room, and the mayor scowled. "The perpetrator will be prosecuted."

Blair spat out her suppressed laughter, and Morgan slapped her arm. "Shhh," Morgan tried not to grin, "you're going to make him mad."

"I'm just picturing a statewide search for the fugitive with the dump truck," Blair said, "on a gravel-dumping spree across the whole state of Georgia."

Morgan saw the mayor's eyes fasten on her, and she punched her sister again. Blair drew in a quick breath and tried to straighten up.

"The Owenses still ain't here?" he asked.

While Morgan glanced back at the door, Blair shot to her feet. "No, Fred, they're not here. Why don't you just move this off the agenda and save it until next week? I'm sure something's come up."

"Maybe they don't intend to come," the mayor said.

"Don't you wish," Blair fired back. "You're threatening to shut down their business. They'll be here, all right."

"Well, I'm tired of waiting," the mayor said into the microphone, causing feedback to squeal across the room. Everybody covered their ears until Jason Manford got down on his knees and fiddled with the knob. "We've moved it down the agenda twice already tonight," the mayor went on. "If we ever want to get out of here, I think we need to start arguin' this right now."

Morgan got up. "Mayor, there must be something wrong. Jonathan went to see if he could find them. Please, if we could just have a few more minutes."

"We're not waitin' any longer. Now if anybody from your camp has somethin' to say . . ."

"What are you gonna do, Mayor?" Blair asked, pushing up her sleeves and shuffling past the knees and feet on her row. "Shut us down without a hearing? That's not even legal. You could find yourself slapped with a lawsuit, and then you wouldn't even have time to worry about jellyfish and gravel. Where would that leave the town?"

She marched defiantly past the standing-room-only crowd against the wall to the microphone at the front of the room.

Morgan got a queasy feeling in her stomach. Blair wasn't the most diplomatic of the Owens family. She was an impatient intellectual who found her greatest fulfillment in the books of the library she ran. People were something of a nuisance to her, and she found their pettiness unforgivable.

Blair set her hands on her hips. "I've been wanting to give you a piece of my mind for a long time now, Fred."

The people erupted into loud chatter, and the mayor banged his gavel to silence them. "As you know, young lady, the city council members and I have agreed that the publicity from the *20/20* show about Hanover House a few months ago brought a whole new element to this town. The show portrayed your folks as willin' to take in any ol' Joe with a past and even exposed some things about one of your current tenants that made the people of this town uncomfortable and afraid. We want to be a family-friendly tourist town, not a refuge for every ex-con with a probation officer. For that reason, we believe Hanover House is a danger to this town and that it's in the city's best interest to close it down under Zoning Ordinance number 503."

Blair waited patiently through the mayor's speech, her arms crossed. "Before we address the absurdity of your pathetic attempts to shut down Hanover House just because my parents refused to help campaign for you—" Cheers rose again, and Blair forged on.

"Maybe I should remind you that Cape Refuge got its name because of the work of the Hanovers who had that bed-and-breakfast before my parents did. It was a refuge for those who were hurting and had no place else to go. I think we have a whole lot more to fear from an ex-con released from jail with a pocketful of change and no prospects for a job or a home, than we do from the ones who have jobs and housing and the support of people who care about them."

Morgan couldn't believe she was hearing these words come out of her sister's mouth. Blair had never sympathized with her parents' calling to help the needy, and she had little to do with the bed-and-breakfast. To hear her talk now, one would think she was on the frontlines in her parents' war against hopelessness.

"Hanover House is one of the oldest homes on this island, and it's part of our heritage," Blair went on. "And I find it real interesting that you'd be all offended by what they do there out in the open, when Betty Jean's *secret* playhouse for men is still operating without a hitch."

Again the crowd roared. Horrified, Morgan stood up. Quickly trying to scoot out of her row, she whispered to those around her, "I'm sorry, I'm so sorry, I didn't know she was going to say that. She didn't mean it, she just says whatever comes to her mind—"

"Incidentally, Fred," Blair shouted, "I've noticed that you don't have any trouble finding a parking spot at *her* place!" Blair added.

The mayor came out of his seat, his mouth hanging open with stunned indignation. Morgan stepped on three feet, trying to get to her sister. She fully expected Fred to find Blair in contempt—if mayors did that sort of thing in city council meetings—and order the Hanover House bulldozed before nightfall.

"She didn't mean that!" Morgan shouted over the crowd, pushing toward the front. "I'm sure she's never seen your car at Betty Jean's, have you, Blair? Mayor, please, if I may say a few words . . ." She finally got to the front, her eyes rebuking Blair.

Blair wouldn't surrender the microphone. "And I might add, Mayor, that your own parents were on this island because of Joe and Miranda Hanover and that bed-and-breakfast. If I remember, your daddy killed a man accidentally and came here to stay while he was awaiting trial."

The veins in Fred's neck protruded, and his face was so red that Morgan feared the top of his head would shoot right off. "My daddy was never convicted!" he shouted. "And if you're suggesting that he was the same type of criminal that flocks to Hanover House, you are *sadly* mistaken!"

Morgan reached for the microphone again, her mind already composing a damage-control speech, but her sister's grip was strong.

"After my parents inherited the bed-and-breakfast from the Hanovers," Blair said, "they continued their policy of never harboring anybody illegally. You know that my father works with these people while they're still in prison, and he only agrees to house the ones he trusts, who are trying to turn their lives around. Hanover House gives those people an opportunity to become good people who can contribute to society . . . unlike some of those serving on our city council."

Again, there was applause and laughter, and Morgan grabbed Blair's arm and covered the microphone. "You're turning this into a joke!" she whispered through her teeth. "Mama and Pop are going to be mortified! You are not helping our cause!"

"I can handle this," Blair said, jerking it back.

Morgan forced herself between Blair and the microphone. "Your honor . . . uh . . . Mr. Mayor . . . council members . . . I am so sorry for my sister's outbursts. Really, I had no idea she would say such things."

Blair stepped to her side, glaring at her as if she'd just betrayed her.

"But I think we've gotten a little off track here. The fact is that Hanover House doesn't *just* house those who've gotten out of jail. It also houses others who have no place to go."

Art Russell grabbed the mayor's microphone, sending feedback reverberating over the room. "I don't think Cape Refuge is very well served by a bunch of people who have no place else to go."

"Well, that's not up to you, is it, Art?" Blair asked, her voice carrying over the speakers.

"If I may," Morgan said, trying to make her soft voice sound steady, "the question here is whether there's something illegal going on at Hanover House. And unless there is, you have no grounds for closing us down."

The crowd applauded again, but Sarah, the swimsuit-clad councilwoman, dragged the microphone across the table. The cord wasn't quite long enough, so she leaned in. "If there aren't any dangerous people staying at the bed-and-breakfast, then how come *20/20* said Gus Hampton served time for armed robbery and didn't even complete his sentence? And how come your husband was at the dock fighting with your parents just this morning, complaining about Hampton? I heard it myself. Jonathan didn't want you working there around Hampton, and he said it loud and clear."

Blair's eyes pierced Morgan. "Why didn't you tell me this?" she whispered.

"It wasn't relevant," Morgan hissed back, "since I didn't think you'd be the one speaking for us."

The council members all came to attention, their rocking stopped, and they waited for an answer. "If there isn't any danger at Hanover House," Sarah repeated, "then how come your own family's fighting over it?"

Blair tried to rally. "Well, Sarah, when Jonathan gets back here, you can ask him. But meanwhile, the question is simple. Do you have the right to shut down Hanover House, and if you do try to close it, are you financially able to handle the lawsuit that's going to be leveled at this town . . . and maybe even at each of you individually?"

"They can't file a lawsuit," Fred said, his face still red.

"Watch us," she bit out. "And the chances of your reelection would be slim at best, since the people of this town love my parents. Most everybody in this town has benefited from their kindness in one way or another."

The crowd applauded again, and cheers and whoops backed up her words. But Morgan realized that it wasn't the cries of the people that would decide the fate of Hanover House. It was those angry members of the city council, sitting there with their hackles up because Blair had insulted them.

"Some call that kindness, others call it naivete," the mayor said. "They'll believe anything anybody tells them. Just because some convict claims he wants to change, doesn't mean he will."

"Thank goodness they believed your daddy," Blair said, "or you might not be sitting on this island in some overpriced chair!"

As the crowd expressed their enjoyment again, Morgan pressed her fingertips against her temples and wondered where her parents were. If they would just rush in right now and take over the microphone, she knew they could turn this around.

While the mayor tried to get control of the crowd again, Morgan looked fully at Blair, pleading for her to surrender the mike and not do any more harm. But Blair's scathing look told Morgan that her sister was in this to the end. The burn scar on the right side of Blair's face was as red as the mayor's face. It always got that way when she was upset, reminding Morgan of her sister's one vulnerability. It was that imperfect half of her face that kept her unmarried and alone—and it had a lot to do with the hair-trigger temper she was displaying now.

"Order, now! Come on, people—*order!*" the mayor bellowed, banging his gavel as if he were hammering a nail.

The sound of sirens rose over the crowd's noise, cutting across the mayor's words and quieting the crowd. Those on the east side of the building, where Morgan and Blair stood, craned their necks to see out the open window, trying to figure out where the fire trucks and police cars were heading. As one after another went by, sirens wailing and lights flashing, Morgan realized that something big must have happened. The island was small, and the sound of sirens was not an everyday occurrence. But now the sound of several at once could not be ignored.

When the front doors of the room swung open, everyone turned expectantly. Police Chief Matthew Cade—whom friends called simply "Cade"—stood scanning the faces, his skin pale against his dark, windblown hair.

His eyes fell on the sisters at the front of the crowd. "Blair, Morgan, I need to see both of you right away."

Morgan's eyes locked with her sister's for a second, terrors storming through her mind.

"What is it, Cade?" Blair asked.

He cleared his throat and swallowed hard. "We need to hurry," he said, then pushed the door open wider and stood beside it, watching them, clearly expecting them to accompany him.

Whatever it was, Morgan realized, he couldn't or wouldn't say it in front of all these people. Something horrible had happened.

Melba Jefferson, their mother's closest friend, stood and touched Morgan's back. "Oh, honey."

Morgan took Blair's hand, and the now-silent crowd parted as they made their way out. Cade escorted them into the fading sunlight and his waiting squad car.

CHAPTER

*J*onathan Cleary pulled his truck onto the gravel driveway at Hanover House and parked in the shade of the wax myrtles that reached up to the cloudless sky. The front door to the big yellow house usually sat open, and from the driveway one could see through the glass storm door into the welcoming front room.

He glanced toward the side of the house, to the three red cedars where Thelma and Wayne always parked their old Buick Regal. It wasn't there now, and neither was the old black pickup that Gus Hampton drove, or the little Honda in which Rick Morrison scooted around town.

He took the porch steps two at a time and rushed through the storm door.

"Thelma! Wayne!" he called as he stepped into the front room. There was no answer, so he went halfway up the staircase and peered up to the second floor. Thelma and Wayne's bedroom looked empty from there.

They were probably already at City Hall, making their speech—undoubtedly glossing over the risks taken in this house each day. He went further up the steps and glanced into his own bedroom. Morgan had left the door open, after he'd asked her repeatedly to keep it closed and locked. He didn't like the idea of his private things being open for anyone to steal. It wasn't as if the tenants around here didn't have clouded histories. At any given time, there was likely to be someone staying here who'd served time for armed robbery. Morgan's trust level in the tenants' "changed lives" bordered on naive. But he supposed she'd come by it honestly. Her parents had spent years instilling that in her.

He closed and locked the bedroom door, then gave a cursory glance around the hallway at the tenants' locked doors. They weren't nearly as trusting of each other as Morgan or her parents were.

He hurried back down the stairs and looked around the phone for a note or message of some kind, but there was none.

He left the house again, this time locking the front door behind him. It was a rule in the house that the last one to leave should lock it, but that rule was seldom enforced even by the Owens themselves. But Jonathan never forgot.

He stepped out onto the porch. From here he could see the beach across the street, with a clear view of Wassaw Sound. Just to the left, the sound opened into the Atlantic. It had always been Jonathan's opinion that Hanover House occupied the best spot on this small barrier island east of Savannah. No wonder the city council wanted to close them down. The council's hope, as far as Jonathan could figure, was that, without tenants, Thelma and Wayne couldn't afford to keep the house. If it ever went on the market, there would be some fierce competition to buy it and turn it into condominiums or a high-priced hotel. As much as Jonathan meant what he'd told Thelma and Wayne this morning about moving, part of him wished he hadn't made that vow. He'd grown to love this huge old house; it had so much more personality than the old two-bedroom home he'd grown up in.

The chairs on the beach that belonged to Hanover House were empty. The tide was low, so the chairs seemed far back from where the waves slapped at the shore, teasing and reaching, then fleeing back out into the Atlantic and chasing back again.

He got into his truck and sat for a moment, thinking. He could drive back to City Hall and see if Thelma and Wayne had made it yet. On the way, he could swing by the dock and see if they had gone by the warehouse where they held church services on Sunday. It would be just like them to find some wayward soul waiting there. They left the door to the building unlocked for that very purpose. Jonathan expected the piano to disappear any day now, along with the carved wooden pulpit that sat at the front of the room.

But you couldn't tell them anything. They were as hardheaded and stubborn as anyone who'd ever put their stamp on this island. And he'd said as much to their faces this morning, in front of God, the breakfast patrons of Crickets who sat listening through screen windows, and his deckhand preparing to take his rig out.

He supposed he owed Thelma and Wayne an apology for the public attack. He should have waited until later when they were alone, but he hadn't wanted to explode in front of Morgan. She had asked him to trust her judgment, and he knew better than to tell her he couldn't. Her faith in their tenants was blinding her to the risks. It was a hard thing to ask a newly married man to stop worrying about his bride's well-being.

He had still been stewing when he'd arrived at the dock that morning and begun preparing his boat for his morning tour. The heat index had already hit record highs, and even at that early hour, humidity rode thick over the Bull River, just a couple of miles from where it joined the Atlantic. A few of the tourists who had hired him to take them saltwater fishing were already waiting near the boat.

He had seen Thelma and Wayne go into Crickets, the hole-in-the-wall restaurant and bar that looked like a rotten screened porch. Crickets did its best business in the early morning or late night hours, when the breeze was cooler as it swept through the place.

Thelma and Wayne often showed up there as the sun came up, hoping to build relationships with the fishermen and dockworkers who took their meals there. Many of them wound up joining the little warehouse church, and some of them became temporary residents of Hanover House.

Jonathan wished his in-laws would just eat breakfast at home with Morgan and stop beating the bushes for ex-cons and strays who had wandered in from nowhere. The sight of them going into Crickets had levered his anger up a notch, so he had decided to confront them right then and there.

He had told his deck hand that he'd be back in a minute, and he'd crossed the pier to the screen door of the old restaurant.

His mother-in-law, dressed in a yellow blouse too bright for this time of morning, was sipping coffee when she spotted him, and her eyes lit up in that way she had, as if he was just the one she'd been waiting to see. But he knew she made everyone feel that way. "Jonathan, have you had breakfast yet? Sit down and let the Colonel fix you some bacon and eggs. Colonel!" she called to the proprietor, "get Jonathan here—"

"I ate," he said, cutting her off.

Wayne grinned up at him. "I swanny, I think he's the only fisherman on this island who gets up and shaves in the morning."

"Oh, hush," Thelma told her husband. "It pays to look nice, doesn't it, Jonathan? And it's good for business. People have more trust in a clean-cut fellow." She reached out for Jonathan's hand. "Come on, honey, sit down and have some coffee."

Jonathan shoved his rough hands through his sandy, wind-blown hair. "I don't want to sit down," he said. "I wanted to talk to you about Gus Hampton. I'm worried about Morgan being in that house alone with him."

Thelma's face twisted in weariness, and she expelled a sigh. "Jonathan, not that again. Gus is a good man, and you don't have to worry about him."

"Are you willing to bet your daughter's life on it?" Jonathan asked her.

She met her husband's eyes, and Wayne got up to face Jonathan. He was a big man, at least as tall as Jonathan, who stood six foot three. "Jonathan, what's the matter with you?" His voice was gruff and way too loud, to compensate for his poor hearing. "Now, I'm proud to call you my son-in-law, and I feel real secure that Morgan has you looking out for her. That's the way it's supposed to be. I know that whatever happens to me, you'll always take care of her. So I don't fault you for your concern. But you knew where she lived and that she helped us at Hanover House before you ever started dating her. You didn't seem to care who lived in our house when you were coming over every night for supper. You got along just fine with everybody then."

"But I see things now that I didn't see then," he said in a low voice, hoping Wayne would take his cue and lower his as well. "And there's something about Gus Hampton that I don't trust."

"Just because he's Jamaican and has an accent—"

"It's not that!" Jonathan said.

"Is it because he's black?" Thelma asked. "Because if it is, Jonathan, I have to say that I'm disappointed in you—"

"No, it's not because he's black! It's because he's as big as a football lineman and sneaks around like a prowler and looks at my wife—"

"Sneaks around?" Wayne boomed. "When does he sneak around?"

"Last night," Jonathan said. "I couldn't sleep. I got up about two-thirty. I was going to go downstairs and read, and here he came up the stairs, walking so quiet you wouldn't have even known he was in the house."

"For heaven's sake," Thelma said. "Jonathan, he was being considerate. Trying not to wake us up!"

"I don't trust him!" he said. "And neither does anybody else on this island, which is exactly why the city council wants to close us down."

"That's not going to happen," Wayne said. "We found out a few things that we're going to bring out tonight at the council meeting, and I guarantee you, those council members will get off our backs."

"What, so you can just keep inviting criminals and rapists and murderers to come and live in the house with my wife?" Now *he* was talking too loudly, and the other patrons were silent, undoubtedly tuning in to every word he and Wayne said.

Thelma sprang out of her seat and grabbed Jonathan by the arm. She was only five feet five, and three inches of that was the curly gray hair that padded her head. But she had a way of making a big man seem small. "Outside, Jonathan," she said through her teeth. "You're about to make me mad."

"*I'm* gonna make *you* mad?" he asked as she escorted him through the screen door. Wayne stalked behind them, his heavy boots clomping on the hollow floor. The door bounced shut behind them.

"Now you look here!" Thelma said, turning him to face her when they were out of earshot of the crowd in Crickets. "We have enough problems in this town with people spreading lies about our tenants and the work we do. But it will not come from our own family. Do you hear me?"

"Why won't you listen to me? I can't sleep nights. I have nightmares about that man hurting Morgan—"

"We can't help your nightmares," Wayne said, loud enough for everyone inside to hear him anyway. Even the tourists waiting at Jonathan's boat seemed to be listening now. "All we can tell you is what we know. I don't invite anybody to live in our house unless I've worked with them for a long time and I know their character."

"Worked with them in jail, you mean!" Jonathan said. "Some of them are con artists. They're going to show you whatever you want to see, if they know you're the one who can get them a job and a place to live when they get out. But what if they're not rehabilitated? What if it's just an act?"

"Jonathan," Thelma said, "those people are saved by the blood of Christ just like you were. Gus Hampton was a drug addict who stole to support his habit, and he's been clean for five years."

"Only because he's been locked up, Thelma." Jonathan shook his head and took a few steps away from her, then turned back. "Are you both telling me that you don't even think it's possible that someone could pull the wool over your eyes? That someone might pretend to have cleaned up his act just to get out of jail?"

"We have to have faith that God will work it all out, Jonathan," Wayne said.

Jonathan's voice rose again. "What if there were clear signs that this guy was bad news? What would it take for you to throw him out?"

"A lot."

"Your daughter's rape? Her murder?"

Thelma grabbed his shoulders and shook him, her eyes flashing lightning. "That will not happen, Jonathan. Do you think you love my daughter more than I do? I have seen that man on his knees, weeping his heart out over gratitude for Christ's redemption," she said. "We would no more throw him out than we would throw *you* out, Jonathan."

"I asked you a question," he bit out. "What would it take?"

Wayne finally stepped between them, as if he feared Thelma might hurt him. "Jonathan, we screen every applicant from the jail who wants to stay in our home very carefully. We don't take all of them. They have to promise a lot of things to stay there. Hours a day of Bible study, a full-time, steady job, work around our house to keep things going, community service, church attendance. They're basically under my thumb while they live there, and you know that I don't let 'em off the hook. Not everybody wants to live by those rules, but Gus did. And he's followed them to a T. He hasn't done anything to deserve your accusations."

"So Morgan doesn't matter?"

"Of course she matters," Wayne bellowed. "If I had an inkling that any of our tenants was going to hurt either of my daughters, they'd be out in a minute."

Jonathan shook away from him and started to his boat. "I get it," he said. "He'll have to hurt somebody before you'll throw him out."

"Jonathan!" Wayne bellowed.

Jonathan swung around. "You people are crazy!" he shouted, not caring anymore who heard. "You think you're brave because you trust people—but you're not brave, you're reckless! And I hope to God that Morgan doesn't have to pay for that!"

He stepped into his boat—only then aware of the gaping tourists watching the drama unfold. He turned back to Thelma and Wayne. "We're moving," he said. "As soon as we can find another place to live, I'm taking my wife and we're moving out."

"Jonathan!" Thelma shouted. "Don't say that. That's her home."

"I mean it!" he yelled. "If you won't do something about it, I will."

He had gone down into his boat's galley then, and Thelma and Wayne had walked over to the warehouse church to lick their wounds.

Jonathan had run that conversation through his mind at least five hundred times today, each time wishing it had turned out better. He should have tried to talk to them in private, should have stayed calm, should have included Morgan in the discussion. As the day wore on, his anger had faded, and remorse had taken its place.

Still, he didn't plan to back down now. He'd made himself clear, and he intended to stick to it. If they didn't ask Gus Hampton to leave Hanover House, then Jonathan would do everything in his power to persuade Morgan to move out and find another job.

He drove around the southernmost point of the island, then up toward the dock at the mouth of Bull River. By now, Thelma and Wayne had probably made it to the meeting and laid all their cards on the table, and the council members were voting to keep Hanover House open and send engraved invitations to the inmates of every jail in Georgia. His in-laws just had that effect on people.

He heard sirens out the window and looked in his rearview mirror for the flashing lights. Some tourist probably had a fender bender. A squad car came up behind him, then whipped past him and hurried off toward the dock.

As the warehouse came into view, he saw that the police cars and fire trucks congregated in the parking lot just outside the building.

In the center of it all sat Thelma and Wayne's twenty-year-old Regal.

Something was wrong.

He started to turn into the gravel parking lot, but a horn and screeching tires made him slam on his brakes. The car passed, and he tried again, stopping his car among the squad cars and fire trucks rumbling out their impatience. Billy Caldwell, one of the rookie cops on the force, broke into a trot and headed toward the warehouse door.

"Billy!" Jonathan called, leaving his car on the street and getting out. The young man turned around.

"What's going on?" Jonathan asked.

Billy looked as if he'd been caught at something. His sunburned face went blank, and he dropped his hands helplessly to his side. His mouth moved as if he couldn't quite get his lips to form the answer.

Jonathan crossed the parking lot and reached him. "Billy, what is it?"

"It's ... Thelma and Wayne," he said. Jonathan stared at him for a moment, trying to make sense of Billy's simple statement. He started toward the door.

"Jonathan, you don't want to go in there," Billy said.

But he had already opened the door and bolted into the big room.

The place had been turned from a place of worship to a crime scene. Four police officers stood taking pictures and dusting the piano and doors for prints, while others spilled out the side door onto the boardwalk that went down to the dock and Crickets.

Joe McCormick, the detective on the police force, stood at the southwest corner of the makeshift chapel. He was sweating and looked shaken. Jonathan started toward him, but Joe saw him and held out a hand to stop him. "Jonathan, this is no place for you right now. Somebody get him out of here."

But Jonathan hurried around the pews, getting closer ...

Between the uniformed legs that blocked his view, a body lay on the floor. He caught a glimpse of the bright yellow sleeve on the small, limp arm ...

"Thelma!" he shouted and bolted forward.

Joe caught him and tried to hold him back. "Jonathan, you can't get any closer. This is a crime scene."

"Let me go!" He wrestled his way out of Joe's grip and pushed someone out of his way. Then he saw them, Thelma and Wayne both, lying lifeless on the bloodstained floor.

His body went limp and he stopped fighting. Billy, the young cop with a more compassionate touch, pulled him back away from the scene and walked him out the side door. He felt dizzy, like he might pass out. His heart seemed inadequate to do its job, and his eyes stung. "How ... how did this happen?" he asked, grabbing Billy's arm. "They were supposed to be at the meeting ... they were on the agenda. . . ." Even as he spoke, he recognized the absurdity of his statement, as if they'd had no right to die when they'd had other commitments.

"*Who did this?*" he screamed. Chess Springer, the old fisherman who had taught him most of what he knew about making a living on the sea, crossed the boardwalk and put his arm around Jonathan's shoulder.

"Come in Crickets and sit down," Chess said in his raspy, smoke-ravaged voice. "I'll get you some water."

Jonathan shook free. "I don't need water, Chess. I need answers!"

The old man rubbed his wizened face. "I saw their car and came over to shoot the breeze," he said. "Found them just like that. Nobody around here heard gunshots or nothing."

"So they were *shot?*" he asked.

"Seems so, though I didn't look too long. I ran to Crickets and called the police."

Jonathan turned back to the scene, his mouth open with the silent wail of gut-wrenching anguish. "My wife. How will I tell my wife?" He brought both hands to his head. "I fought with them this morning! I said things ..."

Horror too deep to voice muted him. Who could have murdered the two kindest people on the island of Cape Refuge? Was it someone they had taken in, a soul so twisted that he would kill the very people who gave him a place to sleep and food to eat, helped him find work, and offered him a reason to live? How many people had they helped over the years? How many lives had they changed? How many hearts had been saved? How much hope had they offered?

And now someone had come in here and murdered them? Cruelly, brutally, cold-bloodedly ... *murdered* them? It didn't make sense.

He stood on the pier, gaping through that door, wondering when they would stop taking pictures and get Thelma and Wayne off the floor. He couldn't let Morgan know until they did. He couldn't let her see them like this.

He heard a new siren coming and the squad car's wheels on the gravel parking lot. He wished they'd turn the noise off before a crowd formed, before Morgan heard it from City Hall.

He wanted to be the one to tell his wife. Just as soon as he could breathe. . . .

But it was too late.

Through the door, he saw Morgan burst through the front entrance of the warehouse. It was clear from her face that she'd already been told. Two cops tried to hold her back, but she was determined to get to Thelma and Wayne.

"No!" she screamed as she saw the policemen clustered near the front of the makeshift sanctuary. "Aw, no!"

Jonathan bolted back into the warehouse, pulled her into his arms, and tried to hold her.

"They can't be dead!" The torment ripped from her chest, shook her body, emptied her. She fell against him, weak and unsteady, just as he'd been moments before. But her need gave him back his strength, and he concentrated that strength on trying to hold her together.

CHAPTER

*B*lair didn't have enough information to accept the deaths as fact. She sat in the front seat of Cade's squad car, staring at a chip on his windshield. He was saying something about the time of death, the murder weapon, the lack of witnesses.

They would know more, he said, when they finished doing the perimeter search for evidence and could examine the bodies.

The thought of her parents lying murdered on the floor of that warehouse short-circuited her mind, and she found herself looking out at the schooners docked at slips nearby, with their masts tall and bare, and scant activity on board some of them. The smell of salt water fish drifted on the warm breeze.

She didn't move, but inside her, emotional troops lined up for battle.

"You okay?" he asked.

The words came soft and unhurried, and she thought of telling Cade that he didn't have to baby-sit her. She just

needed to sit here for a minute. Just needed to get her brain working again.

"You're shaking," he said, and took her hand. "You can't go
in the warehouse . . . but I can take you around to the boardwalk.
Or you can just sit here, or I can take you home. Whatever you
want."

Her mouth was dry, and she found it hard to swallow. His
hand was big and warm over the ice cold of hers. "I don't know
how to do this," she whispered finally.

He didn't ask her what she didn't know how to do. "None
of us does, Blair."

She wished she had her computer with her, that she could
pound on the keys and do a quick search of the Internet and come
up with answers. . . . But she wouldn't even know the questions
until she got out of this car.

She reached for the door handle, and Cade let her hand go
and got out. He came around before she got the door open, and
opened it for her.

She thought of some unnamed killer walking across this
parking lot, going into that building, killing her parents . . . and
rage like a nuclear bomb exploded inside her.

"Cade, why aren't you hunting him down? Why haven't you
caught him?"

"We're trying, Blair. I need to be in there right now, working
the scene."

"Then go," she said through her teeth. "Stop worrying about
me and go. Find him, Cade, before he gets away."

"I'll find him, Blair. You can count on it."

He started into the building but stopped when he saw that
she was following. "Blair, you can't come in here."

She trudged forward until she was face-to-face with him, and
a slow, defiant, desperate agony rose in her chest like a scream.
"Get out of my way, Cade."

He caught her arm. "Blair, you can't. For your own good.
You can see them later, when they've been cleaned up. But right
now—"

She jerked past him and went into the building. An odd thought struck her: she'd never been here when they weren't here too. It was as if the building was an extension of them, a floor built beneath them, walls built around, a roof covering them.

Cade took her arm again. "Blair, please. Don't do this."

"I have to see them," she said, feeling a throbbing beginning in her temple, on the side where the flesh was coarse and scarred.

She heard her sister wailing on the boardwalk outside the door, heard Joe McCormick urging Cade to keep Blair out. But she walked toward them, intent on seeing what some maniac had done to her parents.

Cade took her arm gently, no longer trying to hold her back. His voice broke as he said, "Blair, if you see this, it will be stamped on your mind for the rest of your life. Let me take you outside."

She suddenly went weak, and Cade turned her and walked her to the side door, where Jonathan and Morgan clung together. The room seemed to tip, and shadows shifted on the walls. She was going to faint, she thought. Like some prissy little thing who couldn't stand the sight of blood. . . .

As Cade got her onto the pier and lowered her to a bench, she heard her sister wailing with gut-emptying anguish. She thought of her mother lying on the floor there, with people gawking and probing her. Thelma had a thing about clean clothes. She hated for anyone to see her with a stain. There was bound to be a lot of blood, which meant stains on her mother's clothes and skin. . . . "Their clothes," Blair said to no one in particular. "I have to get them a change of clothes."

She started off the pier and back toward the parking lot, wondering what her mother would want her to bring. "She'll need a dry pair of slacks and a blouse, maybe the pink one, and some clean socks and another pair of shoes . . . underwear too. And a hairbrush . . ."

Someone touched her arm, and she turned. She hadn't known Cade was still with her, but there he was, looking down at her with worried eyes as his hands gripped her shoulders. "Blair, you sure you're all right?"

"I'll be back as soon as I get them, Cade," she whispered.
"Blair."

She swallowed back the panic rising in her throat. "I have to hurry," she said, moving away from him and only then realizing that she had left her car at City Hall.

"They don't need clothes, Blair." His voice was gentle, patient, pulling her back to reality.

She stopped in the parking lot and looked helplessly around. A van with the words WSAV-TV pulled in, and a crew jumped out. The familiar anchor, dressed in a white shirt and tie, with sweat rings under his arms, was trying to hook up his microphone as he headed toward her.

"You can't go in there," Cade said. "It's a crime scene."

"Can you tell us what happened?"

"Not at this time," Cade said, turning Blair back toward the pier.

But Blair resisted. "Don't you take their pictures," she told a man emerging from the truck with a television camera. "Don't you dare. You get back in that van and you leave. Cade, tell them—"

"*Chief* Cade?" the anchor asked. "Chief, could you please confirm the names of the victims? We heard on the scanner that it was Thelma and Wayne Owens."

"Excuse me," he said and firmly escorted Blair away from them.

"Stop them, Cade," she said. "Don't let them put my parents on the news. Not like that."

Cade left her at the bench where she had sat moments before, but she couldn't stay put; she followed him, a few steps behind, as he went through the side door of the warehouse again. Her eyes swept the room—the pews she had squirmed on as a child, writing notes to her sister, then swearing to her father that they were notes on his sermons. Her gaze locked on the piano on which their mother had taught Morgan and her to play. Blair had hated to practice, and eventually Thelma had given up and let her quit. But

Morgan, always the dutiful daughter, had become almost as good at the keyboard as their mother.

Blair wished now that she hadn't quit playing. It had meant so much to her mother for her to learn. She looked at the keys—and at the bare rectangle at the center of the piano above the keys, where an old mirror had once hung, for who knows what reason. Her mother had taken it off when Blair had started to play, because the sight of her own reflection was too distracting to Blair. Mirrors had never been her friends, and her mother had helped her avoid them.

The front door opened, and the Chatham County medical examiner came into the room. She watched as he walked toward the crowd of officers across the room. They stepped away from the body as the man stooped next to them . . .

. . . and as she caught the first glimpse of their lifeless bodies, her stomach lurched. She stumbled to the edge of the boardwalk and threw up into the water.

CHAPTER

Cade wiped the sweat from his brow and tried to remain objective as the medical examiner studied Thelma Owens's wound. Her head rolled back; her chin and neck and chest were covered with blood, and her eyes were open, frozen in some silent horror. He couldn't be emotional now. He had to stay focused.

A metal pin protruded from the back of her neck, straight out her throat. "That's a bulletnose point," Cade said. "From a speargun."

The examiner nodded. "Looks like it. Hit him from the front." He started to turn Wayne over, and Cade turned away. He needed some air, he thought. He walked to the side door, opposite the one where Jonathan, Morgan, and Blair had been sitting, and stepped out onto the wharf.

Billy followed him out. "You okay, Chief?"

"Yeah," he said. "Look, I need to get somebody out to confiscate all the spearguns on the island, so we can determine if they were the murder weapon. There're thirty members in the diving club, including me." He swallowed, tried to steady his breathing. "Only about five who spearfish."

"Know who they are off the top of your head?" Billy asked.

Cade nodded. "I'm one. Also Jonathan, Sam Sullivan, Marty Roberts, and Cliff Cash. There may be others, but those are the ones I know about. Go get Sam, Marty, and Cliff, and collect their spearguns. Treat them as evidence. See if there's blood on any of them, if any are missing, what kind of points they use. Bring those guys to the station for questioning."

"Yes, sir." Billy headed out, and Cade wiped his face on his sleeve. He looked out over the water, trying to think through the men he'd just named. They were all good friends, and two or three times a year they headed down to the Florida Keys and went diving and fishing together. None of those men could have killed Thelma and Wayne.

But it was all he had.

Something clicked against the post beneath his feet, and he looked down through the boards. Something that looked like a brown pole floated in the water there. He got down on his stomach and looked under the wharf.

He recognized it immediately. It wasn't a pole, it was a speargun.

He pulled a handkerchief from his pocket and used it to grab the narrow end of it and pull it out. "McCormick!" he yelled.

Joe came through the door, then froze at the sight of the gun dripping in Cade's hands. "The murder weapon," he said.

"That's it," Cade said and got back up. "It's a Magnum Blue Water." The words lodged in his throat as he realized what that meant. There was only one person he knew who had a Blue Water gun.

"The killer must have panicked and gotten rid of it," Joe said. "May have even had to swim away to avoid being seen."

Cade looked through the door across the building. Blair had bent over the water and was throwing up, and Jonathan had gone to help her.

"I have Billy going to round up everybody who spearfishes," he said. "He's collecting their guns."

"Well, if one of them is missing, we've got our man."

Cade wished he could turn the clock back two hours, when his biggest concern was the car that had been stolen from the Goodfellows parking lot. His mouth was dry, but he managed to get the words out. "I know whose gun this is. I recognize it. I was with him when he bought it."

"Who?" Joe asked.

Cade's eyes were fixed on the three just outside the warehouse. Jonathan had lowered Blair to her knees and was holding her hair back as she retched into the river.

"Cade, tell me whose it is."

Cade tore his eyes from the scene and looked hard at his balding colleague. "This gun belongs to Jonathan Cleary," he said.

C H A P T E R

*J*onathan sat back as Morgan fell to Blair's side and pulled her into a hug. The two women clung to each other.

"Jonathan," a voice called. Jonathan looked up. Cade was standing in the door to the warehouse. "I need to talk to you," Cade said. "You may want to come out front."

"No!" Morgan let go of her sister and looked up at him. "I want to hear. Talk to him right here."

Cade looked down. His black hair flapped in the breeze over a face tight with strain. "I came by Crickets for breakfast this morning after you'd had your fight with Thelma and Wayne. Everybody was talking about it."

Jonathan wished he had the morning to do over. He wished he hadn't left on an angry note, wished he hadn't threatened to take their daughter and leave. . . .

"Were you here this afternoon? Did you come by here before going home?"

"No," he said.

"Did you notice if their car was here then?"

"It wasn't. I looked for it, because I wanted to talk to them. They weren't home, either."

"And did you go straight home when you left your boat?"

"Yes, straight home. I had the meeting to go to, and Morgan was waiting."

Cade looked even more somber than he had when he brought Morgan and Blair here. He set his foot up on the empty bench. Rubbing the sun creases in his face, he said, "Jonathan, where's your speargun?"

Jonathan frowned. This wasn't the time to talk about spearfishing, so he knew that Cade had a purpose for asking. "In the toolshed behind the house," he said. "Why?"

"Because I just found a Magnum Blue Water gun floating in the water on the other side of the warehouse."

"*What?*" Jonathan gasped. "Was that the murder weapon?"

Cade looked down at Blair, who gaped up at him, one side of her face pale, the other dark pink. "Jonathan, let's talk out front," he said.

"Answer him, Cade," Blair said, getting back to her feet. "Were my parents killed with a speargun?"

He rubbed his face and looked away. "They were each hit with a bulletnose point to the neck or throat, which explains why no one heard gunshots."

"The throat?" Morgan choked out. "Oh, dear God . . ."

Jonathan's face twisted, and he took a step toward Cade. "Who besides me has a Blue Water gun?"

Cade shook his head and kept his eyes on Jonathan's face. "You're the only one in our diving group, Jonathan."

Jonathan stood there a moment, staring at his old friend. "There could be others," he said. "Tourists, or someone not in our group. They're not that expensive."

"I'm just asking you where it is," Cade said.

Jonathan let go of Morgan. She looked up at Cade, waiting for the point to his question. Her face was wet, and mascara ran under her eyes. "It's in the storage shed behind the house where

I've always kept it," Jonathan said. "Come with me and I'll show you."

"I'll send McCormick to get it," he said. "Got a key?"

Jonathan nodded and pulled his key chain out. His hands were still trembling as he worked the toolshed key off the chain.

"Tell me about your fight this morning," Cade said.

Jonathan tried to shift gears and think, but the memory crushed him. His mouth trembled with the force of his emotion. "Man, I wish I could take it all back."

"Take what back?" Cade asked.

"The fight. I lost my temper, said things I shouldn't have said. . . . It ended badly. If I'd known it was going to be the last time I saw them . . ."

"What was the fight about, Jonathan?" Blair demanded. "Everybody on this island seems to know but me."

"It was about Gus Hampton. I don't trust him, and I didn't want Morgan around him."

He watched Blair get up, her eyes intense as she grabbed Cade's arm. "Cade, maybe Gus did it. Maybe he's the one. Maybe *he* did this to Mama and Pop." Her voice quivered as her body straightened with purpose. "If he did, so help me, I'll kill him myself. I'm gonna go find out." She started toward the parking lot again.

"Where are you going?" Cade asked.

"To talk to Gus Hampton," she said. The color was starting to return to her face.

"No, you can't go," Cade said. "Blair, you need to stay here."

"Why?" she asked, swinging around. "Am I under arrest?"

"Of course not," he said. "But you're interfering with an investigation. I already have officers looking for Gus. He shouldn't be that hard to find. But when they find him, *they'll* be interviewing him, not you." He caught up to her, touched her shoulder, and leaned down to look into her face. "Blair, I promise you, we're going to find who did this. But you'll have to let us do it, without getting in our way."

"Well, I don't let things rest, Cade," she said.

"I know you don't," he said.

Jonathan put his arm around Morgan. "Cade, I want to see that gun."

"I'm sorry, Jonathan. It's evidence in a homicide case."

"Well, then I'm going with McCormick to show him where mine is. I'll take Morgan with me."

"You can't go, Jonathan," Cade said.

Jonathan gaped at him. "What do you mean, I can't go?"

"I need you here," he said. "We may need to ask you more questions."

"You know where to find me," Jonathan told him. "You can call me at home and ask me."

"Jonathan, you're not going anywhere."

"Why not?" Jonathan asked again. "Cade, what're you saying?"

Cade stood eye to eye with him, unmoving. "I'm saying that if you try to leave, I'll have to arrest you."

He went back into the warehouse, and Jonathan stood there, his mouth open—feeling as if nothing in his world made sense any more.

It wasn't long before McCormick was back at the warehouse with the news. The door to the toolshed was wide open, and Jonathan Cleary's speargun wasn't there.

That wasn't what Cade wanted to hear. He had hoped McCormick would tell him that the gun was right where Jonathan kept it. He'd already heard back from Billy Caldwell, who was at the station with the other three spearfishermen. He'd found each of their guns and brought them in with them. Another officer had checked with every sports store in town. Only one sold spearguns, mostly through catalog orders. He hadn't sold any Blue Water Magnums.

Jonathan's was still the only one they knew of on the island.

"Want me to read him his rights?" McCormick asked.

Cade couldn't conceive of locking up his friend. He tried to think through the possibilities. Someone had taken the gun out of the shed and used it to kill Thelma and Wayne. Then they had left it at the scene so the police would find it. Maybe they wanted it to look like Jonathan had done it.

Or maybe there was someone else on the island who had one, or one of the transient seamen, or a psychotic tourist. . . .

Maybe Jonathan had just misplaced his gun. . . .

Or maybe the most obvious possibility was the truth—that Jonathan had gotten so angry at them that he had acted in a fit of rage, hardly knowing what he was doing. . . .

But Cade had known Jonathan for years, had grown up with him, played baseball and football with him. They had gone to college together, and Cade had been best man in Jonathan's wedding. He knew his friend to be a good person, one who didn't have murder in his heart. Could some set of circumstances have conspired to push Jonathan into a lethal rage?

If there was a possibility, even a remote one, that Jonathan might have done this, Cade had to lock him up. He had no choice.

For the first time since his uncle, the mayor, had appointed him chief of police, he wished he had found another vocation.

"Tell me what to do, and I'll do it," McCormick said.

"I'll take care of it," Cade said. He looked across the warehouse to the open door. Through it, he could see Blair, sitting out on that bench, looking so strong and angry, when inside he knew she was falling apart. And sweet Morgan, still clinging to her husband, shivering from the shock. She would accuse Cade of using Jonathan as a scapegoat. She would claim that he was trying to look effective by making an arrest—any arrest—so the people of the town wouldn't panic. Would she be right?

But Jonathan owned the murder weapon, and he'd had that fight with his in-laws earlier that day. He was a hothead, always had been. He flew off the handle at the slightest thing. Maybe today he'd gotten too angry . . . gone too far . . .

If he could just get Jonathan away from Morgan and Blair, maybe he could soften the blow for them. Maybe Jonathan would come willingly and wouldn't make him cuff him. Or even better, maybe he'd have an explanation for everything, one that made sense and cleared him as a suspect.

He crossed the warehouse, his steps shaking the hardwood floor. Jonathan met his eyes as he stepped outside. "Jonathan, your speargun wasn't in the toolshed."

Jonathan seemed to process that for a moment, and his face changed. "Gus. He ... or any of the other tenants ... could have gotten it out. The key is hanging right there on a hook in the kitchen."

"I have somebody still looking for Gus," he said. "But meanwhile, I'm going to have to take you in."

"Now?"

"Now." Cade looked out over the water. It looked like a storm was brewing in the south, and the water on the river was growing restless. He wished he could get into his boat, ride the river out to the sea, and watch that angry sky open up around him. It would be better to face that storm than the one raging inside him.

Jonathan gaped at him, confused. "Cade, you don't have to take me to the station to talk to me. I don't want to leave my wife right now. She needs me. I have to take her home." He pulled Morgan up and put his arms around her shoulders. "When you get through here, you can come over to Hanover House, and we'll check out the toolshed. If my gun is gone, then that's a crime scene too. There might be evidence there."

"I intend to check out the toolshed," Cade said. "McCormick put one of my men on it. But in the meantime, Jonathan, I got to tell you—you're the prime suspect. And as I see it, I have no choice but to arrest you for the murder of Thelma and Wayne Owens."

"*What?*" Morgan asked, her voice hollow with grief. She was shivering so badly that she needed a blanket. "Cade, you can't!" she cried. "This is crazy."

Jonathan got that wild look in his eyes, the one he used to get when their team was behind. "*My* family has just been gutted, and you're arresting *me?* What are you? *Crazy?*"

"I'm doing my job, Jonathan," Cade said. "You have the right to remain silent—"

"Well, you can do your job on somebody else!"

"You have the right to an attorney . . ." Cade pulled the cuffs off his belt as he spoke, but Jonathan backed away.

"Cade, don't be stupid. People don't take you seriously as it is. They're really going to mock you when they hear about this. They'll ride you out of town."

"Jonathan, I'm asking you to come willingly, without the cuffs. I don't want to make this ugly."

Morgan cried out and clung harder to her husband. "Please, Cade. No! Not now."

Cade had to turn away and look out over that water again. His eyes stung, and a lifetime of history reeled in fast-forward through his mind. His friendship with Jonathan, his affection for Morgan, his love for her parents . . .

And Blair.

He forced himself to look at her. Blair was staring at Jonathan, her face twisted and stunned. "Jonathan, how did your gun kill Mama and Pop?"

"I want to know that too," Jonathan said. "Cade, you're not taking me anywhere. I'm taking my wife home, and I'm going to look in that toolshed, and I'm going to get right in the face of every one of our tenants. I'll see it in their eyes if one of them did this. And when I do, you can arrest me then, because that's when I'll be guilty of murder."

Cade snapped a cuff on Jonathan's wrist. Jonathan tried to pull away from him, but Cade wrestled him to the ground.

Sobbing, Morgan threw herself at Cade. "*What are you doing? Cade, stop it!*"

Cade snapped the other cuff and pulled Jonathan up. He kept the thought of those bleeding bodies at the forefront of his mind as he forced Jonathan across the parking lot and into the back of his squad car.

CHAPTER

*A*n hour later, when he could finally leave the crime scene, Cade pulled away from the warehouse with Jonathan still cuffed in the backseat.

Blair hadn't shed a tear yet. Instead, she stood on the gravel that filled the parking area, between an ambulance and the hearse where her parents' bodies lay, feeling as if she had nothing to do with this scene or this circumstance. She was some detached soul, watching from outside the glass bubble that was her life, filing facts in her mind, filtering them, and coming up with answers.

Only none of them fit. There were more questions for every answer, different answers for every question. It was as if someone had mixed up a couple of intricate jigsaw puzzles and she was trying to fit the wrong pieces into the holes left empty.

Morgan, standing nearby, had a blanket around her now, but she was still shivering so hard that Blair thought she needed medical attention. "He didn't do it," Morgan said as the car pulled out of sight.

"Morgan, we don't know *who* did it."

"My husband did not kill Mama and Pop!" Morgan bit out again.

"He fought with them this morning, Morgan. It was his gun."

Morgan started walking toward Jonathan's truck, which he had left parked haphazardly at the edge of the parking lot. "Where are you going?" Blair asked.

"Away from here," her sister said.

Blair tried to shake herself out of her morbid detachment and think. She had all her faculties—her heart was still beating, her lungs still took in air, her mind still processed the things that were happening. She had to think and act. She had to do what needed to be done. "Don't go home," she said. "You ought to stay away from Hanover House."

"Why?" Morgan turned around. "There are people there who need to know."

"*They* might be the killers!" Blair shouted.

"How can *they* be if Jonathan is?" Morgan screamed back. "Make up your mind, Blair."

"*Somebody* did this, Morgan. We have to be careful. We don't know who it was. Or why."

"We know who it was *not*," Morgan rasped. "It was not Jonathan." She turned around and shook her head, running her fingers through her hair. "I've got to get him out," she said. "I've got to go down there and convince them that he didn't do it. Oh, where are my keys?"

One of the cops who had just come out of the building walked toward her. "Morgan, are you all right?"

She opened the door to Jonathan's truck, and the bell began to ring. Jonathan had left the keys in the ignition.

"Don't let her drive, Doug," Blair said. "She's in no shape to drive."

Morgan was sobbing when she turned back to her sister. "Just tell me one thing, Blair. He's your brother-in-law. You know him. Okay, so you don't get along that well. But you were my maid of honor just a few months ago. You were right there beside me when I married him. How could you give us your blessing and be so happy for us and now turn around and think he could have done this?"

"I didn't think *anybody* could have done this," Blair said. "But somebody did. And the evidence is pointing toward him."

Morgan just shook her head and got into the truck.

Blair stepped up to the window, touched it with her fingertips. "I'll go with you," she said.

But Morgan started the truck and pulled out into the street.

Blair watched her drive away as a smothering sense of aloneness washed over her. Standing here, between the vehicles that held her parents' white-cloaked bodies, she felt like a dot at the center of a massive mountain range, so small and insignificant that some little breeze could blow her off the earth like a flake of dust.

The crowd that had formed outside Crickets couldn't help her now. The police, still working the scene, had other things on their minds. The God to whom her parents had been so devoted seemed distant and far away, too busy with other matters to waste his time with her.

She didn't know what to do or where to go. Taking action seemed as abhorrent as standing idle. But her thoughts were too fragmented, and her organs didn't seem to be working in tandem. Her body was a cage for this tornado that had ravaged her life.

And any moment now, it would all go flying apart.

CHAPTER

7

The Greyhound bus held an odd combi-
nation of smells that made Sadie Caruso feel slightly sick.
The woman behind her had been eating oranges since they
had left Atlanta, and the man next to her who had slept
the whole way snored in her direction, his bad breath
sending up a cloud that was almost visible in the fading
light. The man in front of her had a fierce case of body
odor that spoke of disease and perhaps homelessness, but
she had no room to talk—now, she was just as homeless.

She cradled her left arm across her stomach and
wished she had enough money to spare to buy a bottle of
Tylenol to ease the pain. The bone was broken; she had
no doubt. Her forearm was swollen, discolored and disfigured. But there was nothing she could do about it until
she found safety. For that reason, she kept it under her
shirt. When people saw it, they inevitably gasped in shock
and insisted she get medical help. There would be time for
that later, she told herself. When she had gone as far as

the forty-two-dollar ticket would carry her, then she would see to herself.

Her eyes drifted out the window to the highway, and she scanned the cars, making sure Jack hadn't followed her. She didn't see his car, but that didn't mean he wasn't back there somewhere, waiting to pounce the moment she stepped off the bus. It had happened before. She had once believed she was home free in St. Louis, but he had been standing there just inside the bus station, waiting to descend on her the moment she got off. That time he had broken three ribs and given her a concussion.

She closed her eyes and leaned her head back on the dirty seat. With her right hand, she fished through her bag for a mirror. She couldn't look like a runaway when she got off this bus. She needed to look older, full of purpose, like she knew where she was going, even if she didn't. But the huge black bruise under her eye would attract attention. And the blonde, wispy hair that feathered around her face gave her the look of a fourteen-year-old. That would never do. She would be seventeen next month, but she had to look at least eighteen so she could get a job and support herself while she hid.

With one hand she tried to scrape her hair up into a ponytail, then tried to flip it around so that it looked like some kind of well-planned updo—something a professional woman might wear. Or at least a sorority sister. But Sadie knew better than that. She had never even known a sorority girl. And she wasn't the type to be college-bound, not with a ninth-grade education, a broken arm, and thirty-three dollars to her name.

Abandoning her hair, she threw the mirror back into her backpack and fished around for the thin wallet at the bottom. She opened it, found the picture of little Caleb, only nine months old. In the picture she held, the light hadn't gone out of his eyes just yet, and fragile laughter still rose from that open mouth. His hands were poised as if to clap. He loved to clap.

She closed the wallet and buried it deep beneath her few belongings. She would go back for him soon enough, and then things would change. The bus engine changed its pitch, and she looked out the window again and saw the station up ahead. It was the end of the line, as far east as Greyhound would take her. Savannah, Georgia. Judging from the map on the wall in the Greyhound station, the Atlantic Ocean was just a few miles east from here. Then she would have to decide whether to stay put or go north or south. West was simply too treacherous.

The man next to her grunted awake and turned his smelly mouth away from her. He got out of his seat and she followed, standing in the aisle waiting to get off. Through the window she could see people milling around just outside the station waiting for loved ones ... or not-so-loved ones. She felt alone and cold, but she straightened her shoulders, pulled her bag over her shoulder, and cradled that arm against her stomach.

The passengers began to file off one by one, and as she stepped down onto the hot pavement, she looked around helplessly.

"Hey, baby. Need a ride?"

She turned and saw a scruffy man with dreadlocks, a scraggly beard, and a lusty, amused look in his eyes. She knew that look, and she'd been around enough to know that he was not her answer.

"No," she said, lifting her chin. "I've got it under control."

"'Cause I can fix you up real nice," the man said, "give you a place to stay, even some money. And if you use—"

"I don't use," she snapped back, "and I don't need a place to stay, and I don't need a ride."

She started to go inside but realized that was where Jack had been waiting in the St. Louis station. This time she turned and took off across the street. When she was half a block away, she glanced back over her shoulder. No one had followed her, thankfully, but she wasn't dumb enough to take that for granted. Walking fast, as if she knew exactly where she was headed, she made her way into downtown Savannah.

CHAPTER

*C*ade pulled the squad car into the parking lot in front of the police station, still running murder scenarios through his brain. Someone had thought it through. They had deliberately used a weapon that wouldn't make noise, so they wouldn't draw attention from the people at Crickets or on the dock.

Did that ruin the theory that Jonathan could have lost his temper and acted out of rage?

For the life of him, Cade couldn't conceive of Jonathan *deciding* to kill them, plotting the murders, taking out his speargun, going back to the warehouse, and looking them in the eye. . . .

He had known Jonathan too long. It wasn't like him.

But what if he had had the gun in his car for some reason and in his anger had grabbed it and reacted?

It was a brutal way to die. The spear could kill a large fish at a range of twenty-four feet. When they'd hunted off the Florida Keys, Jonathan had caught a forty-seven-pound amberjack with that gun. At closer range, the point could easily kill a human. But would *Jonathan* do such a thing? Maybe he would scream and yell, maybe even shove Wayne. But raise a speargun to their throats and fire?

No way.

Still, he couldn't base his actions as police chief on gut feelings or on the years of history between him and Jonathan. He had to be objective. And objectively, he knew that the evidence pointed to Jonathan.

"This is just a formality, right?" Jonathan asked from the backseat. "You just want everybody to know you're a big man doing your job, right? You really don't mean to parade me in there in handcuffs and lock me behind bars."

Cade looked over the seat. "Jonathan, what am I supposed to do? It was your gun. There are two people dead on this island. I have no choice."

He slammed out of the car. But before he opened the door to get Jonathan out, Cade stood for a moment on the gravel. Looking back toward the beach across the street, he saw that people had converged—no doubt to talk about what had happened. Word was spreading like a barely controlled fire across the island. There had been two murders. Jonathan Cleary had been arrested. He took a deep breath and opened the back door, helped Jonathan out of the car.

Jonathan met his eyes. "I thought you were my friend."

"I've got to do my job, Jonathan."

"Your job is to find the killer," Jonathan said, "not to go locking up the victims. They were like my own parents, you know." His voice broke off and his mouth trembled. "I loved those people. I *lived* with them."

"But everybody knows about your temper, Jonathan," he said and started toward the door. "Everybody knows that you get raging mad at them sometimes. Until I'm sure what happened, until I sort out what happened with that gun, I've got to bring you in."

Jonathan looked around as if wondering who was witnessing this. Cade didn't even want to know how many across the street were taking pictures, noting every detail for later gossip. He hoped he had done the right thing.

He ushered Jonathan into the small station, converted from an old Laundromat. Three officers sat at their desks in the front room, making the phone calls to track down the information that Cade and Joe McCormick had asked for. The police force was small—only twelve uniformed officers who worked four to a shift, two office workers, three dispatchers (one per shift), and him and McCormick. The twelve lifeguards on the island were under his jurisdiction as well. Under ordinary circumstances, there were no more than five or six people working at the station, but today, all of the uniforms had been called to work to help with this investigation, and the phones were ringing as the cops working the town called in information for Cade and McCormick to process.

Cade put Jonathan in an interview room that had served as a closet in the building's former life. It was only ten by ten, just enough room for a table and a few chairs. Jonathan plopped down, his hands still cuffed.

"You can undo these, Cade. I'm not going to break and run."

Cade leaned toward him and unhooked the handcuffs.

"So much for you blocking for me on the football team," Jonathan said. "When I ran the ball, I always knew you were going to be clearing a path for me. If I'd known someday you'd be arresting me for murder, I wouldn't have saved your life when you were drowning in that lake at scout camp in fifth grade."

"I wasn't drowning," Cade said. "I was faking it. It was a joke."

"It didn't look like a joke," Jonathan said, "when I dragged you out of there and Mr. Martin had to do mouth-to-mouth. And that time I had tickets to the Super Bowl, I wouldn't have taken you."

"That's enough, Jonathan," Cade said quietly. "This is hard for me too. I have a job to do on this island and I intend to do it."

"You have something to prove," Jonathan said, "and you're using me to do it. You want to prove that you're not some lightweight the mayor hired because you were related."

Cade didn't react. He had heard enough of that from every resident of the island who got a ticket or a fine. They all claimed he had gotten the job because his uncle was mayor. No one ever considered the fact that Cade had a degree in criminal justice and ten years on the Savannah police force. At thirty-three, he might be a little young to head up a police force, but he wouldn't have taken the job if he hadn't been qualified.

He started toward the door.

"Where you going?" Jonathan asked. "You're not going to just leave me here, are you?"

"It's your choice," Cade said. "I can leave you here or put you in a cell. I'm just going to get a stenographer, and then we're going to get started answering some questions."

"Fine," Jonathan said, "let's get on with it. I'm ready to get this over and get out of here. My wife needs me. There are two funerals to plan."

Cade stopped at the door and slowly turned back. Jonathan had his hands over his face and was rubbing it roughly. "Those are going to be tough funerals," Cade said, letting out a long, sad sigh as he leaned back against the door casing. "I'm going to figure out who did this, and if it's you, I don't care if we *were* in scouts together. If it's you, Jonathan, I'm going to make sure you pay. And if it's not, you'll go free, and somebody else will fry."

He closed the door and locked it before he lost control of his own emotions. He stood outside it for a moment, swallowing his grief. Then, drawing a long breath, he went out to one of the desks in the front room and picked up the phone. He dialed the stenographer's number, and as the phone rang, he closed his eyes and saw those bodies again. He would see them tonight when he tried to sleep. He imagined he would see them for a long time to come.

After telling the stenographer to come to the station, Cade gathered the information that had come in over the last few minutes. Gus Hampton was still at large; the other tenants were all being questioned at Hanover House; his officers had gotten the manifests of every boat that had come in or gone out from that dock today; they had found two others on the island who owned spearguns; they had done background checks on all of the spearfishermen, and none of them had records.

His mind wandered to the eclectic group of church members who met in the warehouse on Sunday mornings. Many of them *did* have records. Some were drifters, hard to trace.

He rubbed the tense muscles of his neck. What would they do about church services without Thelma and Wayne there to lead things? Would the church just fall apart and scatter? Half the people there would never be welcome at other churches. Some of them were only in town while their boats docked; others hadn't had a bath since they'd gone out to sea. No, they'd never fit in at the other churches in the area.

And what of Hanover House? For so long it had been a fixture on Cape Refuge. Even lately, with the city council threatening to close it down, Cade couldn't picture the island without it. It was why this island was known to be warm and friendly and welcoming, even to the most lost and rootless soul. No—Hanover House wasn't the reason. Thelma and Wayne were the reason.

He got up, telling himself that maybe he should let his old friend go. Maybe he should just tell people he had brought Jonathan in for questioning, then had let him get back to Morgan and Blair to comfort them and do what needed to be done. Cade honestly didn't know the right thing to do.

One of the squad cars pulled up in the parking lot. It was Joe McCormick, his best and only detective. Cade met him at the door.

"Jack wanted me to tell you that the coroner put their time of death at five this afternoon."

"Five," Cade said, raking his hands through his hair. What did that tell him? "Have them check to see what time Jonathan's rig came in."

"I already did, Chief. It came in about four-thirty."

Cade closed his eyes. "He was at the six o'clock meeting tonight. He had showered and shaved. Would he have had time to kill them, shower and shave, and still get to the meeting?"

"Depends," Joe said in a slow southern drawl. "Rage goes fast sometimes. Don't take long to snap. But it seems like somebody would have seen the killer going into the building or coming out. Nobody saw anything."

Cade heard another car in the parking lot and looked out. Melinda Jane, the stenographer, was just pulling in.

"Well, looks like we can get started questioning Jonathan," he said. "Where are the three guys you brought in earlier?"

"The jail was empty, so I put 'em into a cell for now. I have Jim Henry guarding them, with the door open so they can't come back with unlawful imprisonment. We were very clear that we just wanted to question them."

Cade walked to the plateglass window on the front of the building and stared out at the passing traffic.

"You okay, Chief?"

Cade tried to shake off his emotions. He had work to do. "Yeah, I'm fine."

"You want me to do the interview?" Joe asked. "I don't have a history with him. Might be harder for you."

"I'd appreciate that," Cade said. "I'll jump in where I need to."

The door swung open, and Melinda Jane rushed in. "Oh, Cade, it isn't true, is it?" the chubby woman asked. "About Thelma and Wayne? Melba called cryin' so hard I couldn't hardly understand a word. Oh, it's just terrible!"

He swallowed and tried to look unmoved. "Melinda Jane, do you think you can do this objectively and confidentially?"

She dabbed at her eyes and straightened her shift. "Well, yes, of course. I'm a professional, Cade. Are you interrogating the killer?"

"We're interviewing Jonathan Cleary," he said.

"*Jonathan Cleary?* Not Jonathan! Oh, Cade! He's the one fixed my roof last month when it was leakin'. Did it for free, just because I'm a widow and on a tight budget. Well, he wouldn't hurt a fly." She dug into her purse for a tissue, then dabbed at the tears in her eyes. "Oh, that poor man. And Blair and Morgan . . . I just don't know what they're gonna do."

Cade wondered whether Melinda Jane would make it through the interview as he followed her back to where Jonathan waited.

CHAPTER

*M*organ's car seemed to be on automatic pilot. She didn't remember driving to the police station or pulling into the parking spot in front. But here she was, still behind the wheel, trying to direct her thinking, trying to remember . . .

She should have seen something coming. She should have changed just one thing in the afternoon's routine, something, anything—maybe discouraged her parents from leaving the house. She should have sensed the evil waiting. She should have asked more questions about where her parents were going, who they were seeing.

But she had been too self-absorbed, worrying about her fight with Jonathan that morning.

If only she'd paid closer attention.

She thought back a few hours, to the last time she'd seen her parents. They had been in the small office off the kitchen at Hanover House, and she'd been helping them, hurrying to prepare a mailing to the donors who helped support their ministry.

Her father had been stuffing envelopes while Morgan applied the address labels and Thelma stuck on the postage. They had just told her about Jonathan's fight with them that morning.

"I don't want to move," she said. "That's ridiculous. What if he insists on it?"

"Then you'll have to do it," Thelma said. "He's your husband."

"But what if he's wrong?"

"He *is* wrong," Wayne said. "But you've got to keep peace with your husband."

"But if he makes us move out, he's also going to want me to quit working here."

"We'd have to get along without you."

"But what would I do? I don't want to leave, Mama. This is who I am." She stacked the letters she had finished, passed them to Thelma. "It might not matter, anyway. They might close us down tonight."

"Where's your faith, little gal?" Wayne asked her. "The Lord didn't bring us this far to abandon us now."

"Hanover House Ministries was his idea, not ours," Thelma said. "It's been his all along, and he'll take care of it. Those folks at the city council aren't putting one over on God. He's still in control."

"But things do happen, Mama. Sometimes people like that win."

"Well, the Lord would have a purpose for that too. We have to trust him, honey. He does have a plan."

Wayne got up and stretched out his stiffness. "We'd better run if we're going to get these to the post office before it closes. Then we can go by the church for our meeting before we head over to City Hall."

"What meeting?" Morgan asked.

Her mother grabbed her purse off of the hook on the wall. "We'll tell you about it later. We'd better run now. Be praying."

That was it. No good-bye, no farewell hug, no premonition that she would never see them alive again. Now she pressed her forehead against the hot steering wheel, groping for the tissue she had dropped on the seat next to her. She blew her nose, wondering when—and if—there would be an end to these tears.

She had sometimes wondered whether people who died suddenly left clues. Whether there was some subconscious preparation, some hastily scrawled note, a conversation that, when remembered, gave peace and comfort to those left behind.

But there had been nothing like that this morning. Just another few moments in their busy lives, a frustrated exchange, a rushing out the door.

And there was so much unfinished business. Didn't God know that? Didn't he understand?

She forced herself out of the car. Wiping her face, she tried to summon some strength, but she found she was still shaking. If she could just get Jonathan released, she could lean on him—and then she could fall apart, knowing that he would be there to help gather the scattered pieces.

She stepped in the front door and felt the whish of air-conditioning blowing her hair back from her face. She didn't know why they kept it so cold in here. It wasn't as if the police department on Cape Refuge had that much to do. There weren't car chases, foot pursuits, or adrenaline jolts keeping them hot. Not until today.

The few other times she had come in here she had seen police officers with feet propped up on their desks, reading the newspaper. Today, however, every police officer on the island had been called in, and she knew that most of them were working the scene. This would go down as one of the busiest days in Cape Refuge police history.

The day Thelma and Wayne Owens were murdered.

She imagined the residents using this day as a marker. *Where were you when you heard about the murders?* They would each have their own story. The trauma would spread over the island and linger for years.

Her parents never did anything small.

She swallowed a lump in her throat and let the glass door close behind her. She saw Cade standing over a fax machine.

"Where's my husband?" she demanded.

He looked up at her, and she saw the strain on his face. "We're about to question him," Cade said. "You can't go in."

"This is cruel!" she managed to say. "They're my parents, Cade. He is my husband. Why in the world would he want to kill them? You're wasting time when you could be out there looking for the person who did it."

His face changed, and for a moment he was the man who sat on the second row, middle pew, every Sunday, sometimes shedding tears as he praised the Lord. "Morgan, I wouldn't do anything to hurt you for the world. I loved your parents too. You know that."

"Then let their son-in-law go!" she said, surprised at the volume and force behind her words. "Let him out so he can help me get through this. Don't you understand? I'm afraid to go home. I don't think I can do this alone." She covered her mouth and collapsed into a chair. "I'm afraid to do anything, Cade. What if they're after me too? And Blair? What if they're after Jonathan and he's sitting in there like a target?"

"He's not a target," Cade said. "There's nobody in here but us."

"And that's supposed to make me feel better?" Morgan asked. "Who's in there with him?"

"Joe McCormick," he said.

"I went to high school with Joe McCormick," she said. "He has more skeletons in his closet than the tenants at Hanover House. Why does he have the right and I don't?"

"He's got the right because he's a police officer," Cade said calmly. "Morgan, you can sit here and wait. I'll get you something to drink. You can put your feet up."

"Don't coddle me," she bit out. "I have things to do. My parents are dead." Her voice broke off, and grief assaulted her again. She hated to cry in front of other people.

Cade reached out to comfort her. She shook him off.

"Morgan," he said in a quiet voice. "I can promise you we won't hold him any longer than we have to. It made me sick to my stomach when I had to put those cuffs on him. He's the last person in the world I'd want to arrest. But there are two people I cared a lot about who are dead, and somebody murdered them. And he had a fight with them this morning . . . a real public fight. It was his gun that killed them. Can you explain that?"

"No, I can't explain it," she cried. "I can't explain anything. My head feels like it's just been clobbered with a baseball bat. You want me to explain things? Then let me explain what it feels like to know that my parents were the two most cherished people on this island, that they did something for just about everybody who lives here. People loved them. And I can't imagine why anyone would want to see them dead."

Cade straightened up, raked his fingers through his hair. He seemed to struggle with his own pain. Then that hard, professional look returned to his face. He went to the watercooler, got her a cone-shaped cup of water, and brought it back to her.

Staring down at it, she said, "I want to see my husband, Cade."

"Later, Morgan. But I can't let you right now." He backed away and started toward the interview room, which she knew was a converted broom closet. No two-way mirrors, no hidden microphones. This was definitely a no-frills police department. How would they ever be able to find the real killer?

When Cade opened the door, Morgan saw her husband sitting behind the table, hands over his face. Joe McCormick stood in front of him, foot propped on a chair like some television cop.

Jonathan caught her eye and got up. "Honey, are you okay?" he called.

"I'm fine. Just go ahead. Answer their stupid questions so you can get out of here."

The door closed behind Cade, and Morgan sank back into her chair. Anguish overtook her as she recalled the sight of her parents, covered with white sheets, being carried out to the hearse.

People had warned them to be more careful in their ministry, but they had always been completely sold out to Christ, going where others feared to go, loving those who were patently unlovable.

In God I have put my trust, they'd always quoted. *I shall not be afraid. What can man do to me?*

Yet man had killed them . . . brutally, horribly . . .

She grabbed two Kleenexes from a box on someone's desk, wadded them, and pressed them against her eyes. *Where are you, God?*

The question drilled through her soul, leaving a void that she doubted would ever be filled again.

CHAPTER

Sadie made her way up West Oglethorpe, then crossed the street at Montgomery, and walked the block to Liberty Square. It was a charming little park in the middle of the city, one with a statue of someone she didn't know in the center of it, and little park benches placed here and there under massive oaks. She smiled in spite of herself. It was just as she had pictured it.

She adjusted her backpack and headed up West York Street past a parking garage and groomed strips of grass until she reached another park. She had heard that Savannah had been designed and built around parks, each representing some famous part of their history. She had always wanted to visit this city and see for herself, but today she was tired and hungry. She could come back and see it another day. Right now she had to find a place to stay before dark. On thirty-three dollars, it wouldn't be easy.

She saw a diner across from Telfair Square and started toward it. She hadn't eaten since yesterday, before Jack had come home and blown a gasket. She had wound up spending the night in her neighbor's car, hunkered down so he couldn't find her. This morning there hadn't been time to eat. She shoved back her blonde hair and went into the old diner.

She took a stool at the bar and set her backpack down on the one next to her.

"Can I help you, honey?"

A waitress stood across the bar from her. The woman's blonde hair was a little too teased, and she desperately needed to have her roots done. But she had kind eyes even if they were caked with eyeliner and half a tube of mascara. Her lips were red and outlined a little bigger than they really were. Her fingernails, tapping nervously on the Formica countertop, were painted bright red too, with little stars embedded in the center of each. She popped on a piece of gum. "Want to hear the special?"

Sadie shook her head and absently brought her right hand to cradle her left, still tucked under her shirt.

"I'd just like a hamburger," she said, "and a glass of water."

The waitress pulled the pencil from its place over her ear and, chomping on her gum, wrote on a slip of paper as if she couldn't remember the order. "Anything else, honey? A piece of pie maybe?"

"No, thank you," she said.

The woman went on her way and in a few moments came back with a plate bearing an open hamburger and a tall glass of water.

She set the check down next to the plate. Sadie picked it up. "I'll pay now, if that's all right," she said.

"Sure, honey. I'll take it."

Awkwardly, Sadie reached into her backpack with that one good hand and groped around until she came to her wallet again. She pulled out a five-dollar bill and laid it on the counter.

"Who won?" the waitress asked. "If you don't mind my asking."

Sadie glanced up at her. "Won what?"

"The fight you were in, honey." The waitress leaned down conspiratorially on the counter. "That's an impressive-looking shiner,

if you don't mind my saying so. And it looks like your arm might be
even worse. So who won?"

Sadie lowered her gaze to the countertop. "I fell," she said.

"Fell." The waitress laughed. "Yeah, I've heard that before.
Said it myself." Again she bent across the counter and whispered.
"Never met a girl yet who fell on her eye. So what's the matter
with the arm? Is it broke?"

Sadie cradled it again. "I don't know," she said. "I don't
think so. Probably just bruised." She knew better. She could see
where the bone had separated, and the pain had been unbearable
all night and most of the day.

The waitress came around the counter. "Let me see, hon,"
she said.

"I'm okay," Sadie said. "Really."

The waitress drew a deep, laborious sigh, then straightened up.
"Okay, I got you. All you have to say is, 'Tammy, mind your own
business.' They say it around here all the time. Never hurt me yet."

Sadie smiled.

"Eat your hamburger," the woman said, "and if you're still
hungry after, I'll throw in a piece of pie, no charge."

Sadie watched her as she pranced away, her too-tight waitress uniform straining to cover her hips. Sadie devoured the hamburger and felt the energy seeping back into her.

Tammy put a piece of pie in front of her as the door jingled.
Still on the alert for Jack, Sadie glanced back. It was the man with
the dreadlocks who had been waiting at the bus station, the one
who had offered her money and a place to live. He spotted Sadie
and smiled. She hadn't seen him following her from the bus station, but surely it was no coincidence that he had shown up here.
She quickly turned away, but he came and took the stool next to
her backpack.

"You again," he said with a smile. "Thought you said you
had a ride and a place to stay."

She tried to ignore him and turned her body away. Tammy
was there in a moment, popping on her gum and pulling that pencil out from behind her ear.

"May I help you?"

"Just coffee," he said, then he turned back to Sadie. "You don't have to be afraid of me, you know. I saw you get off that bus and look around like you didn't know a soul in town. And you wouldn't be eating in a diner if you had any place to go."

"Slick, you're not trying to bother my cousin, are you?" Tammy asked, leaning on the counter. "Because I get real protective when men come around here hitting on her."

He looked up at her, surprised. "Your cousin?"

"Yeah, my cousin," she said. "You got a problem with that?"

He looked slowly from Tammy to Sadie a time or two, then got back to his feet. "Cancel the coffee," he said. He strolled to the door, glancing one last time at Sadie as he started out.

"Come again," Tammy shouted cheerfully across the room.

Sadie grinned up at her when he was gone. "Thank you. I appreciate it. I don't know him, and he keeps trying to get me to go home with him."

"He wants you to do more than go home with him," Tammy said. "He wants to put you to work. He spends a lot of time over at the bus station waiting for runaways. You ain't a runaway, are you?"

Sadie shook her head hard. "No. Of course not. I'm eighteen. I can go anywhere I want."

Tammy nodded. "Eighteen, huh? Yeah, and I'm twenty-two."

The woman was at least thirty-five.

"Eat your pie," she said. "It's on me."

"I can pay," Sadie said.

"I know you can, honey, but if my intuition is telling me right, you need to keep every penny you got. Just accept it as a goodwill offering welcoming you to the big city of Savannah."

Sadie buried her fork into it. "I'm actually not staying here," she said. "It's just as far as Greyhound would take me. I'm headed east."

Tammy laughed. "Well, not far east. Tybee Island is only fifteen minutes away, and then you're right smack-dab at the Atlantic Ocean. No farther east to go unless you get on a boat or swim. Few minutes south of that and you're on Cape Refuge."

"Cape Refuge?" Sadie asked. The name sounded inviting. "How do you get there?"

"Out Highway 80," she said, "on the Island Expressway. It takes you to the bridge that goes to the Cape."

Sadie had pictured herself at the Atlantic Ocean, sleeping on the beach where no one would bother her, listening to the sound of the waves against the shore. She had only seen that on television, had never experienced it for herself. It sounded romantic and hopeful. How could anyone ever be unsafe on a peaceful beach? And in a beach town she could probably find a job working in a restaurant or a deli or in a souvenir shop of some kind. No high school diploma needed. No college degree.

"Honey, level with me," Tammy said, meeting her eyes across the counter. "It's one thing to lie to old Dreadlocks about having a place to stay, but give it to me straight. You're on your own, aren't you? You don't know the slightest soul here, do you?"

Sadie averted her eyes again.

"That's what I thought," Tammy said. She pulled out her writing pad, jotted something down, then tore off the page and handed it to Sadie.

Sadie looked at the piece of paper Tammy had given her. "'Thelma and Wayne Owens,'" she read aloud. "'Hanover House.' Who're these people?"

"People who'll take you in," Tammy said. "They're known around this area for collecting strays, if you know what I mean."

Sadie didn't like the sound of that. She wasn't a stray. She had a purpose, even though she didn't know what it was.

"They put people up all the time. Mostly, they take people just out of jail, who don't have jobs or places to live, and they help them get on their feet. They have this real cute little bed-and-breakfast on the island. They'll take you in, all right, if you can get there. And let me tell you something. You could do worse than hooking up with Thelma and Wayne Owens and sleeping in that precious place."

Sadie sat straighter. "But I don't have enough money for a bed-and-breakfast."

"You find Thelma and Wayne and you don't have to worry about the money, at least not for a while. They'll give you time to get a job and get set up. Yes, sir, if I had just blown into town on a Greyhound bus, that's the first place I'd go."

Sadie felt a faint sense of hope. "Okay," she said, "I'll look into it. Thanks."

She finished the pie, then got to her feet and slid the backpack onto one shoulder. Reluctantly, she started out of the diner, wishing she didn't have to leave her new friend, but knowing that she had to get wherever she was going before it got dark, so that neither Jack nor Dreadlocks could catch up to her.

CHAPTER

11

"So tell me again why you were at the dock this morning fighting with your in-laws?" Joe McCormick asked Jonathan when the door closed.

Jonathan watched the detective smooth his hand over his shaved head. He had his foot propped on a chair and was looking down his nose at him. A little power was a dangerous thing, Jonathan thought.

"I told you," he said. "We've been all through this. Melinda Jane can read it back to you."

Melinda Jane wiped her nose with a wadded tissue. "Want me to, Joe?"

"That won't be necessary," Cade said.

"The rumor is that you gave them an ultimatum," McCormick said, dropping his foot to the floor and pacing to the window. "What was that ultimatum?"

"I told them that either Gus had to go or Morgan was quitting and we were moving out."

Cade, who sat on a folding chair in the corner of the room, lifted one eyebrow. "Would she have done that?"

Jonathan rubbed his face. "I don't know. It was half bluff. I figured I'd worry about that later. I was hoping they'd just ask him to leave. But they said no, they weren't going to let Gus go. I couldn't believe it."

"And then it escalated into a yelling fight," Cade said. "One witness said you yelled that if they didn't take care of it, you would. What did you mean by that?"

"Just what I said. That I'd take Morgan and move out."

"So you got pretty mad at them," McCormick said. "Were there any blows thrown?"

Jonathan looked up at him like he was crazy. "No, there were no blows thrown. I raised my voice a little, that's all. Several people heard it and got all bug-eyed like they'd just witnessed something real important. And I stormed down the pier and got on my rig."

McCormick's eyes narrowed. "Jonathan, tell us what happened when you brought your rig back."

"Well, we cleaned up, got the boat put to bed," Jonathan said. "And then I had to rush to shower and shave before the city council meeting."

Cade slid his chair closer to the table and leaned on his elbows. "So you were at the city council meeting when they started talking about Hanover House?"

"Right," Jonathan said, "only Thelma and Wayne weren't there. So I took off looking for them."

"Where did you go first?" Cade asked.

"Well, I went by the house, but no one was there."

"Did you go out to the toolshed?"

"No. I haven't been out there for several days." He slapped his hands on the table. "Look, I know I'm a hothead. I lost my temper this morning. I yelled a little too loud. It's my wife we're talking about. I didn't want her around some ex-con who claims he's found God. I was afraid of what he might do. Maybe I was wrong to do and say what I did, but you can't arrest me for that." He stood and leaned across the table, his eyes fixed on McCormick's. "And think about it. Why would I use my own speargun if I was going to kill them? And why would I be so stupid as to toss the gun into the water before I left?"

"Maybe you panicked. Not thinking," McCormick said.

Jonathan turned to Cade. "You can't seriously think I'm capable of this."

"Jonathan," Cade said, "you've been known to have a violent temper before. I remember once before you married Morgan, when you kicked Thelma and Wayne's toolshed until the thing toppled over."

"I was mad because they wanted her to wait a few months before marrying me. Hey, I rebuilt it, okay? It was a building, not a person. I've never been violent with people."

"You've put your fist through walls," Cade added. "Did that at camp. Almost got sent home."

"I was fourteen! Give me a break! What are you gonna do? Haul me into court and tell them you think I killed my in-laws because I lost my temper in eighth grade and tore up a shed once?"

"I don't see how we can release you," Cade said.

"You're going to *lock me up*? Cade, don't you realize my wife just lost her parents? She needs me. If you've ever cared anything about the Owens—"

"I have to do my job," Cade said. "I don't like it, Jonathan, but I can't take any chances right now."

"I did *not* kill them," he said. "Ask my deckhand. I was in a bad mood this morning, but I got over it. I didn't have blood on my mind when I went out this morning or when I came back. I've had fights with Thelma and Wayne, but we've always gotten over it. There were a lot of things about them I didn't understand, and they weren't always willing to explain. But I loved them just the same," he said. "They were good to me and good to my wife. And they wound up with the best-built shed in town, and you know it."

Despite his efforts to hold his emotions back, Jonathan's mouth trembled. "What's this town going to do without them?" "What's going to happen to Hanover House? The whole island is going to change. Not to mention the fact that there's a killer running around. And if you ask me, his name is Gus Hampton. You're going to at least question him, aren't you, Cade?"

"Of course we're going to question him, Jonathan. We're going to question everybody. But meanwhile, we're going to hold you here."

"Cade, you can't. You can't put me in jail and give my wife something else to grieve over."

"Morgan has Blair," Cade said. "She can help her through it."

"And who's going to help Blair?" Jonathan asked.

"Blair Owens is the strongest woman I know," Cade said.

"Oh, yeah?" Jonathan asked. "See if *you* don't have nightmares tonight, and then ask yourself what it would be like to see your own parents that way."

Cade looked down at his hands. "Come on," he said. "I'm going to have to book you and put you in a cell."

"And suppose the real guy gets arrested. Suppose somebody finds out who really did it. You've only got two cells back there, Cade. What are you going to do? Don't you have any drunks or shoplifters in there?"

"Nope. Just some temporary residents waiting to be questioned."

Slowly, Cade got to his feet.

Jonathan wanted to kick the chair over, head-butt his old football buddy, put both fists through this particular wall. Instead he got up, seething quietly, and followed Cade out of the room.

*M*organ thought they might be letting Jonathan go when they brought him out of the interview closet. "They're locking me up," he whispered. "Honey, I'm so sorry."

"No," she wailed. "Cade, what are you trying to do?" She stepped back and looked at the chief. "I'll bail him out," she said. "How much?"

Cade shook his head. "I can't set bail, Morgan. Only the judge can do that, and it's after hours. He's not in his office."

"Then I'll call him at home." There was only one judge on the island of Cape Refuge—a forty-eight-year-old ex-hippie who still wore his gray hair in a ponytail. His name was Randy Simmons, and she knew him well.

She grabbed the phone book and flipped through until she came to the name *Simmons*. Quickly she dialed his number.

"Nancy," she said when his wife answered. "Nancy, it's Morgan Cleary. I need to speak to Randy."

"Morgan," his wife said, "I heard about your parents. Oh, honey, you must be just upside down with grief." Nancy sounded sweet as honey, but Morgan knew she was only after something to run in the newspaper she published, the *Cape Refuge Journal*.

"I need to speak to Randy," she said again. "Please. Put him on the phone."

"He's not here right now," Nancy said. "Are you all right?"

"Where is he?" Morgan shouted.

"Well, he's at soccer practice. He coaches Jimmy's team, you know. And they're over at the soccer field down by the school."

"I need to talk to him real bad," Morgan said. "Nancy, do you think you can get in touch with him?"

"Well, I guess I could drive over to the field and tell him to call you."

"Does he have a cell phone with him?"

"No, honey, I'm afraid not," she said. "You know how it is out here. You can't get a signal no matter what you do. He's thinking about getting one of those satellite phones, but he hasn't done it yet."

"Then, yes, would you please drive over and get him? I really need to talk to him. It's an emergency."

"Well, where can he reach you, hon?"

She closed her eyes and tried to think. She couldn't stay here. She had to go to Hanover House and tell the tenants in case they hadn't heard already. She had to go back to the scene and sort through everything. She had to find out what they were doing with her parents' bodies.

"I don't know," she said. "I'm at the police station right now. Look, Nancy, just tell him that I need for him to set bail so I can get Jonathan out. They're holding him for no reason. He did not kill my parents."

"Oh, my," Nancy said, in that southern drawl that sounded so innocent but packed such punch. "They've arrested Jonathan?"

"When you publish that in your newspaper," Morgan said too loudly, "tell them he didn't do it. He's innocent—they were just looking for somebody to blame. But meanwhile, they'd better realize that there's a killer running loose on this island."

Morgan slammed the phone down. Cade had already taken Jonathan back to lock him up. She felt so helpless that she wanted to break something.

She heard the cell door bang shut and echo throughout the building, then Cade reemerged.

"He'll be all right, Morgan. Just have faith."

"I do have faith, Matthew Cade," she spat out. "Where's *your* faith? You know Jonathan is a Christian, that he could never kill anybody. You're members of the same church. You worship together, pray together. How can you lock up your Christian brother like that?"

"It's not easy," Cade said. He came toward her and put his hands on her shoulders. This time she didn't shake him off.

"Don't worry about him," he said. "He's going to be all right. But Morgan, while you're here, I need you to answer a few questions too."

"Me? You suspect me too?" she threw back.

"No, of course not. But we need to retrace their steps. I need to know what they were doing today, who they talked to, what they said the last time you saw them."

"All right," she said. "I'll tell you whatever I know."

He took her into the interview room, where Melinda Jane still sat with her stenotype machine. She was dabbing at her eyes with her tissue, and Morgan wondered whether she was crying over how they were treating Jonathan or over the death of her parents.

Cade had barely closed the door when she started talking. "They had a regular day, Cade, like any other day. Except that Pop said something about meeting with somebody before going over to City Hall. They said they'd tell me about it later. I should have demanded to know."

"Oh, honey," Melinda Jane said. "You didn't know. How could you know?"

"Melinda Jane," Cade warned, and she got back to her work.

"Morgan," Joe McCormick asked, "what do you think about Gus Hampton? Is Jonathan right about him?"

She leaned back. All she had to do was tell Joe something negative about Gus, something that would cast him in a bad light and get Jonathan out of trouble. But she couldn't. It wouldn't be true.

"My parents knew Gus was an ex-con. They weren't harboring him illegally at all. He came here, a broken soul trying to start over, and they gave him a place. I've seen them do wonders with him," she said. "I've seen him transformed. I don't think he killed my parents, but I don't know who did. All I know, Cade, is that you won't find him by sitting in this building."

"We're looking," Cade said. "As soon as we find him, we'll bring him in."

He questioned her further about her parents' activities of the day: people they called, places they had gone, things they had said. When she had told him everything she knew, he finally walked her back out to the front door.

"I appreciate your help."

She wiped her eyes. "I want you to find the killer," she said. "I'll cooperate in any way I can. But I want my husband out of here."

"I know you do," he said. "Morgan, you just go do what you need to do, take care of yourself and Blair, and let me take care of this."

"Right," she said, and turned away from him. She started to the front door, opened it, and stood at the threshold. "My parents would want me to forgive you," she said, "but it's going to be hard when this is all over."

"I know it is," Cade said. "I'd have trouble too. Believe me, Morgan. This is the hardest thing I've ever had to do."

She pointed at Cade, her finger trembling. "You protect my husband. Whoever did this, whoever stole his speargun and set him up, might have it in for him too. So help me, you'd better protect him, Cade."

Sobbing into her hand, she headed back out to her car.

CHAPTER

*A*cross Cape Refuge, Blair stood in front of the warehouse, fighting nausea. Someone had brought her car over from City Hall, so she got into it and sat behind the wheel.

Alex Johnson, one of the police rookies, came to her window. "You okay, ma'am? Sure you can drive?"

"I'm fine," she said. "I'm going to follow the hearse and see that my parents get there safely."

The absurdity of her words struck her, and she looked away, fighting despair. What could happen? Could the hearse run into a tree and kill her parents all over again?

She started her car and pulled off the gravel, following the hearse back across the bridge to Tybee Island, then to the causeway that led into Savannah.

Morgan would say that her parents were in heaven, that their souls had ascended instantly, that they would never be unsafe again. But Blair couldn't buy it. She had trouble buying into anything that she couldn't see and feel and taste. If it couldn't be explained with physics and chemistry, if you couldn't look it up on the Internet or find it in a book, spelled out all nice and neat with foolproof formulas and definitive explanations, then she couldn't accept it.

But that created a problem. That meant that her parents were no more, that she would never see them again, that the last time she had seen them, sometime yesterday, had been a farewell and she hadn't even known it. What good had it done them to be so spiritual and so godly, only to have their lives end so cruelly?

She didn't cry, didn't even blink back tears, as she followed the hearse into town. Even so, sorrow crushed her with such heaviness that she almost couldn't breathe. There were too many things her parents had left unsaid, too many equations that hadn't yet been solved.

She had known for years that she hadn't been told the whole story about those red, hideous scars on the side of her face, which repulsed the men who were attracted to her other side. Her parents had insisted as long as she could remember that she had been burned as a baby when a grease fire erupted in their kitchen. The story had made sense when she was a child, but as she'd grown older, she had begun to recognize their evasions about the fire and their reluctance to talk about it even when she'd pleaded for details. She had had screaming arguments with her parents, demanding to know the truth, but they had insisted they had told her everything there was to know. She had left home in a fit of anger, taken the job as the town librarian, and set up her own house. Eventually, she had gotten over that anger, trying to convince herself that her parents would never lie to her.

Her mother had once told her she was lucky to have the scars, that the man who finally fell for her would see her inner beauty and the outside wouldn't matter. Her mother hadn't meant it in a cruel way, but it had felt cruel to Blair.

Even so, Blair agreed with her mother. She was *glad* she hadn't been caught in the whirlwind of dates and dances to which Morgan, with her delicate beauty and gentle spirit, had seemed enslaved. Blair had always had more important things on her mind. A man would have just held her back.

She could get through this night and this grief without one. She was strong. She was intelligent. And if she could just get back to Cape Refuge and lock herself inside her office at the back of the library, somehow she would be able to figure out who the killer was. Then everything would make sense.

At the funeral home, Blair followed the hearse around to the covered area at the back door. She sat frozen in her car, watching through the windshield as they took the bodies out and carried them in, as carefully as if they were still alive.

She thought about the last time she had come to this place, when Roland Ball died of a heart attack at forty-two, leaving behind a wife and three children.

"What do you say to somebody who's going through a thing like this?" she had asked her parents as they walked across the parking lot for the visitation.

"You just hug them," her mother had said. "Tell them you're sorry. Scripture sometimes helps, but that's better for after the funeral, when you can write it down so they can look at it when they're ready."

"What good does Scripture do?" Blair asked. "Seems a little shallow, to bombard hurting people with platitudes when they're at their lowest point."

Her father, who had been walking a few steps ahead, stopped midstep and turned to face her. "Blair, you know better than that. Scripture is not platitudes. It's life."

"Not for Roland Ball."

"You're wrong about that too, darlin'. He does have life. His wife'll see him again."

"And what if you're wrong?"

"Oh, Blair," her mother had said with genuine despair in her eyes.

Her father got that look in his eyes that she had seen so many times, when he witnessed to a lonely dockworker or an aimless ex-con. It was easy for her to understand why people responded to him so as those soft, doleful eyes fixed on her. "The better question, Blair, is what if *you're* wrong?"

She wasn't wrong, she thought now as she watched them close the door to the hearse. If there was a God, he would have rescued her parents from the evil that defeated them today.

The driver of the hearse saw her car and started toward her. She rolled her window down.

"Ma'am, is there anything I can do for you?"

"No," she said. "I ... I'm coming in ... just as soon as I get back with some clothes. Please ... don't touch my mother."

He leaned down and set his arm on her window. "Ma'am, we have to touch her."

"Don't ... dress her, I mean." She swallowed, wondering why the words came so hard. "She's very modest. She hates it when people see her dressing. Even in department stores, she makes me stand in front of the dressing room door and hold it shut. But it's okay. I can do it."

"Ma'am, the medical examiner needs access to them. Let us take care of things. There's enough for you to do."

She stared through her windshield, and focused on an azalea bush at the edge of the parking lot. The pink blooms had all wilted. Someone needed to pinch them off, so that new ones could grow back. She didn't know why people left wilted blooms.

She looked back up at the man. "I told you," she said, her voice louder now. "I don't want you to touch her. What about that don't you understand?"

"Ma'am, you're upset." He spoke like one would speak to a rabid tiger, circling and growling, waiting to pounce. "Maybe you'd like to come in and sit down, and I can explain the process to you."

"I told you, I have to get her some clothes. Him too."

"It's no hurry. You can bring them later today or even tomorrow."

She couldn't understand why the man was so obtuse. Her knuckles whitened as she clutched the steering wheel. "I will bring them today, and I will dress her myself, and if you so much as open a button on her shirt, I will get a lawyer and sue you for everything you're worth!"

He nodded then. "Yes, ma'am. We won't touch her, then. We'll just wait."

"Good." She sat there staring at him for a moment, wondering where she would direct her anger now. She shifted into "drive." "I'll be back."

She didn't wait for his response, just rolled up the window and pulled out of the parking lot.

The drive home seemed longer than it ever had before, and when she finally crossed the bridge to take her back to Cape Refuge, she felt the sudden chilling sense that there was nothing here for her anymore. Still, she navigated her way through her town until she got to the little library. It was on the west side of the island, just north of the dock.

Her home and her library sat side-by-side among pine trees and mimosas, across the street from the water.

Next door, Sally Hanfield's Marine Museum sat, sharing an empty parking lot. She hoped Sally wasn't there ... she couldn't deal with questions and pity.

She hurried to the library door. She had closed it a little early today so she could make the city council meeting, and she walked in and locked the door behind her. For a moment she stood there, breathing in the scent of the books and the dust.

She shouldn't have come here, she thought. She should have gone to Hanover House to get the clothes. She should have hurried back to the funeral home, as she had said she would, to attend to her mother's body.

She stood frozen, running faces through her mind, wondering who on this island had the potential for murder. Maybe Jonathan had done it. Maybe it was someone else running free on the island waiting to do it again. Maybe it was revenge, or just plain evil.

She stood there a moment, staring into space, while all the questions reeled through her mind like microfiche from the back room. Anguish bled into trembling rage, bubbling up, boiling over, shaking her . . .

Finally, she erupted. She grabbed the edge of the bookshelf in the center of the room—and pulled it over.

The books hit the ground first, and then the wooden structure crashed to the floor. She grabbed another set of books, knocked them off the shelf. One shelf at a time, she pulled the books off, then kicked the shelves over. Rage played out of her in violent form, book after book, shelf after shelf, crashing on the hard floor, wreaking havoc on the little building she kept so carefully. Vintage books, antiques, out-of-print books that no one could ever find anyplace else, all went flying in clouds of dust. Shelf after shelf—books landing open, facedown, pages flapping. Every last one crashed and banged.

It sounded like justice. Like broken dreams. Like flattened hopes.

Like she was murdering that thief, Death, who had robbed her of her parents.

She had to upend every one. Destroy them all. Every last one. Then maybe she could cry.

CHAPTER

*T*ammy took off her apron an hour later when her shift ended, freshened up her lipstick, then waved her long groomed fingernails at her boss before heading out. When she got to the parking lot, she looked around for any sign of the young girl who had been in there tonight. She hadn't been able to forget that black eye or the way she cradled her arm. She reminded her of herself when she was that age. She wondered if she'd been beaten by a boyfriend—or worse, her father. She had no doubt the girl had fled for good reason.

She got into her old Ford Escort, started it up, and pulled out into the traffic, but instead of starting home, she took off toward Highway 80, driving slowly and glancing at each side of the road for the girl with the backpack. She looked at her watch. Clarence, her boyfriend, would be expecting her any minute now, hungry and waiting for her to cook supper. But this seemed more important now than maintaining his paunch.

She saw the girl crossing a street up ahead, trudging east as if she thought she could actually walk all the way to Cape Refuge before dark. Carefully, Tammy pulled up to the curb and leaned over the seat to roll down the window.

"You ain't gonna walk all the way, are you, honey?" Tammy asked.

The girl swung around, startled. Then recognition flickered to her eyes. She stepped to the car window and leaned in. "I was going to hitchhike before it got dark."

"Scared, huh? Don't blame you. You never know who'll pick you up. Hop in," Tammy said. "I'll take you myself."

Sadie straightened. "You live on Cape Refuge?"

"No, I live about three blocks from here," Tammy said. "I would walk to work, but your dreadlocks friend has buddies, and sometimes they keep the streets from being all that safe. But I can't abide the thought of you walking all the way or even hitchhiking with strangers. Didn't your mama teach you better than that?"

Sadie slid off her backpack and got in, slumping into the bucket seat.

"I appreciate it, but if this is out of your way, really, I can—"

"Honey, I wouldn't be able to sleep tonight knowing you weren't settled. It'll be just fine. I'll take you across the river and drop you right at the front door of Hanover House, then I can go on my merry way knowing you'll be all right."

Sadie was quiet as they crossed the causeway onto Tybee Island. Tammy hoped Thelma and Wayne Owens were home and that they wouldn't let Sadie down.

"Do you know these people, Thelma and Wayne Owens?" Sadie asked her, as they drew closer to her destination.

"No, not personally," Tammy said, "but my sister lives on Cape Refuge and goes to church with them. I'd take you to her house, but her husband is mean as a snake, and it probably wouldn't be any better than where you came from. And I couldn't take you home with me, 'cause Clarence likes blondes a little too much, and I'd be shooting myself in the foot, if you know what I mean."

The beach came into view, and Sadie's eyes lit up as if she had just rounded a corner into some kind of glittering wonderland. The sun was going down over the horizon, and waves

frothed and billowed as they hit against the shore. "It's beautiful," she said. "Just like I pictured it."

"Oh, honey, you should see it in the morning," Tammy said.
"It's a right pretty little island, nice place to visit and all that. Not
for me, though. Things move slower than I like."

Tammy drove along the beach, then crossed the bridge to
Cape Refuge. She slowed the car as she got closer to the bed-and-
breakfast, and she pulled onto the long graveled driveway in
front of the yellow house with its massive front porch and huge
yellow Victorian turret. A frilly little sign in the front yard said
"HANOVER HOUSE."

"Well, here you are. This is it, the end of the line."

"It's perfect," Sadie whispered.

Tammy looked around to the side of the house. "Doesn't
seem to be any cars here. We might have come at a bad time.
'Course, somebody could be inside. If not, I guess I could take you
on back with me—"

"That's okay," Sadie said. "There are rocking chairs on the
porch. I'll just sit up there and wait until somebody gets home."

"You're sure now?" Tammy asked.

Sadie nodded. "Thank you, Tammy. I really appreciate what
you've done."

Tammy reached into her purse and pulled out a receipt,
marked her phone number down on the back of it, then thrust it
at the girl. "Now, if you find yourself in a jam, you give me a call,
you hear? There might be something I can do."

"Okay," Sadie said with a smile. She took the receipt, then
grabbed her backpack and got out. "Thanks again."

She closed the door and started up to the porch. Tammy
waited as she knocked on the door, but no one came. Finally, Sadie
sat down in one of the rocking chairs and waved that it was all
right for her to go on. Tammy felt a little better about herself as
she pulled her car out of the graveled driveway and headed back
home.

CHAPTER

15

*M*organ found the judge on the soccer field, but she couldn't make herself get out of the car and walk through the spectators who were all probably buzzing about the murders. *"Did you hear that Jonathan Cleary did it? I always said that boy was trouble...."*

Those who had counted him the town hero as a quarterback when he led the high school team to a state championship would swear that they had always known he had violence in him.

Judge Simmons ran along the field, yelling at the teenage boys as they kicked the ball toward the goal. Morgan wondered if Nancy had reached him yet. If she had, why hadn't he already gone to the police station?

Someone knocked on her window. She jumped. It was Hattie Brumfield, motioning for her to roll her window down. Morgan did and looked up with dull eyes.

"Darlin', I'm so sorry about your folks," she said. "How did it happen? They know who did it?"

That lump of emotion blocked her throat. "No." She swallowed and drew in a deep breath. "Hattie ... would you please . . . go tell the judge I need to speak to him? I just can't get out of this car and . . . walk through all those people."

"Well, of course I will. But, honey, how did they die? Were they shot or beaten . . . ?"

"Hattie, please." She opened her car door. "Never mind, I'll do it myself."

"No, no, honey. I'll do it. Just get back in."

Slowly, Morgan got back into the car. "Hattie, it's real important. Please. I need to talk to him right now."

"I'm going." The woman left the car and waddled down to the soccer field.

Morgan watched her approach the coach, and he turned back, looking for her. Hattie pointed toward her car, and several heads turned her way. She absently locked her door, as if that would protect her from their curiosity.

Finally, the judge barked a few more orders at the team, then headed toward the car.

He was sweating when he reached her, and his gray ponytail looked as if it hadn't been washed in days. "Hey, Morgan. Nancy came by and told me you needed to talk. I was gon' call you soon as the game was over. You okay?"

She didn't want to answer that question. "Randy, I know you're aware of . . . what happened to . . . my parents. Cade arrested Jonathan. I need for you to do something. Set bail or whatever . . . so I can get him out."

"Why Jonathan?"

"Someone took his speargun and . . . killed them. . . . " She stopped and took a deep breath. "That's all. Circumstantial evidence. Please, Randy . . ."

He straightened and set his hands on his hips. "I'll go right down to the station, but I can't promise anything."

"Why not?" she asked. "You're the judge! You can promise whatever you want."

"I don't like to interfere with Cade's investigations. If Jonathan owned the murder weapon—"

"He is not a murderer!"

"I'll see what I can do, Morgan."

She started her car and jerked it in reverse. "I'll see you at the station."

"No, Morgan. You don't need to be there while I'm reviewing the case."

"Reviewing the case?" she asked. "Randy, the case is about two hours old, and you probably heard through the grapevine everything Cade knows about it. What's to review?"

"I have to take Cade's opinion under advisement. I can't just let people out on the street because their wives don't want them in jail."

"They were *my* parents! Why would I want him released if I thought for a minute that he did it?"

"Go home, Morgan. Take care of yourself. I'll have Cade call you when I've finished." He started back to the game, dismissing the discussion.

Morgan tried to pull herself together. What was she going to do? She thought of going home, walking into that big house with her parents' things everywhere, right where they had left them. And the tenants . . . and the friends who would start coming by, meaning well . . .

She couldn't go home just yet. She needed to be with Blair, who understood the storm in her heart and needed shelter from it too.

She saw Blair's car parked on the gravel parking lot in front of the library next to her house. She got out and went to the library door. It was locked, so she knocked and waited. Blair didn't come, so she knocked again, harder this time. Still no answer. She stood there, bewildered by the peaceful serenity of the shade trees and the blooming crepe myrtle and the sound of the water washing against the river wall just across the street. You would never know someone had been murdered just a couple of miles from here, that her family had been destroyed, that nothing would ever be the same again.

She heard something crash inside and ran to the front window to peer in through the glass. The shelves were on the floor and there were books everywhere. Alarms went off in her head. She ran around to the back of the building, feeling for the brick that Blair kept there with a key underneath. She scraped her fingers trying to pull it off, then found the key and bolted back to the door.

By the time she got the door open another shelf was flying over and books were catapulting down. She looked around for the culprit, for anyone who might be hurting her sister, when she saw Blair reach for the next bookshelf and pull it over. The books flew out and the shelf smashed to the ground.

"Blair!" she shouted, and Blair spun around. Her face was raging red and wet, and her eyes had a wild, desperate look. The scars on the right side of her face were crimson.

"Blair, stop it!" Morgan ran to her as Blair reached for the next shelf. She pulled her away and pushed her against the wall where she couldn't do further harm.

"Let go of me," Blair cried. "Let go of me *now!*"

"You're going to hurt yourself," Morgan cried. "You need to calm down."

"Who did it, Morgan?" Blair screamed. "Who murdered them?"

"I don't know."

"They won't get away with it." She started to weep and put her arms around Morgan, and they held each other for a long time, standing against the wall, surrounded by books lying open and facedown beneath heavy bookshelves.

"How can you not suspect everybody on the face of this island?" she cried. "How can you walk into that bed-and-breakfast and look in anybody's eye and not suspect them? They shot them in the *throats*, Morgan! Mama and Pop must have looked the killer in the eye and feared for their lives. One of them saw the other one die! The horror they must have felt!"

Morgan couldn't speak. She just clung to her sister and cried, hating where this day had brought them, hating the uncertainty, hating what lay ahead. "What are we going to do?" she asked.

"That's easy," Blair said. "We're going to find the killers. And when we do, I'm going to kill them myself.

CHAPTER

*A*n hour later, Morgan paced Blair's office, clutching her cordless phone to her ear. She had finally gotten the judge on the telephone at the police station, but he wasn't cooperating. "What do you mean, you can't release him?" she asked him.

"I'm sorry, Morgan. But Cade had good reason to arrest him, and for a murder case like this, I think it's appropriate to keep him in custody. If I were you, I'd get a lawyer as soon as possible."

Morgan clung to the phone, speechless, then finally set it back in its cradle without another word. She stepped back into the library with its toppled shelves and books scattered like debris from some kind of explosion. Blair still sat on the floor among the fallout. "I've got to get a lawyer," Morgan told her in a dull voice. "I don't even know where to look."

"What about the lawyers who were advising Mama and Pop about Hanover House?" Blair's voice was quiet and without inflection. "We could use them."

"Are they criminal lawyers?" Morgan asked. The words seemed to stick in her throat. It was absurd that she needed a criminal lawyer for her husband.

"No, they're not criminal, but maybe they could recommend somebody."

Morgan called the law firm but got a recorded message that they were closed for the day. She hung up and rubbed her face. "Guess I'll have to wait until morning."

"You can stay with me tonight," Blair said. "I've got the guest room, and I don't think either of us should be alone."

Morgan just looked at her. "You have a queen size, don't you?"

"Yeah," Blair whispered.

"I'm too scared to sleep alone in the guest room. They're out there somewhere, Blair, laughing because the keystone cops in this town have the wrong guy locked up."

Blair swallowed. "Yeah, we can share."

"Just like when we were kids," Morgan managed to get out. "We would sleep together, all huddled up. Two peas in a pod, Mama called us."

Blair stared off into the air, as if she saw something there that Morgan couldn't see. "I have to go back to the funeral home. I have to get Mama out of those clothes, and Pop—"

"Blair, let them do that. That's what they do."

"No, I'm doing it. You don't have to come."

"Good," Morgan said, "because I'm not. I can't."

Blair got off of the floor and looked helplessly around her. "I'd better get going."

"Don't go, Blair. Just tonight, let's stay together, okay? I don't want to be alone, even for a little while, and I can't go with you. . . . Please, you're not thinking clearly."

"Someone in the family has to do it, Morgan."

"No, they don't. That's what the funeral home is for."

"Mama is modest! She doesn't want—"

"She's not there, Blair!" Morgan cut in. "She's not in that funeral home, and she's not in those bloody clothes! It's not her!"

Blair stared at her as if she were the enemy—as if those words exposed her.

"Then who is it?" Blair demanded.

"It's her shell," Morgan said. "Mama is somewhere else, and she doesn't care what clothes she's wearing or who sees her. Neither does Pop. They would want us to huddle together and get through this, Blair, and not torture ourselves with things that don't even matter."

Blair stared again, helplessness and hopelessness tightening her face. "It's something I can do. I need to do it."

"No, you don't. You want something to do? Then stay here. Get through the night. Wake up and help me with all the details tomorrow."

"I told them I'd come," she said quietly.

"I'll call them. I'll tell them to go ahead and do what they need to do. Blair, you know Mama wouldn't want you torturing yourself." She reached out a tentative hand and touched her sister's arm. "Come on, Blair. Stay here, okay? We'll just leave this mess and go over to your house where we can think."

Blair's eyes had no luster as she kicked some of the books aside and made a path to the door.

Blair saw Melba Jefferson the moment she stepped outside, and almost turned back. Her mother's best friend stood at her door with tears streaming down her face, and she clutched a casserole dish in her chubby hands. When she saw them, she set it down on the hood of her car and pulled them both into a fat embrace.

"Oh, you poor things!" she wailed. "It's just so awful."

Wiping her tears, she went back to her trunk and pulled out several more casseroles that she had made. Blair wondered if she kept a freezerful of the things, and took them out to thaw when someone died.

"Now just tell me what you need me to do," Melba said, her voice wavering. "I can answer your phone, or clean up your house. Or I can just sit here all day tomorrow while you take care of the arrangements. I'm available. I want you to know that."

Blair wanted to tell her that she preferred to have her sit at her own house and leave them alone, but Morgan piped in, "I just can't think of anything right now, Melba. But we appreciate it."

"If you're not hungry, it'll keep," the woman said. "You'll need it after the funeral." Her voice broke off again and she swallowed. Her ample chest heaved with grief. "I could go to the funeral home with you tomorrow," she said. "You know your mama and daddy wouldn't want anything fancy. They weren't like that. But sometimes in our grief we overextend ourselves, choose coffins that we can't quite afford."

Blair lifted her chin. "We can afford to bury our parents, Melba."

"Of course you can, honey. I'm just saying, don't you get talked into anything. Now if you need me to go, I've had plenty experience with this sort of thing."

"You've had parents who were murdered?" Blair asked. Morgan squeezed her arm to silence her.

"Why, no, I've never had a murder. Just death, that's all. The older you get, the more you deal with death, you know. They weren't just your parents. They were my good friends. I don't know what I'll do without Thelma." She turned back toward the car, as if she didn't know whether to stay or go.

Morgan shot Blair a scathing look and touched Melba's back. The woman turned around, and Morgan pulled her into a hug and held her there just like her mother would have done.

"Oh, darlin'. You've got Thelma's heart," Melba said. "You always have."

Blair had heard that before. Morgan was the one with the heart. But she didn't care. She wasn't out to impress any of the socialites of Cape Refuge. She didn't even care about those who attended church with her parents. They had nothing to do with her, she thought. As far as she was concerned, Melba was among those who stared at her when she was a little girl and clicked her tongue and said what a shame it was that such a pretty girl would be so terribly marred. She had caught Melba's own son shuddering once, sitting next to her in class. It was his way of showing off for his buddies, but Blair had never forgotten it.

"You take care now, Blair," Melba said before Blair walked inside. "I'm going to be praying for you whether you like it or not."

*T*he warm breeze whispered from the Atlantic and ruffled Sadie's hair as she sat on the porch at Hanover House. She could see the beach across the street and the waves rolling in, and her heart soared at the idea that she had actually made it here. Jack would never find her.

A van pulled up into the driveway, and she got to her feet slowly, suddenly nervous at the prospect of meeting these people face-to-face. What if they weren't like Tammy said? What if they were impatient and angry? What if they insisted on calling the police and reporting her as a runaway?

But it wasn't an old couple that got out of the car. Instead, it was a young man of about twenty, with sandy blond hair a little too long and wire-rimmed glasses. He got out of the driver's side and went around to the back, pulled out a big wreath with flowers all over it, and carried it up across the yard. Sadie stepped to the post and met him as he came up the porch steps.

"Hey," she said, awkwardly. "Do you live here?"

The young man shook his head. "No, I just work for the florist. My boss told me to stop by here and put this wreath on the door."

Sadie backed away. "Oh, okay."

He found the nail that was, no doubt, there to hold the Christmas wreath and gently placed it on the door.

"I'm Matt," he said, reaching out to shake her hand.

She took it. "Sadie," she said. "What's the wreath for?"

"Don't you know?" he asked, frowning. "About Thelma and Wayne?"

Sadie had had bad news many times in her life, and it was always preceded by a tightening in her chest, a closing of her throat, a headache starting behind her eyes. She felt all of that now.

"No. What about them?"

"You haven't heard about them being murdered?"

Sadie felt suddenly dizzy, and she stepped back against the post, reached out for it to steady her. "They were murdered?"

"Found dead," he said, "just this afternoon."

She groped back to the rocking chair and sat down. "I was waiting for them. I didn't know."

"I'm really sorry," he said. "They were nice folks. Real nice folks."

That was it, she thought. There went her chance of finding shelter and safety. Thelma and Wayne Owens, the two people in the area who could have helped her, were no longer here.

"Are you all right?" Matt asked.

She nodded absently.

"Your arm, I mean? And that bruise on your face. What happened?"

She got up and slipped the backpack over her good arm. "I've got to go," she said.

He stood there on the porch, then followed her down the steps, but before he could catch up to her, she had crossed the street and was headed out across the sand.

"Nice to meet you," he shouted. She didn't turn back, and after a moment she heard him driving away.

She tried to calm herself, tried to tell herself not to panic. She would be all right. She had pictured it this way, anyway—sleeping on the sand at night under the stars, the warm breeze blowing across her body, the sound of the ocean lulling her to sleep. It looked like the safest place in the world, she thought. If she could get the murders out of her mind, she could sleep here and find the public showers in the morning where the beachcombers washed off. Maybe she could come across a bar of soap and wash her hair, then head out looking for a job.

She stood on the edge of the beach and saw the condominiums and hotel rooms five stories deep for as far as she could see. There were rooms everywhere, empty beds, linens, fresh and clean, but she didn't need them, she thought. She was here and she wasn't afraid.

At least, not yet.

She walked along the beach, carrying her backpack on her shoulder, looking for an inconspicuous place where she could lay her head. She walked until darkness began to fall over the water and the few remaining beachcombers had gone in. Then she found a place between two decks, pulled out a light jacket that she had brought, and slipped it on. The pain in her arm tormented her, and she examined it for a moment, realizing it was turning black and blue, that the bones still didn't quite meet. It throbbed all the way up to her shoulder, but she couldn't get medical help just yet, she thought. She didn't have the money. And besides, whoever treated her would want to know where she had come from, how the accident had happened. She would have to think of a story first, but not now. Now she just needed to sleep.

She made herself a little nest in the sand between the two decks and lay down, then covering herself with a shirt from her backpack, she fell into a light sleep to the sound of the ocean and the wind.

CHAPTER

18

Billy Caldwell's nervous radio call was broadcast on every police scanner in Chatham County. "Chief, I found Gus Hampton."

"Where is he?" Cade asked.

"In the Owens's boathouse, about a mile down from Hanover House. His truck's parked out front. Want me to go in?"

"No," Cade said. "Just wait there for backup. But if you hear him starting the boat, go in. We can't let him get away."

Cade cut off the radio and began barking orders to the dispatcher. "Call the other three patrol cars and have them meet me there. No one's to act until I get there."

He heard her dispatching the other three officers, who were all out beating the bushes for leads. Cade ran out to his car, turned on his blue light, and headed for the southern tip of the island.

They had been looking for Gus since the bodies were found. His boss had sworn that he'd been at work until a little after six, probably an hour after the murders, and that he hadn't left all day. He had been there when Gus heard about the killings and said he had been visibly upset. Then Gus had rushed out.

Relief flooded through Cade as he flew across the island, traffic separating to the sides of the road to let him through. Maybe this was the break they needed. Maybe it would clear Jonathan.

The boathouse was a mile north of the bed-and-breakfast, not visible from the street. The woods were thick there, maple trees and mimosa, loblolly pines and sassafras, standing sentry at the dirt road that led down to the water.

Cade pulled in and saw that the other three cars had beaten him here. They had stopped near the entrance, not wanting to alert Gus that they were there. He saw Billy with his weapon drawn, standing near the door of the boathouse. Cade signaled the others to follow him, and he ran quietly down the side path.

They reached the boathouse, a simple wooden building with only three walls. Inside, Wayne Owens kept his small fishing boat, which he allowed his tenants to use as they wished. Cade had been there before. It held only the boat, a couple of toolboxes, some bait and tackle, and his fishing rods.

He stood to the side of the door and drew his own gun and listened hard. There seemed to be no movement inside.

He turned back to the others and signaled for two of them to go to the water side of the building, made sure they were ready, then he put his hand on the doorknob.

He threw the door open and lurched inside.

Gus, crouched on the floor at the corner of the building, sucked in a breath and held out his hand. "Don't shoot, mon. It's just me."

Cade could see that the man had been crying. His eyes were red and his face was wet.

"It's just me, mon."

"Gus, I need for you to get to your feet, and if you're carrying a weapon, drop it right now."

"You crazy, mon?" he asked, getting up. "I ain't got a weapon. What you think? That I'm the killer?"

"Turn around," Cade ordered. "Put your hands over your head."

Gus did as he was told and turned facing the wall. The other officers came in as Cade frisked him. He wasn't armed.

"Gus, what were you doing here?"

"I was trying to get off by myself," he said. "To think things through ... to pray ... I didn't want to be around nobody."

"Gus, I'm gonna have to take you in for questioning about the murders of Thelma and Wayne Owens."

"Who did it, mon?" he asked, beginning to sob. He turned around to Cade, his black face twisted in anguish. "Who would *do* that kind of evil? Who would do it?"

"That's what we're trying to find out."

"Am I under arrest? Do you suspect me?"

"We just want to ask you some questions," he said. "You're not under arrest."

"I'll answer whatever I can, mon. I want that killer found. I want to look him in the eye and ask him why he done this."

The man looked like a linebacker for the NFL, but he was as compliant as a kitten as Cade walked him back to the car.

They questioned Gus for a little over an hour, but his alibi was clear. He'd been at work when the murders were committed, and his boss had been there with him. There was no evidence at all that he had committed the crimes.

It wasn't until Cade released Gus that he realized how much he had wanted him to be guilty. Then he could have released Jonathan.

But as it stood, he had a serious problem.

And so did his best friend.

CHAPTER

*I*t didn't really matter what size Blair's bed was, because she couldn't sleep anyway. Blair got up and wandered through the house, feeling dazed and light-headed. She wondered why she had knocked over all the shelves in the library, how she would ever put it all back together. She hoped the mayor didn't pay her a visit there in the next couple of days. She might lose her job. Then again, he'd probably understand. She was surprised at herself, surprised to think that she would lose control of her emotions that way and snap like some raging kid throwing a temper tantrum. She would have thought she was stronger than that.

Her head ached, so she went to the bathroom, opened the medicine cabinet, and found a bottle of Tylenol. She poured some into her hand, then caught her reflection in the mirror. As she often did, she held her hand up in front of her scars, imagining what she might look like if she didn't have them. She could have won beauty pageants, she thought. She could have been homecoming queen. She would probably be married by now, have babies.

Thank goodness those weren't things she wanted.

She threw the Tylenol into her mouth, filled her cupped hand with water, and washed them down. Finally, she went back to her bed and lay down next to Morgan. But sleep would not come.

On the outskirts of sleep's netherworld, Morgan sank into a dream of flames dancing around her, someone pulling on her hand. She felt the heat of it on her face, on her arms, on her legs, her bare feet. She heard the sound of her feet running, running, running away, looking back over her shoulder at the flames dancing and prancing around. And then she saw someone coming through—a little girl, wreathed by the flames. She pulled away and took off running toward the child, but hands grabbed her and wrestled her back.

She saw that the little girl was Blair, and the flames were closing in.

She caught her breath and sat up straight in bed, pulling herself out of the quicksand of that dream. She looked over at her sister, saw that her eyes were closed and she was lying still. Blair wasn't three years old anymore, but twenty-five. But there were scars on that face, scars that she didn't think had been put there by a grease fire in the kitchen, as her parents had always maintained. It was a much bigger fire, she thought. She had dreamed about it too often for it not to be real.

Why would her parents have lied about such things?

The truth was there somewhere in the recesses of Morgan's memory, but she couldn't quite get to it.

She got out of bed and wandered around the house, hoping that Jonathan was all right, that someone guarded him at the jail, someone reliable who wouldn't let anybody in. She reeled through the possibilities of killers in her mind.

There was Gus Hampton. She wondered if the police had found him yet. The idea of him killing her parents seemed ludicrous to her. Instead, he was probably grieving like the rest of them.

And then there was Rick Morrison, the gentle, tormented man who'd come to Hanover House to get his bearings after a tragedy had hit his family. A tragedy much like this one.

She went into the living room, curled up on the couch, and tried to pray. She was thankful that Jesus interceded for the saints. Sometimes she couldn't find the words to pray herself. How did one pray when something so hideous and violent preyed on her mind? How did one find that peaceful, joyful feeling that came with salvation when Satan had been so victorious?

Where had God been when her parents were fighting for their lives? Where had their guardian angel messed up? Why hadn't Jesus interceded for them at the moment when they had needed deliverance? She fought the anger welling up inside her at her Lord, for she knew it was irreverent and disrespectful. But she couldn't fight those feelings coursing through her, making her anxious and sick.

"Eat something," a voice in her head seemed to tell her. Maybe she would feel better, she thought. Maybe then she wouldn't feel so queasy, and she could sleep and wake up rested enough to do the business she had to do tomorrow.

She looked in the refrigerator and found the casserole that Melba had brought. She got a spoon and dipped out one scoop, put it into her mouth, and forced herself to swallow it. It went down smooth and tasteless. It didn't settle her stomach or her heart. Nothing was settled, she thought.

She walked around her sister's house, feeling the oppression of some dark force weighing down on her, crushing the breath out of her, keeping her from sleep or rest or peace, reminding her of violent, horrible things like flames dancing around her sister, spears flying into her parents, bars hovering around her husband.

She went to the couch and curled up on it, her knees at her chest, dropped her forehead, and wept hard, knowing that tomorrow, somehow, she would have to get hold of herself. There was too much to be done, and only the two of them to do it.

CHAPTER

20

*M*orning dawned with a stark brightness that contrasted the grief in Cade's soul. But he didn't have time to grieve. He arrived early at the station but, instead of going in, walked across the street to the sand and the beach. He needed to breathe the sea air, to experience the morning when it felt so much like midnight.

He walked to the hard, wet sand and stood there a moment, looking out over the clear sky. Seagulls swooped and squalled, attending to the business God had given them. He needed to do the same.

In this same bright morning, with the sea pounding against the shore, the sun shining with blinding brightness, and the sky clear and blue, a brutal killer lurked. As temperamental as Jonathan could be, he didn't fit that description.

But if he didn't do it, then who killed Thelma and Wayne?

Cade turned around and scanned the homes and condos and rooms along the beach. Something caught his eye between two decks side by side. Someone sleeping in the sand.

Probably a drunk who forgot where he lived, he thought. He trudged across the sand to the two decks with just three or four feet between them, ready to wake the drunk and make him move on.

But instead he saw a girl, scrawny and bruised, sound asleep, with a backpack for her pillow and one shirt as her cover. Her eye was black and swollen, and she held her mangled arm close against her.

He thought of waking her and sending her on her way, but she looked so young. She was probably a runaway and needed to be reported. She also needed medical help.

He bent over her and shook her. Her eyes shot open. She squinted in the sunlight and quickly sat up.

"It's against the law to sleep on the beach," he said. "Can I see some ID?"

She clutched her arm, as if it gave her intense pain, and looked around, disoriented. "I—didn't know it was against the law. I won't do it again."

He held out his hand and repeated the question. "Can I see some ID, please?"

Looking helpless, she got up and dusted the sand off of her clothes and her hair. She put the strap of her backpack in her teeth and with one hand dug into it as if looking for her wallet. She kept the other hand bent against her ribs.

"Oh, no," she said. "My wallet. It's gone. It had my driver's license. It must have been stolen."

He had heard that before. "What's your name?" he asked.

"Sadie," she said. "Sadie—Smith."

He grinned. "Smith, huh? That's convenient. How old are you?"

"Eighteen," she said.

"You're not eighteen. You're not a day older than fifteen."

"I am," she said. "I swear."

He saw the despair on her face and felt sorry for her. He stepped closer, touched her arm. "Let me see that."

Carefully she pulled off the windbreaker she was wearing. He winced at her disfigured arm.

"How'd you get hurt?"

"Fell down some stairs," she said.

"It looks broken. You need to see a doctor."

"Well—I don't have much money. I was going to look for a job and a place to live today, and then I plan to see one."

He frowned. He wondered if someone was looking for her, frantic that she wasn't at home in her bed. The wind whipped up, blowing her hair, disheveled and tangled. She pulled it down from its haphazard ponytail and combed her fingers through it.

"Where are you from, Sadie?"

She hesitated a moment. Clearly, she wasn't used to lying. "Birmingham. I just moved here yesterday."

"Moved here, huh? You got a U-haul somewhere or did you just 'move' that backpack?"

She looked down at the sand. "I was going to stay at that Hanover place—but when I got there I found out the people who ran it were killed. I didn't know what else to do."

He stared at her for a moment, wondering if such a coincidence was even possible, or if she knew something about the murders. "Come with me," he said.

She looked frightened and backed away. "No, I didn't mean to do anything wrong. Please."

"I just need to talk to you at the station across the street."

"Am I arrested?" she asked. "Just 'cause I didn't have a place to stay?"

"No," he said. "Get your stuff and come on."

She turned back and grabbed the shirt that had served as a makeshift blanket, stuffed it and the windbreaker into her backpack, and trudged across the sand.

As they crossed the street, he watched the way she cradled her arm. Fell down the stairs? Likely story. She had obviously been in a struggle, with that eye and arm. Had it been with Thelma and Wayne? Had she been the one who stole the speargun? If she knew how to use it, and stood close enough, it was possible . . .

And here she was sleeping on the beach, thinking she was hidden between the decks of two condominiums. . . . Her story didn't add up, and he was almost certain she had lied about her name and age.

He got her into the small interview room with another cop to witness, then asked her if he could search her backpack.

"Sure," she said, and handed it over.

There wasn't much there—just one shirt, a few school supplies, her wallet. "Thought you said you'd lost this."

"Oh," she said. "It must have been under something."

He opened it, and didn't find a driver's license. "No ID," he said.

She just looked at him.

That had been no big surprise. He had run her name through his database, but found no match for Sadie Smith. She fit the description of a dozen missing persons, but that proved nothing.

"Tell me how you knew Thelma and Wayne."

"I didn't know them," she said. Her eyes were big and round, blue as the sky today. But one of them was swollen almost shut.

"Then how were you going to stay with them?"

"A waitress at a diner in Savannah told me they might take me in. I didn't know they were dead."

"What time did you come into town yesterday?"

"I don't know," she said. "Maybe seven. It was still light out."

"How'd you get here?"

"Tammy, the waitress, brought me. I don't know her last name. She was nice. She said Thelma and Wayne were good about helping people with no place to go. She dropped me there, and I waited on the porch for somebody to get home. Then a florist guy came with a wreath . . ." She dropped her eyes to her arm, and her voice trailed off to a whisper. "He told me."

He leaned back in his chair and rubbed his face. He hadn't slept since they had found the bodies, and he was dog tired.

Her story sounded true. He thought about what Thelma and Wayne would have done for this girl, how Thelma would have embraced her and brought her into the House, seen to her wounds, and taken care of her needs. He wondered if he should call Blair and Morgan, but then he thought better of it. They had too much on their minds. They didn't need the burden of a teenage runaway. But he couldn't just send her back out on the street, and he wasn't too anxious to throw her back to the person who had beaten her up.

He stood up. "Come with me," he said.

"Where?" she asked.

"I'm taking you to the doctor."

"I don't have any money. I can't—"

"I'll pay for it," Cade said, "but you can't just walk around with a broken arm. You need medical attention. Thelma and Wayne would have done that for you."

She was quiet as she followed him out to his car, and when he opened the passenger door on the front seat, she slipped in. He started the car, and she looked over at him.

"Are you going to arrest me after he fixes my arm?"

"I don't know what I'm going to do with you," he said, "but I can't very well send you back out there to fend for yourself."

"It's better than being in jail," she said. "I swore I'd never go to jail. And I meant it. I didn't mean to break the law. I won't do it again."

He wondered why a child her age would swear she would never go to jail. Girls dreamed about being movie stars, models, mothers. Jail didn't cross the average kid's mind.

"I can get a job," she said. "I can find a place to live."

"Let's just take care of one thing at a time," he said. He drove a couple of blocks, then pulled into the driveway of an old Victorian house, painted purple. A sign out front said, "Cape Refuge Medical Clinic."

"Doc Spencer is a good man. He'll fix you up."

She looked pale as she got out of the car and followed him in.

CHAPTER

*D*r. Spencer was a kind old man who looked like somebody's grandfather. In the waiting room, he had one whole wall filled with pictures of babies he had delivered and children he had treated. In the examining room, he had a model of a skeletal backbone, and a Norman Rockwell print of a goofy boy getting a shot.

He was gentle with Sadie's arm, though any pressure at all felt like a knife stabbing into it. "The X-rays show that it's broken in two places," he said. "I'm going to have to set it and put a cast on it." He took off his glasses and rubbed his eyes. "Tell me, honey. How'd it really happen?"

She decided to stick to her story. "I just lost my balance and fell down some stairs."

He breathed a disbelieving laugh. "Your legs don't look bruised."

She knew she shouldn't have let the nurse talk her into putting on that gown. "I don't know—I—"

"When a young girl like you turns up on this island, sleeping on the beach, with breaks and bruises—I can't help thinking that she might be a runaway who was abused at home."

She swallowed and looked down.

"You *were* beaten up, weren't you?"

She blinked back the tears stinging her eyes. "Okay," she said. "But that doesn't mean I'm a runaway. I'm eighteen. I can go anywhere I want."

"Who beat you up? Your boyfriend? Your father?"

"I don't have either," she said.

"Your mother?"

"No. . . ."

He started to clean his glasses with the edge of his lab coat, then shoved them back on. "Whoever it was, they need to be locked up. They don't need to get away with this."

Sadie looked at the ceiling, trying not to let those tears fall. Jack always got away with it. She had called the police before, but he had threatened to hurt Caleb if she told them what had happened.

"I just want to start a new life," she whispered. "This place looks like a dream I had once. If I could just start over here."

The old man patted her shoulder and offered her a compassionate smile. "Well, let me get that arm cast, and you can get on with starting over."

The funeral director in Savannah was good at his job. His soft, gentle manner suggested that he grieved over their parents too. But Morgan knew he had never met them.

"Will you be having two services, or just one for both of them?" he asked in that cautious, soft voice.

"Just one," Morgan said, and Blair nodded agreement.

"And who would you like to preach at the funeral service?"

Morgan looked at Blair. Their father was the preacher of their little church. "I don't know," she said. "I hadn't thought about it."

"Who preaches at the funeral of the preacher?" Blair said in that weary monotone she had used all day.

"Well, you could choose a member of the congregation, or a preacher from a nearby church, or someone from your past. Or we could provide a preacher—"

"No," Blair cut in. "A lot of people loved our father. We don't need to get a stranger."

Morgan was having trouble swallowing. "That—that man who ran that shelter in town. You know, where Pop went to help out. He brought some of those people home," Morgan said. "Yes, maybe he would do it. His name was Frank. Frank Jordan, I think. It was the Gateway Missions in Savannah."

"I'll contact him for you," the man said. "Now, would you like to have the service here or somewhere on Cape Refuge?"

"At our warehouse, where we had church," Morgan said.

"No." Blair's mouth trembled. "Morgan, that's where they were killed. There's still blood on the floor." Her voice broke. "I don't want it there."

Morgan looked down at her hands in her lap. She wished that Jonathan was here or that they had brought Melba. They needed someone objective to help with the million decisions to be made.

"There's also the problem of seating," the man said. "It's very likely that a lot of people will turn out for this. Probably way too many to fit into a warehouse."

"All right," Morgan said. "Maybe the Calvary Baptist Church would let us use their building."

"I'll take care of it," he said and jotted that in his notebook. "Now, about visitation. When would you like to hold the viewing?"

"I don't want a viewing," Blair said. "I don't want people gawking at my mother and father."

"Then we could close the caskets and simply have a visitation."

"No," Blair said. "I don't want to see people and talk to them and answer their inane questions and hear their empty platitudes. The funeral's enough."

"But, Miss Owens, most families find the visitation to be comforting. People can come by and tell you what your parents meant to them."

"I know what my parents meant to them," she said.

He looked at Morgan, as if hoping she would reason with her sister. But Blair's logic made sense to her. "Just the funeral," she said.

"And the burial, of course," he said. "Would you like to bury them at our cemetery?"

Blair leaned back in her chair and looked up at the ceiling. Morgan knew she was fighting tears. She still hadn't seen her cry.

She wished she were that strong. Her tears hadn't stopped since yesterday.

"I know this is difficult," the man prompted.

Finally, Blair answered. "I don't want them in the ground."

Morgan took her hand. "Blair, they're not in those bodies. It doesn't matter where we bury them."

"I can't do it. Maybe we should bury them at sea. They loved the sea. We could take a boat out and have a small, private service out on the ocean."

Morgan considered that for a moment. "I think they would have liked that."

"Then you'll want them cremated," he said, jotting on his notepad.

"No, we certainly do not," Blair said. "Can't we have a sea burial with caskets?"

"Of course we can," he said. "We'll have to get permission, but it shouldn't be a problem."

"Then we'll do that," Blair told the man. "We can use Jonathan's boat and have a private burial at sea."

"But won't your parents' friends want to come? Your church members? The people of the community? There's comfort in closure. . . ."

"The people can worry about their own closure," Blair said, her voice too loud. "I don't have the energy to do it for them."

Later, as Blair drove home, physically exhausted and mentally drained, Morgan gazed out the window. "Did we do the right things?" she asked.

"We did the best we could," Blair said.

Morgan sighed. "There are still so many decisions to be made. The music, the eulogy—I wish Jonathan was here."

"Maybe they'll let him out in time for the funeral."

Silence lay heavily over them as they drove home. Morgan leaned her head against the window and sniffed and wiped tears. After a while, she said, "I've got to start thinking of them in heaven. Pop's hearing restored, his arthritis gone, Mama's laughter like music in Jesus' ears."

Blair wanted, more than ever, to believe in an afterlife. If heaven was real, were they singing praise songs and running through meadows? Were they reunited with that AIDS patient they had harbored at Hanover House, or Sam, the man in the last stages of cancer when he had come?

She wished she could believe she would see them again. But her mind wouldn't allow herself to believe. Yesterday was the end of them, and that was all there was to it.

If she could only make herself say good-bye.

CHAPTER

*T*he cast itched, and Sadie's arm ached. Gritty sand had worked its way into the cast, and it coated her clothes and her skin. Hot sun lasered down on her with blistering intensity, but she couldn't seem to escape it.

She had spent the afternoon walking along the beach, picking up change left by sunbathers. A quarter here, a nickel there. Once, she had found a dollar rolled up inside a paper cup. She managed to collect a little over ten dollars, half of which she spent on a hot dog and drink. Strength seeped back into her muscles and bones with every bite, but dread overwhelmed her. Night would fall soon, and she still hadn't found a job or a place to stay.

And who in their right mind would hire a girl who hadn't bathed in days, who looked as if she had been in a fight and lost, who didn't have a toothbrush or clean clothes or a hairbrush?

Back home in Atlanta, there were homeless people all over the streets, sleeping in doorways, begging on the curbs, walking the sidewalks, looking for cans or change or handouts. She had walked down those streets with fear and distaste, thinking there was something wrong with people like that. Why don't they just get a job and a place to live like everyone else, she had often thought. If they spent half as much time looking for legitimate work as they spent begging or digging through trash cans, they'd have nice homes and plenty of food.

Now she knew better. She was one of them, a homeless stray hunting for nickels and pennies. She had often guessed what she would do in their position, how she would rise above her circumstances, how she would never allow herself to get that low.

But she had been proven wrong.

Weary, she sat in the sand and watched a group of children playing in the surf. The waves were too tall for them, and she worried that they had gone out too far. She searched for their parents, saw that the mother was on her feet, yelling for them to come back.

The ocean's response was to slap more waves on the shoreline, its loud roar mocking the lone voice of the mother. But the children came back, jumping and challenging those waves, laughing and splashing.

Overhead, a gull squawked in a flat, off-key note. Behind her, someone played a radio too loudly, a vulgar, angry rap song.

Her first sight of the beach, just yesterday, had filled her with such hope, as if nothing bad could ever happen in a place like that. Now it seemed violent and unforgiving, threatening her hope and weakening her resolve. She longed to get away and find a place without sand where she could sleep tonight.

She tried to get her thoughts in order. First, she needed a bath. She needed to wash her hair and get presentable. Then she needed to wash her clothes. Once that was done, she might be able to get someone to hire her. If it was in a food place—a fast-food restaurant, maybe—at least she might be able to get her meals for free. If it was in a hotel, she might be able to get them to let her rent a room.

She turned around and looked at the motel just off the beach. Rooms faced the water, and maids moved with their carts along the rail of the upper floors. She could be one of them, she thought, if she could only convince the manager that her broken arm wouldn't hinder her work. Maybe she could do that work in the daytime and get something else at night.

Armed with purpose, she got up and walked to the concrete sidewalk that led around the pool to the stairs. She went up one flight and looked along the walkway that led in front of the doors. A maid was coming out of a room to drop dirty towels into her cart.

"Excuse me," Sadie said.

The Latino woman had her hair pulled back in a ponytail. She wore a crisp gray uniform, with a white apron. "Yes?" she asked.

"I'm looking for a job," Sadie said. "I wondered who I could talk to about working here."

The woman grabbed a stack of white towels to put into the rooms, and Sadie eyed the cart. A bucket of shampoo bottles, soaps, hand lotions were piled there. "My boss, she on the third floor, behind vending machines," the woman said in a thick Mexican accent. "She not hiring, though."

"She's not?" Sadie asked. "Why not?"

"She have all she need," she said.

"Okay," Sadie said. "I'll try somewhere else." She started to walk away, then stopped and turned back. "Uh ... would it be possible ... I mean ... would you mind ..." She cleared her throat. "I was wondering if I could take one of these bars of soap and a shampoo? I could really use a bath."

The woman eyed her for a moment, then finally gave her the ones in her hand. "That's all I can give," she said. "I get in trouble."

"Sure, of course. Thank you." Sadie unzipped her backpack and stuffed the items down into it. Now, if she could just find a place to shower.

She went back down the stairs but stopped before descending completely. Her eyes scanned the beach, looking for a shower. There was one near the pool of this very hotel, meant for washing off sand. There were probably others, she thought. She could wash her hair there, and scrub the sand off of her skin.

But then what would she wear?

Her eyes fell on a girl strolling down to the beach, wearing a breezy, pale blue sundress. Her blonde hair flew in the breeze behind her, and her skin was bronze, as if she came here daily to soak up the rays. She looked like a homecoming queen, Sadie thought with admiration. Like a cheerleader or a lifeguard.

She probably had a pink bedroom with flowered wallpaper and a mother who waited up for her at night. She probably talked on the phone for hours each day, went to movies, had boyfriends.

She watched the girl drop a towel onto the sand. Then she shed that dress, revealing a bikini beneath it. She kicked off her sandals, left them there with the dress on the towel, and headed for the water.

Sadie's heart quickened. If she had a dress like that, she knew she could get a job. It would be easy. With her hair washed and those clothes, she would look so much more respectable. That girl probably had twenty others like it in her closet. She probably had a pair of shoes for every outfit.

She hurried down the stairs and out across the sand, intent on taking the girl's clothes while she was in the water. She had never stolen before, so her hands trembled and her heart raced, but she told herself there was no other way. She just wanted a job, a place to stay, food to eat.

Basic things. Wasn't it all right to steal for basic things?

She reached the sand, and her step slowed as she watched the girl get doused by a wave. She stood there, sweeping her hair back.

She had sworn she would never wind up in jail like her mother. Not for anything, she had told herself. It was easy to avoid. All she had to do was keep the law.

But that dress was what she needed, and those sandals that hadn't yet been covered with sand. She would look pretty in them, clean, respectable. Not at all like a runaway.

Her mouth went dry, and her legs grew weak. The girl dove into a wave, came up on the other side, and swam out toward the next one.

There was plenty of time, she thought, and no one was looking. But if they were—if someone saw her—that police chief might have to arrest her, and he would shake his head and say he might have known, that nothing good could come from a girl sleeping on the beach....

She reached the clothes, stood over them, and watched the girl swimming further. The clothes lay in a wad at Sadie's feet. She could swoop them up, stuff them in her bag, walk on, as if nothing had happened. She could just reach down . . .

Her body froze, and she thought of her mother in jail, warning her never to break the law. *Don't wind up like me, Sadie. You're better than that.*

Her resolve suddenly melted like chocolate in the sun.

She would have to find another way.

As if she feared being caught in her intentions, she turned and ran down the beach, away from the dress and the shoes, away from the girl who probably dominated the pages of her high school yearbook, away from the eyes that might have seen her, had she succumbed.

And as she ran, she began to cry, for she didn't know what to do next.

CHAPTER

*T*hey held the funeral service two days later in the Calvary Baptist Church on the island. Jonathan was not allowed to leave jail, so Morgan and Blair clung together, alone on the front row of the church. The city council sat near the front like government dignitaries, as if no one remembered that, just three nights ago, they had been trying to ruin those for whom they mourned today. But the congregation of their warehouse church, and most of the town of Cape Refuge, turned out and sang praise songs exactly the way Thelma and Wayne would have directed them.

Morgan closed her eyes and sent her mind on a mission to pull up every Scripture verse she knew to get her through this moment.

Absent from the body, present with the Lord.
We do not grieve as those who have no hope.
Precious in the sight of the Lord is the death
of his saints.

Her mind captured one after another, like lifelines keeping her from sinking into the muck of despair.

She had Blair's hand in hers and thought how cold it was. Her sister's face was pale and expressionless, a blank slate for fertile imaginations who would gossip that Blair had not cried at her own parents' funeral. But they hadn't seen her in the library that night.

The preacher addressed the two of them as if they were the only two in the room, with sweet stories about her parents that made the crowd chuckle nostalgically.

But Morgan couldn't laugh. She wanted to leap up and scream out that they could come here and wipe a tear or two, tell a funny story, laugh, change the subject, network, gossip, catch up, then go home and sit down to eat with their families. Their lives would go on. It was too cruel.

She had often wished that God offered us each one chance to turn back time, one chance to do things over. She would have wasted hers years ago, when she dyed her brown, curly hair blonde and it came out orange, or when her tenth-grade boyfriend broke her heart. Or if she had made it to the age of twenty-eight without using it, would she know how far back to turn the clock to prevent her parents' murders? Would one day do it? Two days? A week? Or had it started years ago, when they began their ministry and started taking risks for the Lord?

God was merciful for not giving us that time-turning option, she supposed. She wasn't wise enough to use it well.

The very act of sitting in this building with this sniffing crowd indicated her acceptance of their deaths. But she did not accept it. Her heart lashed out now with the same screaming, crashing fury that Blair had shown in the library. Only no one knew it.

She quenched her loud, heartbroken, raging grief in quiet nods and weak smiles, as if there wasn't a hole burning right through her center.

We do not grieve as those who have no hope.

If hers was the grief of hope, then she knew that her sister's grief was even more consuming. Blair had no hope.

She squeezed her sister's hand more tightly, trying to warm its icy chill.

But Blair sat stiff, like a statue, vacant and blank and pale, except for the crimson color of her scar.

Blair came back to herself about a mile from shore, as Jonathan's boat took them out to bury the bodies at sea. They had only invited a handful of people to join them—the preacher conducting the funeral, Jay Riley to pilot the boat, and a few of Thelma and Wayne's closest friends.

They rode out for two hours into the deeper ocean, then had another short service. The men Morgan had chosen as pallbearers lowered the coffins over the side of the boat. The friends and loved ones who had been granted the honor of coming out with them came by Blair and Morgan and paid their respects in turn.

When it was finally the crusty boat pilot's turn, he took off his hat and held it over his heart. "I'm sorry for your pain," he said awkwardly.

Morgan took his hand and thanked him. Blair thought he smelled like fish, and she wondered if he hadn't bothered to wear clean clothes for the funeral.

But the boat, itself, had a rank fish odor. Morgan had gotten some friends to wash the deck and clean up the boat before they used it, but the smell was impossible to get rid of.

Jay came to Blair next and took her hand. "Your parents were good people," he said.

He sounded like he was reading a script, and the thought made Blair angry. She'd rather he said nothing at all.

"Ironic, ain't it?" he said to both of them.

"What is?" Morgan asked.

"That we'd take Jonathan's boat out to bury his victims."

Morgan's mouth fell open, but that scar on Blair's face reddened instantly. "Jay," she said. "why don't you just go back and drive the boat, since that's the only reason you were invited to come?"

He looked shocked at her outburst, then shaking his head, as if he didn't know what had set her off, he went back to the helm.

Later, as she and Morgan sat side by side in the back of the boat, Morgan looked over at her. "Everybody thinks he did it."

"They ought to have sensitivity training for people like that before they allow them to walk around in public," Blair said.

Morgan started to laugh quietly, and finally Blair joined. They leaned against each other until that tired laughter played down.

"I'm sorry I thought he did it at first," Blair said. "I know Jonathan didn't kill anybody."

"Thank you," Morgan said, her eyes growing serious again.

"We're going to get him out of there," Blair said. "And we're going to find who did this."

"I know we are," Morgan whispered.

As they pulled back up to the dock, their faces sobered again. "I've got a lot to do tonight," Blair whispered. "I've got to put the library back together."

Morgan was quiet for a moment as the dock grew closer. "You're not going to have to do it alone," she said. "I'll be there to help you."

Blair looked over at her and registered the statement. Somehow it seemed right that her sister would be there beside her, picking up the pieces, putting them all back together. Quietly, she accepted that as the trip to bury their parents came to an end.

CHAPTER

*T*he visitation room at the Cape Refuge jail was combined with the kitchenette where the officers heated up their honey buns in the mornings. One of the rookie officers stood near the refrigerator, guarding Jonathan and Morgan as they visited. Her eyes were red and puffy, and she looked like she hadn't slept in days.

"J.J., could we have a little privacy?" Jonathan asked.

The young man shook his head. "Sorry, Jonathan. Can't do it. Cade told me I had to guard you."

"Well, you can guard me, but couldn't you put on some headphones or something? I mean, I'm entitled to a little conversation with my wife."

J.J. Clyde, an officer who had played defensive tackle for Cape Refuge High just a year ago, thought it over, then went over to his locker and pulled out his headphones and his Walkman.

"I'm going to put these on," he said, "but you won't know when I've turned down the volume. I'm going to be listening in and out."

Jonathan rolled his eyes. "Okay, J.J."

J.J. put on the headphones and went back to the refrigerator as if he considered raiding it.

Jonathan focused on Morgan. "Are you okay?"

"It was hard without you."

"It was hard not being there," he said. "My own in-laws. I couldn't even go to their funeral. That beats everything. I can't believe how stupid this police department is."

"Jonathan." Morgan's word cut into his, silencing him. He glanced up at J.J. whose hand gravitated to the Walkman as if he was about to turn it down and tune in to their conversation.

"You don't need to make them mad," she whispered. "It's already bad enough."

"Arraignment is tomorrow," Jonathan said. "If I'm arraigned, they'll probably move me to Chatham County Detention Center."

"No!" She sat up straighter. "Jonathan, they can't put you there."

"It's gonna be okay," he said. "I'm not afraid of jail, baby. I've ministered there with your pop enough to know what it's like. I never wanted to be one of them, but I'll survive it until this is all straightened out."

"But how can we get it straightened out when everybody's focusing on you?" She rubbed her eyes. She hadn't even bothered to wear makeup today. She had barely managed to shower and get dressed for the funeral. Melba had gone to get her clothes from the house, because she couldn't manage to face it just yet. "If I'd only asked who they were meeting . . ."

"They must have written down something," Jonathan said. "Your pop wrote everything on those little index cards he kept in his pockets."

"The police have everything that was on him."

"Maybe he left some on his desk at the house. There's got to be something there. Cade will get phone records, and find out who he talked to that day. Maybe there are some papers or something.

Maybe they have some information about Gus Hampton that could prove he did it. I can't believe they let that guy go."

Morgan sat straighter as a sense of purpose filled her. "I need to go look to see what I can find."

"No, not you," he said. "I don't want you there with Gus Hampton in the house. Cade will look. He's probably already searched the place by now."

"But they obviously didn't find anything," she said. "It might be the only way to get you out of here, Jonathan."

He touched her face and looked hard into her eyes. "Look at me, and listen hard. I don't want you anywhere near that place, do you understand me? I want you safe. Let Cade do the investigation."

She swallowed, not certain she could make that promise. His face softened, and he scooted his chair closer to hers, hugged her, and kissed the top of her head.

She closed her eyes and soaked in the feel and smell of him. "They feeding you okay?" she asked.

"Let's just say they're feeding me."

"Are you eating?" she asked.

"Yes, don't worry about me, baby. Just take care of yourself." He cupped her chin, made her look up at him with her wet eyes. "You're the prettiest girl I've ever known," he said.

She smiled, knowing it wasn't true. But it was true to him.

"Don't you be alone," he said. "I don't want you to be an open target for whoever it is walking around out there."

She closed her eyes. "Jonathan, you're scaring me."

"Good," he said. "I mean to scare you. We don't know who it is or what they want. But you and Blair, you stick together, okay? You'll be okay if you're with her."

"Jonathan, I'm not some weak little spineless creature. I can be strong too."

"I know you can, honey," he said, "but Blair can be a barracuda."

"She's real upset, you know," Morgan said. "She tore up the library out of pure rage. I promised to help her put it back together tonight."

"As long as you're together," he said. "And don't stay at Hanover House. I don't trust anybody there anymore."

"I know," she said. "I won't."

They heard footsteps on the building floor, then Cade came to the door and peered in like a teacher checking on one of his students. "J.J., what're you doing?"

J.J. jumped and pulled off his headphones. "Just listening to the news, Chief," he said. "I thought maybe it would give us a clue."

Cade looked disgusted. "You need a clue all right, but you're not going to get it from the news. Now pull off those headphones and get back to work."

He shot Morgan an apologetic look. "Sorry, Morgan, but I'm going to have to ask you to leave now. Your visitation time is over."

"It's not like anybody's keeping track," Jonathan said. "You're the boss around here last time I looked."

"We have rules," Cade said, "and I abide by them, just like I expect you to."

"I never expected to abide from this side of the bars," Jonathan muttered. He got up and bent over and gave Morgan a kiss.

Cade waited respectfully until she let him go, then he led Jonathan back to the jail cell.

Morgan didn't wait to say good-bye to Cade or anyone else in the station. She just headed out to her car, determined to find Blair so they could clean up the library, then head over to Hanover House to search their parents' things.

CHAPTER

26

*M*organ was full of plans and purpose by the time she found Blair at the library. They hadn't been there since the other night when Blair had torn the place up.

Blair stood in the middle of the room, surveying the damage. She had a blank look on her face as she stood in profile, the pale, pretty side of her face closest to Morgan.

"You okay?" Morgan asked.

"Yeah," Blair said absently. "Just wondering whatever possessed me to do this."

"I told you I'd help you clean it up. But I want you to do something else first."

Blair turned around. "What?"

"I want you to go with me to the house. I want to look through Mama and Pop's things for clues."

Blair frowned. "But you know the police have already done that. Wouldn't they have found something if there was something to find?"

"Maybe," Morgan said, picking up a book and smoothing out the pages with her hand. "Maybe not.

There may be something that would ring a bell for us but not for them. Besides, Cade's shorthanded for the investigation. They might not have done a thorough job." She looked around at the floor, wondering where to start. Blair didn't seem to know, either. "I was thinking that maybe we could go over there now, then clean this up when we get back."

"I guess we could," Blair said. "Hanover House is ours now. I guess we have to decide what to do. Maybe we should just give everybody notice and close the place down."

"No," Morgan said. "Mama and Pop fought too hard to keep it open."

"Well, we can't just keep it going to spite the city council. It's more than you can handle by yourself."

"But where will they go? No one on the island would take Gus, what with all these rumors. Rick isn't ready to leave yet. He's still not over the death of his wife and daughter. And Mrs. Hern is just in the beginning stages of Alzheimer's. She relied so on Mama."

"Still," Blair said, "I have a full-time job. I can't help with it."

"Yeah," Morgan said. "You've got your hands full with this mess."

Blair looked helplessly around her again. "Do you have any idea how heavy these bookshelves are?"

"I think I'm going to find out."

Blair stepped over some books. "Let's just go. It'll still be here when we get back."

The home in which Blair had spent most of her childhood years looked different as she pulled into the driveway. A wreath hung on the mailbox, offering grim notice of their bereavement. She looked up at the front door and saw another, larger wreath hung on the door in the place reserved for her mother's handmade Christmas wreath.

"We're going to need to write some thank-you notes," Morgan said softly. "The funeral director said they were bringing all the flowers here."

"Why didn't you tell him we don't want them? He should have thrown them away."

"That would have been rude," Morgan said. "Besides, some people sent pots of flowers that I want to plant in the yard. Kind of a memorial garden for them."

Blair's gaze drifted to the yellow Victorian house. White rocking chairs and a swing adorned the front porch. Full-bodied ferns spilled over hanging baskets at intervals along the eaves, and green azalea bushes lined the front lawn, a breathtaking addition to the groomed yard when they were in bloom each spring. Petunias of pink, white, and yellow filled the beds in front of the azaleas.

That was their memorial garden, she thought. Her mother's love shone in every blossom, in every carefully chosen color, in every placement, and her father's care gave them a healthy, hydrated look. He had watered them every morning after returning from Crickets. Sometimes he pulled up a lawn chair and sat down and prayed right out loud, as if God was in a chair next to him as he fed the garden.

"There shouldn't be flowers in bloom," Blair whispered under her breath. "When people you love die, it seems like every flower in the world ought to just die with them."

"It's nice that they don't," Morgan said.

Blair sat there a moment, staring up at the house. Fresh new anger surged through her.

Someone inside could be responsible for their deaths, or someone who had once passed through. Maybe the city council members' concerns had been prophetic. And there she'd been, spouting off at that microphone, defending the house and its tenants while her parents bled to death.

Morgan got out of the car. Blair followed her up to the front porch steps, climbed them one at a time. Morgan opened the front door. The parlor was empty. It was dark except for the Tiffany lamp in each corner, and the piano light that illuminated the sheet music for "It Is Well with My Soul."

So many times, her father had told the story of the man who had written that song. His four children had drowned in a storm at sea, all of them, and his wife sent a telegram home to him. "Saved alone," it said. Later, the man had sailed to that very spot where his children had lost their lives and, standing on the deck of the ship, had penned the song.

Blair didn't know where he got his peace or how he had managed to speak, let alone sing, those words. Her chest tightened in resentment at his misguided faith.

It was not well with her soul, and it never would be.

Someone had brought the mail in and left it in a stack on the coffee table. Condolence cards and notes had already begun coming, and she wondered if people really expected them to read all of them and answer.

Almost reverent in her silence, Morgan went into the kitchen. Blair went with her. Through the back window to the screened porch, Blair saw Mrs. Hern, the old woman who had moved there after serving three years in prison for embezzlement. She sat slumped in front of an easel propped at the corner of the porch, her back to them.

Blair didn't want to see anyone, for the thought of making small talk seemed worse to her than the empty silence of the house. But Morgan opened the door and stepped out. Mrs. Hern turned around, her unbound gray hair swinging around her shoulders and sticking to her wet face. She had been crying for hours, it was clear. Her nose was so red and her eyes so swollen that Blair had to look away.

"Oh, Mrs. Hern." Morgan took the old woman into her arms.

The woman's frail body shook as she clung to Morgan. "I know she was your mama and all," she wept, "but I sure loved her."

"I know," Morgan whispered. "I know."

Blair looked away from the two clutched together, trying not to get pulled into that maelstrom of despair again. Her grief had a different manifestation that she didn't quite understand. It came up in rage, like a cracking, furious storm, rather than a soft drizzle. She had to fight it.

She stepped over to the painting, trying to get her mind off of Mrs. Hern's grief.

There were clouds everywhere, and in the center of the canvas was an unfinished white horse and someone riding it.

When Morgan finally let Mrs. Hern go, the woman turned her tormented face to Blair. "You're not going to close the house down, are you?" she asked, taking Blair's hand.

Blair didn't pull away. "We don't know, Mrs. Hern."

"Please, you can't," she said. "I don't know what I'll do. There's no place else I can stay. They'll put me in a nursing home, only I'm not that far gone yet. My memory goes sometimes, but I think the medication's helping. I don't know how much longer they'll let me work at Goodfellow's because I've been making too many mistakes lately. Thelma told me she wouldn't throw me out if I couldn't pay, that I could help around here to earn my keep."

"I know," Morgan said. "She told me all that. You don't have to worry. We're not going to run you off. When we make a decision, we'll make sure you're taken care of."

Blair wished Morgan wouldn't make such promises. Hoping to change the subject, she looked back into the house. "Where is everybody?"

"Gus is up in his room playing his guitar," Mrs. Hern said, "and I think Rick is across the street at the beach. He likes to go over there by himself and think. Lana and Harry both left. They checked out after the funeral when the police told them they could leave."

"The police questioned them?" Blair asked.

"Oh, yes," Mrs. Hern said. "They questioned all of us here."

"Then they've been through Mama and Pop's things?"

"Seems like they did," she said. "They went upstairs while we were being questioned in the front room." She let Blair go and took Morgan's hand. "I know you don't feel like doing what you usually do around here," she said, "but I wanted you to know that I learned a lot from Thelma. She taught me how to cook some of her best recipes, and I'd been helping her clean up. I can take care of the place if you want until you feel like coming back. I know with Jonathan in jail and all, you've got a lot on your plate."

The woman hadn't even remembered to brush her hair this morning, Blair thought. How could she take care of the house?

"Feels like I ought to do something, the way Thelma and Wayne took care of me." Mrs. Hern burst into tears again and turned back to her painting.

Morgan stroked the old woman's hair. Blair almost envied her sister. This was the strongest she had seen her since they had learned of the murders. Leave it to Morgan to find strength in reaching out to others.

"I was just painting that verse in Thessalonians," Mrs. Hern said. "The one about the Lord coming back from heaven for us."

"First Thessalonians 4:16," Morgan said softly. "Pop's favorite verse: 'For the Lord himself will come down from heaven, with a loud command, with the voice of the archangel and with the trumpet call of God, and the dead in Christ will rise first. After that, we who are still alive and are left will be caught up together with them in the clouds to meet the Lord in the air. And so we will be with the Lord forever.'"

Blair let those words float like a balloon in her mind, bouncing gently off the sides, never quite settling in. She had heard her parents quote it many times. She could probably have quoted it herself.

It made sense that Mrs. Hern would want to be reminded of it now. It did offer comfort. If it was true, then there would be a reunion someday. She wished she could believe it.

She didn't want to think about the crude, amateur painting anymore or the words it represented, so she went back into the house and started up the staircase.

She heard the sound of a guitar playing in one of the rooms, and saw that Gus's door was open. She stood frozen on the stairs, listening, thinking, trying to sort through the things she knew about the man—the 20/20 report, the mayor's accusations, Jonathan's concerns . . .

She heard Morgan's footsteps behind her. When she reached the second floor, she looked inside and saw the big black man sitting on his bed with his red bandana tied around his head. He stopped playing the moment he saw her.

"Blair," he said in his throaty Jamaican accent. "Ah, Morgan." He set down the guitar and came to hug them. Blair was stiff, and she could see that Morgan was cooler with him than she was with Mrs. Hern.

"I'm so sorry," he said in that deep bass. "Who would kill those kind people?"

"We don't know," Blair whispered.

"I know what you be thinking," he said. "I know you are suspicious right now, with all this talk about me. But I tell you, I would never hurt Thelma and Wayne."

Neither of them said a word, and Blair tried to process his statement in her mind. Would a guilty person broach the subject head on or avoid it completely?

He went back to his guitar. "I was just playing 'How Great Thou Art.' Wayne taught me. I played it in the church two weeks ago. You remember that, Morgan?"

She nodded and looked at her feet.

"'Praise the Lord,' Wayne always be saying. So I'm tryin'. Wish I'd known about it in the prison. Instead o' cursin', I coulda been prayin'. You know how I came to be here, don't you, Miss Blair?"

Blair shook her head. "No, Gus. Tell me."

He strummed a few chords. "I just got my release from the prison, and I had no place to go, mon, absolutely no place. Rescue mission took me in and let me sleep there at night. And Wayne and Thelma would come there and do Bible studies with us. After the rescue mission told me I'd been there too long, I had to move on and make room for somebody else, Wayne let me come to stay here and got me a job. Best mon who ever lived."

Blair let her eyes wander around the room while he spoke. It was neat, and he had only a few personal items on the dresser. Some pocket change, the keys to the house and his truck, his billfold.

"The police interviewed me, and let me go. I was at work all that day. I know Jonathan didn't do it, either, Miss Morgan. He wouldn't do that to them."

"No, he wouldn't."

Blair only stared at him, running every expression on his face through her mental lie detector. Did his body language suggest he was telling the truth? Was he hiding something?

She couldn't say for sure.

They left him alone in his room, and Morgan crossed the hall to her parents' doorway. The room was just as they had left it. Everything was neat and in its place, freshly dusted and fluffed. The bedroom was the most lived-in room of the house, and the least elaborate. Her mother's things graced the tables and stand, and family pictures hung in collections on the walls.

Blair went in, but Morgan froze in the doorway. "I can't do this," she said. "I can't go in there and rifle through their things. I'm not ready for this yet."

"Neither am I," Blair said. "But I haven't been ready for much of what's happened in the last few days."

"Maybe Jonathan's right. Maybe we shouldn't have come."

"We're here," Blair said. "Let's just get what we need and take it back to my house."

Morgan took a tentative step into the room. "I feel like I'm invading their privacy."

"We are. But they're not in a position to care." The words came out on a cruel note. She didn't know where that flip tone came from.

She bent down and looked under the bed. She pulled out the boxes in which her parents archived their most important papers. "Let's take these," she said.

"Okay," Morgan said. "And we can take the file cabinet downstairs, if the police haven't already taken it for evidence."

"Do you know where the key to the file cabinet is?"

"She kept it in her jewelry box," Morgan said. She crossed the room slowly, anguish on her face, and went into the closet where her mother's modest jewelry box lay. She opened it, found the key.

"Okay," Blair said, "help me carry the boxes down."

"We could get Gus to help," Morgan said.

"Leave the tenants out of this. It's just us."

Blair grabbed one box, and Morgan took the other.

When they had loaded the car, Blair saw Rick—the other tenant—sitting in the sand across the street, watching the ocean. "There's Rick," she said as a warm breeze picked up and whispered through the trees, blowing her hair against her mouth. She pushed it back. Morgan came up beside her. Her long curls bounced in the breeze.

"He does that a lot," she said. "Just sits out there staring out at the waves. Mama said it's how he grieves."

Blair had heard the story from her mother about how he had lost his wife and daughter in a drunk-driving accident and how he had come here seeking refuge while he tried to endure the pain.

"I'm going to run back in and get a few things together to bring back to your house," Morgan said. "I'll be right back."

Blair waited at the car, watching Rick as the waves lapped up close to his feet. He was a suspect too, as far as she was concerned. She needed to talk to him, read his face. She needed to see if he grieved over her parents.

She crossed the street, and her feet rocked across the sand as she walked toward where he sat. The waves hit hard against the shore. A storm was probably blowing in, she thought. It was appropriate—more so than the bright sunshine that mocked her pain. She wanted thunder and lightning, howling wind, dark skies.

She walked up behind Rick and set her hand on his shoulder. He jumped and almost knocked his chair over.

"Blair!" he said. "You scared me."

"Sorry."

He sat back in his chair, trying to steady his breathing. He looked pale, tired, just like the rest of them, and his eyes looked raw and red.

"I was waiting for Morgan," she said. "I thought I'd come over and speak."

He leaned forward, his elbows on his knees. He was familiar with grief, she thought, and knew what not to say. "I like to come out here sometimes," he said. "There's something healing about sitting here and listening to the waves, knowing that God is still in control even when it seems like he's not." His voice faded out and he swallowed and got to his feet. He was a head taller than she and looked down at her with sorrowful eyes. "I'm going to miss your parents," he said. "I'm going to miss them real bad."

Blair turned the scarred side of her face away and gazed out over the water. A schooner was coming in, slowly making its way to the shore. There had been times in her life when she had sat on this beach herself and watched those boats come and go, wondering what it would be like to be on your way to some distant country, not knowing when or if you would return. She had dreamed of sailing away. But she never had, simply because the scars would have gone with her. And wherever she wound up, they would still be the ball and chain that held her to her past. And thwarted her future.

"I've been sitting here for a couple of hours," he said, "watching for that boat to come in. I didn't see it until just now."

He slapped his hands against his thighs, then let them hang limply to his sides. "I thought I was healing; I thought I was coming to terms with what happened to my family." His voice blended with the sound of the wind and the waves. "Now I have to grieve over the people who were helping me heal. Sometimes you just wonder how many more people are going to have to go before God thinks you've had enough."

Blair swallowed and kept her eyes on that boat.

"I'm sorry, Blair," he said.

She shook her head. "Don't be. It's okay. I feel the same way."

The water began reaching farther as the tide rose. She backed up so it wouldn't rush around her feet. "Sometimes I feel like somebody's just walloped me in the stomach and I can't catch my breath," she said.

"That's it," he said. "That's exactly it. I can't catch my breath. I haven't caught it yet from what happened a year ago."

He sat back down in the chair and dropped his face into his hands. Slowly he rubbed them down his face and looked up at her.

"How do you do it, Blair? How do you not cry? I saw you at the funeral service today. Your eyes were dry."

That boat looked so peaceful, floating toward home. But behind it, dark clouds closed in, moving faster than the boat. "Crying doesn't do much good," she said.

She didn't want to tell him that if she ever got started, her tears might never stop. "I have to go," she said. She started back across the sand.

"Blair." Rick's voice stopped her. She turned back. He had stood up again, taken a few steps toward her. "Yeah?"

"I hope they find them. Whoever did that to your parents, I hope they find them soon."

"Me too," she said.

"You know what your mama would tell you right now?" he asked. "She would tell you to cling to the Lord with all your might. And she would tell you to forgive."

Blair's hair whipped into her face. "That's a tall order when you don't know who to forgive."

"It's a tall order even when you do."

She knew he was talking about his family and the drunk who had killed them. For the first time she felt something of the pull that Morgan had toward the tenants, a little connection of understanding, an affinity that she hadn't expected to feel.

"Your mother wouldn't say it was easy," he said, "but you know she'd say it."

"Yeah," Blair said, "she'd say it, all right."

She met his eyes for a moment, saw the genuine grief pulling at his face, rimming his eyes. Finally, she turned away and hurried across the street where her sister waited.

CHAPTER

$\mathcal{S}$adie had gathered enough change to buy a toothbrush and some toothpaste, so she went into Goodfellow's Grocery and closed her eyes in pleasure at the rush of cool air conditioning. Though she had bathed daily at the outdoor showers, she still felt sticky and sandy. She had washed her clothes in the swimming pool at one of the hotels last night, but they still smelled of perspiration.

She had slept in a boat bobbing in the water near the dock, curled up on the floor so no one would see her. It was comfortable, and she had found a life jacket for a pillow, and a tarp with which to cover herself. The act of surviving had become a full-time job, the only one she could get.

She found the toothbrushes and chose the cheapest one, grabbed a small tube of toothpaste, and counted out her change. There was enough, she thought with gratitude.

She headed for the front and waited in the short line. The people in front of her had obviously been on the beach all day. Like her, they looked sandy and sweaty, and their clothes were rumpled and damp.

Maybe people would think she was a sun-drenched tourist instead of a homeless runaway.

She got to the front of the line and set the items down.

"You find everything all right?" the checkout girl asked.

"Yes," she said, trying to smile. "It sure is hot out there."

"Yep," the girl said. "Humidity's like five hundred percent." She rang the toothbrush and toothpaste up. "That'll be two dollars, thirty-six cents."

Sadie counted out her change, dropped it into her hand. "You wouldn't have any openings here, would you? I sure could use a job."

The girl shrugged. "Sometimes they do. You could ask over there. The guy with the mustache. He owns the place."

"Mr. Goodfellow?" Sadie asked with a smirk.

The girl laughed. "No, Mr. Jenkins." She lowered her voice. "And he's not that good a fellow, either."

Sadie thanked her and headed for the man. He was surveying his stock of soup, and she came up behind him and cleared her throat.

He turned around.

"Excuse me," she said. "I know I look awful. I've been on the beach all day. But I was wondering if you had any job openings. I'm a real hard worker, and I really need the money."

He looked down at her cast. "You live around here?"

"I'm new in town," she said. "I was in a car accident a couple of days ago. Great way to start a vacation, you know? Anyway, I like it so much that I wanted to try to stay. I graduated last month, so I can really go anywhere I want. . . ."

She stopped, realizing she was saying too much. Lies were best told in bits and pieces, not with long explanations.

"You can fill out an application," he said. "If anything comes up, I could call you."

"Okay," she said. "Only, I'm not sure where I'll be staying, so I'll just check back every day. Will that be okay?"

He shrugged like he didn't much care. "Fine." He got her an application. "Just leave it with the cashier when you're done."

She filled it out, lying about her home address, her age, her school. Then she left it with the girl at the front. Brimming with hope, she left the store. Maybe he would hire her. It would be a nice place to work. She could make friends with the cashier, buy the food she needed, and stay in air conditioning.

She crossed the busy road and went back down to the beach to walk along the shoreline. When she reached the end of the sand, she walked further, up along the river side of the island. She crossed through the yard of a house on the water and saw a boat-house at the end of a drive.

It looked like a little house, with a front door and a roof, but only three walls. A boat probably floated inside it, she thought. It would be safer to sleep in a boat that was docked in a boathouse. She would be out of the wind and the sand and the morning dew, and no one would be as likely to find her there.

The idea blossomed in her mind as she walked further, looking for one that wasn't so close to a house. There were several, scattered out along the river, but most were too visible.

Finally, she came upon one situated in a woodsy area, with nothing but a dirt road leading to it. She tested the doorknob, but it was locked, so she took off her shoes and dropped her back-pack and slipped into the water. She swam to the opening of the little house. Just as she thought, a boat sat there in the opening of the boathouse floor, and around it was enough room to walk, and various items hung on the walls.

She pulled up onto the floor and looked around. Yes, this place was lonely enough to keep her hidden tonight, and it wasn't likely that anyone would want to take the boat out tonight. Tomorrow morning, she would leave early, then come back when it was dark again.

It was an answer, she thought, until she could get a job and find a better place.

Things were starting to look up.

CHAPTER

28

Morgan was quiet as they drove back across the island with their parents' boxes and file cabinet in the car. Blair seemed pensive too, lost in her own thoughts.

A massive magnolia tree blocked the view of Blair's house, the library, and the marine museum, as they came up the street.

As the place came into view, they saw police cars filling the library's parking lot. Morgan's heart jolted. "Oh, no," she whispered. "What now?"

Blair pulled haphazardly into the gravel parking lot and jumped out of her car. Cade came to the open door of the library.

"What is it, Cade?" she asked.

"Someone's broken into the library and vandalized the place," he said. "The mayor came looking for you, and he used his key to get in. It's a mess in there. We're dusting for prints."

Morgan touched Blair's back and saw that her facial scars flamed with shame. She started to speak up for Blair, but her sister lifted her chin defiantly. "I did it," Blair said.

Cade frowned. "Did what?"

"I'm the one who made the mess. I was—a little angry the other night," she said. "I kind of took it out on the books. I was going to put them back together before anybody saw it. I didn't think it would hurt for the library to be closed for a couple of days. Didn't count on the mayor using his key."

Cade stared at her in stunned silence. Finally, he said, "You did *that*? Shelves on the floor, books everywhere, tables knocked over?"

"Yes," she said. "I was just coming home to put it all back together. I'm sorry, okay? I was upset."

He gave her a long, contemplative look, and she turned her scars away from him.

"Okay," Cade said quietly. "It's no problem. One less crime to solve."

He stepped back to let her in. Melba stood among the books, her massive chest heaving. "Oh, honey, you're not safe anywhere around here," she cried. "They've come into the library and ransacked it—"

"It's okay, Melba," Cade cut in. "We know who's been in the library. Case solved."

Joe McCormick turned from where he was dusting. "Solved? Cade, what's going on?"

Cade motioned him into Blair's office at the back, muttered a few words, then they both came back out.

"Well, aren't you going to tell us who did it?" Melba demanded. "Don't we have a right to know? This could be the same person who killed Thelma and Wayne!"

"It was me," Blair cut in. "Cade's being polite. He doesn't want to embarrass me, but I'm the one who did it, Melba."

"Did what, honey?"

Blair was getting angry again, and the smooth side of her face was coloring to match the scar. "I'm the one who knocked the books over, okay? My parents were murdered that day. I was having a little trouble coping."

"Oh, honey." Melba brought her hand to her chest. "And here we thought you weren't—"

"Weren't what?" Blair asked. "You thought I wasn't grieving for my parents because I didn't cry out in the open where everybody could see and gossip about my tears like they were some kind of cheap entertainment? Is that what you thought?"

Horrified at Blair's outburst, Morgan touched Melba's shoulder. "Oh, Melba, she doesn't mean it. It's just been a really hard week."

The woman drew in a breath, raising her big chest. "Well, you don't have to tell me that now, honey. I understand completely. Just don't you worry another little bit about it."

"I came with Blair tonight to help her start putting things back together," Morgan said. "The library will be good as new before you know it. As organized as Blair usually keeps things, I'd say she has a right to blow a fuse every now and then."

Blair met Cade's somber eyes across the room. "I need to go call the mayor," he said. "You going to be all right?"

"Of course," she snapped. "I'll be fine."

Cade looked over at Morgan. "You'll stay with her?"

"I'm not leaving," Morgan said.

The exchange set Blair off again. "Don't talk about me like I'm unstable. I don't plan to destroy any more public property."

He looked wounded. "No, Blair," he said, "that wasn't what I was thinking at all. I just don't like to see you hurting."

Blair bent over and started snatching books off the floor. "Find someone else to feel sorry for, Cade."

Cade just watched her for a moment. Finally, he and Joe headed for the door.

Melba kissed Morgan, leaving a pink lipstick smear on her cheek. She touched Blair's hair and looked tearfully into her face. Blair moved away and grabbed another book.

When they were alone, Blair stooped down and began stacking books. "I can't blame the mayor for jumping to conclusions," she said with a sigh. "Wonder why he would use his key to get in? He's never done that before."

"Probably saw the mess through the window and got worried," Morgan said.

Blair lifted her stack and set them on a table. "I don't know what came over me. It's going to take us days to put everything back together." She bent over and picked up a rare, ancient book she had bought at an auction with her own money. "What am I saying? Days? It took me *years* to get it as organized as it was in the first place."

"Well, I'll work as long as it takes," Morgan said.

"What about going through Mama and Pop's things?"

"I don't think I'm up to it right now," Morgan said. "It's like rubbing alcohol into a wound. This kind of physical work is just what I need." She went to the top of one of the toppled bookshelves. "Give me a hand with this."

Blair got the other side, and with great effort, they managed to get it standing again.

They worked for twenty minutes trying to get the next one up, when they heard another car pull up.

"What now?" Morgan asked.

Blair went to the window. "It's Cade again."

Morgan looked out over her shoulder. Cade was getting out of his car, wearing blue jeans and a T-shirt with the sleeves cut off. "What does he want?"

Blair went to the door and flung it open. "What?"

"I thought I'd come help out," he said. "I knew you'd need some muscle to get these shelves back up."

Suddenly speechless, Blair turned to Morgan.

"I think we can do it ourselves," Morgan said. "Maybe you need to get on back to the jail and keep an eye on your prisoner."

"The prisoner's in good hands," he said. "I got a few minutes to spare."

"Well, maybe you should be out looking for whoever killed our parents," Morgan said. "The real murderer."

He looked down at Blair. "Do you want help or not, Blair?"

She turned back to the bookshelves lying like dominos across the floor. "I guess we could use his help," Blair said to Morgan. She glanced at Cade. "I appreciate it."

"No problem," he said, then he clomped back across the wooden floor to the bookshelf furthest in the back, the one on the top of the domino pile, and pulled it upright. When he had gotten the third set of shelves up, they heard another set of wheels on the gravel outside.

"Now what?" Morgan mumbled.

Blair went to the door and looked out. Melba and several ladies were getting out of the car.

"It's the cavalry," Cade said. "I asked Melba to get some people together to help with this."

Blair gave Cade a belligerent look. "They're not bringing food are they? We don't have any place to put it."

"No, they're not bringing food," Cade said with a grin. "They're just bringing a few more hands to help."

Melba came in, wearing stretch pants and a big floppy T-shirt. The other ladies were dressed for work, as well. "I couldn't get the whole auxiliary," she said, "but I did get ten of us."

Blair grunted. "Melba, it really isn't necessary. . . ."

"It certainly is," Melba said. "There's no reason you and Morgan should have to do this all by yourself." She stepped into the building and smiled at Cade. "And I see our police chief is already hard at work. Don't you worry about a thing," Melba said. "With thirteen of us working, we'll get it all done tonight. Might even get the place vacuumed and dusted too."

Morgan saw that Blair was about to object again. They both wanted to do it alone, quietly, without people trying to make them feel better. But it was impossible. "I can't argue with that," Blair said finally. "I appreciate it."

The ladies came in one by one with their condolences and hugs, and Blair and Morgan accepted them as each one started to work.

CHAPTER

*A*fter several hours, the shelves were standing, the books were stacked, and the ladies went home.
Cade lingered behind, as if there might be some last-minute
lifting for him to do. He didn't want to leave as long as he
could make anything easier for them.

Morgan had remained distant from him and avoided
speaking to him, but Blair seemed moved by the help he
had brought.

"Looks like maybe I can open again tomorrow," she
said. "That'll be good ... getting back to work."

Cade leaned against the wall, crossing his arms as he
looked down at her. "Tomorrow? Don't you think that's
too soon?"

"No, the sooner, the better," she said. "Besides, I'll
be here, anyway, at my computer. Figuring out who killed
my parents."

"Blair, come on. Let me take care of this."

"You're *not* taking care of it, Cade," she whispered,
glancing back at Morgan who was still dusting in the back.

149

"You've got the wrong guy." She started to walk away, but he touched her arm, stopping her.

"If Jonathan didn't do it, then we're going to find who did," he said.

"Well, I'm going to help you," Blair told him. "If there's anything I can do, it's research. I can find anything you want to know faster than anybody you know can do it."

"I'm sure that's true, Blair, but it could get dangerous. If Jonathan is not the guy, then somebody else is. I don't want you walking into any traps. And I'll tell you something. I'm sure not anxious to investigate another homicide."

He realized instantly that the words had been insensitive. Her face went pale.

"You're not going to talk me out of it, Cade," she said quietly. "I'm going to find out who killed my parents if it's the last thing I do. This killer has met his match."

He looked down at her, pensive. She had pretty, thoughtful eyes, the same color as the water off of Cayman Island. It was the only place he had ever seen that exact color. Her eyelashes were long and always looked a little wet. She was prettier than Morgan, he had always thought. Only she would never believe it.

As he gazed down at her, her hand came up to cover the scar on her face. It always did. He had never looked seriously at her when she didn't raise her hand up to scratch an itch just under her eye.

"Well, just do me one favor," Cade said. "If you find anything, let me have a look. It might help."

"Will you do the same?" she asked.

"No."

"I didn't think so. Cade, I'm not interested in sharing information with you if you won't share it with me."

"Well, are you interested in catching the killer?" he asked.

"Of course I am. Aren't you?"

"My point," he said, "is that it could happen faster if we share information."

"My point too."

"Yeah, but I'm an official. I am the police chief of Cape Refuge."

"And I'm the official librarian," she said.

"I don't want you and your sister playing detective and getting into trouble. We have a police force in this town. We can do this."

Blair looked up at him, her gaze sinking deep. "I know you loved them, Cade. They were your friends, even your mentors. They meant a lot of things to a lot of people. But they were *my* parents."

He swallowed and looked at his feet. "I know."

"And you know me," she said. "You know what I do. I look things up. I chase things down. I get the facts."

"I always said you should have been a detective."

"I prefer to chase my facts down on the computer or the telephone."

"Well, just don't fool yourself into thinking you're safe," Cade said, "that nobody's watching or listening or reading. Because you and Morgan could be pretty vulnerable right now."

"Funny. That's what Jonathan told her."

"Well, he's right," Cade said. "I'm going to have my men patrol your house a lot more than usual. You two need to stay together, and you need to watch your backs. Call me if anything happens. If you hear a noise in the night, if a dog barks that you're not used to hearing, if the wind even blows too hard, you call me. You hear?"

Blair looked up at him. "I hear."

"But will you do it?" Cade asked.

She thought about that for a moment. "Of course I will. I don't have a death wish."

"Middle of the night, two in the morning—I don't care," Cade said. "I'm there in minutes."

She looked up at him, met his eyes. "You talk real scary for a man who thought he had the crime solved," she said. "If you're so sure we're in danger, why is Jonathan still behind bars?"

"I'm covering all my bases," he said.

Blair just stared at him. "I do have a .22 in my closet. By Georgia law, I can carry it in my purse, since I have a license. I've never really felt the need to carry it, but maybe I should start."

"As long as you use it for self-defense," Cade said, "and don't go off half-cocked, taking the law into your own hands."

"Who me?" Blair asked.

Cade sighed. He stood straighter and caught Morgan's eye in the back of the library. "See you later, Morgan," he called back.

She only turned away. He wondered if Morgan would ever speak to him again, but he couldn't worry about that now. He had a job to do, and he needed to get back to the station and do it.

CHAPTER

30

*M*organ was seething when Blair came to the back room. "We could have put the library back together ourselves," she muttered. "We didn't need his help. Coming in here like he's still a football star, his arms all pumped up . . ."

"Well, we got it. And now it's done. I'm glad it's behind us."

"He arrested my husband," she said. "On the worst day of my life he took my husband away from me."

"He's just trying to do his job."

"It's not his job to arrest innocent private citizens in their moments of grief."

"He means well, Morgan." Blair realized the irony of the role reversal. She couldn't remember when she had ever defended anyone to Morgan. She was usually the fault-finder.

Morgan swept the last of the dust into a pan, dumped it, then dusted her hands off. "Well, at least it's done. I'm ready to go through Mama and Pop's things."

They carried the boxes into Blair's office and set them on her desk. "I figured out a way to do this," Blair said as Morgan sank into a chair. "I was thinking that the first thing we need to do is get information on the tenants at Hanover House. I can be doing that on the computer while you start digging through the files."

Morgan reached into the box and withdrew a stack of papers. Her face betrayed her fatigue and dread as she began flipping through them.

"The first thing I'm going to need is some information about the tenants," Blair said, tapping the keys. "I need full names if I can get them, social security numbers, birth dates. Do you see a tenant file in there where Mama might have kept up with this stuff?"

Morgan pulled a file out and looked through the contents. "Yeah, this might be it." She took it over to Blair's table and pulled up a chair. "Here's some stuff about Gus."

"Perfect." Blair took the sheets out of the file and entered the information onto the database that she used. Then she entered Rick Morrison's.

Before she had gotten it all entered, the computer chimed, telling her that Gus's profile was already complete. Quickly, she pressed *print* and waited as the pages came off of her printer.

"Okay, look at this," she said. "His rap sheet. Looks bad."

"Well, we knew he had a past," Morgan said. "That's no surprise."

"But he's a three-time convicted felon," Blair said. "He served more time in prison than he's been out of it. Car theft, drug dealing. There's one here for beating his girlfriend back in the eighties. Armed robbery was just the latest."

"Let me see that," Morgan said, snatching the paper out of her hand. "Spent ten years just for the armed robbery," she said. "Paroled six months ago. No surprise there." Morgan scanned the rest of the list, then handed it back to Blair. "Okay, so he abused his girlfriend, stole cars, committed armed robbery. It doesn't say he killed anybody. And he's changed."

Blair flashed a look at her. "What is it with you and this guy? I've just shown you that he has a terrible history of criminal behavior. And you're trying to tell me that since he hasn't been in jail for murder, then he couldn't be a killer?"

"No, that's not what I'm saying," Morgan told her. "I just can't see it. I know Gus. I've been there since he moved in. When he first came to Cape Refuge he was really confused and quiet. He was the most depressed and troubled man I'd ever seen in my life. And I've seen Mama and Pop turn him around. I've seen how they ministered to him, and he's slowly changed. He does things for other people now. He thinks of the other tenants. He cried at Mama and Pop's funeral service."

"Of course, he cried. If he had anything to do with it, maybe he was feeling remorse over it. Or maybe he's just a good actor."

"I just don't think he did it," Morgan said.

"Well, your own husband thinks he did."

Morgan got to her feet and crossed the room, looked out the window. It had started to drizzle, and the sky was darkening with the promise of more. "You keep flipping sides, you know that, Blair? It makes me dizzy just to be around you. Yesterday you thought Jonathan might have done it, and today you're telling me to listen to him because he's right about Gus."

"Okay, I admit it," Blair said. "Everything's a little confusing right now."

Morgan turned back from the window. "I'm not saying that we should just give up the possibility that Gus could have done it. I think everybody's got to be a suspect. And if you show me any viable evidence that he did, I'll believe you. But until then, I'd rather think the best of him."

It was clear that fatigue, grief, fear, and hunger were all combining to take its toll on Morgan. "Look," Blair said, "I know that you've spent an awful lot of your life trying to get Mama and Pop's approval, and that you look at everybody like they have some kind of halo around them, but when your parents have been murdered, it's okay to think badly of people."

"What do you mean, I was always trying to get their approval? So were you. That's what daughters do."

"Yeah, but I didn't make it my life's work."

Morgan turned on her. "I did *not* make it my life's work. If you think that, you don't know me at all. I just wanted to be like her."

"Well, you succeeded," Blair said, beginning to type again. "At least one of us did."

Though Blair kept her eyes on the screen, she could feel Morgan's anger as she stood over her. "Why do you do this?" Morgan asked. "All I'm doing is digging through these files to find the information that *you* think we need."

"And *you* don't think we need it?"

"What is wrong with you?" Morgan demanded. "I'm here with you for comfort, for security, and for my own sanity, but I'm beginning to wonder if it's a safe place."

That sent Blair's own anger up a notch, and she set her mouth and typed faster. "Another one of Mama's words," she said. "*Safe place.* She and Pop made a safe place for everybody in the world. Everybody but—" She stopped before the word was out of her mouth.

"Everybody but who?" Morgan asked. "*You?*" She said the word as if she couldn't believe it, and Blair wished she hadn't even started this. She kept typing, harder, faster.

"They always provided a safe place for you, Blair."

Blair shoved her keyboard away and got up, facing her sister. "It wasn't safe for me, okay? Cape Refuge—the haven for everybody in the world who needed a safe place—was not a safe place for me."

Morgan's voice was as loud as Blair's now. "Why wasn't it, Blair? Because of the scar?"

"I don't want to talk about it," Blair said. She started to sit back down, but Morgan grabbed her arm and turned her around. "Mama and Pop offered you a lot of safe places. You just chose not to take them. And it's not fair for you to have so much contempt toward me just because I did."

"I don't have contempt for you, Morgan," she said. "I'm just speaking my mind. I'm sorry if it hurts you."

"Oh, give me a break." One of Morgan's tears spilled over her lashes and raced down her cheek. "You're not sorry, Blair. It's your intention to hurt me, and I'm not sure why." She sighed and sank back into the chair next to the file cabinet. "I'm sorry I mentioned the scars."

Blair breathed a mirthless laugh and plunked back into the chair. "I know I have scars, Morgan. I can handle your mentioning them."

"No, you can't. Every insecurity in your life, every regret, every disappointment, goes back to those scars."

Blair didn't say a word, for her anger was rapidly escalating into fury. "Don't psychoanalyze me, Morgan. I'm not one of your projects."

Morgan set her arms on the file cabinet and dropped her face into them. "This is crazy. We're supposed to be supporting each other, and instead we're tearing each other down. I hate this. If I had anyplace to go, I'd leave right now. But I need you, and you need me. We're kind of stuck together for a while, until this murder is solved. We need to get along. But when this is over, Blair, I'm going to do everything in my power to make a safe place for you."

Blair was desperate to change the subject. "While you make it for Gus Hampton?"

"When you work in Hanover House every day like I do, and you see the people and get to know them as your friends, it's not easy to think of them as killers, okay? I've heard their stories, Blair. They've shared their hearts with me. I've sung with them in church and praised God, and I've watched them change."

"Hasn't Jonathan?" Blair asked. "If he's watched them change right along with you, then why wasn't he so keen on Gus?"

"You know Jonathan's temper," she said. "Gus made him mad. He saw me comforting Gus when he had just shared something really personal with me, about how he felt like he was never good enough for Christ, and how forgiveness seemed like something he could never quite have. And I gave him a hug. It was spontaneous, Blair. It didn't mean anything except that I was a

Christian sister who loved him and cared about him. And Jonathan walked in and went ballistic."

"Why wasn't he mad at you?" Blair asked.

"He was at first, until he understood the way I felt about it, that I hadn't done anything wrong. I was trying to comfort a friend. But then he started thinking that Gus had ill motives."

"Why didn't you tell me this before?"

"Tell you what? You knew what Jonathan thought. Gus didn't do anything wrong." She flipped idly through the files. "But that's when Jonathan decided he wanted him out of our house. That's all there is to that story. But in my mind, Blair, Gus Hampton is the same man I've watched grow over the last few months. He has the same past now that he had when he came to Cape Refuge. It's just that we weren't all privy to it. But Mama and Pop were. You mark my word. People told Mama and Pop things that they didn't tell ordinary people. They shared their lives and their hearts with them. I want to be like that, Blair. I like people, and I can love them. I can empathize with them; I can relate to what they're thinking. Mama always said it was a gift, but you act like it's a curse."

"It's not a curse," Blair said, typing again. "I never meant it was a curse. At least not your curse."

"Then who does it curse?" Morgan asked. "You, Blair? Does it curse you?"

The keys clicked at record speed. "I'm not like you, Morgan. I've never been like you."

"Of course you're not," Morgan said. "You'd go nuts. You'd pull your hair out. You're not supposed to be like me."

"But you're the one most like Mama. You're the one people love."

"That's because I'm out there," Morgan said. "I'm not hiding away in a library trying to keep anybody from ever getting close to me." Morgan's voice broke, and she dropped her forehead against her palm. "Oh, Blair, I miss them so much. I miss Mama's hug every day. Have you thought about that, Blair? Both of us, we had her hug every single day of our lives. I wake up in the middle of the night and just hunger for it."

Blair stopped clicking and just stared at the screen.

"And I miss Pop," Morgan said. "I miss the way his jaw felt at the end of the day, like sandpaper—and that twinkle in his eye. Whenever he looked at you, you just felt it going into you, warming you up somewhere deep. I miss his corny jokes. I miss how much he loved us."

Blair set her hands on her desk. She didn't want to cry, not here, not now, not in front of Morgan while they were fighting. But it took a valiant effort not to.

"And I miss Jonathan," Morgan said. "I miss my husband because I need him now. And there he is, locked up behind bars for something he didn't even do. All I have is you."

Blair turned and started to say something cryptic about how she was sorry to be the last resort, but Morgan beat her to it.

"And here you are, taking potshots at me like I'm the one who kept you from having a safe place."

"That's not what I meant," Blair said.

"I know what you meant," Morgan bit out. "It's the same thing you've meant for years, that I follow my emotions. You're too smart to have any. But maybe sometimes my heart clears things up for my head, Blair. Have you ever thought of that? Maybe it makes me see things a little clearer than you do."

"And maybe it blinds you," Blair said.

Morgan wilted and leaned against the cabinet. Blair hated seeing her cry. She thought of crossing the room and pulling her sister into her arms just the way her mother would have done. Maybe it would have made up for the lack of hugs they had gotten lately. But it would be too hard to be that soft, and it might lead to Blair's breaking down. She couldn't take that chance.

"Maybe it makes me wise," Morgan said.

Blair couldn't entertain that possibility, but she was weary of the fight. "Maybe it does. And maybe if we put our strengths together, we can get through this. And maybe, if we leave our emotions out of it, we can figure out who did this."

"I can't," Morgan said. "I can't leave my emotions out of anything."

"Well, I'm asking you to try. I'm asking you to give me your brain instead of your heart and see people through a filter of facts."

Morgan sniffed and wiped her eyes again. "All right, Blair. I'll make a deal with you. I'll give you my head with as little emotion as possible, if you'll give me a hug every day like Mama did."

Blair just looked at her as if that was an uneven swap. It would cost her so much, and she wasn't sure she had the deposits to cover it. But she saw no way out.

She got up and pulled her sister into a hug. They clung to each other for a long moment, Morgan weeping into her shoulder, wetting her hair and her shirt. Blair's mind started down a path of no return, a path toward the emotions taunting and luring her, daring her to step over the line.

Finally, she let go and stepped back. "We have work to do, Morgan," she said. "We need to get to it."

Morgan went back to the files she was working on. It took Blair a moment to gather her wits, but finally she went back to the computer to see if there had been any rap sheets sent on Rick Morrison and Mrs. Hern, or the Andersons, who had left right after the murders. There was nothing on Rick, since he had had no arrests. Mrs. Hern's one conviction for embezzlement came up, and the Andersons each had several convictions for drug dealing.

"What's this?"

Blair looked down at Morgan and saw her puzzling over a paper in her hand.

"Looks like a death certificate," Morgan said. "Only you'll never believe whose name is on it."

Blair leaned over to see. "Whose?"

Morgan pointed to the name. "Richard Morrison."

Blair's mouth came open, and she gaped at her sister. "What does this mean?"

Morgan shook her head. "I don't know. Maybe it's Rick's father."

"But why would Mama and Pop have it?" Blair took the certificate out of Morgan's hand. "Let's think this through," she said.

"Mama and Pop have a tenant named Rick Morrison who claims his wife and daughter were killed in a drunk-driving accident. He's steeped with grief so he comes to Cape Refuge. Now how do you explain Mama and Pop having a death certificate with his name on it? Okay, so it could be his father. Or someone else with the same name. But why?"

"Maybe it's fake," Morgan said.

Blair went back to the computer. "That would be pretty easy to check out." She banged on the keys, found the public records that could tell her who had died and when. "Unless this person died in the last few weeks, it should be listed."

Morgan came to look over her shoulder as the answer came up on the screen. Four Rick Morrisons emerged with various middle names. Blair clicked down each one until she came to the one that matched the death certificate.

"He was a real guy, Morgan," Blair said. "Died at the age of fifty-eight."

Morgan frowned. "Can you find out things like where he went to high school, where he lived, what he died of? We need a picture."

"I'll try," Blair said. "Just give me a few minutes."

CHAPTER

*B*lair and Morgan spent the entire night looking for information about the Richard Morrison who had died. They had compiled a dossier on the dead man, including a picture that looked nothing like their tenant. Now, mentally and physically exhausted, they vowed to finish it before they laid their heads down to sleep.

Just after six-thirty in the morning, they drove to Hanover House, intent on getting in Rick's room and finding what they could.

"What if he's still there?" Blair asked as they pulled into the driveway.

Morgan shook her head. "He's an early riser. He walks on the beach every morning. He does that every day before he showers for work."

"We can go in with a vacuum cleaner," Blair said, "and pretend we're vacuuming. Maybe something's lying around."

"He's pretty neat," Morgan said. "Makes up his bed every morning, picks up after himself. But maybe there'll be something. Do you even know what you're looking for?"

"If I see his wallet left out I'm going to dig through for his driver's license, credit cards, anything. Maybe a checkbook or some of his mail."

"This feels wrong, somehow," Morgan said. "Mama was always real respectful of their privacy."

"It's not snooping," Blair said. "It's an investigation. It could save people's lives and might get your husband out of jail."

Morgan knew it was true. "Okay, so which do you want to do, make breakfast or vacuum?" Morgan asked.

Blair looked at her like she was crazy. "I don't intend to do either."

"Well, you have to do one or the other," Morgan said. "I mean, if we walk in there after not being here for days and start vacuuming, it's going to look awfully suspicious. Besides, it's a bed-and-breakfast. We're supposed to provide breakfast."

Blair grunted. "I think they understand why they haven't been given breakfast. Besides, they have full run of the kitchen. They can get anything they want."

"I was just thinking that if we acted like things were normal, that we had come to make them breakfast, that would get Mrs. Hern and Gus out of their rooms, so they wouldn't see what you were doing."

Blair sighed. "Well, okay, but you'll have to cook."

"All right. But that means you have to be the one to go into his room."

"That's fine," Blair said. "Let me at it."

A while later, Blair smelled the scent of scrambled eggs and bacon and her mother's favorite biscuits downstairs while she vacuumed the upstairs hall. The smell brought back a mourning so deep that it bypassed tears entirely.

So did the house. She vacuumed around and under things, trying not to let the images bring back a flood of emotions—but it was hard to fight them off.

When Rick finally opened the door, and yelled "Good morning" over the noise of the vacuum cleaner, she watched him head down the stairs. This was her chance, she thought. She vacuumed her way into his room, her eyes darting back and forth at the personal objects he had out.

A Swiss army knife, a couple of keys on a key chain, his wallet—

She grabbed it up and started going through it, looking for some kind of identification. There were no credit cards, no driver's license, nothing with his name on it. She looked through the billfold for a receipt—anything . . .

The vacuum cleaner shut off, and Blair swung around.

Rick stood at the door, looking at her with somber eyes. "I didn't want to scare you, so I turned it off."

She swallowed and dropped the wallet. "You didn't scare me."

He bent down and picked it up, keeping his eyes on her. "Need a loan?" he asked.

Her mind reeled for an explanation. "Of course not," she said. "I was just dusting that table and it fell off." She knew it was a lame explanation, and that he had seen her rifling through it. "I'm sorry. I was looking to see if you had pictures of your wife and daughter."

That seemed to satisfy him, and the suspicion on his face quickly melted away. He went to the bed table and picked up two framed pictures. "Here they are."

Right out in the open, she thought. She gazed down at them, feigning interest. "They were beautiful," she said.

He looked genuinely mournful as he set them back down. When he turned back to her, she saw a glimmer of tears in his eyes. "Well, thanks for vacuuming in here."

"Sure."

He shoved his wallet into his back pocket. "I'm going walking. I always stop by Crickets for coffee. You want to come?"

"No," she said quickly. "Too much to do."

"Okay. See you later."

She turned the vacuum cleaner back on and watched him go down the stairs. When she was sure he was gone, she wilted on his bed. That had been too close. She would have to be more careful.

She looked around again. His trash can had recently been emptied, his bed had been made. The only thing out of place was a lone water glass sitting beside his bed, next to the pictures. *Fingerprints*, she thought. Maybe she could take them to Cade and have him run them down to discover who he really was. She held it with two fingers, careful not to smear the prints, then pulled the vacuum cleaner out of the room and headed down the stairs.

She could hear voices in the kitchen and knew that Gus and Mrs. Hern were there, helping with breakfast and reminiscing about Thelma and Wayne, but she headed out to the car, set the glass carefully on the floorboard, and drove off.

Morgan would wonder where she had gone, but she couldn't stop now. She headed to the police station. It was only seven-thirty; she hoped Cade had made it in by now.

Carefully carrying the glass, she pushed through the door and crossed the room to Cade's office. He sat at his desk, studying something on his computer with a cup of coffee in his hand. He looked as if he had been going without sleep too.

Blair didn't knock. She just bolted in and leaned over his desk. "I want you to get the fingerprints off this glass," she said. "I want you to tell me whose they are."

He looked down at the glass. "Where'd you get that?"

She reached into her pocket and pulled out the death certificate with Rick Morrison's name on it and slapped it down in front of him. "One of my parents' tenants, Rick Morrison. It's his glass. And last night as we were going through my parents' . . . ," she hesitated, avoiding the words "file cabinet." She didn't want to give him the idea to confiscate it. "We were going through some of their things, and we found this."

He looked at it. "A death certificate."

"With his name on it. Only he doesn't look that dead to me. He also doesn't look fifty-eight years old."

Cade sat back hard in his chair. "Interesting . . ."

"I found out that the Richard Morrison of the death certificate had a heart attack, had three grown daughters, two married,
and worked as a banker in Atlanta. He left behind a wife who's
already remarried."

"And the one staying at Hanover House claims to be here
after losing his wife and child in a drunk-driving accident." He
nodded, as if this was pertinent information. "We'll run the prints
on the glass, Blair. I'll let you know what we find out."

Blair straightened. "Will you, Cade? You promise?"

"I said I would, didn't I? I always keep my word."

That had to be good enough for Blair. She followed him out
of his office. "Do it quickly, Cade. Don't waste any time. If this
guy's a murderer, we need to know. Morgan's served the guy
breakfast this morning."

"I'm aware of the urgency. I'll take care of it, Blair."

Feeling as if she had left her firstborn in the hands of a
stranger, she hurried back to Hanover House to tell her sister.

CHAPTER

*D*ebilitating fatigue was setting in by the time Blair got back to Hanover House. "Where did you go?" Morgan asked, keeping her voice low.

"The police station. I had to talk to Cade." They glanced back at Mrs. Hern, knowing she could hear every word. Morgan held her hand up to silence Blair, and Blair nodded that she would wait until later.

When the kitchen was as clean as Thelma would have left it, they got back into the car. "Rick came in while I was going through his wallet," Blair said.

"Oh, no. I thought he went out to walk."

"He needed his wallet for Crickets. I told him I was looking for a picture of his wife and daughter," Blair said. "The fact that there were two framed pictures next to his bed didn't help my story. But I guess he bought it."

"Oh, thank goodness. I wouldn't have thought of that. I probably would have broken down and spilled my guts and told him I was looking for his identification."

"There wasn't any. But when he left, I found a glass, and I figured it had fingerprints. I didn't really know what to do with it. I mean, when police take evidence from a crime scene, they usually have a paper sack to put it in, and I didn't have anything. I knew if I came in the kitchen I would call attention to myself, so I just got in the car and took it over to Cade's office."

"Was he interested?" Morgan asked.

"Yeah, he was real interested. I showed him the death certificate. He's going to run the prints and get back to us."

"Okay, that's good," Morgan said. "Did you see Jonathan while you were there?"

"No, I didn't take the time to."

"Maybe they'll decide Rick is the prime suspect, and let Jonathan out today," Morgan said.

Blair looked at her with tired eyes. "Why are you so much more willing to have it be Rick Morrison than Gus Hampton?"

Morgan shrugged. "We didn't find a death certificate for Gus. It's made me real suspicious. When does Cade think he'll have the prints identified?"

"I don't know," she said. "I didn't ask. But I know he'll get it as fast as he can. I'm thinking sometime this morning. Meanwhile, we can go back home and lie down, maybe get a couple of hours' sleep before we hear from him."

"And then I'll go see Jonathan."

Blair was quiet as they got back to the house. She wanted Morgan to think she was settling down to sleep, but she merely waited in her bedroom until she knew that Morgan was sleeping, and then she got up and sneaked through the door. As tired as she was, she couldn't turn things off just yet.

There had been many nights in her life when she had stayed awake all night researching a topic that interested her, then spent the next day following up on the things she had learned. How could anyone sleep when they were waiting for the fingerprints of the person who may have killed her parents?

She went into the kitchen and called Cade. When he came to the phone she said simply, "Anything yet?"

"Blair?" he asked.

"Yes. Have you gotten the fingerprint report?"

"Not yet," he said. "I'm still working on it. I told you I'd call you as soon as I have something."

She sighed. "All right. How long do you think it will be?"

"Two or three hours," he said. "Not before that. I dusted the prints and sent them in, and now the computer has to do a search through every fingerprint on file. It takes a while. Why don't you get some sleep? You didn't look like you had had any."

"Neither did you," she said.

"I'll call you, I promise."

She hung up and sat for a moment, staring at the telephone. She should sleep or eat, she realized, but her mind was still racing, and she had no appetite. The normal body functions like sleeping or eating or crying seemed like weaknesses she couldn't entertain.

But she wasn't sure what to do with herself.

Finally, she stepped out the front door and stood in the shade of the warm breeze coming from the water. The sun was already bright in the sky, and though it was only eight-thirty, it was already hot and humid. The trees around the house whispered and rustled, and birds squawked and cooed overhead. She slid her hands into her jeans pockets and crossed the street to the water's edge.

It was low tide. She could walk way out into the place where, later today, the water would be knee deep. She looked to her right and saw the dock about a mile up the road, right next to the building where worship and murder happened under the same roof. The beach was no more than four miles around, and from where she stood, she could see this side of the Cape clearly. In front of her and to the left was the Wassaw Sound. Across it was Cabbage Island, a marshy place full of marine animals and rabid raccoons that wreaked havoc on the island pets.

The ocean sounds calmed her nerves, made her feel that maybe there was some peace in the world. Desperate to soak up more of that peace, she started walking the island's perimeter, back toward Hanover House.

The wind picked up her hair and feathered it across her face. She pulled it back and slipped it behind her ears, then pulled it out again, trying to make it cover her scar. As she walked, a plan began to form in her mind. It wasn't much after nine. Most of the establishments on the island didn't open until nine. She would hide and watch both Gus and Rick as they left for work. Even though they had cars, both men worked within walking distance of the house. Maybe she would have the opportunity to see what Rick did in the mornings.

She reached the part of the beach across from Hanover House and stepped back behind a magnolia tree near the street. Rick Morrison was already taking his garbage out to the street. She watched as he closed the garbage can carefully, then went back for a few more bags. She wished she had her car with her so she could grab those bags and go through the trash to see if she could find any clues.

When he had finished, he dusted off his hands and started across the street toward her. She let him get a safe distance ahead, then she followed. He didn't go far, just walked along the shore for about a mile or so, to the dock near where her parents had been killed, past the church warehouse and to the Madison Boat Shop, where he worked.

He didn't go right in but went to the boardwalk skirting the bay side of the island, and he stood there, quiet and mysterious, his hands in his pockets, his face somber. She didn't know what she hoped to see in him. A nervous twitch maybe, or a gun packed beneath his shirt. Maybe a bloodstain on his clothes. But she saw nothing except a man who seemed as pensive and troubled as she.

She watched until he went in. Then she turned around and started back. Her eyes strayed to the few people already on the beach. The lifeguards were distributing the chairs they rented in neat little rows on the sand. City workers picked up trash left behind from the night before. A few residents walked at the water's edge, getting their morning exercise.

She gasped as her gaze collided with Gus Hampton's. He stood among the trees near the street, watching her. The big, ebony-colored man was smoking a cigarette, taking long, deep drags, then flicking the ashes to his side.

A chill ran through her, and she quickly looked away and moved closer to the water, and headed home. What had Gus seen? she wondered. Had he realized she was watching Rick Morrison? Or had he been following her for some other reason?

She hurried into her house, locked the door, and stood there for a moment, trying to catch her breath. Finally, she went to the closet that held her gun, got it out, and loaded it. From now on she would have it handy, she thought. From now on, she would be ready.

CHAPTER

*B*lair finally gave in to sleep shortly after noon. Since Morgan had gone to visit Jonathan, Blair slept with the gun clutched in her hand.

The sound of knocking awoke her. From the stupor of deep sleep, she looked at the clock. It was nine in the evening. She hadn't meant to sleep that long, but her body needed the rest after the events of the last few days. Darkness was invading the room, and Blair reached for the lamp.

When the knocking started again, she grabbed her gun, slipped it into her pocket, and stumbled to the front door. With groggy eyes, she looked to see who it was. She couldn't make the visitor out in the darkness. She leaned against the door. "Who is it?"

"Rick," the voice said from the other side. "Rick Morrison."

Blair caught her breath and her hand closed over the gun again. What did he want? She knew better than to let him in here alone. She wondered if he realized she had taken the glass from his room and given it to Cade to dust

172

for fingerprints, or if he'd come to ask her about why she was snooping in his room.

She took a moment to compose herself. "Just a minute," she said through the door. She pulled the gun out and reassured herself that it was loaded. Her hands trembled. She was glad she had pockets. She had to act normal. If he hadn't heard that they suspected him, then maybe they could keep him from bolting and running before Cade had enough evidence to arrest him.

She took a deep breath, put her hand on the knob. Slowly she opened the door. "What can I do for you, Rick?" she asked.

He made no attempt to walk in but seemed to linger back, as if he knew his presence might have caused her consternation.

"Sorry to bother you, Blair. I know things can't be easy for you right now, but I wondered if we could talk. I have some things I need to tell you, things you need to know."

Curiosity mushroomed inside her like a nuclear explosion, and she found herself anxious for the fallout. She stepped out into the night and pulled the door shut behind her. "Let's talk out here," she said.

"That's fine, Blair. You don't have any business letting some strange man into your house, anyway, when you're alone."

She swallowed and wondered how he knew she was alone. The fact that Morgan's car was gone had probably clued him. She kept her hand on the gun in her pocket and went to a porch swing hanging from an arbor between her house and the library. She sat at the right end, leaving the other for him. Slowly, he sat down, his solid weight making the chains creak.

The sound of the surf combined with the calls of the insects chirping in the trees. Wind stirred her hair and rustled her wrinkled clothes. She wiped the sweaty palm of her free hand across her blue jeans and swallowed hard as she looked across the street toward the ocean rolling up onto the shore with foamy moonlit eagerness. She remembered just yesterday, looking out at the beach with him as he talked about grief.

She had felt such an affinity with him then, as he talked of his own grief. Had it been an act? Was he playing her?

"Your parents taught me more than I ever knew about God," Rick said, setting his elbows on his knees and folding his hands between them. "Mostly, they taught me about his love. But I got to tell you, I'm having a hard time with why he had to take them."

"I don't believe in God," Blair said.

"Then what do you believe in?"

If he had asked the pointed question a week ago, she would have proclaimed a belief in herself. She would have said that she believed there was a direct correlation between her effort and her results. She would have said that she believed in the basic goodness of man, and the determination of man's spirit. She would have said that she believed in science and mathematics, with their facts and their certainty, and the tangible manifestation of all they represented.

But now she couldn't say any of those things. Nothing was certain, least of all her own autonomy. The facts were hazy, at best, and the goodness of man was seriously in question.

The truth was that the murders had derailed her entire belief system, but she didn't want to share that with him.

He waited. "You must believe in something, Blair. I didn't believe when I first came to Cape Refuge. Your father told me that by not believing in anything, I was choosing to believe in something. He said that all people believe in a god—whether it's the god of hopelessness or the god of circumstances or the god of ourselves or the god of some other person. It took me a long time to figure out what my god was. I finally realized that I was believing in the god of hatred, the one that seemed to feed the thoughts I had toward the drunk driver who killed my family. I couldn't get that hatred or that desire to destroy him out of my mind. But it was only destroying me."

He leaned back hard on the swing. "That hatred robbed me of my memories. It robbed me of my peace, because I couldn't stop going through the if-only's in my mind. If only Karen hadn't been coming to meet me that day. If only I'd left work early and picked them up myself. If only I'd told her I loved her that morning. If only I'd had one last hug from Katie. *If only* . . . The two most hateful words in life."

Those same two words had played like a mantra in her mind for the last few days, over and over and over, tormenting her.

"Your father showed me that if-only's deny the power of the one true God. He said God was in control when that drunk driver ran over the median and head-on into their car. He was in control when I came so close to putting a gun to my head. He was in control when I heard about a place called Cape Refuge."

He shifted on the swing, put his arm on the back and looked at her for a long time until she had no choice but to return his gaze. He didn't have the look of a killer. He looked like a father and a husband. He looked like a grieving man with blue, bloodshot eyes and pink rims around them, and the way he always stared off into the ocean, as if there were some answers there . . . or maybe some joy coming up just over the horizon, if only he watched long enough. There was something about their common feelings and the way he stared at her now that made her wish he was genuine.

But she hadn't forgotten that death certificate with his name on it. "You said you had something to tell me," she said. "Was that it?"

He rubbed his eyes roughly with his fingers, then looked back across to the ocean again, and cleared his throat. "No," he said. "It's about my name."

Her eyes flashed back to his. "Your name?"

"Yeah," he said, "my *real* name."

Blair's hand clamped over that gun. "What do you mean?"

"I know that's why you were going through my wallet this morning, Blair. You found out somehow that I'm not really Rick Morrison."

She slowly got to her feet, and put some distance between them. Her hand was slick over the gun in her pocket.

"I know what you're thinking," he said. "You're thinking that if I'm not who I say I am, then maybe I should be a suspect. Right?"

"Well, the thought had crossed my mind."

"But it's not like that," he said. "Rick Morrison was a friend of mine who died. I borrowed his identity. I had this mountain of debts back in Atlanta, and when my wife and daughter died, I was such a basket case I couldn't fulfill any of my responsibilities. That mountain of debt just kept growing and growing. I tried to function, Blair. I really did. I got up every day and I went to work and I sat there and tried. But my head wasn't in it. I was grieving. My whole life had changed and nothing mattered anymore."

Blair stared down at him as the wind brushed her hair across the scar on her cheek. The story seemed real. The expressions on his face left no clues that he was feeding her a lie. It even made sense.

"And then my friend died," he said. "His kids were grown and off on their own, and no one knew where his wife was, so no one really cared, and I started thinking about getting away from it all, from all the things that reminded me of my family. I just had to get away and I didn't want to do it hounded by bill collectors. In my twisted thinking back then, I started to believe that, if I took his name, I could *be* someone else for a while."

"And what's your real name?" Blair asked.

"Richard Dugan," he said. "I've always been called Rick. It's only the last name that's different. That's why it was so easy."

She kept her eyes on his face. "Did my parents know about this?"

"Yes, they did," Rick said. "I told them at the very beginning. When a tenant comes to Cape Refuge, Thelma and Wayne have quite an orientation. They don't want any lies and they don't want any surprises. After I was here for a couple of weeks and had a job under that name, your father found some discrepancies in my story. He told me to either be straight with him or pack up and leave. So I told them the truth and gave them a copy of Rick Morrison's death certificate. As far as I know, they checked out my story and decided to let me go ahead using Morrison, just so I wouldn't wind up losing my job. I expected to have problems with the Social Security Administration soon, since I was using his social security number to get paid. It was getting really complicated and tangled, but they agreed to let me work it out. They had a lot of compassion, your folks did. They really wanted to help. I was at a place in my life where I felt so numb and paralyzed that I just wanted to escape everything, including me. If I could have stepped out of my own skin, I would have."

The moon was rising, casting its own light over the trees and the ground and the swing where he sat. The light caught the edge of his eye, and she could see a tear glistening there. Yes, she did understand that desire to escape. She had felt that way many times.

"I miss Thelma and Wayne," he said, and his voice broke. He touched his finger to his eyebrow and began to cry. Slowly she let go of the gun.

"I guess it was selfish," he said. "I just needed to get it off my chest. I just wanted to explain. I thought maybe you'd understand."

"Thank you," she whispered. "I appreciate your coming and telling me this. I did need to know."

Rick swallowed and raked his hands through his hair. "Jonathan Cleary did not kill Thelma and Wayne."

Blair nodded. "Try telling that to Cade."

"I can't imagine anybody doing that to them," he said.

She thought back to this morning, and the way Gus had watched her as she watched Rick. But before she could bring it up, she saw headlights coming up the street. Her sister's car pulled onto the gravel driveway. Cade was right behind her in a squad car. Blair stiffened as Cade's headlights illuminated her and Rick.

Morgan got out. Her face was pale as she looked at Blair, as if asking if she was in trouble.

Cade wasn't so discreet. "What are you doing here?" he asked Rick.

"I was talking to Blair," Rick said. He met Morgan's eyes. "How's Jonathan?"

Morgan looked too shaken to speak, but she managed to get out, "He's fine."

"He didn't do it, Cade," Rick said. "You've got the wrong guy."

"So I've been told," Cade said.

Rick looked at Blair again, then down at his feet. "I think I'll go now."

"Okay," Blair said. "Thanks for explaining."

He nodded as if it was no problem, then got back into his car. As he pulled away, Blair went into action. "Cade, why didn't you call me back about those fingerprints?"

"Because I told Morgan. I thought she'd pass it on. Either Rick's never been arrested or the prints just weren't clear enough."

"I think it's the first," she said. "He told me why he changed his name." She related his story almost verbatim.

"And you believed him?" Morgan asked.

"You would have too," Blair said, "if you'd heard his confession."

"And why would he make it?" Cade asked. "What did he have to gain?"

"He figured out that we already knew," Blair said.

"So you still believe the story about his family?" Morgan asked.

"I do. It rings true, Morgan. The look on his face, the tears in his eyes, the things he says, they all ring true."

Cade started back to his car. "I'm going back to the station to run a check on Richard Dugan."

"Let me know as soon as you come up with something," Blair said.

He opened his car door and stood there before getting in, looking over the door at her. "You need to be more careful, Blair," he said. "Things could have gone bad just then."

"I didn't let him in the house," Blair said. "I went outside to talk to him." She pulled the pistol out of her pocket. "I had this the whole time, Cade. I'm not stupid."

"Well, I hope you're not naive, either. All it takes is a nice genuine-sounding, tear-jerking story to get you to let your guard down. We don't know enough about him, Blair." He let his eyes roam the trees around her property. "Why didn't he come to me with the story? If he knew he'd been caught, why wouldn't he come straight to the police?"

Blair shrugged. "Maybe he wasn't sure we'd told you. Why get himself into legal trouble if he didn't have to?"

"Maybe he knew we'd have the capacity to check that story out, and he didn't want to go that far with it," Cade said. "And maybe even tonight, he had some other purpose up his sleeve. Maybe my showing up thwarted things a little."

She couldn't help being a little disturbed. "Cade, something kind of weird happened this morning. After I took the glass to you, Morgan and I came back here, and I went for a walk. I saw Rick leaving for work, and I followed him at a distance. When I turned back, I saw that Gus was following *me*, standing back in the trees and watching. It gave me the creeps."

Cade stepped away from the car and slammed the door. "Blair, why didn't you tell me that?"

"Because it wasn't like anything *happened*. I wasn't sure it meant anything."

"Everything means something."

"Well, I've told you now."

Morgan, who had been nursing her own thoughts, couldn't stay quiet any longer. "Cade, if you're so doggone sure that the killer is still out there, then why do you have Jonathan locked up?"

"Because there's still more evidence against him than any-body else. But I'm not betting your lives on it, okay? I *want* Jonathan to be innocent. I want to find out somebody else did it. But if that's what happened, then the killer is still roaming around. I need every bit of information you have, when you get it, so that I can do my job effectively. Got it?"

Blair nodded. "Got it. I'm sorry I didn't tell you, Cade. I was exhausted and upset and real focused on those fingerprints. And then I fell asleep and the day got by me."

He softened a little, and she realized that he could use a few hours of sleep himself. There were dark circles under his eyes, and his face seemed to have aged in the last few days. He gazed down at her, emotions battling on his face. "Well, you needed the sleep," he said. "You need to take care of yourself."

Something about the worried look in his eyes and the gentle entreaty warmed her. She met his eyes and realized that his pres-ence made her feel safe.

She was losing it, she thought. In the space of an hour, she had allowed two different men to move her. She was too vulnerable, too unguarded. Even with a pistol in her pocket, she was exposed.

She hated that feeling.

Finally, he got into his car, started the engine, and rolled his window halfway down. "Let me see you go into that house and lock the door before I leave, Blair."

She lifted her chin. "I'm a big girl, Cade. I've been taking care of myself for a long time."

"So did your parents," he said. "Like I told you before, I don't want any more crime scenes involving people I care about. Get in the house."

She didn't argue. She slipped the gun back into her pocket and followed her sister into the house. When the door was closed and locked, she heard his car pulling away.

CHAPTER

Cade didn't like the feeling in his gut as he pulled out onto the street between Blair's house and the water. The sight of Rick in the dark with Blair had set alarms off in his head. He wished he could hang around a little longer, maybe go inside, check out the locks, test the windows, see to it that they knew what to do in an emergency. But Morgan was still nursing her anger at him and had been cool about his even following her home from the station tonight.

And Blair seemed disturbingly defensive about the man she had begged him to check out that morning.

The trees made a canopy across the road, blocking out the light of the moon. He drove slowly, his headlights illuminating his path.

A shadow crossed the road up ahead. He flipped on his brights and tried to follow it. Had it been a deer crossing the road? No, it was tall. The size of a man.

He pulled his car over and got his flashlight, shone it into the woods. He saw the back of a man retreating through the trees. "Stop! Police!" he yelled.

But the man seemed to run faster into a cluster of magnolias and cedars, disappearing in the brush. Cade drew his weapon and sprinted after him, as he called for backup on the radio clipped to his shoulder.

He shone his flashlight through the woods, listening for the sound of those retreating feet, but he heard nothing. He tried to think where the woods would take him. If he could get cars to the other side, maybe they would get him as he emerged. He radioed his orders to the other four cars on duty and shone the light back and forth across the trees. There were too many places to hide and too many directions to run.

Cade's mind reeled with possibilities. Had Rick come back to linger outside Blair's home, hoping to catch them unaware?

Was it Gus, hoping to finish the work he had started with Thelma and Wayne?

Or was it someone else—a dockworker, a tourist, a resident with a beef against the family?

Realizing that he wasn't going to catch anyone with a head start in the black of night, he backtracked to his car. Already, two other officers had joined him on the street. Bruce Allen met him, his flashlight zigzagging its spotlight across the trees.

"See anything?" Cade asked him.

"No, Chief," Bruce said. "Didn't see a thing. You sure you saw somebody?"

"Positive." He glanced back at Billy, who was out of breath with excitement. "You?"

"Not a thing, Chief."

He radioed the other cars. No one had seen anyone emerging from the woods. Either he had gotten out before they arrived or he was still in there.

"All right," he said. "Bruce, I want you to do me a favor and just hang around here tonight. I'm a little uneasy about Morgan and Blair being alone. Just keep an eye on things, will you?"

"Sure thing, Chief."

Cade got back into his car, pulled back onto the street. Quickly, he drove the perimeter of the island to Hanover House.

No lights were on in the house, nor were any vehicles in the driveway, neither Gus Hampton's truck nor Rick's car.

He drove around town through parking lots of bars and past Goodfellow's looking for either of the two vehicles. Finally, he found the truck parked at Barracuda's, the town's most popular bar. He put his hand on the hood to see if it was warm. It was, but that didn't necessarily prove that Gus had driven it in the last few minutes.

He strode inside, where a live band played sixties tunes at an earsplitting volume. The air was heavy with the smell of liquor and cigarette smoke. His uniform called attention to him, and people turned and looked, whispered and pointed. He could feel the tension falling over the room as he searched the faces for Gus.

He saw him sitting at a table near the front, wearing jeans and a tight white T-shirt, and that trademark red bandana on his head. He smoked a cigarette as he tapped his feet to the music. Cade knew he would have noticed if the man running away from him tonight had been wearing a red bandana and a white shirt, but he supposed that Gus could have changed if he had really wanted to create an alibi. There was mud caked on the sides of his shoes, as if he could have been recently strolling through the woods or running away from someone who was after him. He was sweating, but so were many of those in the warm, stagnant air.

Cade went to the end of the bar, and motioned the bartender toward him.

"Hey, Cade. Don't usually see you here." The bartender was a short, heavyset man, with white-bleached hair.

"Sam, how long has Gus Hampton been here tonight?" he asked, pointing to the big Jamaican.

Sam looked across the room. "Didn't even know he was here," he said. "Might as well not be, for all I care, since all he drinks is water when he comes. Sits up there at the front of the room and listens to the bands, but doesn't contribute one thing to the running of this bar."

"So he just got here?"

"I'm not saying that," Sam said. "Just that I hadn't noticed him before now. Why? Is he involved in the murders? I heard you had Jonathan Cleary—"

Cade left him in the middle of his question and crossed the room to Gus. The song ended just as he reached him, and quiet settled over the room. He knew that everyone in the place had their eyes on him. He tapped on Gus's shoulder. The big black man turned around and looked surprised.

"Yeah, mon?"

"I need to talk to you outside, Gus," he said.

Gus looked around and saw that all eyes were on him. He put his cigarette out and got up.

"You got the curiosity up now," Gus said. "Why you need to talk to me again?"

"Outside, I said."

Gus acquiesced and started through the crowd to the door. He led Cade out of the bar and into the fresher air. "What is it, mon? Something else happen?"

Cade looked over his shoulder and saw that several of the bar's patrons had come to the door and were peering out.

"We can't talk here," he said. "Just leave your truck and ride with me to the station."

"Okay, mon. I got nothin' to hide."

Gus got willingly into the front passenger seat, as if to let anyone watching know that he wasn't under arrest. Then he adjusted the red bandana on his head, as Cade drove to the station.

CHAPTER

*C*ade made Gus wait in the interview room while he touched base with each of the cars prowling the island and waited for the court reporter to show up.

Melinda Jane arrived in her bathrobe, with rollers in her hair. Though he had asked her to hurry, he had expected her to get dressed first. He hoped he could conduct a serious interview with her sitting there like that, but he had no choice.

When he had finished the preliminaries, he dove right in. "Gus, tell me about the dirt on your shoes."

"Dirt on my shoes?" Gus asked. He looked down at his feet. "What dirt?"

"There's dirt on your shoes, Gus. It's not on the path between Hanover House and where you work, and it's not sand from the beach. Where did you go to get dirt on your shoes?"

"I like walkin', mon."

"How long have you been at Barracuda's tonight?"

Gus shrugged. "Hour or so. Friend o' mine be playin' the bongos."

Cade had already sent an officer back to the bar to find someone who knew how long Gus had been there.

"Where were you before that?"

"At Hanover House. Why, mon? What's happened?"

"Were you, at any time tonight, in the woods near the library?"

"No," Gus said. "Why I be walkin' around in the woods at night?" He sat straighter. "That be near Blair's house. Nothin' happened to her did it, mon?"

"No, she's fine."

"You know it ain't me you need, mon," Gus told him, leaning his big elbows on the table. "I got nothin' to hide. But Rick . . . he got the secrets."

Cade stood back against the wall, frowning down at the man, and remembered what Blair had said about Gus watching her that morning. He had so many reasons to suspect him, yet no evidence, and you couldn't arrest a person for watching someone in a public place, or even for having dirt on his shoes.

There was a knock on the door, and McCormick stuck his head in. "Chief, can I speak to you a minute?"

"Sure," Cade said. He started to the door, but Melinda Jane jumped up.

"I'm coming too," she said.

He gave her a questioning look as he closed the door.

"Well, you didn't think I was going to stay in that room with a potential killer while you and Joe huddle, did you?"

McCormick looked down at her robe and hair rollers. "What in the world—"

"I was in bed," she announced, thrusting out her chin. "Cade said he needed me right away, so here I came."

McCormick grinned and turned back to Cade. "Mrs. Hern says that Gus had been with her at the House until just an hour or so ago. And the band members are friends of Gus, and they confirmed that he had been there an hour."

"Any word on Rick?"

"Still haven't been able to run him down," McCormick said.

"Well, now that's odd," Melinda Jane said, patting her rollers. "Don't you think that's odd?"

Cade shot her a look. "What's odd?"

"That he's missing," she said. "Looks to me like he must be guilty if he'd run off like that."

Cade couldn't believe a woman dressed for bed was advising him.

"Melinda Jane, leave the police business to us."

He went back into the room, and Melinda Jane took her seat. "I'm going to let you go, Gus," Cade said, "but I don't want you to leave town. I might need to ask you some more questions."

Gus opened his palms. "No problem, mon. I got no place to go."

Cade got one of the officers to drive Gus back to the bar. Cade went to his office and leaned back in his chair, wishing he could go home and catch a few hours of sleep. But he couldn't leave until Rick had been found.

He spent the evening on the phone and his computer, working to get information on Richard Dugan. There were no arrests, no convictions in the man's past. His fingerprints hadn't even been registered. For all he could tell, Rick had been a devoted father and husband until the day a drunk driver changed everything. He had even managed to find a picture of Rick Dugan from a newspaper article about the deaths of the wife and daughter. It matched the man who was staying at Hanover House.

But if he was who he said he was and had no ill motives in visiting Blair—then who had been in the woods?

It was midnight when they finally found Rick, pulling back into the driveway of Hanover House. They had brought him in, and Cade had gotten Melinda Jane to come back. This time she had taken the time to get dressed, but she still had a head full of rollers.

Cade was in no mood to beat around the bush as he faced the man who had disrupted his night. "I want to know where you went when you left Blair's house tonight," he said.

"I drove to Savannah and caught a movie," he said. He pulled the torn ticket stub out of his pocket. "Here's proof. Why? Did something happen? Are Blair and Morgan all right?"

"They're fine," Cade said. Rick's shoes were clean, and he was still wearing the clothes he had been wearing earlier. He looked down at the ticket's showtime, and mentally calculated the time it would have taken to go straight from Blair's to the theater. They didn't normally sell tickets much after the show had begun.

"Tell me about your name," he said.

Rick looked down at his hands. "I imagine Blair has already told you. That's what this is really all about."

"I want to hear it from you."

"All right. I'm not really Rick Morrison. My name is Rick Dugan. Rick Morrison is dead."

Melinda Jane gasped and began coughing. The rollers in her hair wobbled.

Cade waited until she could breathe again. "Why did you feel the need to go to Blair to explain that tonight? Why didn't you come to me?"

"Because I'm not stupid. I didn't want to get into any kind of trouble for stealing someone's identity. But I knew Blair knew, so I wanted to explain. I knew I'd have to account for it someday, but I was hoping to put that off as long as possible."

"I find it hard to believe that Thelma and Wayne would have covered for you, knowing you were breaking the law."

"I didn't use it to get credit or money or anything. I just used his social security number to get a job. If I hadn't, my creditors probably would have found me and garnished my wages."

"Why didn't you file bankruptcy?"

"Because that would have involved getting a lawyer, paperwork, money. I didn't have the presence of mind or the energy to do any of that. I didn't care if I dropped dead, so why would I care if my credit was ruined? I just wanted to be someone else." He closed his eyes and rubbed his face hard. "I don't want you to get the wrong idea about Thelma and Wayne. They kept a close eye on things to make sure I didn't use that name for any personal gain. They wanted me to tell my boss what I'd done, but they didn't force it. They just waited for me to do the right thing."

"Was there some kind of confrontation over it? An ultimatum?"

"No, not really."

"They didn't tell you to confess what you'd done or else?"

"Look, if you're trying to use this to pin their deaths on me, you're crazy. I didn't kill them."

Melinda Jane's fingers tapped wildly on the keys of her stenotype machine.

"But I'll do whatever I can to help you find who did. That is, if you don't lock me up."

Cade tried to think. Fatigue set its claws into his brain. Rick's story sounded convincing, but he couldn't ignore the fact that he had broken the law. He wasn't ready to let Rick go back out on the street until he had at least checked a few more things.

"I'm going to have to arrest you for identity theft," Cade said.

"What? But I didn't hurt anyone."

"It's against the law," he said.

"So you're putting me in jail?"

"Yes. You have the right to remain silent . . ."

Rick moaned as Cade read him his rights, then opted to call a lawyer. Even as he locked Rick into the cell next to Jonathan, he knew that the judge would probably set bail the next day. He couldn't prove that Rick was guilty of any kind of violent crime, so he couldn't hold him longer.

But at least the man was off the streets tonight.

CHAPTER

36

*S*adie's hopes for the next day were shot down when the manager of Goodfellow's had told her that she needn't come back asking for a job. He wasn't going to hire her. He hadn't given a reason, but she knew it had to do with the dirty clothes she was still wearing, the broken arm, and the bruises. She looked a little too rough, despite her efforts not to.

And though she had applied at every establishment along the four-mile stretch of beach, no one else had offered a job either. As a result, she hadn't eaten all day. She scraped together just enough for a stale sandwich at a convenience store, which she scarfed down on the way back to the boathouse.

She had left the boathouse door unlocked so she could come back in without getting wet. She went in, took off her shoes, sat on the floor at the open end of the structure, and hung her feet in the water. She zipped open the backpack and pulled out her picture of little Caleb, so small and trusting, and she prayed that he was all right.

She should have waited until she could take him with her, she thought. She should never have left him.

She wiped the tears on her face, and wondered if she should go back for him. Maybe Jack's wrath was worth it.

Her body was heavy with exhaustion, so she got into the boat. Lying down on the cushioned bench seat at the back of the boat, she fell into a deep sleep.

Morgan's despair loomed heavy, like a fog from which she could not escape. Her visit with Jonathan had simply tangled her in more frustration, grief, and loneliness. There was no pastor to counsel with, no clergy from her church who could minister to her in this dark time. Her father was the pastor, her mother the most attentive counselor. And they were both gone.

She longed to sit in the warehouse church that meant so much to her parents, but their blood still stained the floor, and the police had sealed it off. She longed to stare up at the pulpit where her father used to stand, Christ's ambassador to the lost and wounded who wandered here from the jails or the sea or the highways leading to this place.

She didn't want to go to Hanover House, where Mrs. Hern would need gentle attention. She didn't have it to give right now. And she didn't want to answer all the questions about why Rick had been arrested last night.

And she didn't want to be around Blair right now. She needed quiet, a few moments alone with God.

So she drove to the boathouse down the road from Hanover House. As she pulled onto the dirt road, she saw the building standing idle and alone among the trees and bushes at the edge of the river. The perfect place to sit and pray, the perfect place to get her bearings.

She went in and stood for a moment in the place where they had found Gus after the murders. The air was damp and muggy, and a fish scent blew in from the water. She breathed in the scent of cedar that reminded her of her father and tried to picture him stooped over his tackle box, puttering before going out to fish.

She wiped the tears on her face and stepped further inside. If she could just sit down here for a moment, soak in the scent and the familiar air of her father's life, maybe he would come back to her. But as she stepped across the floor, something in the boat caught her eye.

Morgan screamed.

The teenage girl in the boat sprang up. "I'm sorry!" she shouted.

Morgan grabbed a paddle hanging on the wall and held it like a weapon. "Who are you?"

"Sadie," the girl said. She stood up, and Morgan saw her casted arm and the bruises on her face. "I was just sleeping. I didn't have any place to go."

"What are you doing here?"

"I found it a couple of days ago," she said. "I've been trying to get a job, but no one will hire me, and the police won't let me sleep on the beach. It was the first boathouse I saw that wasn't next to a house. I just needed a place for a couple of days."

Morgan slowly lowered the paddle.

"Please don't call the police," Sadie said.

"Why would you sleep here?" Morgan asked, her heart still racing. "Where'd you come from?"

"West," the girl evaded.

"You a runaway?"

"No," the girl said too quickly. "I'm eighteen. I came here because it seemed like a wonderful place. Just the name—Cape Refuge. I thought it would be a nice place to live. But I can't find a job, and I don't have any money."

Morgan knew the girl was lying, that she couldn't be a day over fifteen, sixteen at the most. "How'd you get here?"

"I rode the Greyhound to Savannah," she said, "and there was this waitress in a diner, and she told me about Hanover House here and the nice people who owned it, Thelma and Wayne Owens, only I didn't know they were dead. And she brought me here and dropped me off thinking they would give me a place to stay."

Morgan gaped at her for a moment. "Thelma and Wayne were my parents."

Sadie brought her hand to her mouth. "Oh, I'm so sorry. I didn't know." She got out of the boat, grabbed her backpack, shoved her empty sandwich bag into it. "I'm leaving. Please, don't be mad. I won't come here again. I'm sorry I scared you, and I'm sorry I came in when I wasn't supposed to."

"Where'll you go?" Morgan asked.

"I don't know," she said. "I'm sure I'll find a job before long, and maybe then I can get an apartment on the beach—I've always dreamed of living on the beach."

The girl sounded like Dorothy dreaming of what lay over the rainbow. She was clueless about the price of beachfront property and had no resources of her own. She might get a job with hourly wages, but until she had a deposit for an apartment, no one was going to lease her a place.

For the first time, Morgan realized what her parents had felt each time they discovered a stray soul looking for refuge.

But she told herself the danger wasn't worth it. She didn't know this girl or anything about her. She was sure she had lied about her age. And she was certainly a runaway.

But she couldn't escape the fact that she needed a place to sleep, a roof over her head. There was a killer on the loose, and this child could be perfect prey for him. She couldn't send her back out there alone.

She set the paddle back on its hook and touched the girl's shoulder. "Look, you did scare me, but a lot of things are happening around here that I can't explain. I'm still upset about my parents' murders, and I'm a little on edge. But your waitress friend was right. My parents wouldn't have turned you away—and I won't either."

The girl looked so small and wounded, so innocent with her wispy blonde hair stringing around her face. "I'll be okay. Really."

"I know you will," she said. "You seem like a very enterprising young lady, very independent. But it would help you a lot if you had a place to lay your head tonight, and I have that big old house."

The girl's eyes filled with tears and hope, and she stepped toward Morgan. "You mean it? I could stay there?"

"I'm not promising it's safe right now," Morgan said. "There are other tenants there. Two of them are ex-cons, and the third one is in jail right now for identity theft. We don't know who killed my parents. But you could lock your door. It's better than sleeping out here. And meanwhile, there would be a place to take a bath and eat. I could loan you some clothes, so you'd have a better chance getting a job." She regarded her broken arm and the big bruise beneath her eye. "Or you could even just hang low for a while, let yourself heal before you start beating the bushes."

The girl's face reddened and twisted as she began to cry. "I'll pay you," she said. "Even for the time when I don't have a job— I'll pay you back as soon as I have money. I don't expect this for free."

"It's okay," Morgan said. "We have a whole list of donors who contribute to the Hanover House ministry. It makes it possible for us to take people in without pay until they get on their feet."

She took Sadie's backpack, slipped it over her own shoulder. "Come on," she said. "It's probably time you got settled. We have an empty room on the beach side of the house. I think you'll like it."

The girl couldn't stop crying as Morgan put her arm around her and escorted her out.

CHAPTER

*A*s Sadie showered upstairs, Morgan called Blair at the library to tell her about the girl. Blair went ballistic and told her she was coming over to talk some sense into her. She pulled into the driveway moments later, her face full of indignation.

"What are you thinking?" she asked in a loud whisper when she found Morgan in the kitchen. "We don't even know if we should be keeping the tenants we have, and you're bringing new ones in?"

"You would have done the same thing," Morgan said. "She was sleeping in the boathouse. She has a broken arm and this big bruise under her eye. What did you want me to do, send her back to the people who did that to her?"

"She's not your problem," Blair said. "She's not *our* problem."

Morgan checked the oven, where she had pork chops baking.

Blair grabbed her arm and stopped her. "Morgan, we have to find her another place to stay. We have to tell her to leave."

Morgan swung around and leveled her gaze on her. "Mama and Pop would have done just what I did, Blair."

"Maybe that's why they're dead!" Blair said. "And if we've learned anything from it—"

"I learned more from their lives than I did from their deaths, Blair," Morgan threw back. "I learned that sometimes it's important to do the right thing, even if there's uncertainty."

Blair paced across the room, rubbing her temples. "I don't understand this treacherous compassion you have, just like they had. I guess it's a religious thing, something you feel you have to do to score points with God."

"It's not about scoring points," Morgan said. "We rescue others because God rescued us. We're grounded enough in reality to know that we could be floundering, just like them."

"Reality?" Blair asked. "There's no reality involved here, Morgan. You think you'll bring Mama and Pop back somehow by taking in lost souls like they did. But it's not going to happen. You're just going to have a lot more stress on you, a lot more responsibility."

"I can handle it," Morgan said.

"Well, can you handle moving back into this house? Because you can't bring a teenage girl home and leave her alone here. You have to stay and watch over her."

"The doors have locks on them. And Rick's in jail."

"Didn't you hear?" Blair asked. "The judge set bail this afternoon. He's already out. He'll be coming back here."

"I thought you didn't think he did it!" Morgan said. "You're the one who was all friendly with him last night."

"I *don't* think he did it," she said. "But Gus might have. *Whoever* did it is still out there."

"All right, then, you've made your point. We could bring her to your house to stay with us—"

"No!" Blair cried. "I'm not entertaining some teenage kid!"

"Then I'll have to stay here," Morgan said, picking up a dish towel and rubbing a wet spot on the counter. "And you too because I don't want you alone at your house."

"This is crazy, Morgan!"

"Go up and meet her," Morgan challenged. "See if you could have turned her away. You might think you could, Blair, but I don't think you're that cold."

"Well, that's great, Morgan," Blair said, her lips compressed. "I'm cold just because I think clearly while you think with your emotions."

"Sometimes emotions matter!" Morgan said. "They're not all just whims, you know. Sometimes your heart tells you the truth."

"And sometimes it doesn't. It didn't that day Mama and Pop were murdered. Whatever they had done that day, whoever they had seen, it did them in. And it doesn't matter how good they felt or how emotional, they're still just as dead."

Morgan started to cry, and she flung down the dish towel. "I just want their legacy to be worth it," she said. "I don't want it to end right here. I want some of it to stay!"

"Pass it on," Blair said. "There are other people who can love stray people. If Hanover House doesn't get closed down, we can find somebody else who will want to run it."

"Maybe we don't need to," Morgan said. "Maybe I can do it."

"Yeah, if you don't wind up dead yourself. And if you think Jonathan's going to sit by and allow it, even from jail, you're cracked."

"He'll get over it," she said. "He'll understand as soon as he meets her. He couldn't turn her away either. That's why I married him, because of the compassionate man he is."

Blair pulled out a chair and dropped into it. "All right, Morgan. I can see I can't talk you out of letting the girl stay. But will you at least honor *your* husband's wishes and stay with me tonight? You don't need to sleep in this house, and I won't."

Morgan leaned against the cabinets and crossed her arms. "All right," she said. "I'll ask Mrs. Hern to look after Sadie—if she can remember to—and I'll make sure she locks her door. After I take care of a few things around here I'll go on over," she said.

"You promise?" Blair told her. "You won't get all warm and fuzzy and decide to stay here, will you?"

"No," Morgan said. "I won't. I just want to make sure Sadie's settled."

Moaning, Blair left the house, muttering under her breath about her sister's lethal compassion, and the complications this girl had just added to their lives.

CHAPTER

*B*lair left her car at Hanover House and crossed the street to the beach. She needed to walk, to get the anxiety and frustration out of her mind. She needed fresh air and a moment to think.

She walked around to the river side of the island, past her own house, and farther up to the dock where her parents had been murdered. The front door of the warehouse was sealed with crime-scene tape. She walked around to the pier where she had waited as they had searched the building and photographed their bodies. She sat down on the boardwalk, her legs crossed Indian style as she looked between the slats to the water beneath her.

Despite the heat, a chill ran through her. Looking across the water, she saw Jonathan's boat docked in its place. It was a good day for sailing. A schooner moved out from the dock, making its way toward the sound. Another was coming in, slowly drifting home. She knew some of them brought back sweet secrets of faraway places. Others would move on forever out of her sight, taking their secrets with them.

She wondered if any of those secrets had to do with murder.

She looked at the side door of the warehouse. It too was locked, but it didn't have any crime-scene tape across it. She pulled her keys out of her pocket and found the one her parents had given her long ago. She studied the door and wondered if she had the strength to go in and see the blood still on the floor.

She wanted to go in, not because it was the place of her parents' death, but because it was the place of their life.

Slowly, wearily, she got up and unlocked the door.

The building was as they had left it only four days ago, with its donated pews and the makeshift pulpit her father had put together. It smelled of mold and cedar and the faint scent of fish brought in by travelers and seamen who had sought out her parents for help with their sagging spirits.

She stepped across the room, to the stain on the floor where her parents had bled to death. She forced herself to look down at it, but that tornado of emotion whirled up in her again. Queasy, she went to the other side of the room and slipped onto the back pew.

She sat there quietly, wishing she had come to more of their services and watched as her father led in the singing, his deep bass voice ringing with authority and enthusiasm over the crowd, and her mother skittering here and there, greeting everyone who came in with hugs and encouragement.

She hadn't shared much of it with them. More than once her mother had cornered her and tried to talk her into coming. "But I don't believe what you believe," Blair had said. "It doesn't even make any sense to me."

Thelma had looked at her with genuine pain in her eyes. "How could you have grown up in our home and feel that way? Didn't you see all the ways God worked in our lives?"

"He works differently in mine," Blair said. Her hand came up and touched that scar on her cheek. Everything in her life had been filtered through that mangled scar. She didn't see the blessings they saw, for they were not always blessings to her, and she couldn't understand their reason for faith.

But now, as she sat in the pew and looked up at the pulpit from which her father had preached, she couldn't help wishing that she believed.

The front door opened, and she swung around, startled.

Cade stood in the doorway, squinting in as his eyes adjusted to the dim light.

"Cade," she said, catching her breath. "You scared me."

"Someone from Crickets called and said they saw you coming in here. It's still a crime scene, Blair. You shouldn't be here."

She sighed. "You know I'm not going to disturb anything. I just wanted to sit here for a minute." She pulled the pistol out of her pocket. "I've still got my friend with me. You don't have to worry."

He was quiet as he walked down the aisle and sat down next to her. "I know you want to be alone, Blair," he said, "but if you don't mind my saying so, there's got to be a better place."

"I didn't come here enough when they were alive," she said carefully. "I guess I just thought . . . that there would be some answers here."

He looked around at the dim building, its shadows speaking of death instead of life. She knew he wasn't going to leave, not until she came with him, but she wasn't ready to go. She just sat there, her eyes trained on that pulpit, trying to picture her father, his bright eyes laughing and full of life. She had never expected to see them shut in death.

"They changed lives here, Blair," he said softly. "There are people all over the world who've come through here."

"So I've been told."

"Some day when we get to heaven, you're going to see your pop surrounded by all kinds of people who are there because of him."

"I wish I could believe in heaven," she said. "You have no idea how I wish that."

Cade looked at her, and she was glad her scar was on the other side. "You can believe, Blair."

She shook her head. "It's not that easy for me," she said. "I need more evidence, more facts. I don't do well on faith alone."

"Your parents' whole lives were a testimony to Christ. *They* were the evidence."

"But they're dead," she said in a flat voice, "and now none of it really matters, does it? None of the hard work or the love they showed. None of the people they took into their home or the lives they sheltered. *They* weren't blessed or sheltered or protected. They were murdered."

"I see things differently," Cade said. "I knew them to be a couple that is still bearing fruit. Their faith multiplied into lots of other people, and it's still multiplying because those people are out there helping other people. They *were* blessed. You know, if you could sit down with your father and talk to him about this now, that's what he would tell you."

"My father would tell me a lot of things," she said. "But he could never adequately explain to me how God's control works with man's free will. Is God some kind of divine terrorist who uses homicidal maniacs to carry out his will? Or did that person wrench control from God in the time it took for him to get the speargun and shoot them? Was God sleeping when my parents were murdered? Or did he *cause* their murders? And if he did, then why should I pay homage to him? Why should I do anything for him? If there really is a God like that, it wouldn't matter whether I worshiped him or not. It didn't matter that my parents spent their lives serving him."

She hadn't meant to say so much, but her words were fueled by days of thought.

"I don't have all the answers, Blair," Cade whispered. "But your father taught me that God is not a 'divine terrorist.' He's a loving father, with purposes we don't even have the capacity to understand."

She breathed a bitter laugh. "There is no purpose in my parents' murder."

"Not from your vantage point," he said. "You may never see the purpose in it. But I bet they already know the good that will be done through it. Life is such a short little blip on God's timetable. He has all eternity to show them how the plan worked."

It was as if Cade parroted her father's exact thoughts, as if Wayne himself had sent him here to say these things to her.

But she didn't want to hear them. "How convenient, to believe that," she said. "To look at evil and decide that it's somehow good."

"That's not what I said."

"For me to decide to look at this as no big deal," she said, "as just another mysterious part of God's plan, would be the ultimate betrayal. I've earned my anger, and if I ever find out who killed my parents, you can bet that I've earned the right to get my revenge. How could *anyone* see any good in this? My parents were so convinced of a sovereign God. So this sovereign God *planned* to cut my parents off when they were doing so much good for so many people? I never could believe their stories, and I believe them even less now."

Cade shifted on the pew to face her. "What do you mean, their stories? Your parents never told a lie in their lives."

"Yes, they did," she said. "They told lies. Some intentional, some not." She tapped on the scar on her face. "This is the biggest one."

Cade only stared at her.

"They told me I was burned in a grease fire when I was three. But they wouldn't talk about it beyond that. So I'm left wondering why there's so much secrecy attached to a grease fire. It was a lie. But I don't know why they told it."

"What do you think happened?" Cade asked.

"I have no idea," she said, "just like I have no idea what happened to cause their murders. I may just have to add it to that long list of questions I have that I'll never have answers to."

She expected Cade to turn away, to act awkwardly, as if he hadn't noticed the scars. She didn't know why she had shared these things with him. She usually kept the terrible secrets of her heart wrapped up, never to be opened.

But Cade didn't turn away. Instead, he looked harder at her, his eyes cutting deep.

She hated herself for mentioning the scar. She didn't want to be vulnerable, not here with him, when he was sitting so close and looking at her with those eyes that used to make her nervous when she was fourteen. She had had a crush on him then, but she had countered it by acting as if she couldn't stand him, the jock who wouldn't have given her the time of day.

She wouldn't have him feeling sorry for her now. She thought of getting up and walking out, saying something rude and cryptic, something that shifted his focus off of her face.

But she felt tears rising in her throat, her nose, stinging behind her eyes. One move, one turn of her head, and her control would shatter, she was sure.

Cade touched her shoulder. "Hey," he whispered. "Look at me."

She forced herself to meet his eyes.

Slowly, his hand moved up her neck, into her hair . . .

She swallowed, but didn't allow herself to look away.

With the featherlight touch of his thumb, he stroked her scarred cheek.

No one had ever touched it before, no one besides her mother or father. Even Morgan had never intruded on that private part of her.

She felt herself recoiling, knowing it was blood red and testifying to the heart slamming out its cries that this was her scar and no one else's, and he couldn't just reach out and touch it like it didn't repulse him. He couldn't sit here and pretend—

"I know the scar bothers you, Blair," he whispered, stilling her thoughts. "And I know it's caused you a lot of pain. But I don't really see it anymore."

Her eyes misted, so she closed them, holding back those tears. But the hard protective shell over her heart seemed to melt, and one tear escaped, tracing its way down the crusted, blistery skin. He wiped that tear with a sweet, gentle pressure that made her heart break.

"I've known you for so long, Blair," he whispered, "that all I see when I look at you—is the prettiest girl on Cape Refuge. I don't see scars anymore. I know what you *really* look like."

She felt exposed, undressed, as if he could see things about her that she didn't want revealed. Slowly, she slipped back out of his touch.

He kept his hand suspended in the air.

She tried to say something logical, meaningful, something that would make light of what had just happened, but there weren't words like that inside her right now.

Finally, she blurted the only thing that came to her mind. "You really know how to kick a girl when she's down."

She could see that he wasn't fooled. "Blair—"

"I have to go." She launched out of her seat and crossed the floor, her heels pounding with vengeful purpose. She left Cade there and pushed through the hard wooden door.

As she quickly walked away, she told herself she could not look back. What had just happened had no meaning to her, and she would not think of it again.

CHAPTER

39

*A*fter Morgan had gotten Sadie fed and settled, and had made sure she was locked in her room, Morgan kept her word and headed back to Blair's house to spend the night. Though Blair's car was still at Hanover House, she wasn't there. Morgan figured she had gone for a walk, so she used her key to get in.

Quiet had become a friend to her, a comfort during these painful days. She had no heart or stomach for the radio or television, and even conversation with her sister could be an unwelcome intrusion. She lay down on the couch, closed her eyes, and slipped into a light sleep.

Some time later, she woke with a start. The house had grown dark as night fell over the island. She turned on a lamp and listened for the sound that had awakened her. Something scratched on the side window of the house. She lifted her head and looked toward it. The blinds were drawn, so she couldn't see out. She heard it again, so she got up and started toward the window.

The noise got louder, a scratch, scratch, scratching, like someone was cutting through the screen.

An animal? she wondered. Perhaps a bird tearing it, or some kind of rodent? She reached for the blinds and was about to pull them back when the glass broke. She jumped back and screamed.

Her mind reeled, and she grabbed the antique hutch that Blair kept near the window. She pulled it with all her might, shoved it in front of the window to keep the intruder from crawling through. Then she dove for the telephone.

Frantically, she dialed the number for the police department—but the line was dead.

She stumbled into the kitchen, groped for the silverware drawer, and pulled out a butcher knife. Holding the knife in her teeth, she turned the kitchen table on its side and pushed it against the back door. Then, with Herculean strength she didn't know she had, she slid the kitchen island against it.

She wasn't a strong person. Jonathan and her father had always done the heavy lifting in the family, but adrenaline surged through her as she ran around from window to window, grabbing the piano and shoving as hard as she could until it rolled against the front door. She backed away, and held the knife as she frantically scanned her fortress for a breach.

She heard a noise at the back door. He was trying to come through.

"Get away from here!" she screamed. "The police are on their way. I have a cell phone!" She knew that if the man outside was an islander, he would know that most cell phones couldn't get a signal here.

Her screams only seemed to make him try harder to get into the house. Terror pumped through her veins. She knew Blair had a gun somewhere in the house, but she didn't know where she kept it.

She heard a back window breaking, heard the scraping back of the cedar chest she had shoved against it on its side.

He was coming.

She stumbled and fell as she ran to Blair's bedroom, got up and groped for the closet door. She backed up into the corner of it and hunched down, clutching that knife in her hands, determined to use it.

Suddenly, she knew some of the terror her parents must have experienced in those last moments before their death.

As she crouched there, she prayed that Blair would not be the one to find her dead.

CHAPTER

40

Blair didn't go right home. She walked down the beach, trying to shake off the feelings that had come over her. Night was falling over the water, and the lights of Cape Refuge were coming on. She walked faster and faster back to Hanover House where she had left her car, hoping her speed and her determination would slow the surging of her blood and the racing of her heart. She hoped the blood pumping through her brain would purge her mind of the thoughts of Cade sitting next to her and seeing through the scars. There was too much pain that came on the heels of hope. She had enough pain in her life.

She got to her car, and stared at her windshield until her emotions were under control. Finally, she started home.

Morgan's car was parked in her driveway, and for a moment she wished she hadn't insisted that her sister spend the night there. She needed to be alone to think.

She went to the door and unlocked it, but it wouldn't open more than an inch. Something blocked it. She shoved harder. "Morgan!" she cried. "Morgan, let me in!"

There was no answer, so she rang the bell and banged on the door. "Morgan!" she cried. "Open the door! It's me." When there was no answer, she went to the window.

The screen was cut, and someone had broken the window. She called for her sister again, but no one came. Beginning to panic, she ran around to the back of the house, unlocked the back door. It too was barricaded.

Frantic, she went back to the broken window, knocked more of the glass out, then shoved the cabinet in front of it until she was able to climb through.

"Morgan!" She hit the floor and turned on the light. "Where are you?"

She sucked in a breath as she saw the furniture shoved against the windows and doors, a feeble effort to create a fortress. Panic rose like acid in her throat, and she clutched her gun and dashed for the bedroom.

Something moved in the closet, so she threw the door open.

Morgan crouched in the corner, a knife clutched in both hands.

"Morgan!" she cried, and Morgan looked up and began to wail.

"He was coming in," she cried, still clutching the knife. "He broke out the glass, and the back door, and he was coming around . . ."

She was shivering in terror, and Blair took the knife out of her hand and pulled Morgan out of the closet.

"The phone line . . . I couldn't call . . ."

"I've got a gun," Blair said. "I can protect us. We need to get Cade."

Morgan's eyes darted from window to window. "We can't go out there."

"My car must have scared him," she said. "Come on. We'll go outside together. We'll get in the car and go to the police."

Morgan clung to her and followed. Blair shoved the piano away from the front door and held Morgan with one arm as she clutched the gun with the other.

They flew to her car and tore out of her parking lot. Within minutes they were at the police station.

Cade was standing at the door to his office when Blair and Morgan rushed inside.

"Somebody tried to break into the house," Blair cried. "They cut the phone lines. I found Morgan in the closet with a knife."

Cade didn't waste any time. "Dispatch all four cars to 214 River Road!" he shouted to the dispatcher. "Stay here," he ordered Blair. "Don't go *anywhere.*"

Cade rushed to his car and headed toward her house with his lights flashing. Then adrenaline and wrath beat through his head as he walked around the house and saw how close Morgan and Blair had come to death. The intruder had believed they were both at home, and he had been intent on getting to them.

"I got something," McCormick called from the other end of the garden.

Cade crossed the yard and looked over his shoulder. A red bandana lay in the dirt.

"Gus Hampton always wears a red bandana," McCormick said.

Cade didn't answer. "Bag this evidence," he told Joe, then he turned to Billy Caldwell and Alex Johnson. "Both of you, follow me over to Hanover House to arrest Gus Hampton. If he's not there, we're gonna tear up this island 'til we find him."

Leaving two officers to help McCormick, Cade and a convoy of police cars flew down River Road toward Hanover House.

CHAPTER

It didn't surprise Cade to find that Gus's truck wasn't parked at Hanover House. He was probably cowering somewhere or scheming to go back to Blair's and finish the job.

Cade's urgent knock shook the house, and he heard footsteps. A woman's voice called, "Who is it?"

"Chief Cade. Open up."

The door slowly opened, and Cade saw the girl he had found on the beach. "What are you doing here?" he asked.

She was startled. "Morgan invited me," she said. "I haven't done anything wrong. She brought me here, and—"

"Don't worry," he said. "I'm not here for you. I'm looking for Gus Hampton."

"I don't know Gus," she said. "I just got here a little while ago. Mrs. Hern is the only one here."

He stepped inside, his eyes darting across the room. "I need to speak to Mrs. Hern, then."

"She's in the kitchen."

Cade found the woman standing at the sink. When she looked up at him, her face lit up.

"Hello."

He knew the woman had probably forgotten his name. "Mrs. Hern, I'm looking for Gus Hampton. Do you know where he is?"

"I can't say," she said, "but he could be over at . . . uh . . . that place on the dock. He likes to go there for supper sometimes. You know the place . . ."

"Crickets?"

"Yes, that's it. He likes that place."

"Mrs. Hern, when's the last time you saw him?"

"Well, uh . . . this morning, I guess. Why? What's wrong?"

"Blair's house was broken into tonight."

"You think it was Gus?" she asked. "Oh my, Gus wouldn't do that."

"I just want to ask him a few questions," he said. "But take my advice and lock your doors tonight, just to be on the safe side."

He could see the fear on Sadie's face as she inched back to the stairs as if she was ready to hide in her room and lock the door even now.

He got back into the squad car and crossed town to the warehouse where he had sat with Blair a little over an hour before. The parking lot at Crickets was full, and he could hear music from inside. Life went on, even though the murder was just a few days old—not more than a few dozen yards from this place. No time to mourn during tourist season, he supposed.

Followed by the officers who had met him there, he went into the restaurant and looked around the bar. He stood there a moment, scanning the smoke-blanketed tables and the faces of diners and drinkers. Finally, he saw a man with his back to him sitting alone at a corner table reading the paper. He had a red bandana tied on his head. He had expected Gus to be without it, with his bald head shining. But he supposed Gus had more than one.

Cade turned to the officers who had come in with him. "Caldwell, go check with the bartender and waiters to see how long he's been here. Johnson, come with me."

Caldwell headed through the people to the bar, and Cade started toward Gus. He ignored the greetings of those who called out to him and kept his eyes instead on the man who may have just broken into Blair's house.

Gus looked up. "You again, mon?"

"I need to talk to you," Cade said through tight lips. "Come with me. *Now.* If you do it quietly and peacefully, I won't arrest you here."

"Arrest me?" Gus asked. "For what?"

"Are you going to come with me or not?" Cade asked.

Gus stood up. He was a good six inches taller than Cade and had at least fifty pounds on him, but Cade was angry enough to tear him limb from limb. "Mon, nothing's changed since the last time."

"In the car, pal."

Gus looked around uncomfortably, then decided to do as he was told. He stalked out of the building, closely flanked by Cade and Alex Johnson.

He got into the passenger seat of Cade's car and propped his elbow on the window. "I be sitting here minding my own business, mon. You making me look bad."

"We can talk about it at the station," Cade said.

As he drove back across town, Cade told himself that he wasn't going to let this man back on the streets tonight. Even if he didn't have the hard evidence he needed, he would lock Gus up and make sure that Blair and Morgan were safe for the rest of the night.

CHAPTER

I was set up, mon." Gus Hampton paced across the interview room, a fine sweat shining on his brown skin. "I never even been near Blair's house."

"Okay, let's just go with your story that you weren't the one who tried to break into Blair's house. Where exactly were you?"

"I be at work, mon. Then I went straight to Crickets."

Cade looked hard at the man. He wanted nothing more than to beat the truth out of him. He pictured him sawing through Blair's screen, breaking the glass, cutting the phone line, going from window to window in a murderous attempt to get at her and Morgan.

The justice system wasn't enough for people like that, he thought. He needed something more brutal.

Knowing his mind was taking him down the wrong path, he got up and stalked to the door. "McCormick!" he shouted.

Joe came to the door. "Yeah, Chief?"

Cade stepped out into the hall. "Help me out here, man, before I hurt this guy."

McCormick nodded. "Glad to."

"He claims he was at work, went straight to Crickets, never been to Blair's house in his life."

McCormick went in and dropped into the seat next to Melinda Jane. He leaned up on the table, looking at Gus with hard, weary eyes. "Gus, take off your shoes. There were footprints near the windows. Big ones."

Gus took his boots off and plopped them on the table. "Check them out, mon." He set his jaw and peered at Cade. "If that was my do-rag you found, it was planted there to make me look guilty. Rick's the *bandooloo*."

"He's the what?" Cade asked, irritated.

"The trickster, mon. He's dishonest, that Rick Morrison."

Cade didn't bother to confirm Gus's statement with what he'd learned about Rick.

"Ask him about the money he be stealing from his boss man," Gus said. "Even better, ask them. He be walking around all misty-eyed and mourning. 'Tom drunk but Tom no fool.'"

"What?" McCormick asked. "Who in the blazes is Tom?"

"It is a Jamaican expression, mon," Gus said. "Meaning things are not what they seem."

"Speak English, Gus, and we'll move along a lot faster." Cade got up and set both hands on the windowsill. He could hear Melinda Jane's fingers clacking on her stenotype machine.

"So tell me what you know about the thefts," McCormick said.

"What I know is that Rick Morrison stole money from his boss man," Gus said. "Check it out. You'll see, mon."

"How do you know that?" McCormick asked.

"I listen good," Gus said. "It's not that hard in Hanover House. You hear things and you put them together."

"And what did you hear?"

"That Rick stole money from his boss man, but he gave it back before they caught him."

"Oh," McCormick said without belief. "So there wouldn't be any evidence at all? No stolen money, no angry employer, no nothing? What does that prove?"

"That he is not an honest man. He has secrets. And if he be involved in this terrible thing, maybe he be trying to make me look like the one. He could have got my bandana out of my room. Or found it after I dropped it somewhere."

When they had finished questioning him, they let Melinda Jane go, and Cade stepped out with McCormick. "I want to lock him up," Cade said. "Too many things point to him. But you've got to get me more hard evidence or the judge will let him out tomorrow. What about the boots?"

McCormick turned them over and studied the soles. "These weren't the shoes used in the break-in attempt. The footprints weren't this big."

"So he changed shoes. Get a warrant to search his room. Call the judge at home."

"Will do."

"So what do we have? A bandana that may not be his, the fact that the argument between Jonathan and the Owens was over him, his access to the speargun, the fact that his shoes were muddy last night when I saw someone running in the woods near Blair's house . . ."

"But we have statements from his coworkers and the folks who saw him at Crickets. Basically, we have nothing to base an arrest on," McCormick said.

"But everything to base an arrest on. I'm locking him up. It's my job to keep the community safe, and there's no way I'm letting him back out there tonight."

He went back in and read Gus his rights. The big man took his arrest with a moan of resignation and allowed himself to be escorted to the jail cells.

As Cade walked Gus past Jonathan's cell, Jonathan came to the bars.

"What's going on?" Jonathan asked.

"You're going to have company," Cade said.

"What did he do?"

Cade didn't answer.

"I asked you, what did he do?" he yelled.

"He's a suspect in an attempted burglary," Cade said. He knew he would find out tomorrow as soon as Morgan visited him, but he wasn't going to get it out of him tonight.

"Whose attempted burglary?" Jonathan demanded.

Cade ignored him.

"Who did you rob, Gus Hampton?" Jonathan yelled as Cade locked him into the cell next to Jonathan's. "Did it have anything to do with my wife?"

"I did not do it, mon."

Jonathan rammed his hand into the cell bar. "Is my wife hurt? Cade, you let me out of here!"

Cade turned back to Jonathon with resignation. His friend was too scared for his wife to accept Cade's evasion.

"She's fine, Jonathan. Just a little shaken up. Somebody tried to break into Blair's house, but they didn't get to either of them." He started to walk out, but Jonathan wouldn't be silenced.

"You're going to leave me in here with him? Man, if he did it, doesn't that clear me?"

"Not yet," Cade said. "Just hold tight, Jonathan."

CHAPTER

*T*he next morning, Morgan tried desperately to keep busy. She paced the second floor of Hanover House, going from room to room and straightening up. The police had searched Gus's room but hadn't seemed to find anything.

She shivered at the thought of him being the one trying to get into Blair's house, so relentless in his efforts. She had no doubt that he would have been brutal if he had gotten in.

The bandana had convinced her that Gus was the culprit and that Jonathan had been right about him all along. She was glad Cade had him locked up.

Today might be the day that her husband was set free.

When she couldn't find anything else to do, she drifted to the door that hadn't been opened since she and Blair had taken the files out of the room and closed it behind them. She touched the knob, turned it, and stepped into her parents' room.

The fresh, clean scent of her mother's shampoo and father's shaving cream drifted on the air, and her heart swelled. She ran her hand along the bedspread, trying to picture them lying there and watching the news before turning in. How many times had she seen them like that?

She pulled the comforter back, took her father's pillow, and buried her face in it. It smelled of salt air and sea breeze, second-hand cigarette smoke from Crickets, and the slightest hint of after-shave—the unique combination of scents that she would always associate with him. She wondered if, later, when all the linens had been washed and the room had been cleared of their things, she would ever smell that scent again.

She climbed onto the bed and curled up, clutching the pillow against her chest. She felt as if she lived in a dream, one with no logical order, that made no sense. But it was no dream.

After crying for a while, she pulled herself off the bed and made it up, hiding any evidence that she had climbed onto it like a child onto a parent's lap. She went to her mother's closet and looked around at all the things stacked so neatly there. There were shoes in one corner in orderly rows on a shelf unit her father had built. On one side hung the dresses and pantsuits her mother had worn. She touched them each with reverence, feeling the fabric and the softness, picturing the way they had hung on her mother.

She looked up onto the shelves of the closet and saw an old teddy bear stuffed into the corner. It had been Blair's when she was a child, and she remembered her sister clutching that stuffed animal with all her might after skin graft surgeries that had left her weak and in pain. She had thought the teddy bear was lost. It had never occurred to her that her parents had kept it.

She went out and got a chair from the bedroom, pulled it into the closet, and stood on it carefully. She reached for the teddy bear. As she pulled it, some papers rustled beneath it. She stretched to look over the shelf and saw that the papers were in a shallow box and the teddy bear sat on it. She pulled the box out with it and got down.

She got down. Sitting on the edge of the bed, she held the teddy bear. Maybe it would give Blair comfort, she thought.

In the box there were letters from family members she had never met, people her parents had rarely spoken of. She skimmed the first one, saw nothing of importance, then turned to the second and third. Clutching the teddy bear, she tried to fathom why her parents had saved these letters over the years, what significance they might have had to be kept tucked in a box at the corner of their closet.

And then she came to one addressed to the little South Carolina town where she had been born.

Dear Thelma and Wayne,

I've thought long and hard about writing this letter to you. It's always easier to put the blinders on and keep quiet about the sins you see in the lives of loved ones, but you have those two children involved, and as their grandmother, I can't help telling you that one day your lifestyle is going to catch up with you and fall back on your children. You can't live a life of deceit and think that God will bless it. Now I know you don't believe in God, not because you weren't taught to, Thelma, but because you want to rebel as hard as you can against what your family embraced. But in your heart I know you know better. I won't lie to the police for you anymore. But I will pray for you, and mostly I'll pray for those little girls who don't deserve parents on the wrong side of the law.

You have a choice to make, Thelma and Wayne, a choice about how to spend your lives, a choice about how your girls will grow up. You've spun them into a dangerous web of lies and schemes, and the thought of it makes me ashamed and afraid. Turn back now before it's too late, before your children suffer, before you wind up in jail and someone else has to raise them. They don't deserve that. You know it's true.

And it was signed simply, "Mama."

Morgan slowly got to her feet, clutching the paper in her hand. She felt as if a hand had reached in and grabbed her heart, squeezing it so tightly that the blood would not beat through.

Her parents on the wrong side of the law? She looked back at the date of the letter and saw that she was only four at the time. That couldn't be, she thought. Not her parents. Always upstanding, model citizens, always willing to help others. How could her grandmother have thought that her parents were doing anything wrong? Yet, here it was, and her parents had kept it for all these years. Her grandmother had died two years later.

She heard Sadie coming out of the bathroom and crossing the hall, and she tried to pull herself together. Quickly she folded the letter up and stuck it in her pocket, clutched the teddy bear tighter, and went to the door.

"Sadie, do you need anything?" Her voice quivered as she spoke.

"No, thank you," she said. "It felt so good to sleep so late. I needed it."

"Good. Just make yourself comfortable. If you get hungry, you're welcome to eat anything in the kitchen." The words came out of her mouth by rote, almost amazing her because she didn't feel like being helpful or generous. Instead, she felt like finding a dark place and weeping again for the double loss she felt now. The loss of her parents' lives—and even worse, the possible loss of her image of them.

She stumbled downstairs to the telephone in the kitchen and dialed Blair's number.

"Hello?"

"Blair." Morgan's voice was soft, breathless. "I found something in Mama's closet. I want you to come over here. Meet me across the street on the beach."

Then without saying anything to anybody, she stumbled out of the house and off the porch, clutching the teddy bear to her chest and the letter in her fist. She crossed the street, out onto the sand and to the edge of the water. One of the chairs her father had built and put out there for the guests was damp with the spray of water. Without drying it off, she sat down and studied the letter again, then put it back into her pocket.

The wind whipped through her hair, slapping it into her face, and she shoved it back and wiped the tears from her eyes. After a while she heard Blair's car pull up into the driveway. Her sister came over, her loose dress flapping against her body in the wind.

Blair saw the teddy bear at once, and her step slowed. "Where'd you find that?" she asked quietly.

Morgan tried to swallow back the knot in her throat. "In Mama and Pop's closet."

Blair reached down and took it, looked at it almost objectively, for a moment, like someone analyzing a piece of evidence. Then she sat down in the chair next to Morgan and slowly pulled the teddy bear against her. "I've wondered where this was. I think about it every now and then."

"They kept it for you," she said. "I guess they knew that you'd need it again."

Blair looked out on the water, her eyes fragile and shadowed.

"There's something else." Morgan pulled the letter out of her pocket again, slowly unfolded it. "It's a letter from Grandma."

"Which one?" Blair asked.

"Grandma Simpson. It's to Mama and Pop. Back when I was about four and you were one."

Blair took the letter out of her hand. "Why did they keep it all these years?"

"Read it," she said. "You'll see."

Morgan watched as Blair's eyes scanned over the letter. At first they were objective, as they had been when she had taken the teddy bear. Then they changed to surprise, then to astonishment, and then to a deep sadness. She brought those grieving eyes back up to her sister.

"Mama and Pop—on the wrong side of the law? That's just not possible. I can't even picture it."

"There are other letters in that box," Morgan said. "I haven't gone through them all. I saw a few of them. They were pretty benign. But it was almost like Mama and Pop kept them because they were some kind of connection with their family. And think about it, Blair. All these years we've never really known any of them. It was like they cut them off years ago. And this letter kind of tells us why."

"Our parents have never broken the law," Blair said, brooking no debate.

"But they haven't always been Christians, Blair," Morgan said. "What if there's something about their past that we don't know, something that happened before they changed?"

"People don't change *that* much," Blair said. "I know you believe in that new creature thing, but I don't. We're talking about inherent personality traits. Our parents have never had that kind of deceit or scheming in them. Maybe Grandma had it all wrong. Maybe she just misunderstood."

"Mama used to grieve every year on her mother's birthday," Morgan whispered. "One time I caught her crying, and she said she missed her, that they'd had a fight before she died and she never had a chance to reconcile."

Blair looked back down at the letter. "Well, it shouldn't be that hard to check out. I mean, there are other family members we could call."

"But you have to wonder how much they knew."

"If our parents were con artists or something, people in the family would talk."

Morgan pulled her feet up on the chair with her and hugged her knees. "Do you think this has anything to do with their murders?"

"It couldn't possibly. This was twenty-four years ago. They've done too much good since then. But I'm still going to check it out. I'm going to find out what Grandma thought, anyway. There must be cousins, nieces and nephews, people who heard something. And then there would be police reports and a rap sheet on them if they'd ever been arrested." Her eyes drifted back out across the water as if the words "rap sheet" associated with her parents didn't quite fit. "This is all absurd, you know," she said. "Our parents never broke a law in their lives."

"But we don't know that much about them before we moved here," Morgan whispered.

Blair's hand came up to cover the scar on her face, as if that was the most critical evidence of all that her parents had a secret past. She looked back down at the letter again as if somewhere embedded in the message there might be an answer about the scars she had carried most of her life.

"I'm going to get to the bottom of this, Morgan," she said. "Trust me. If there's something to know, we're going to know it."

Morgan sighed. "I don't know if I feel right about that. Maybe we're just supposed to let our memory of them rest as it is. It doesn't seem that respectful digging into their past, looking for things they obviously didn't want us to know. And if they did have some kind of criminal past, I'm not sure I want anyone else finding out about it either. If we get on the phone with relatives and start asking questions, it might stir up a hornets' nest."

"We need to know," Blair said. "I need to know. And when we get to the bottom of this, then we'll decide what to do. Agreed?"

Morgan looked out over the water as a sense of dread crushed down on her. She knew she couldn't talk her sister out of this. It was a quest that she needed to embark upon, and Morgan had no right to stand in her way. "All right," she said finally. "Agreed."

CHAPTER

*T*he Madison Boat Shop stood on the coastal side of the highway. Cars zoomed by just yards from its front porch. Behind the shop was a dock where four boats sat in various stages of disrepair. Everyone in the area who had a boat that needed working on brought it here.

And it was where Rick Dugan worked.

Gus's words about the money being stolen from the boat shop had nagged at Cade since he had arrested him, and now he stepped into the shop and looked around, breathing in the scent of lacquer and wood stain. He saw Rick out on the back deck sweeping, and he stepped across the wooden floor and into the smaller room toward the back of the building. He found Gerald Madison at his desk with a pile of paperwork spread out in front of him.

"Hey, Gerald. How's it going?" Cade said.

The old man looked up and rubbed his mustache. He was always rubbing his mustache as if it itched, and Cade didn't know why he didn't just shave the thing off. The man looked as ragged as a homeless man, even though he was probably one of the richest men in town. Cade always wanted to point him to the nearest barbershop.

"How's it going, Cade?" he said. "Hear you been busy the last few days."

Cade shook Gerald's hand and took the seat across from the cluttered desk. A big picture window at the back of the office drew his gaze, and he looked out on the boats that some of the employees worked on.

"Hear you already arrested two people about the killings," Gerald said. "Do you know yet why they did it?"

Cade shrugged. "I can't think why anybody would do a thing like that. But I had a couple of questions to ask you."

The man stiffened and leaned forward on his desk. "Fire away."

"I heard a rumor," he said. "A rumor that you had a theft recently, that a good bit of money was stolen, but that you didn't report it."

Gerald's mouth fell open. "Now who told you a thing like that?"

"Doesn't matter," Cade said. "Is it true or isn't it?"

"Don't matter now," Gerald said. "The money was returned. There was never a need to file a report."

"Returned?" Cade asked. "How much money are we talking about?"

"Ten thousand."

Cade whistled under his breath. "Ten thousand dollars? What, was it in the cash register?"

"No," Gerald said. "It was embezzled."

"Embezzled?"

"That's right," he said. "I discovered it in the bookkeeping."

"Then you must know who did it," Cade said.

Gerald's eyes shot to Rick out on the deck, and Cade didn't miss it. "I have a few people who have access to my books. Maybe I trusted them a little too much. But the bottom line is it was returned."

"Did the thief confess?" Cade asked.

"No, never did. Still not sure who did it." He sighed and leaned back, picked up a cigar, and lit it. "I have a few ideas, but since he turned honest, I don't see no reason to press the issue."

"So you're still trusting him with the books?"

"I didn't say that," Gerald said. "But I figure everybody has temptation now and then. Long as their conscience turns them around, I reckon it's all right."

Cade got up and strolled to the window, looked out at Rick working. The rumor was that he had good carpentry skills that had translated well to this business. But he'd asked Rick once what he did before coming to Cape Refuge. Rick had said he was an accountant.

"Tell me about Rick Morrison," he said.

Gerald got quiet. Cade turned around and saw the closed look on his face. "If you think Rick Morrison had anything to do with Thelma and Wayne's murder, you're wrong. He's a decent man."

"You sure of that?" Cade asked.

"I'm a good judge of character," Gerald said. "Yeah, I'm sure of it."

Cade held his eyes for a moment too long. "Is he the one who stole the money?"

Gerald looked away. "I told you I don't know who stole the money. All I know is somebody put it back, and I can't very well go firing people when I don't have any evidence, especially when no real harm was done."

"You should have filed a police report," Cade said. "It could happen again."

"I don't think it will," Gerald said. "Besides, like I said, I'm taking over the books. It's about to kill me," he said. "But I'm doing it."

Instead of going back to his car, Cade walked out the back door and down the deck steps. He watched Rick Morrison work on the boat for a while, then strolled along until he got near the pier and the warehouse where Thelma and Wayne had been found. A family sat fishing for crabs from the pier just outside the warehouse. He watched as a tawny-haired boy slowly pulled up his line. A crab was wrapped around the chicken neck he used for bait. He scooped the crab up with his scoop net, examined it, saw it was a female, and threw it back in, holding out for a male with more meat. The kid's little sister laughed, her sound lilting across the wind.

Cade stood there a moment, listening to the sound of a sand-hill crane flying overhead and the gentle roar of the surf.

He walked back up to his squad car, got in, and sat behind the wheel. He wondered if either of the two men he had behind bars at the station really had anything to do with the killings, or if Rick Dugan out there on that boat was the culprit. He wondered if Rick had, indeed, stolen the ten thousand dollars and put it back. And he wondered how Gus really knew about it.

He started his car and pulled back onto the highway, made his way around the island back to the station. He had a lot of work to do tonight, he thought, but he was going to get answers before this day was over.

CHAPTER

45

*T*he letter from her grandmother about her parents' lifestyle plagued Blair into the night, and finally when she had given up on sleep, she got dressed and went next door to the library. She used her key to get in, then locked the door behind her, nervous about who might be lurking in the shadows. She kept her gun hidden in the pocket of her skirt, her hand curled around it. Then she went to the computer.

What lifestyle was her grandmother complaining about? And did it have anything to do with the scars on Blair's face? All she knew was that her parents had come from Charleston and that the burns had happened when she was three and Morgan was six. Her parents had never wanted to discuss it or dwell on those years. There were no pictures of that time, no fond memories, no traditions from that time etched in their family's consciousness.

She pulled up a file she had scanned into her computer a year or so ago, when she had ordered copies of her medical records from all the hospitals who had treated her.

She read back over the list of her injuries at age three. She had been burned in a house fire, it said, and had suffered third-degree burns on twenty percent of her body. The scars were still there, despite surgery after surgery, multiple skin grafts, new scars to fix old ones.

She checked the date of her injuries, jotted it down, then went to a database at a Charleston newspaper and pulled up its archives. If there had been a house fire in which a child had been injured, it would have likely been in the newspaper, Blair thought.

Quickly, she did a search of the newspapers in Charleston, searching for any articles with her name. Her heart pounded as she watched the bar move across the screen, and the hourglass telling her to wait. She didn't realize she had been holding her breath until the newspaper article loomed up on the screen. She saw the title: "THREE-YEAR-OLD INJURED IN HOUSE FIRE." She clicked it and waited as the small article filled her screen.

Three-year-old Blair Nicole Owens suffered multiple second- and third-degree burns in a house fire Tuesday. Officials said that the child was rescued from a second-story bedroom. Her parents, who had discovered the fire and gotten the family out earlier, were not aware that the child had run back in to rescue a pet cat. The child was transferred by helicopter to the Anderson Burn Center where she is listed in critical condition.

The cause of the fire is yet unknown, but arson is suspected, according to fire department sources.

Blair sat back hard in her chair. Arson? If it had been a simple grease fire, why would they suspect arson? And from the sound of things, it had been so much more than a small grease fire. It had been a raging house fire. Why had her parents failed to tell her that?

Her hands trembled as she bookmarked that page. She turned off the computer and paced around the room, her shoes clicking on the wooden floor. Wouldn't Morgan have remembered a blazing house fire and Blair going back for the cat? Why wouldn't she have told her?

Her heart sped with aerobic force, and she closed her hand around that gun again and headed out of the library, locking the door behind her.

The clock on a shelf in her living room said 3:00 A.M., but time had little meaning to her now. She found Morgan sleeping deeply in Blair's bed, just where she had left her. She flicked on the light. "Morgan, get up."

Morgan squinted up at her. "What is it?"

"We have to talk. About the fire."

Morgan pulled her feet out of bed and sat up, squinting her eyes at the light. "What fire?"

"The one that did this to me," she said, pointing to her scars.

Morgan blinked and got up, staring at her sister. "Blair, I don't remember much about it."

"You were six!" Blair shouted. "You remember who your first-grade teacher was! Don't tell me you don't remember a fire that almost destroyed your sister. I found a newspaper article, and it said I had run back in to get the cat and that arson was the suspected cause—"

Morgan slowly sank back onto the edge of the bed. "The dreams," she whispered. "I have dreams at night of you running through flames . . . screaming . . . I have vague memories of you in the hospital and everybody thinking you were going to die. I remember holding your teddy bear, and Mama and Pop pacing the floor. But I just don't remember the fire." She stared at her sister as her mind reeled. "Why wouldn't I remember it if I was there?"

The look of genuine despair on Morgan's face convinced Blair that she was telling the truth.

"Maybe I blocked it out somehow," Morgan said. "I do remember having a cat, though. She must have died in the fire."

Blair pushed off from the wall. "Why did they say it was just a grease fire? Why didn't they tell me it was arson? Why was it they never wanted to talk about it?"

"Could it have anything to do with the letter we found from Grandma?"

"No," Blair said. "That letter was dated before the fire. But there are so many secrets, Morgan. Why? And now their murders . . . and more secrets."

Morgan took her hand. "These things happened twenty-something years apart, Blair. I doubt if the murders had anything to do with their past, don't you?"

"I don't know what anything has to do with anything," Blair said. "All I know is that I can't crack the code of my past, and nobody else seems to be able to either. There was only that one article that came up when I typed my name in. And it had so little information."

"Maybe you can talk to Cade. Maybe he has other resources."

She thought about that. "Maybe so. But he's got an awful lot on his plate already." Blair suddenly felt exhausted, as if the energy had bled out of her. But she didn't want to sleep. "I'm going to go to Hanover House," she said. "I want to see what else Mama and Pop have in their closet."

Morgan got up and grabbed the jeans she had laid over a chair. "I'll come with you."

"No, you don't have to. You need to sleep."

"Then why did you wake me up?"

Blair saw that Morgan was smiling. "I'm sorry. I was just a little upset."

"It's okay. I'm awake now. Let's go."

Everyone at Hanover House slept, so Morgan and Blair went in quietly and climbed the stairs. They closed themselves inside their parents' room. Then Blair went into her parents' closet where her teddy bear and the letters had been discovered.

Morgan brought a chair in, and Blair stepped up onto it and looked around at the top shelf. She found three shallow boxes full of papers. Some of them were just bills that her father had kept over the years in case of an IRS audit or dispute over the donations that kept the house running. Another was a box of papers on past tenants, and she flipped through and saw that none of the more recent ones was even represented there. The other was full of Bible studies and notes taken at church and at Christian meetings, useless things as far as Blair was concerned, but Morgan grabbed hold of the box as if it was a treasure she hadn't expected to find.

Morgan placed it on the middle of the bed and climbed up next to it. She pulled out her father's notes on the book of Romans, his extensive study on the book of Revelation, his *Experiencing God* book, several Precept courses—

Blair sorted through the papers, her eyes scanning her father's handwritten notes. She picked up one of the books and flipped through, and saw his notes jotted on every page. In a section on forgiveness, her father had written extensive notes on a chart entitled "Things He Forgave Me For." She looked down at the list, curious at the sins that had plagued her father.

Number one knocked the breath out of her.

"Morgan, look at this."

Morgan scooted across the bed and looked at the chart. "'Causing Blair's burns'?" She brought her astonished eyes up to Blair's. "How did he cause them? It was a house fire. You ran in to get the cat."

"There's more," Blair said. "He wrote, 'Because of my own choices, my little girl will suffer with scars for the rest of her life. She almost died. But even as she lives, each time I look at her face I realize what a wretch I was, how selfish and self-centered, how greedy. And even though Christ has forgiven me, I don't think I'll ever forgive myself. Her burns stand as a constant reminder of the enormity of the debt that was paid for me when Christ died on the cross. And knowing the cost of that, how could I ever deny anyone else forgiveness? I only hope that if Blair ever finds out, she'll forgive me too.'"

Blair set the book down as if it had burned her, and locked her gaze on her sister.

"How could it be his fault?" Morgan asked. "What could he have done?"

"I don't know," Blair said. "Do you think he started the fire? Maybe he was smoking in bed or something."

"Pop never smoked."

"But it had to be something. Maybe this story about me running back in for the cat wasn't true. Maybe he didn't really rescue me."

"He would never have forgotten you," Morgan said. "You know better than that. Pop loved us. I remember every time you had a surgery, he'd stay at the hospital with you around the clock, pacing the room and making sure the nurses didn't come in and disturb you when you finally slept, making sure your medicine was given on time, that you didn't have any unnecessary pain. He doted on you, Blair. I was even jealous a few times."

"Then how could he blame himself for this?"

"I don't know," Morgan said, "but maybe that's why he kept it secret. Maybe he didn't want you to know his part in it."

When they had exhausted the possibilities, they both crawled up in their parents' bed. Morgan fell off to sleep, but Blair only lay there, breathing in the scent of her father, resting in the sweet memory of his love for her and wondering how in the world he had almost killed her.

CHAPTER

46

*T*he stolen money at the Boat Shop plagued Cade all night, and he couldn't help thinking that, somehow, it tied in to the murders of Thelma and Wayne Owens. The night had not been a good one for Cade. He had lain awake trying to put together Jonathan's part in the killings, Gus's, or even Rick's. He went to the police station before the sun had even risen and sat behind his desk trying to figure out what he had missed, whether he should let Jonathan and Gus go, whether he should bring Rick in for questioning.

But he didn't have to wonder any more, when Rick Dugan showed up to talk to him.

"I heard you were at the Boat Shop yesterday asking about me," Rick said, taking a seat across from Cade's desk. "I thought maybe you'd like to ask me those questions face-to-face."

Cade rubbed his jaw wearily. "Tell the truth, I was about to come question you."

"Then I saved you a trip," Rick said. "Is it about the murders?"

Cade didn't know if he wanted to go that far just yet. He leaned on his desk. "It was actually about some money that was stolen from the Boat Shop a couple of weeks ago. You know anything about that?"

Rick's eyes shot to the side, a sure sign of guilt in Cade's book. "Yeah, I remember. Gerald told us that the money was missing and that he was going to report it to the police. But before he did, a deposit for that exact amount showed up in his account. So he never reported it."

"Don't you find that odd?" Cade asked. "I mean that somebody who apparently worked for him would have stolen money and then returned it?"

"Well, if it was returned, then the person turned out not to be dishonest, after all. I guess he figures there's no point."

"Apparently that's exactly what he feels," Cade said. He watched the man try to get comfortable in his seat, and he thought of Blair sitting outside talking to him that night so quietly and intimately. A surge of resentment had washed through him at the sight of it. He hadn't trusted Rick Dugan since.

"Look," Rick said. "I know that every little thing matters when you're investigating a homicide. But it's not the theft of Gerald Madison's money or my name change that really bothers you. You want to know if I killed Thelma and Wayne, and I've told you that I didn't. I could never do that. I was at work until four that afternoon," he said. "The whole crew saw me."

"So somebody was with you every minute?"

He shrugged. "Well, I can't promise that. Sometimes we get to working on a section of the boat by ourselves. I mean, we don't work right on top of each other, if that's what you mean."

"Then it's possible that your every moment wasn't accounted for?"

"It was accounted for," he said. "And for all I know, somebody did see me every minute. I'm just telling you that I don't always work side by side with somebody else. I'm not on a chain gang. And after work, I started to go home, but then I decided to go by the Owens's boathouse and take the boat out. I fished until about six."

The same boathouse he'd found Gus in hours later, Cade thought.

"Thelma and Wayne Owens were the most decent people I've ever met in my life," Rick went on. "I don't know what I would have done without them. When I brought the boat back that day, I stopped by Crickets to get a bite, and I heard about the murders there." His voice broke and his eyes filled. "If I ever get my hands on the pitiful soul that killed them, I might just commit the first violent act of my life."

He drew in a breath and went on. "I went by Cricket's for lunch too that day. Got a hot dog. I don't remember seeing anybody at the warehouse when I passed. No cars, nothing. I keep thinking that I should have gone home or stopped by the warehouse instead of going to the boathouse. Maybe I could have stopped the killer. Maybe I could have changed things somehow."

When he had finished questioning him, Cade walked him out to his car and leaned in the window. He glanced around at the contents inside and saw a Delta Airlines envelope stuck in the visor pocket.

"Look, I'm more than willing to answer any questions you have," Rick said. "I'm in enough trouble for the name thing. I have to go to court about that next month. That's why I came by here today. I don't want anymore secrets, and I don't want to worry if you're going to come break my door down in the middle of the night and arrest me like you did Gus and Jonathan."

"I didn't break anybody's door down," Cade said.

"I'm just saying I'll answer whatever you want to know."

"Then tell me about that airline ticket."

Rick looked up at the ticket in his visor pocket, slipped it out, and handed it to Cade.

"I've been planning a visit to see my mother. She's in a nursing home in Atlanta," he said. "She has advanced Alzheimer's. She doesn't know whether I'm there or not, but I feel like I need to go see her. And while I was there, I was going to pay off some debts to clear the slate." He looked down at the steering wheel. "I've also been struggling with how to forgive the guy that killed my wife and child. Thelma and Wayne kept telling me that until

I forgave, I was never going to heal. They were the ones who encouraged me to go back."

"Well, I'd rather you didn't leave town right now," Cade said. "I might want to question you again."

"Fine," he said. "Look at the tickets. They don't even have a date on them. They're open-ended. Thelma and Wayne bought them for me."

"Thelma and Wayne?"

"Yeah. They also provided the money to pay off the debts. You can look in their bank account. They wrote the check right to me."

Cade frowned. "For how much?"

Rick looked reluctant to tell him the amount, but finally the words came out. "Ten thousand dollars."

That familiar alarm blared in Cade's head. "Thelma and Wayne gave you ten thousand dollars?"

Rick's eyes misted over, and he swallowed. "They were good people."

"Where did they get ten thousand dollars?"

"They said they had it in savings. For all I know, they may have borrowed it."

"Is that why the Boat Shop's stolen money turned back up, because Thelma and Wayne gave you the money and you didn't need it?"

For a long moment, Rick stared at him, his eyes dull, as if he struggled with whether to offer the truth or a lie. "If there's no police report and no money is missing, then there wasn't a crime committed, was there?"

Cade stared at him. "Let's just say the crime was undone. I'm thinking somebody's conscience got to them."

"Well, if that's so," Rick said, "then they wouldn't be much threat as far as murders were concerned, would they?"

"Maybe," Cade said. "Maybe not."

Rick started his car. The engine hummed to life, clicking and moaning. "You know where to find me if you have any more questions," Rick said. "And you know, you really ought to let

Jonathan and Gus go. Neither one of them has murder in them. I'm not telling you how to do your job or anything, but let's get real. I've lived with both of them, and they're not killers."

Cade took a step back as the car pulled out of the parking lot and watched the man drive out of sight.

CHAPTER

*C*ade's phone call to Hanover House woke Blair up. It was late, past time for her to open the library, but he was glad she had gotten some sleep. "Sorry to wake you, Blair," he said. "I called your place first. I figured you were there. I need to go to Hanover House and look in your parents' office."

"What are you looking for, Cade?" she asked in a hoarse voice.

"Their checkbook," he said. "I want to know where Thelma and Wayne spent their money. I need to account for every penny."

"Why?"

"It's part of the investigation, Blair," he said. "Do you know where their bankbook is?"

"Yes," she said. "We'll be waiting."

*C*ade and McCormick got to Hanover House and knocked, but there wasn't an answer right away. He figured Blair and

Morgan were still getting dressed. It had only been a few minutes since he woke her up.

He slid his hands into his pockets and looked out at the water across the street. So much had happened since he had sat in that warehouse with Blair and touched her scars. Life seemed to have sped into fast-forward ever since.

You really know how to kick a girl when she's down.

The words clanged through his heart, a stark accusation. He hadn't meant to hurt her. They had just been sitting there alone, and he had felt so close to her. He shared her grief, her anger, her confusion.

He had only wanted to touch her. And he had meant what he said. He didn't see those scars anymore.

But she did, and her perception of herself was cruelly filtered through him.

The door finally opened, and Blair leaned out. "Come on in, guys." He could see that she hadn't gotten much sleep last night. Her eyes were puffy and red and so were Morgan's.

"Why do you need their checkbook?" Blair asked as she followed them into the office.

"I need to check the deposits. And I want to look through their other papers."

Morgan came down the stairs and followed them into the house. She led them into the room off the kitchen that their parents had used as an office. "It's just like they left it," Morgan whispered.

Cade saw the checkbook sitting on their desk, and he picked it up and thumbed through. "Where are their bank statements?"

"I don't know," Morgan said. "We have their file cabinet at Blair's house. I didn't see them in there." She opened a small cabinet in a hutch on her father's desk. Several notebooks were lined up there. "Here," she said. "I think they kept them in one of these."

Cade took a notebook and began flipping through the pages.

Blair came up beside him, her puffy eyes pleading. "Cade, please, take the bank statements, but leave the other papers where they are. I need them."

"What for?"

Blair looked at McCormick as if she didn't want to answer in front of him. Cade didn't want to make her. "Come here," he said. He took her arm and escorted her out to the sunporch at the back of the kitchen. The smell of oil paint filled the room, and a half-finished painting sat on an easel in the corner.

Blair looked up at him, and he could see the pain in her eyes. He hated that pain, and wished he could exorcise it from her heart.

"Tell me, Blair," he whispered.

She swallowed and looked out at the shed in the back of their yard, where her father used to putter. "I was looking into what caused my scar," she said. "There's some secret in my parents' past, some way my father was involved with what happened to me. Last night I found some notes he'd written. He said he'd caused my scars, but he didn't say how. And I found out that it was a raging house fire, not some little grease fire like they said, and the police thought it was arson. I have so many questions. I haven't finished going through all their papers yet, but I need to, Cade." Her eyes shone with her plea. "If I find anything that will be of interest to you, I'll give it to you, I promise. You know I'm trying to find who the killer is too."

"I need to go through them first," Cade said quietly. "Don't worry. If I find out anything about your past, I'll let you know. Besides, now that I know you're looking, maybe I can do a little snooping around on my own. I have a few resources you don't have."

She turned back to the glass door into the house. "Not many."

He knew that was true. With her library skills and command of the Internet, Blair was usually able to come up with information as fast as he could.

"Promise you'll tell me if you run across anything?" she asked.

"Promise," he told her.

"And do you swear that you won't mess up the files? I don't want anybody but you going through them, Cade. You get a bunch of hands on them, there's no telling what's going to become of that information, and it might have some link to my parents' past."

"You have my word," he said.

She sighed with resignation. "All right, take them," she said. "I'm trusting you, Cade. And I hope you'll hurry because I need them back as soon as possible."

"If I don't find anything vital in there, I'll give them back to you," he said. "But if I do, I'm going to have to hold it as evidence."

She didn't like it, he could tell, but he could see the trust in her eyes. That made his work a little less difficult as he went back to riffle through her parents' things.

CHAPTER

48

*B*lair was in no mood to take the phone call that came that afternoon from East Coast Properties, Inc., the company who had approached Thelma and Wayne weeks ago about selling Hanover House.

The caller identified himself as James Clark. "I'd like to make an appointment with you and your sister," he said. "I'd like to discuss the possibility of my company purchasing your property."

"It's still not for sale," Blair said, though she knew they should listen to the offer.

"We're prepared to offer you fair market value. There's no harm in discussing it with us. We'll come there, if you'd like."

Blair's eyes were tired from staring at the computer screen for so many hours as she tried to get more information about her parents. She swiveled her chair around and rubbed her eyes roughly.

She supposed he was right. There *was* no harm in listening. They could always say no. But in case money got

tight or Hanover House became too much of a burden for
Morgan to handle alone, it would be good to know what their
options were.

"All right," she said. "We'll meet you at Hanover House at
seven tonight. I'll make sure my sister is there."

James Clark was a tall man in a thousand-dollar suit. His pitch
to buy the house was more persuasive than Blair had expected.

The offer was generous, too generous to ignore. But Morgan
sat quietly through the whole conversation, her lips compressed
with distaste.

When Clark left, Morgan started up the stairs without a
word.

"Where are you going?" Blair asked. "Aren't we even going
to talk about this?"

Morgan turned around at the top of the stairs. "Blair, this is
my home," she said. "It's where we spent most of our childhood.
It was our parents' dream. We have no business selling it."

"Morgan, the city council may not even let us keep it open.
Contributions from our donors are bound to drop as they hear
about the murders. And if it's not making money, the property
taxes will do us in. Besides, who will run it?"

"I can," Morgan said.

"How can you say that?" Blair asked. "It took four people
to run it before. Mama and Pop and you and Jonathan. And who
knows when Jonathan is going to get out? It's just you now. And
I don't want to help, Morgan. I don't want to take this on."

"You don't have to," Morgan said. "It's not going to be your
problem."

She disappeared across the top floor, and Blair followed her
up. Morgan had gone into their parents' room. So Blair rushed
behind her. "It's my problem just knowing it's here," she said, "just
knowing it's something that we own and that we can't manage."

Morgan sat down on the edge of the bed and ran her hand
over the bedspread that her mother had made. "Jonathan and

I will manage it. He'll get out and come home, and we'll manage it."

"Jonathan will want us to sell it," Blair said. "You know he will."

Morgan wiped the tear rolling down her cheek. "Why would you say that?"

"Because he's been wanting the two of you to get a home of your own since you got married. He's done nothing but complain about this place. Just ask him."

"All right, I will," she said. "When I visit him tonight I'll ask him." Her eyes glimmered with tears as she stood up again. "I love this place."

"But let's face it," Blair said. "We're trying to solve their murder. We're trying to deal with the stress of what's happened in our lives. Keeping this place up is going to be a major burden, not to mention the questionable character of some of the tenants who come here. I mean, Sadie alone is going to drain you. And then there's Gus, if he gets out of jail. Mrs. Hern will be a handful before long. And Rick Whatever-His-Name-Is."

"I can do it," Morgan bit out.

"They're offering an awful lot of money," Blair said. "Think about it. We wouldn't have to fight city council anymore. We wouldn't have to deal with these tenants and all the questions flying through town. We could start over and try to put this awful thing behind us. We could invest the money and live off of it. And you and Jonathan could have your own place and start a family."

"We could have a family here."

"All right, just ask him. That's all I ask," Blair said.

"I said I would."

"Just see what he wants to do," Blair said. "But if he agrees with me, we'll sell it, right?"

Morgan looked down at her feet, struggling with the emotions on her face. "I don't know," she said. "All I'm promising to do is ask him."

CHAPTER

"Let's do it, Morgan," Jonathan told her when she visited him later that day. "Come on, we could get our own little place, maybe right on the beach, and not have the burden of always taking care of other people. We can't do what your parents did. I can't."

Tears filled her eyes, and her mouth trembled with the effort of holding them back. She didn't want him to know how disappointed she was in his answer.

"Think about it. Do you want to be a mother to everybody in town at your age, to every transient who comes up on a boat, to every prisoner released with no place to go?"

"Somebody has to do it," Morgan said.

"No, somebody doesn't," Jonathan threw back. "Your parents did it and it was wonderful. They filled a need. But they were *called* to fill that need, Morgan, and we weren't. You can't inherit a ministry and expect to be as passionate and adept at it as the people who left it to you. And whether you like it or not, the bed-and-breakfast is a ministry. It was their ministry. But not ours. There are other things we can do."

"But what about the tenants?"

"Well, Gus is here," Jonathan said. "He'll be in prison for the rest of his life, I hope."

"But there's Rick and Mrs. Hern, and now Sadie."

"Then give them notice," he said. "Give them time to find a place to live, and then we can sell."

"What if they can't find a place?"

Tears rolled down her cheek, and he wiped them, tipping her face up to his. "Of course they can find a place," he said. "There's real estate all over town, people renting places out. We're not the only game in town."

"We're the only ones who take in the refugees," she said.

"The what?" he asked.

"Mama used to say we took in spiritual refugees. That's what they are, you know."

He pressed his forehead against hers. "You have a sweet heart, baby. That's why I love you. I know God's going to use it somehow, but it doesn't have to be at Hanover House."

"Is it just the money?" she asked. "Is that what means so much to you?"

He leaned back. "That was a low blow," he said. "I just want a fresh start with you, Morgan. I'm being accused of your parents' murders. There will be people in this town who'll always think I did it. I'm not sure how it's going to be, living in that house without them—the shadow of their murders hanging over us like that. And I've never been comfortable with you being around what you call the 'refugees.' Call me overprotective, but that's what husbands are for."

She dropped her face in her hands. "I'll think about it," she said, "and I'll pray about it. It's just so hard. Too many changes all at once. And you're still in here. I thought you'd be out by now."

"I'm going to get out soon," he said. "As soon as Cade comes to his senses."

She got up, and he pulled her into a crushing embrace. Alex Johnson, the cop guarding them, turned his back to give them some privacy.

"I miss you," she whispered.

"Me too," he said. "It's going to be all right, okay?"

"I know."

"We're going to find who killed your parents. Beyond a shadow of a doubt, and they're going to be punished, and we're going to get our lives back to normal."

She nodded, trying to believe.

She wept all the way back to Hanover House, then ran inside, hoping to avoid any of the tenants until she got to her room. But Sadie was sitting at the top of the stairs.

"Hi, Morgan," the girl said brightly.

"Hi, Sadie."

Sadie's face changed as she saw the tears. "I was waiting for you, but if you're not in the mood—"

"What is it?"

"Nothing."

"Come on, it's okay."

"Well, you had some apples in the refrigerator. I was just wondering if I could have one."

"Of course you can. You can have anything you want in the kitchen. I told you that."

"But I don't want to take advantage," Sadie said. "I mean, it is a bed-and-breakfast, and this is a snack."

"The guests have full run of the kitchen, all the time." Through the blur of her tears, she regarded the bruise around Sadie's eye. It was healing to a yellow hue, and her arm, in its cast, still hung in a sling. The girl had been no trouble since she had come. She picked up after herself, helped Mrs. Hern, and kept quiet. "You can have all the apples you want."

"Thank you," Sadie said. She stood up and looked awkwardly at Morgan, as if she didn't know what to do next. "I'm still looking for a job, but when I get one, I promise to pay you back for all this."

"Don't worry about it," she said. "Just go eat."

The girl ran down the stairs.

Morgan was emotionally drained by the time she closed herself into her room. She lay on her bed, staring at the ceiling and wondering what she would do if they sold this place. What would it be like to have a home of her own with Jonathan, knowing she could never come here again and walk through these halls and into her parents' room?

The phone on her bedside table rang. She picked it up. "Hello."

"What did he say?" It was Blair's voice, soft and familiar.

Those tears assaulted her again. "He wants to sell," she said. "But I have to pray about this, Blair. I'm just not ready."

"Morgan, Mama and Pop wouldn't want you saddled with this."

"Have you and Jonathan been comparing notes or something? Mama and Pop loved these people. They would be proud if I followed in their footsteps."

"Of course they would," Blair said, "but they'd never ask you to. They wouldn't expect it of you. I don't want to spend the rest of my life taking care of people just because they did, and I don't think you do either. And your husband sure doesn't."

She closed her eyes and wished for sleep. "He thinks he might get out tomorrow, maybe the next day."

"That's great," Blair said, "but I guarantee you, he's not going to want to come back to that house. That money could help with a lot of things, Morgan."

"What would Sadie do?" she asked. "And Mrs. Hern?"

"Sadie'll find someone else to help her, just like she did this time. And so will Mrs. Hern. Maybe a nursing home—"

"I'm *not* putting her in a nursing home! She's a long way from needing that!"

"All right, then. We can help her find a place. I'm not suggesting we throw her out on the street."

Morgan closed her eyes. "What's the hurry?"

"Well, they might withdraw the offer," she said. "I mean, come on. It's a good offer. I say we go ahead and sign on the dotted line while we still can."

Morgan rubbed her forehead. It was beginning to ache. "I can't commit to this," she said. "I have to pray about it. You have to let me do that."

And with that she hung up the phone, no longer interested in what her sister had to say.

CHAPTER

*L*ate that night, Jonathan lay on his cot, staring at the jail's stained ceiling tiles where a leak had come through. He had hoped to get out that day, but Cade still seemed intent on keeping him locked up. Even with Gus in the cell next to him, Cade's resolve hadn't weakened.

The anguished look on Morgan's face when he told her to sell Hanover House had haunted him since she left. He wondered if he was doing the right thing to ask her to sell. Was it selfish, or was he really thinking of her?

The thoughts kept him from sleep, and he wished he had the luxury of a telephone so he could call and check on her. He hadn't meant to give her something new to grieve over. She had already lost her parents, had practically lost her husband, and now he wanted her to lose her house too?

He wished he could see her again tonight and undo the damage he had done.

The silence was getting to him, and he wished he had a radio or a television to watch, something to get his mind off of his thoughts. But there was only Gus, and he had avoided talking to him since they put him in the cell next to him. The man had mostly slept since he had been here, and he hadn't seemed interested in conversation either.

But now, in the quiet of the night, he heard a soft sound.

"Amazing grace, how sweet the sound . . ."

It was Gus, singing quietly in his bed. He looked over at him in the darkness, saw him lying there on his back, staring at the same ceiling tiles. He listened as the man got to the end of the verse, and quiet settled back over the room.

"Do you mind?" he asked out loud, his voice echoing over the room. "I'm trying to sleep in here."

"Sorry," Gus said in that deep Jamaican accent. "I just be trying to pull a Peter. You know, when they sang in the jail and the walls fell down?"

Jonathan let that sink in for a moment.

"I always liked the mon Peter," Gus said. "He be saying the wrong thing, all the time, like me."

And like me, Jonathan thought, though he didn't want to engage with the man.

"And then there was Paul, killed all them Christians. God forgave him that."

Jonathan wondered if he had killed Thelma and Wayne, if his conscience was bothering him now, if he was consoling himself with the memory of forgiveness for a similar crime.

Soon he heard Gus singing again, quietly, in the night. Jonathan fell asleep to the sound of "Amazing Grace."

CHAPTER

Cade sat at the computer in his den that night, a yellow light illuminating the place where he worked. He had done a search on Gus Hampton in an attempt to find out what he could about the ex-convict he held in his jail cell, and now he tried to put the pieces together.

But as hard as he tried to concentrate, he couldn't get his conversation with Blair today out of his mind.

Abandoning his work, he decided to do a search through his databases for Blair's name. One article came up. He scanned its contents, about a house fire and the injuries sustained by the little girl who lived there. This was, no doubt, the article Blair had already found.

He typed in "Wayne Owens" and another article emerged. The article was titled "Man Arrested for Insurance Fraud." Frowning, he clicked it and read as it filled the screen.

Wayne Owens, 28, was arrested today follow-ing an investigation into the fire that consumed

*his house and injured his three-year-old daughter. The
charge was insurance fraud. A spokesman for the district
attorney's office cited evidence that Owens and his wife,
Thelma, allegedly plotted to set fire to their house in order
to collect the insurance money. Owens made no comment
as the police arrested him.*

Cade felt as if a fist had just belted him in the gut, and he sat
staring at the screen. Wayne Owens, arrested for arson? Had he
really caused the fire that did that to Blair?

He looked at the phone and thought of calling her, but he
wasn't sure there was any purpose in sharing this with her. Did
she need to know that her recently murdered father had been
arrested for setting their own house on fire? Was there any purpose in telling her that her own father had caused her injuries?

Yes, there was a purpose, he thought. He had promised Blair
he would tell her whatever he learned. He intended to keep that
promise.

He picked up the phone and dialed her number.

"Hello." She sounded groggy, and he knew he had awakened
her again.

"Blair, it's me, Cade."

"Cade?" she asked.

"Yeah. Sorry I woke you, but I just found something I
thought you'd want to know."

"About my folks?" she asked.

"Yes," he said. "I did a search for your father's name in the
Charleston newspaper, and an article came up about his being
arrested for insurance fraud."

There was a long pause. "I never thought to do a search on
his or Mama's name. I only entered mine. Give me the date of the
article," she said. "I want to see it."

He read it out to her.

"Thank you, Cade," she whispered. "I've got to go."

She hung up, and Cade sat holding the phone, despising himself for bringing her more pain, and wishing he could rush to her

side to help her through this. But he knew she wouldn't accept his help. This was something Blair would insist on dealing with alone.

Blair got to the computer as quickly as she could, and within moments had the Website with that article: "Man Arrested for Insurance Fraud."

Blair read the article, her heart beating against her chest. She sat there, stunned, for a moment, then forced herself into gear and found another article. Then she scanned the next article and the next until she had enough pieces to discern the whole story.

Her father had served time in jail. He had served several months, then their family had moved to Georgia.

Had *they* been refugees coming to Hanover House for shelter and safety from staring eyes and pointing fingers? Had Thelma and Wayne been trying to escape a rap sheet that told too much?

She got up and moved away from the computer, staring at the screen as if it radiated danger. This was too bizarre to fathom. It couldn't be possible. Her parents had never done a deceitful thing in their lives. They had always been in ministry. They had been helping people as far back as she could remember.

Blair took the chair across the room and sat in it with her knees pulled up, her arms hugging them to her chest as she stared at the screen. It couldn't be true. They were all lies.

After a moment she got up and forced herself back to the computer, quickly printed out the articles, then snatched them from her printer. Morgan had to see these, she thought. She had to help her discern what was truth and what was not. Morgan would know.

She ran back across the gravel to her house, the articles gripped in her fist.

Morgan sat upright in bed at the sound of the door opening, and she saw Blair's silhouette in the light of the hall lamp.

"Morgan, I've got to talk to you," Blair said.

Morgan reached for the lamp and squinted up at her. "Blair, I don't want to talk about selling the House anymore. I told you—"

"It's not that," Blair said. She came and sat on the bed and laid the articles out. "I've found out about Pop and Mama."

"What are these?"

"They're articles that fill in the blanks," she said. "Mama and Pop started the fire to collect insurance money."

"No." Morgan's word cut through the night, and she got out of bed and stood staring down at her sister. "If it says that in those articles, then they're lying."

Blair's eyes glowed with intensity, anger, sorrow. "Think," Blair said. "Think back when we were kids. Was there ever a time when Pop was gone for months at a time? A time when he could have been in jail?"

"*Jail?*" Morgan asked. "Blair, you've got to be kidding. Our father?"

"It says here he was arrested for insurance fraud. And then in this article," she flipped through the pages and found the one she needed, "it says that Pop was sentenced to a year. And then later on I found this little clip that tells that he was released early for some reason or another."

"Let me see that," Morgan snatched the articles out of her hand. "This can't be. I would remember."

"How?" Blair asked. "You don't even remember the fire. Morgan, don't you see? They lied to me about the grease fire because they didn't want us to know they had done such a terrible thing and that it resulted in these scars. And they didn't want us to know that Pop had served time, that when we came here *we* were the refugees and that the Hanovers had taken us in."

"It's not possible," Morgan said, "and you know it. It's just not."

"Do you remember Pop ever disappearing for a few months, when you might have been given some explanation about where he was?"

Morgan sat down and racked her brain. "I remember you in the hospital. You were there for months. I remember the surgeries, and Mama cried and paced the floors back and forth, back and forth. I remember you coming home and Mama being so glad . . ."

"So where was Pop?"

Morgan looked up at her, and her voice fell to a whisper. "I remember him coming home from a long trip, my being shy about seeing him again. I remember him picking me up and swinging me around."

"Then he was gone a long time."

"I remember him putting me down and looking up at the upstairs window and seeing you looking out. He burst into tears, then ran up the stairs to see you. He was careful picking you up, but he held his face against yours . . ."

"He'd been in jail, Morgan," Blair said. "He served time. The article says they were both charged, only Mama got off."

Morgan closed her eyes against the truth and ground her teeth together. "Stop this," she said, flinging the articles down. "I want you to stop looking for dirt on our parents. They haven't done anything wrong. They were murdered, and it wasn't because of some fire twenty-two years ago."

"That wasn't just 'some fire,'" Blair blurted. "It was my face."

"Pop would have never done anything to hurt you, and you know that."

"But he did," Blair said.

"Something's wrong here," she said. "This just isn't right. I don't believe any of it."

"Then I'll get more evidence." Blair started out of the room.

"And what'll you do then?" Morgan asked. "Are you going to be glad that our parents are dead?"

Blair turned back from the open door and leveled her dejected gaze on her sister. "I'll never be glad they're dead. I just want to know the truth, Morgan. And that's been real hard to come by."

She closed the door and hurried back to the library.

CHAPTER

52

*M*organ got to Hanover House early. In a fog of depression, she made breakfast for Rick, Mrs. Hern, and Sadie. When the dishes were washed and put away, she sat down at the kitchen table, staring at her coffee.

"Do I look all right?" Sadie asked from the doorway.

Morgan looked up at her. The girl had washed and ironed her clothes—a pair of khakis and a bright pink shirt that Morgan had given her.

"You look fine. Why?"

"I'm going to look for a job," she said. "I'm not coming home until I get one."

Morgan smiled and got up. She pulled herself out of her mood and gave the girl a more critical look. "I think we could do something to cover that black eye, Sadie," she said. "A little makeup would do wonders."

Sadie shrugged. "I didn't bring any."

Morgan turned her toward the stairs. "Let's go to my room and see what we can do."

They went into Morgan's room, full of Jonathan's things, exactly where he had left them. Morgan ushered Sadie to a small makeup table in the bathroom. Around the sink were Jonathan's razor and shaving cream, a bottle of aftershave, some Lava soap.

"I heard about your husband," Sadie said. "I'm really sorry."

Morgan nodded. "I'm hoping he'll get out today. It's absurd, their keeping him in there." She pulled out the drawer in the table and got a small jar of foundation. "I think this might be close to your color." She got a sponge pad and began applying the makeup to the bruised area of Sadie's face. "Let me know if it hurts," Morgan whispered.

"It doesn't hurt," Sadie said. "I really appreciate this."

Morgan smiled. "It's fun. I haven't played makeup in a long time. My sister never wanted to when I was young. She hated mirrors."

Sadie was quiet.

"Sadie, did a boyfriend do this to you?"

Sadie seemed to struggle for an answer. "I was in a wreck."

"Really." It was a statement, not a question. She stopped dabbing and regarded the girl who had so many secrets. "It looks great. You can't even see it."

Sadie looked in the mirror, surprised at the change. "Wow."

"How about a little blush?"

"Okay."

She applied the makeup with a deft hand. "You're a pretty girl, Sadie. I have a feeling you don't know that."

Sadie looked embarrassed. "Thank you."

"When you apply for jobs, tell them to call me if they need a reference. I'll put in a good word for you."

"I will," she said.

When the girl had gone, Morgan decided to pray. It had been difficult the last few times she had tried. Anger and despair over what God had allowed to happen to her parents had paralyzed her. But Sadie needed intercession, so she went to the throne. And she found open arms and peace washing over her like a warm tide.

While she was there, she prayed for the decision about the house, and for Blair too, and her destructive quest to find out things about her parents that neither of them really wanted to know.

CHAPTER

*W*ith the clothes Sadie had borrowed from
Morgan, her hair clean and brushed, and her bruises carefully covered, Sadie had her hopes up that someone would
give her a job. She walked down Ocean Boulevard, going
from establishment to establishment. Commercial businesses crowded both sides of the road, tourist traps with
colorful, useless products to sell.

She stopped at a hotel half a mile down the beach and
inquired if they were hiring. She was politely but firmly
told there were no positions open. She crossed the busy
street to a gift shop where several tourists milled around.
Swallowing back her tension, she approached the counter.

A tall woman, who resembled Popeye's Olive Oyl,
stood beside the cash register, arranging a point-of-purchase
display.

"Excuse me. Are you the manager?"

The woman looked up at her with her big eyes. Her
voice lilted as she said, "Well, yes, I am. The owner, actually, if that makes any difference."

Sadie liked the sound of her voice and the kindness in those big eyes. "I'm looking for a job," she said. "I'm a hard worker. I'm staying at Hanover House, and Morgan Cleary can vouch for me."

"Oh, honey, I'm so sorry about Thelma and Wayne," the woman said. "Terrible, terrible thing." She sighed heavily, then seemed to shake her thoughts back to the question. "I'm afraid I can't afford to hire anyone. I run this place by myself. Where you from?"

Sadie stood straighter and lied. "Hilton Head."

"Hilton Head?" the woman asked, giving her a surprised once-over. "You don't look like anybody from Hilton Head."

She didn't know what that meant, but she didn't appreciate it.

"Are you an ex-prisoner?"

Sadie frowned. "No. I've never been to jail, and I never will."

"So how'd you break your arm?"

"I was in a wreck," she lied again. "I just came here because it seemed like a wonderful place."

"Oh, it is. I didn't mean to offend you. It's just that you don't look like an ex-con either."

She didn't know what ex-cons looked like. She thought of sweet Mrs. Hern. Would anyone have guessed that she had served time? And would her mother come out of prison someday with a tainted, used-up look that told people where she'd been?

"I'm sorry to bother you." She started back to the front door, but the woman stopped her.

"You know, there's an opening over at the paper."

Her eyes widened. "The newspaper?" she asked.

"Yep. Nancy Simmons was telling me yesterday she was looking for someone who could help her put the paper together. Her assistant had a baby and quit. Doesn't pay a lot, just a little over minimum wage, but it's something."

Sadie wanted to kiss her. "It sounds perfect. Can you tell me where the office is?"

After getting directions and being sent on her way, Sadie had more of a bounce to her step. When she arrived at the little house with the *Cape Refuge News* sign out front, she stepped onto the porch and knocked. There was no answer. She tested the doorknob and found the door was open. She stepped inside.

"Hello?" She waited a moment and heard machinery in the back, no doubt cranking out the latest issue. They probably hadn't heard her. She stepped tentatively inside, looking around at the little desk at the front and the cluttered office off the hallway. Then she stepped to the archway at the back of the house and peered inside.

"Hello," she called again. This time she caught the attention of a woman standing behind the machinery.

"I didn't hear you come in," the woman yelled over the noise as she came around the machine. "Can I help you?"

"The lady down the street at the gift shop told me that you were looking for someone," she said. "To hire, I mean. I'm looking for a job."

The woman led her back out of the room and closed the door as she surveyed Sadie's broken arm. "Don't know how much help you'd be with a broken arm."

"It's okay," Sadie said. "I'm right-handed, so it doesn't affect most of what I do. I'm pretty good with just one hand."

"You new in town?"

"Yes, ma'am," she said. "I'm staying at Hanover House."

"Ah," the woman said, nodding her head knowingly.

Sadie wondered if she was thinking the same thing that the woman at the store had. Maybe she shouldn't have told her where she lived.

"Hanover House, huh? So Morgan and Blair are taking care of you?"

"Mostly Morgan," she said. "I haven't seen Blair much."

The woman shook her head. "Horrible thing that happened to their parents. Who'd have ever thought?" She clicked her tongue, as if she wasn't all that sorry. "Do you have any experience in the newspaper business?"

Sadie wished she could tell her that she had worked on the high school paper as she had wanted to, but the day applications were due she had been in the hospital with a broken jawbone.

"No, ma'am, but I learn real fast."

The woman assessed her again with that critical eye of hers. When Sadie expected her to show her the door, she said, "You can start tomorrow."

Sadie caught her breath. "Really? You're giving me a job?"

"You'll have to work hard," the woman said, passing her in the hall and heading to her office. Sadie followed. She searched her desk for something, then turned to the file cabinet and pulled out some papers. "Here's an application. Fill it out and bring it back tomorrow. And here's a Social Security form and a few other things. The job mostly consists of running errands and helping me with the layout. If you can write, sometimes I might even have you write an article or two."

Sadie's eyes lit up. It was too much to believe. "It sounds wonderful."

She started out of the room with the papers in her hands, when the woman caught her by her good arm and turned her back around.

"How old are you, anyway?"

"Eighteen," she lied.

The woman stared at her for a moment. "You don't have anything shady in your past, do you, 'cause my husband's the judge of this town, and it wouldn't do for me to have any shady characters from Hanover House working for me."

Sadie frowned. "No, ma'am. Nothing."

"So you just blew into town one day, and they took you in at Hanover House?"

"It wasn't like that exactly," Sadie said. "I've always thought it would be nice to live at the beach. As soon as I graduated from high school I headed out. They said I could stay at Hanover House until I got on my feet. So I'm trying to get on my feet."

"All right," the woman said brusquely. "Be here at eight tomorrow ready to work. When are you getting the cast off?"

"Another month or so," Sadie said.

"Well, I guess it's all right," the woman said. "We'll just work around it."

Sadie wanted to dance and turn a cartwheel as she headed back to Hanover House, but she didn't want the reputation of a crazy reprobate before she started her new job as a newspaperwoman.

CHAPTER

The next morning, Morgan scrambled eggs for the Hanover House guests with one hand as she filled glasses with orange juice with the other. When the phone rang, she grabbed it up and held it to her shoulder.

"Morgan, it's Cade."

She froze, bracing herself for news about Jonathan. "What is it?"

"I've been going through your parents' bank statements," he said, "and I have their canceled checks. And there's one here for ten thousand dollars, and the notation on the memo says, 'Paid debt RM.' Did they mention this to you?"

She turned from the stove and gave her full attention to the phone. "No. Where would they get ten thousand dollars?"

"It came from their savings account," Cade said. "And RM is Rick Morrison. He told me they'd given it to him to pay off some debts. I'm not sure I'm buying that story."

"I don't know anything about it, Cade. They never said a word to me."

"All right," he said. "Thanks."

"Cade?" Morgan clutched the phone. "When are you releasing Jonathan?"

"I have no plans to do that, Morgan."

"Come on, Cade. You suspect Gus, and you suspect Rick— you know Jonathan didn't do it. Let him go!"

"I still have more evidence on him than anybody else. He owned the murder weapon."

"Well, then why are you holding Gus?" she asked. "You can't have two suspects for the same crime, unless they were working together, and you know that wasn't possible. Jonathan didn't even like Gus."

"I'm holding Gus for possible breaking and entering into Blair's house. Two different crimes."

"But you know that break-in was related to the murders."

"Morgan, I can't talk about this with you right now."

"Cade, I *need* my husband. He has no business being locked up in a jail cell."

"I'm keeping him until I'm satisfied that he's innocent," Cade said, "and I'm not completely satisfied yet."

Morgan slammed down the phone and pressed her forehead against it. She was soul-weary of this whole thing. The mystery of her parents' murders, Jonathan's incarceration, Blair's anger, her parents' past . . . Smoke rose up from the pan and she swung around. She had burned the eggs.

When the doorbell rang, she felt like screaming, "What now?" She moved the pan off the burner, then wearily went to the door. Melba Jefferson stood there holding a steaming casserole.

"I know I'm early, honey," she said, "but I wanted to get this to you so you could feed the guests for breakfast if you wanted."

Morgan's eyes rounded with relief. "A breakfast casserole," she said. "Melba, you're a treasure. Come in. I had just burned breakfast."

The woman bustled into the kitchen behind her. Morgan turned on the stove's fan to suck the smoke out of the room.

"I need coffee," she said. She poured them each a cup and urged Melba to sit down.

"So why are you up so early?" Morgan asked.

Melba shrugged. "I didn't sleep good last night. I was thinking about Thelma and Wayne." Her voice broke and she reached for a handkerchief in her pocket and dabbed at her eyes. "I'm sorry. I don't mean to get you going too. I know you're having worse trouble than I am."

Morgan sank down across from her and reached out to hold her hand. "Melba, you've known my parents a long time, haven't you?"

"Since the day they came to Cape Refuge," she said.

"Tell me about that," she said, her eyes riveted on the woman. "I mean, what were they like then?"

"Well, they were just the sweetest people I've ever known. Precious through and through."

"Really?" Morgan asked. "I mean, were they Christians then?"

"The genuine article," Melba said.

Morgan sat back in her chair, trying to decide whether to be honest with Melba in hopes of getting some information—or just trying to pump more out of her. She finally chose honesty.

"Melba, Blair and I ran across some information that was very disturbing to us. It had to do with my father being in jail. Do you know anything about that?"

Melba didn't look surprised. She dabbed at her eyes again. "Oh, honey, I promised your mother I'd never say a word...."

"Then she confided in you?"

"Well, of course she did," Melba said. "She was my best friend."

"Melba, it would mean a lot to us if you could tell us whatever you know. Our imaginations are running wild. All we know is that Pop was accused of starting the fire that burned Blair— and that he wound up in jail for it."

"Oh, they didn't want you to know that," Melba cried. "What am I going to do now? I can't betray their confidence."

"You don't have to. We already know it. I just want you to clarify a few things."

Melba gave a sigh of resignation. "They changed, you know. Your father changed when he was in prison. There was a Christian group that came there and ministered to them. He accepted the Lord, then led your mother to Christ. They came here to start their lives over clean, where nobody knew them and they could work for the Lord unhindered. The Hanovers, who owned this place at that time, took them in right here in this house. And they started that seaman's ministry down on the dock, and then their prison ministry, and it was such a success. And then the church. Why, your parents hit the ground running as Christians and never looked back."

"Melba, did my father go to prison for insurance fraud?"

Melba looked down at her hands, as if trying to decide whether to tell her the truth. "Yes, but you know he changed. You know that in your heart."

"Did he start the fire that gave my sister her scars?"

Melba's face twisted. "Oh, honey, that plagued him till the day he died. God forgave him, but he never forgave himself for that. It was the defining moment in his life. The thing that brought him to his knees and made him realize that he had to change."

Morgan wilted. Blair was right. The newspaper articles were real. She looked around, trying to find something to do with her hands, something to keep her busy and get her mind off of this horror. Her parents putting her family in harm's way, almost killing Blair, altering her life.

She didn't want to break down in front of Melba, so she breathed in a cleansing breath. "Jonathan and Blair want to sell Hanover House."

The woman expelled a heavy sigh, then dabbed at her eyes again. "I kind of thought you would. It's a lot to handle, even for someone as young and energetic as you."

"I don't feel young or energetic right now," Morgan said. "I feel empty and numb, like I've been beaten up and shot with morphine or something. I don't want to be in this position. And I don't want to sell."

Melba looked around at the big, homey kitchen. "This was your folks' dream. They loved it so. It was a miracle when the Hanovers left it to them."

The woman got up and stuffed her handkerchief back into her pocket. "Well, I'd better be getting on now. I've got things I have to do." Morgan could hear the emotion still quaking in her voice. "You take care now, you hear? And let me know if there's anything I can do to help you."

Then pulling that handkerchief back out of her pocket, she headed out to her car.

CHAPTER

55

*C*ade needed a break. He wasn't sleeping well, and the workload that greeted him each morning kept him keyed up and worn out. Today, he got up with the sun, put his kayak into the river, and paddled out through the Wassaw Sound. He reached the Atlantic as the sun rose and warmed his bare shoulders.

The act of stroking, front to back, front to back, riding up over the waves, worked some of the tension out of his muscles. He drifted farther out, where the only sounds were rushing waves and birds swooping down for their morning meal. He paddled until the waves calmed, until he was floating alone on the current.

Questions swirled through his mind as he drifted. Did he really need to keep Jonathan locked up? What did Gus know about the money the Owens had given Rick? Why had Thelma and Wayne withheld the truth from Blair?

Why had Blair been so offended when he had touched her scars and told her she was the prettiest girl on the island?

You really know how to kick a girl when she's down.

He wished he could set her free from the prison of her life—
the slavery to her philosophies, her beliefs about herself, her lack
of belief about the God he believed in. Blair was the toughest
woman he knew, but he wasn't fooled by that toughness. It was a
cover. Like those scars were a cover for the beauty behind them,
her toughness hid the soft heart inside. The heart that hurt. The
heart that feared.

He knew these thoughts weren't helping him, so he turned
the kayak around and paddled back the way he had come. He
moved more easily this time, as the current took him in. When he
got back to the river, it was only seven, so he put the boat up,
showered, and got to the station by eight.

He got Gus out of his cell and took him into the interview
room. "I want to ask you something, Gus," he said. "You knew
about the money that Thelma and Wayne gave Rick. How did you
know?"

"I overheard. The walls are thin at Hanover House. My
room be next to his."

"Did they give him the money voluntarily, or was there some
manipulation involved?"

"It was their idea," he said.

"Why would they do that?"

The big black man looked down at his feet and rubbed his
eyes roughly. When he looked up at him again, Cade saw that
his eyes were red with tears. "They told him that Christ paid for
his sins, and the least *they* could do was pay for his debts." He
swallowed back the emotion in his throat. "That be when I
really came to Christ."

"I thought you were a Christian before they brought you here."

"Me too, mon. But I knew it up here." He tapped his temple. "That day they gave Rick the money, I got it down here." He
put his hand over his heart.

Cade didn't say anything. He didn't want to believe Gus had
been transformed by the same Holy Spirit that had changed his
own life.

"So you heard all this firsthand?"

"Yeah, mon," he said. "They never knew. Too bad it didn't change Rick."

"What makes you say that?"

"He set me up, mon. Took my do-rag while I showered, then left it for you to find. He be your mon, not me."

When Cade had locked him back in his cell, he saw Jonathan sitting beneath the one lightbulb in the room, studying his Bible as if seeing it for the first time. Cade stood at the cell door, watching for a moment. Jonathan never looked up to see him. Finally, Cade went back out to his desk. He dropped his face into his hands and rubbed hard, wishing he knew what to do.

There Jonathan was, studying his Bible while sitting in a jail cell for murder—and another possible suspect sitting in the next cell, talking about how Christ had changed his life. He went to church with both men, believed the same things they seemed to believe.

But he had a job to do. So shaking those personal feelings out of his head, he went back to his office.

CHAPTER

56

*S*adie started her job at the *Cape Refuge News* that day. Morgan loaned her a blazer to wear with her khakis, so she felt mature and professional. Judge Randy Simmons, her boss's husband, was at the paper when she arrived that morning. He was a good-looking man who had a long gray ponytail, and wore jeans and tennis shoes even though he was on his way to the office. Sadie tried to picture him making serious decisions about people's lives. The judge who had sentenced her mother was a stern-looking older man with a bald head and an angry scowl on his face. Nothing like this old hippie who reminded Nancy to order the new T-shirts for the soccer team he coached.

Nancy Simmons, Sadie's boss, was a driven, ambitious woman who took her job seriously. She and the two writer/photographers who worked for her ran from telephone to file cabinet, from the grand opening of the new souvenir shop to the police station—with stops at the office in between. Nancy kept Sadie hopping with a list of things to do, but Sadie met the challenges head-on. She loved the pace of the office, the deadlines they were trying to meet before going to press, the drama of fielding new stories, and deciding what to tell their readers.

The first copies of tomorrow's edition were coming off the press as Sadie prepared to leave. Nancy tossed her a copy. "A memento of your first day's work," she said. "Congratulations."

Sadie clutched the newspaper against her chest as she walked back to Hanover House. As she passed the establishments that had refused to give her jobs, she held her head higher. She was gainfully employed now. She could support herself. And her fear that Jack would hunt her down and drag her back was diminishing. Things were working in her favor now, and she felt she could do anything.

Maybe someday she could even go back and get Caleb.

Hope burgeoned inside her, and she pictured herself playing on the beach with him as he started to walk, teaching him to float in the water, signing him up for a "Water Babies" class at the Y. Now that her feet were on surer ground, she dared to dream of security for the baby too.

She reached Hanover House and trotted up the stairs to the porch, slipped in through the screen door, and found Blair, Morgan, and Mrs. Hern in the kitchen.

"Hi," she said brightly.

Morgan looked up at her and smiled, like she was genuinely glad to see her. "Sadie, how was your first day at work?"

"Fantastic," Sadie said. "I did everything. I proofed articles, filed, and even took information for articles over the phone. It was fun. And look at this." She tossed the newspaper down on the kitchen table. "My first issue."

"Tomorrow's paper?" Blair asked.

Morgan smiled as she looked down at the headline, but her smile quickly crashed. The glass she was holding slipped out of her hand and shattered on the floor. "Blair, look!"

Blair grabbed the paper. "Convicted Killer Living at Hanover House."

TERRI BLACKSTOCK

"It's Rick," Morgan said, starting to cry. "Look at that picture."

"A mug shot," Blair said. She brought her eyes up to her sister. "I thought there were no arrests. I looked under both names. There was nothing."

Sadie's hands were shaking as she pulled out a chair and sat down. She shouldn't have brought the paper home, she thought. She couldn't believe she had been so stupid, so insensitive. But she hadn't even noticed the headline. She had just been so excited about the feel of the paper in her hands and the knowledge that she'd had a small part in it.

"Read the article," Morgan said. "What does it say?"

"'Rick Morrison is not who he says he is,'" Blair read. "'In fact, sources tell us that is not even his real name. The supposedly grieving man living at Hanover House, the place where ex-cons and criminals like to live, is really Rick Dugan.'"

"Ex-cons and criminals?" Morgan asked. "Give me a break!"

"'But according to police, Rick Dugan is not a suspect in the murders of Thelma and Wayne Owens. Two other residents of that home are, and they are currently in police custody. But should Rick Dugan be free to roam around Cape Refuge at will?

"'*Cape Refuge News* has recently uncovered information that Rick Dugan is already a convicted killer, who has been serving time at Angola for the murder of Rick Morrison. He escaped while on a work detail last year, and has never been apprehended.'"

"This can't be right," Blair said. "Cade would have told me."

"Mama and Pop would have known," Morgan said. "They would have checked out his story. They knew about the name change."

"Where did Nancy get this information?" Blair turned to Sadie. "Sadie, do you know who her sources were?"

"No, ma'am," Sadie said. "I didn't even know she was working on this story. We were working on things about the Tybee Beach Bums Parade and a groundbreaking for a new hotel and a grand opening for a new souvenir shop near the pier."

Blair slapped the paper down and stood up. "Well, there's only one thing to do. I'm going to ask him how much of this is true. And I'm going to ask him about the money Mama and Pop gave him. Something's not adding up here, Morgan."

She headed up the stairs, and Morgan followed.

"I shouldn't have brought that home," Sadie told Mrs. Hern. "It was stupid. I should have looked at it first."

"It's all right, dear," Mrs. Hern said, peering up the stairs. "Let's just stay down here and let them handle it."

Sadie was glad to do that, for she didn't want to be in the middle of a confrontation with a killer.

Blair got to the top of the stairs and felt for the gun in her pocket. She stormed across the floor to Rick's room and banged on it.

"Rick? Rick, it's Blair. I need to talk to you." Her voice left no room for debate.

But there was no answer.

"Rick, open the door!" she said. When there was still no answer, she turned the knob and saw that it was unlocked. She pulled the gun out of her pocket and slowly pushed the door open.

The room was spotless, and the bed was made up. His family picture still sat on the bed table, next to his clock and a notepad.

He had scrawled a note there.

"What does it say?" Morgan asked.

"It says, 'Dear Morgan, I know I'm not supposed to leave town with the investigation going on, but I just found out my mother's in the hospital, and I have to go see her. I'll be back when I can. Rick.'"

The scar on her face burned as she turned back to Morgan. "He's gone," she said.

Morgan tried to think. "Maybe he knew the article was coming out. It shouldn't be that hard to verify that his mother is in the hospital."

"I don't think she is," Blair said. "I think he dreaded being exposed and skipped town."

"You don't think he's the killer, do you?" Morgan asked. "All this time, living in this house? Acting all grief-stricken about his wife and child?"

"It sure does look suspicious," Blair said. "He got ten thousand dollars out of Mama and Pop. Maybe they found out about his background, so he killed them."

"Why would he leave us a note if he was running from the law?"

"To throw us off. To give him a head start."

Morgan brought a trembling hand to her forehead, and her eyes darted back and forth across the room as she tried to sort through the evidence. "That does it," she said. "I'm going to the police station. I'm going to tell them that Rick left and make them let my husband go."

CHAPTER

57

*M*organ and Blair flew to the police station, and Morgan shivered with determination and anxiety as she marched into Cade's office and dropped the newspaper down in front of him.

"I thought you were looking into this," she said. "I thought you said you hadn't found an arrest record on Rick."

Cade picked up the newspaper and frowned as he skimmed the article. "I hadn't," he said. "They didn't get this information from me."

"Well, it's too late to do anything about it because Rick—whatever his name is—has already left town."

Cade stood up. "How do you know that?"

"Because he left us a note that he was going to visit his mother in the hospital. He's gone."

Cade pushed past them into the squad room. "Livvie," he said to the dispatcher. "Put out an all points bulletin for Rick Dugan, alias Rick Morrison. Six feet tall, blond hair, 175 pounds. Driving a white Honda Civic, '95 or '96 model."

"You have to let Jonathan out," Morgan said. "It's madness to keep him in here when you know he's not the killer. Rick has money that my parents gave him for no explicable reason. He had access to the speargun. Mama and Pop may have discovered he was a fugitive and threatened to turn him in. You have all the evidence you need. Now this is coming out, and he's disappeared. Instead of sitting here twiddling your thumbs—"

"I'm not twiddling my thumbs," Cade said over her ranting.

"—you should be out looking for him, tracking him down, and bringing him in, putting him in the cell where my husband is right now." She slammed her hand down on the table. "Let Jonathan out, Cade!"

"No, Morgan," he yelled back. "The district attorney is working on it now and the judge doesn't want to release him."

She wanted to scream, break a chair over Cade's head, make him listen to her. She had never felt such rabid rage before. "Well, I want to see him. Now!" she cried. "Let me see my husband!"

Blair touched her arm to calm her, but she jerked away.

Cade nodded to J.J. Clyde, sitting behind a desk. J.J. got up and escorted her to the back. She knew she was in no shape to feign strength for Jonathan today. He would have to take her as she was—shaken, frightened, and as angry as she had ever been in her life.

Cade was visibly shaken as he turned back to Blair.

"I know how it looks, like I've got some grudge against Jonathan and I'm trying to get even. But it's nothing like that. If I had it my way, I'd let him out. But I don't."

"Get real, Cade," Blair said. "If you told Randy Simmons that his own wife's article pointed to the killer, you know he would let Jonathan out."

"Maybe he will," Cade said. "But unless he does, I have to keep him here."

His face softened as he looked down at her. "Sit down, Blair," he said. "You look pale."

Slowly, she did. Her mind raced with the new facts whirling around looking for a place to fit. She remembered the night she had sat outside with Rick, and he had explained his past to her. She had foolishly believed every word. She had even defended him to Morgan and Cade.

"They'll catch him," he said. "They'll bring him back."

She swallowed and set her chin on her palm. "I got to tell you. He was good. He sure had me going," she said. "I thought he was a decent man. I liked him. I should have known it was an act."

Cade stared at her for a long moment, the concern in his eyes making her want to run away.

Finally, he slid his hands into his pockets and jingled his keys. "We're going to catch Rick Dugan and bring him in. You have to know, though, that I didn't discover the same information about him that was in the paper. I'll have to find out what their sources were and why it didn't come up on my search. Mine didn't show any past convictions, nothing out of the ordinary, except for his changed name. He explained that. I did find evidence of his wife and daughter being killed. Everything I found went right along with his story. He even told me about the money."

"Yeah, well, he explained a lot of things to me too," Blair said. "Apparently none of them were true."

She couldn't sit there and do nothing, she thought. She had to get home and do her own computer search, see what had failed in her attempts to learn about him. She wanted to see his police record for herself. She got up. "Tell Morgan that I've decided to walk home."

Not waiting for Cade's response, she took off across the parking lot and across the busy street to the beach.

CHAPTER

58

*C*ade double-checked his databases that night and the next morning, trying to find the information Nancy Simmons had cited in her article, but he could verify none of it. Angola had no one by the name of Rick Dugan who had escaped. He couldn't even find evidence that Rick Morrison had been murdered. His sources said that the man had died of a heart attack, just as Rick alleged.

The paper's sources were wrong.

He was about to pay Nancy Simmons a visit, when he got a phone call. The city council had scheduled an emergency meeting for that night. They wanted to discuss Hanover House in light of the news that day.

"Here we go," he whispered under his breath. They were going to use this article to put a scare into the people of Cape Refuge so they would want to close Hanover House. He hoped Morgan and Blair were strong enough to withstand it.

He headed over to the newspaper and found Sadie sitting at the front desk. She looked well groomed and energetic, like any other teenager on the island. Morgan had done wonders with her.

"Chief Cade," she said, coming to attention. "Is something wrong?"

He smiled at her and tipped his hat. "No, Sadie. Everything's fine. I just came to ask Nancy something."

She seemed relieved and wilted back into her chair. "Oh, good. I thought I was in trouble again."

He smiled and glanced around the desk that she had made her own. She had brought some fresh flowers from Morgan's garden and put them in a Coke bottle; a framed picture sat on the corner of the desk. It was a snapshot of a baby.

"Nancy's in the back," she said, "in the printing room. Want me to show you?"

"I know where it is." As he headed to the back, the sound of the printers grew louder. From the hallway, he saw Nancy standing in the hot room.

"Nancy," he said, "I need to talk to you."

She looked up. A thin film of perspiration covered her face. "Now, Cade? I'm kind of busy."

"It's police business," he said.

She sighed as if she wasn't impressed and stepped out of the room. "Okay," she said, leading him into her cluttered office. "What is it?"

He cleaned a few papers off of a chair and sat down. "That article in the paper this morning. I want to know where you got that information."

"What? About the beauty pageant?" she asked.

He didn't find that amusing. "You know very well what I'm talking about."

"Oh. Rick Morrison," she said with a grin. "Yes, the killer. Must be frustrating when the local paper solves the murder before you do."

"Where did you get the information about him being a convict?"

"I have my sources," she said. "I can't reveal them."

"Well, does it matter to you if they're false? I checked with the prison you mentioned and they've never had a Rick Dugan there. I ran that picture through my database and it didn't come up. I've even run his fingerprints through my database, and from the looks of things, he's never even been arrested."

She didn't seem too concerned. "Well, I can double-check it."

"That's it?" he asked. "You're not upset that you slandered a citizen who's done nothing wrong? That you cast fear into the hearts of the islanders, and that the city council has new ammunition to close Hanover House down? They've called a meeting tonight to discuss it."

"Really?" She grabbed the pencil from behind her ear and starting to take a note. "What time is that meeting? Where?"

"It's at the City Hall where it always is," he said, "at seven. Surely your 'sources' could tell you that."

"Look, I'm busy," she said, getting to her feet. "If you don't have anything else to say—"

He stood, appalled at her attitude. "You're not the least bit worried that the front page article in your paper today might be a bunch of lies?"

"I'm upset about it, okay?" she said. "I'm going to check with my sources. I'm going to find out what's going on."

"You need to ask your husband about slander and libel," he said.

She rolled her eyes.

"Show some judgment in your reporting, Nancy, or I'll make sure that every resident of Cape Refuge knows that they can't trust the *Cape Refuge News* anymore. You'll be out of business in two weeks. And when I find Rick Dugan, I'm going to encourage him to sue you for so much that you won't be able to keep it running anyway."

She gaped up at him. "What do you want from me, Cade?"

"A retraction would be nice. Something that tells the towns-people that you lied about this story, that you created a panic unnecessarily."

"Okay," she said. "I'll print it right underneath the article about how Rick Dugan extorted money from Thelma and Wayne before their deaths, how he skipped town the day my article came out, how he's still at large, how our pitiful police force wasn't able to catch up with him yet—"

"You're walking on thin ice, Nancy."

"Fine," she said. "Arrest me. See how long my husband leaves me locked up."

Cade's jaw popped. "If I could lock you up even for an hour, Nancy, it'd be worth it."

As he stormed out into the hall, he heard Sadie talking on the telephone. He stopped and tried to calm himself, taking a deep breath. Sadie's voice was low, as if she didn't want anyone to hear. "Atlanta, please. Miss Tina's Day Care?"

He looked up at her from his place in the hall. There was a pause as she got the number and dialed. "Uh, yes. I just want to check on Caleb Caruso," she said. "He's in Miss Jane's room. Nine months. Could you check on him for me? Tell her it's Sadie calling." Her voice broke, and he saw the tears on her face.

"I just want to know that he's all right," she said into the phone, "that he's not sick or anything, that maybe he doesn't have any bruises or cuts. Yes. So—has he been there every day?"

He saw her listening, her eyes intense as she took in every word.

"You're sure? I appreciate that. No, that's all right. Thank you." She hung up the phone and dropped her face into her hands.

Cade stepped out of the hall. "You okay?" he asked.

She wiped her face quickly. "Sure. I was just working on a story for Nancy."

"A story," he said. "It didn't sound like a story."

"I know," she said. "It's kind of silly. I get all emotional over nothing."

"She has you writing stories?" he asked. "How long have you been here, a couple of days?"

She straightened and lifted her chin. "I'm a good writer. I made straight A's in English."

"Journalism major?" he asked.

She shook her head. "No. But Nancy didn't ask for that."

"Yeah, she doesn't have real high standards, does she? You didn't by any chance write the article on Rick Dugan, did you?"

"No, of course not."

He knew she hadn't, but he was still angry. He nodded to Nancy's office. "Keep an eye on her, Sadie. She's ruthless."

Sadie looked at him as if she didn't know what he was talking about.

Sighing, he went back to his car and told himself that he needed to do some digging into the girl's past. She was calling about a baby named Caleb Caruso. Maybe he was her own child. Maybe her name was really Caruso too.

As soon as he had a moment to breathe, he would see what he could find out.

CHAPTER

59

*J*onathan sat up late in his cell, studying his Bible with a zeal he hadn't had many times in his life. He had convinced Cade not to turn off the light yet, and Gus hadn't made any protest. He read with a new hungriness, searching for something, though he didn't know what. Finally, he heard Gus moving around in the cell next to him.

"Hey, mon," Gus said through the bars.

Jonathan looked up at him. "What?"

"We both be Christians, mon, am I right?"

"I know I am," Jonathan said.

"Well, I guess you don't be trusting that I am. I was thinking maybe we could pray together. "

Jonathan turned back to his Bible and stared down at the page. Had someone he considered an enemy really asked him to pray with him? The thought sent a cold chill through him. Then, suddenly, he was ashamed of himself. He set the Bible down and put his hands on his knees, staring at the concrete floor. Finally he turned around.

"You want to pray with me?"

"The Bible, it says whenever two or more—"

"Yeah, I know what the Bible says," Jonathan threw back.

"I heard Cade tell you about that city council meeting tonight," he said. "We need to pray on that."

Jonathan only looked at him for a moment. The gulf between them seemed as big as the lake out on his granddaddy's farm. He didn't want to do it, but he was supposed to be the big Christian. And Gus, well, what was he? Jonathan wondered. Another ex-con? A threat to his wife? A beloved man Thelma and Wayne had taken under their wings? Had he been the one to try to break into Blair's house when Morgan was there, or had he really been set up as he claimed?

"What is the harm?" Gus asked. "We both be behind the bars."

Jonathan realized that was true. "All right," he said, "I'll pray with you."

Gus nodded and sat down on the one chair in his cell, folded his hands, and dropped his elbows onto his knees. Jonathan did the same, and they both bowed their heads and closed their eyes. After a few seconds of silence, Jonathan looked up.

"You go first," he said. He wanted to hear Gus pray, wanted to hear if it sounded like Gus was used to talking to God, wanted to hear if his words sounded sincere.

Gus's gruff voice grew soft, and he began to speak in a tone that was reverent and awestruck. "My gracious Father, the God of the universe," he said, then paused for a moment as if catching his breath at the awe inspired by such a statement. "I be amazed at you," he went on.

Jonathan opened his eyes, looked over at Gus, and saw the tears on his face and the struggle he was having to keep his voice steady. A sure knowledge came over him that this man in the cell next to him was no threat at all. His heart was sincere. He was, indeed, a brother.

Jonathan closed his eyes and bowed his head in earnest this time, joining his heart with Gus's in prayer.

CHAPTER

60

*T*he standing-room-only crowd at City Hall that night made Blair feel like a movie star whom people had come to gawk at. It was a minidrama, she thought. The daughters of the murder victims having their property snatched out from under them. Adrenaline rushed through her as she prepared for the fight.

"I don't care if we're going to sell the place," she whispered to Morgan. "I'm not going to honor them with that announcement tonight. It's the principle of the thing. They have no right to do this."

Morgan touched her hand. "I wish I knew what Mama and Pop knew that day. They were so confident that they were going to win. They had some information, they said. I wish they'd told me what it was."

"Well, if it was important, we'd have found it by now."

Morgan looked around uncomfortably. "Blair, why don't you let me do the talking?"

"Oh, no," she said. "It's me they're going to contend with. They're counting on our not having the strength to fight. I resent their tactics, and I won't let them get away with it."

The mayor hammered his gavel and drew the microphone too close to his mouth. It produced instant feedback, and people moaned and yelled for someone to fix it. It was like the opening bell in a boxing match, only she didn't intend to shake hands.

"This meeting will come to order," the mayor said. He had dressed up for the occasion in a Hawaiian tourist shirt and a pair of khakis with sandals on his feet. At least Sarah Williford hadn't worn her bathing suit to the meeting, Blair thought.

"As everyone knows," the mayor began, "we're here to discuss Hanover House and the fact that polls show that seventy percent of the citizens on Cape Refuge want to see it closed down."

"Give me a break!" Blair sprang up and pushed through the crowd to the microphone. "Don't give us that stuff about polls," she said. "You know good and well this island doesn't have a pollster. What did you do, go out on the beach and ask random people? Did any of them happen to *live* here?"

She didn't get the cheers that she got the last time she had done this, the night her parents were murdered. The townspeople were scared now and weren't on her side anymore.

"Blair and Morgan, first of all, let me offer my greatest sympathies in the death of your parents," Fred Hutchins said. "The whole island has felt the loss. It's with great sorrow that we called this meeting tonight."

She didn't have the patience for condolences. "Yeah, I'm sure you cried your eyes out as you were putting on your Hawaiian shirt and rehearsing how you were going to twist the knife. Could we just get on with this?"

The council members looked at each other uncomfortably, then went on. "Very well," Fred Hutchins said. "As you know, we're a little upset about the article on the front page of the paper today. It's about one of your tenants being a convicted killer and a fugitive from the law. Your family has been harboring him. He is a danger to the community."

"Cade told me this afternoon that he can't confirm that anything in that article was true."

"I understand Rick Dugan has left town. Is that true?" the mayor asked.

"He left," Blair told him. "But that certainly doesn't implicate Hanover House in any way. It's not a reason to close it down."

"Blair, we all understand your pain," Sarah said, her saccharine voice carrying without the mike. "We understand about the grief that you and your sister must be going through. Having Jonathan on his way to prison for murder, and then Gus and now Rick—"

"My husband is not going to prison," Morgan said from her seat. "He is not guilty!" She stood up. "Do you hear yourselves? You just named three people you think committed these murders. What do you think it was, some kind of killing club?"

"Might have been," the mayor said. "As a matter of fact, there's been quite a bit of speculation that's just what Hanover House is."

"Why are you out to get us?" Morgan demanded. "What do you want?"

"I'm not out to get you," he said. "We just want to make Cape Refuge a safe island for everybody."

Blair wasn't going to let that go. "Well, you don't care about making it safe from tourists. You want more of them to come through, not fewer. And you don't know anything about them. They could be from anywhere. It's your *plan* to have strangers roaming this island. And you can thank the *20/20* piece on Hanover House for tourism picking up thirty percent already this summer. At least the tenants at Hanover House work in the community and contribute to it. People get to know them. They're not just phantom convicts roaming around mysteriously."

"They might as well be," the mayor said. "Rumor has it that you're now harboring a teenage runaway."

"She's not a runaway," Morgan shouted. "She says she's eighteen. She can live anywhere she wants to. She came here with a broken arm and a bashed face, and I wasn't going to turn her away."

"Maybe if you did start turning people away you wouldn't be here before us tonight," he said. "We wouldn't have to close you down. But since you refuse to be discriminating about who you keep in that place—"

"That place is my home," Morgan shouted as tears twisted her face. "It's where I live. It's where my parents lived. How dare all of you treat their memory like it was nothing?" She stumbled across the people in her way, and grabbed the microphone in front of her sister. "My parents did something for every one of you, and you know it. They took in people with problems, even some of you. You have no right to stomp dirt into their memory like this. They were coming here to fight for Hanover House the night of their deaths, but they never made it here. And if they had made it, you would have seen a fight like you'd never seen before. Hanover House was their dream and they loved it, and it was the best thing they'd ever done. We have the right to do whatever we want with our own property, and you don't have the right to choose that for us."

Silence fell over the room as Morgan's impassioned speech hung in the air. Under her breath, Blair whispered, "Way to go, Sis."

"Well, we appreciate your plea," Fred said. "Now, we have a few residents who would like to speak."

Blair shot a look around, daring anyone to get up and speak against them. No one did.

"I think you're mistaken, Mayor," she said. "Looks like these fine folks are here to support us."

"I have something to say." Sam Sullivan got up at the middle of the room, and slid his hands into his pockets. "Mayor, Council Members. . . ."

"Would you mind going to the microphone, please?" Fred asked.

Blair relinquished it to him but didn't sit down. If he was going to trash Hanover House, then he was going to do it standing right beside her.

"Uh . . . Mayor, Council Members . . . I just want to say that ever since Wayne and Thelma's death, I've been afraid to leave my family alone. I don't want my children playing outside. I want to go back to the life we knew before this tragedy. And I think we can do that if Hanover House no longer harbors criminals."

"Hanover House never harbored criminals," Blair said. "And as for wanting to go back to the way things were before the tragedy, you don't know the half of it, Sam. But the fact is that closing Hanover House won't solve anything. We're still going to need a police force because there are still going to be people who come and go with evil intentions. But Hanover House is one of the good things about this island." It had gotten hard to talk around the lump in her throat, so she forced it down and forged on. "Most of you know I'm not a religious person. But I've got to tell you, I do believe in good and evil. Hanover House is a light in this town. It's a beacon and a symbol of all that Cape Refuge should be. A symbol of all it can be. If you shut Hanover House down, then what hope do any of us have?"

She met Morgan's eyes and saw the tears on her face. She fought valiantly to keep her own emotions at bay. "We're a community of kind, warm, caring people. That's what our name represents. Sadie, the teenager who is staying at Hanover House, told us she chose Cape Refuge because the name sounded inviting. It sounded like a pleasant, beautiful place. And she found that it was. Hanover House drew her here because some stranger in a café in Savannah told her that she wouldn't be turned away. Don't you want to live in a place that opens its arms to people like Sadie, instead of a place that shuts them out?"

Hattie Brumfield, who sat near her, got up and waddled to the microphone. "I just have to say that Blair makes a good point, but I feel that we can be a sweet, warm, inviting town without Hanover House. In fact, we might be more inviting if we didn't have the reputation that Hanover House brings us."

Blair rolled her eyes. "What reputation? You've never had a problem with Hanover House until the 20/20 special came out. It's always been known as a good place, not a breeding ground for killers."

"Then explain what's happened with that Rick fellow," Hattie said in her deep drawl. "There he is, a fugitive convict

TERRI BLACKSTOCK

who's already killed once, and now he's disappeared. He could be anywhere, and all because your parents, rest their souls, invited him here."

"I told you, the article is probably a lie. We haven't been able to confirm it."

"Well, Nancy couldn't print it if it wasn't true," she said. "Could you, Nancy?"

Nancy, who sat taking notes on the front row of chairs, said, "We're in the process of confirming the story, but I can tell you that I do trust my source."

"Your imagination is your source, and you know it!" Blair bit out. "Since when has anyone put any stock into what she writes? She makes a hobby of misquoting everybody on this council, and you're telling me that she prints truth? *She's* the one who ought to be shut down!"

Fred banged his gavel. "That's enough, Blair. I think we've heard enough. It's time we took a vote."

She didn't sit down, just crossed her arms and watched as the council members settled in to cast their votes.

Fred got his pen and pad, as if he wouldn't be able to add the five votes up in his head. "To give thirty days' notice to close down Hanover House, vote yes. To keep it open, vote no. Sarah Williford, what is your vote?"

"Yes," Sarah said.

He made the notation. "George O'Neill?"

"Yes."

"You're kidding me!" Blair shouted. "George?"

George looked down at his hands.

"Harold Delaney?" the mayor said.

The man leaned forward to the microphone. "I have to vote yes." He shrugged. "Sorry, Blair."

"Cowards," Blair said. "That's what you all are."

"Ron Helms?"

Helms raised his hand. "Count me as a yes."

"And finally, Ken Adams?"

"Yes, I believe so."

"I can't believe you people! You're not worthy to serve this island! I'll spend every cent I have campaigning against each one of you!"

"Please, Blair," the mayor said. "Don't make me call the police to escort you out."

"Why don't you do that?" Blair asked. "Call Cade to escort me out. He'll probably love reliving the whole thing. I'll just wait right here."

She had called his bluff, and the mayor just sighed. "As you know," he said, "I only vote in the event of a tie if one of the council members is absent—but since we have a unanimous vote to shut down Hanover House, my vote will not be needed."

"We'll get a lawyer," Blair said in a flat voice. "We'll get a *team* of lawyers. We're going to fight this with every resource we have."

"You'll wind up paying more than Hanover House is even worth," the mayor said.

"It would be worth every penny," Blair told him and tore out of the room with Morgan behind her.

The wind was whipping hard from the east as she stepped outside, and she swung around to her sister. "We'll sell that bed-and-breakfast over my dead body. Those people are not going to decide what we do with our own property. And they *won't* tell us who we can have in our home."

Morgan was silent as Blair got behind the wheel and drove them back to Hanover House.

CHAPTER

61

Cade and McCormick spent half the night
going over the evidence they had on both of their prison-
ers and trying to figure out where Rick fit in. They had
located the nursing home where Rick's mother lived and
learned that she was indeed in the hospital with a case of
pneumonia. They called the Sheriff's Department in
Atlanta and asked them to post a man near her room, to
catch Rick if he happened to show up there.

It was too much of a coincidence that he had left
town to visit her on the very day the article had come out.
And why hadn't he been found yet? Every police force in
Georgia was looking for him.

Cade slept for three hours, then got up and showered. Feeling weary to the bone, he called the DA and went
over the evidence with him.

"I'm holding them for two different crimes," he said.
"Gus for breaking and entering, and Jonathan for murder. But I haven't been able to build a very strong case
against either one of them. In fact, if you took what I've
got to a jury, they'd both be acquitted."

The DA agreed. "The speargun was big, but a good defense attorney could refute that with the evidence of the shed being broken into. And it looks like his alibi holds. What's your gut feeling about Gus?"

"I don't know," Cade said. "I was absolutely sure that he was the one who'd broken into Blair's. So far, the bandana is the only evidence we've got, but I'd like to keep him in custody. I don't want to take any chances. But I feel sure that we're barking up the wrong tree with Jonathan."

The DA thought for a moment, then let out a heavy sigh. "The more I look into it, the less of a case I have. I'll go along with Jonathan Cleary's release."

Cade headed to the judge's office, a brand-new sprawling building overlooking the water on the north side of the island. The office buzzed with activity. Judge Randy Simmons had many enterprises other than law. Cade tried to catch the secretary's attention as she flitted from room to room, delivering memos and picking up mail.

"Whatcha need, Cade?" she asked as she hurried past him.

"I need to see the judge."

"I'll tell him you're here." But she headed to the back of the offices, instead of to the judge's office.

Irritated, Cade went to the judge's door and knocked, then pushed it open. Randy had his feet propped up on his desk, holding the phone with his shoulder. He wore Reeboks, faded jeans, and an Atlanta Braves baseball cap. Randy gestured for him to sit.

Cade remained standing.

After a moment, Randy got off the phone and dropped his feet to the floor. "It's a madhouse around here today. Want a Coke or something?"

Cade shook his head. "Has the DA called you about Jonathan Cleary?"

"Yeah," Randy said. "I can't do much about it if he doesn't want to press the issue, but I sure don't want him leaving town."

"I think we can trust him."

"Right," the judge said. "We can trust him—just like we could trust Rick Dugan, who I hear has fled and can't be located."

"You know, your wife's article didn't wash. I checked and Rick Dugan has no prison record. Where she got her information I have no idea, but it was slanderous and inflammatory."

"You sound like a defense attorney now," Randy said, propping his feet back up. "Whose side are you on?"

Cade didn't honor that with an answer.

"If you're wrong, and we let Jonathan out, he could kill again."

"I wouldn't recommend releasing him if I thought he did it. I'm convinced now that he didn't. Enough's been done to the Owens family. I'd like to undo some of it."

"You're telling me. That house must be cursed. Two of them murdered, and three of them suspects. It's a good thing they're closing the place down. Nothing good can come out of Hanover House."

Cade didn't want to get into an argument right now. "So do I let him out?"

Randy rubbed his jaw, as if giving it deep consideration. "So you have people out looking for Rick Morrison or Dugan or whatever his name is?"

"Yes," Cade said. "We have some leads. I think we'll have him by day's end."

The judge sighed heavily, then stretched and got up. "I'm not going to make a decision right now, Cade. I'll get back to you."

Cade had to be satisfied with that, but by the time he got back to the police station there was already a call for him from the judge. He picked up the phone and dialed the number, waited until the call was routed to the judge.

"Randy," he said, "did you call?"

"Yeah. Go ahead and release Jonathan."

Cade was surprised. "All right."

"Just send the paperwork over so I can sign it. I have to leave at three for soccer practice."

"I'll be there as soon as I can," Cade said.

CHAPTER

"So how does a Jamaican wind up in Georgia?" Jonathan's question didn't offend Gus at all. They had been talking for hours, enough for Jonathan to realize the man wasn't touchy about his past.

"The drug smuggling," Gus said. "I came here with a crateload of cocaine, and they didn't let me leave."

"You got caught then?"

"Served ten years, mon."

"But I thought you were in for armed robbery."

"Got out, couldn't find a job, and didn't have the money to get home to Jamaica. A friend from jail decided we could get fast money at a convenience store. Got us some guns, and we went in the place waving them around. Got fast money, mon, then fast jail time. Another five years."

"So when did you meet Thelma and Wayne?"

"When I got out, I had no place to go. So I stayed at the Gateway shelter in Savannah. Wayne came there, and he preached to us. I had a lot of questions, mon. Down in

Jamaica, I was a Rastafarian. We followed the teaching of the mon Haile Selassie."

"Who?"

"An Ethiopian emperor. He dead now, mon. But that was my religion, and this Christianity was hard for me. Wayne helped me with it, then invited me to come to Hanover House. He told me I could stay there if I would read the Bible and study with him every day. That I did. I owe my life to them."

Jonathan heard the catch in the big man's voice and saw the tears he wiped away in his eyes. He doubted tears were commonplace for the man. He did seem to love Thelma and Wayne. And he really did love Christ.

It was so hard to fathom that this hardened ex-con, who looked like he could break Jonathan in half, had the same hope, the same spirit.

He heard footsteps, and Cade appeared. "Okay, Jonathan. Your charges were dropped. You're free."

Jonathan got up and gaped at him. "You kidding?"

"Nope," Cade said as he opened the cell doors. "You want to stay?"

"No!" Jonathan grinned. "I'm going, I'm going."

Gus stood up and looked at him through the bars. "Good for you, mon. Good for you."

Jonathan gave him a high five as he hurried out of the cell.

CHAPTER

*J*onathan's been released!" Morgan shrieked at Mrs. Hern, dancing her around in a circle. Then she grabbed her purse and headed out.

"Call Blair and tell her I'm going to pick him up!"

Morgan sped to the police station. Leaving the car running in the lot, she dashed in. Jonathan was waiting in the front room, looking as victorious as he had after leading his team to the State Championship. She threw her arms around him, and he picked her up and swung her around.

"I can't believe it," she squealed. "You're coming home! Thank you, Cade! Thank you, thank you!"

Cade smiled as if he hadn't expected to be the hero in all this. He just stood back and grinned as they rushed out of the station.

Morgan hopped into the passenger seat, and Jonathan drove. "Free, at last," he said. "I thought I might be looking at a long sentence. Things weren't looking good."

He pulled her against him, and they drove home, clinging together like teenagers who couldn't stand to be apart.

His mood changed as they pulled into the driveway of Hanover House, the first time he had seen it since the murders. For a moment, he sat behind the wheel, staring at the yellow house. "It won't be right without them," he whispered.

Morgan shook her head, and her eyes glimmered with tears. "It isn't."

"But we're going to be all right," Jonathan said. "I'm home now."

CHAPTER

*A*fter a few hours at home, Jonathan craved the sunshine and salt air. While Morgan scurried around the kitchen, making all his favorite dishes, he walked to the dock to check on his boat. The sun burned its welcome on his face, and the smell of the sea made him long to get back to work . . . that is, if he still had any. Being a murder suspect wasn't exactly good for business.

His shirt stuck to his skin as he stood on the deck of his schooner, recalling his last words to Thelma and Wayne. He would give anything to erase the memory of his angry accusations that morning. Why hadn't he just sat down and had breakfast with them? Why hadn't he accepted their explanations about Gus? Why hadn't he enjoyed them a little while longer?

He got off the boat and stood on the pier, looking at the warehouse where they had worshiped and died. He pulled his keys out of his pocket, found the one to the warehouse. He went in the side door.

The bloodstain was still on the floor, and as he stood over it, he remembered what their bodies had looked like lying there limp and empty.

Did that memory ruin the church they had worked so hard to build? Did the blood taint it somehow? Could the Holy Spirit still work here?

He sat down on the old secondhand pew that he and Morgan occupied on Sundays. He looked up at the pulpit and realized that he would never see Wayne behind it again. What would become of their seamen's ministry and the church? Where would the congregation go? He couldn't bear the thought of the church closing down. And all those new, struggling Christians with no one to disciple them.

It was Wayne's calling, Wayne's vocation, Wayne's church . . .

His thoughts screeched to a halt, as if the Lord had thrown up a roadblock. It wasn't Wayne's church—it was Christ's. And the Holy Spirit could still work here.

He started to pray for direction for the church, for guidance for the people, for a preacher who could keep it going. Suddenly he got a glimpse of himself standing at the pulpit, preaching to a crowded room.

No way, he thought. He wasn't preacher material. It had never even crossed his mind.

He wasn't called like Wayne was. He wasn't ordained, anointed. . . .

And yet he saw the need and heard the Lord's voice clearly telling him that the church wasn't finished. Somehow, he had to keep it going.

Maybe he could clean the spot up tomorrow, he thought. Maybe he could get the church ready for Sunday. Maybe he could find some kind soul to preach. In honor of Thelma and Wayne, someone would come. And he couldn't imagine their regular church members staying away.

But as his mind struggled with the concept, his heart swelled. "I miss you, Thelma and Wayne," he whispered. "I'm sorry I was a jerk."

He knew they would have forgiven him, probably had even before they died. And as the relief of that flooded through his mind, he realized that he had someone to forgive, as well.

His oldest, closest friend, who had arrested him for something he hadn't done. Cade, who had done his job despite his personal feelings.

He could do that, he thought. He could forgive Cade. He had no other options.

He got up and walked to the pulpit, stood where Wayne used to stand, and touched the order of worship Morgan had typed for them the Sunday before they died. Thelma had sat at the piano, playing her old favorite hymns.

No one could ever replace them. Their shoes were too big to fill.

But they would have church this Sunday, and the Sunday after that, and the Sunday after that.

He took a deep breath, wiped his face on his sleeve, and left the building with new purpose—one that felt strangely like a calling.

CHAPTER

65

Cade rose before dawn, feeling as bone-weary as he had when he had gone to bed. Questions and clues whirled in his head, keeping him from the deep, restoring sleep he needed. There was too much to do.

Before the sun came up, he had made the decision to go to Atlanta. He couldn't keep Rick's airline tickets out of his mind. He had already checked with the airlines and learned that the ticket had not been used. Why would an innocent man disappear on the day that lies were published about him? Wouldn't he stay and fight? Set the record straight?

Cade had learned that Rick's mother did not have pneumonia, though his boss confirmed that Rick had gotten a phone call the day he left, telling him she was hospitalized. Had Rick lied about the call, or had someone else lied to *him*?

He had never shown up to visit his mother in the hospital. They were still watching the nursing home in case Rick showed up there.

Rick's disappearance created suspicion that Cade might not have had otherwise. His all-points bulletin had turned up nothing, and he wasn't sure he could trust the Atlanta PD to be diligent enough to catch Rick. He had to search for Rick by himself. Going to Atlanta would be a start.

But Rick wasn't the only reason to head for Atlanta. Cade couldn't get Sadie's phone call off his mind. She had called an Atlanta day care, Miss Tina's, to ask about a nine-month-old named Caleb Caruso. With that information, he knew he could fill in a lot of blanks about the girl.

One way or another, he would come back from Atlanta with information he sorely needed.

By the time he ended the four-hour trip to Atlanta, McCormick had called him with the name of the nursing home where Rick's mother lived. After arriving in the city, it took Cade another hour to navigate the traffic and find it. He wore jeans and a golf shirt, a baseball cap and sunglasses so that Rick wouldn't recognize him.

He found the home, a one-story building in an L shape, with a sign out front that said "Treasure Oaks Rest Home." He went in and approached the woman behind the nurse's desk. She had a powdered donut in her hand and a telephone at her ear.

Cade waited for her to get off the phone but quickly realized she was gabbing with a friend, and it could be a long wait.

"Excuse me," he said.

She turned around as if seeing him for the first time. "Hold on," she said to the phone, then to Cade, "Yeah?"

"I understand you have a resident here named Marilyn Dugan. Could you tell me what room she's in?"

The nurse dusted the powdered sugar off of her hands. "Yeah, room 432."

Cade waited for her to point him in the right direction, but she went back to her phone conversation instead. "Which way is it?" he asked, annoyed.

She looked at him as if his last question had pushed her over the edge. "It's that way, okay? The number's on the door."

He flashed his police badge and leaned on the counter. "I need to ask you a few questions. You might want to call your friend back later."

The woman looked insulted but picked the phone back up. "Sue, I'll call you back." She turned back to Cade. "Police, huh? Marilyn do something wrong?"

"Could you tell me if she's had any visitors lately?"

She set her hands on her hips and sighed. "Marilyn hasn't had visitors since her son moved away a few months ago."

"Are you sure?"

"You calling me a liar?"

Cade wondered if the woman was married. She must be a delight to come home to. "No, I'm not calling you a liar," he said patiently. "I was actually looking for someone who may have visited her in the last couple of days. But if a fine upstanding woman like yourself says no one's come, then I'll just talk to Marilyn myself."

"Good luck," she said, then added, "she thinks she's living in 1955."

Cade left the nursing home fifteen minutes later, no closer to finding Rick than he had been before. He got into his car and sat there, staring at the wheel.

Rick's mother was not an old woman. In her late fifties, perhaps. Early sixties at the most. He had expected someone old, in her last days of life. Alzheimer's had gotten her early.

"Samuel," she said when she first caught sight of him. Her face lit up like a little girl's, and she sprang up and threw her arms around him. "Samuel, you're almost late for pictures. Where's your suit?"

He felt as if he had stepped into someone else's life. "I'm not Samuel, ma'am," he said. "You have me mixed up with someone else."

She stepped back then, and her face went slack. "I thought we were dancing. I got you a boutonniere."

He felt sorry for her and thought of pretending to be Samuel just to light her face back up. "Ma'am, my name is Matthew Cade. I'm looking for your son, Rick. Has he been here?"

She sank into her chair, her eyes growing vacant. Just when he thought she might answer, she began to sing, in a soft, haunting voice . . . "Where have all the flowers gone, long time passing . . ."

"Ma'am," he said softly. He pulled a chair up next to her and leaned in close. "I need to find your son."

She stopped singing and smiled again. Her hand came up to stroke his cheek. "You're as handsome as ever, Samuel."

He knew then that he wasn't going to get through to her. Her life was somewhere in the past, in a world that couldn't be penetrated by police investigations or her own son's trouble.

He had been glad to get out of there.

He decided to wait a while, in case Rick Dugan showed up. Rick had laid low a couple of days, but eventually Cade knew he would come to check on his mother. With his car hidden among the others in the parking lot, Cade sat and waited.

CHAPTER

*C*ade waited until late that night, until the lights began going off in the nursing home. Then he returned early the next morning and waited some more. Rick Dugan never showed up. Realizing his trip had been for nothing, he decided to see what he could find out about Sadie.

He looked up the number of Miss Tina's Day Care, got the address, then made his way through town. He found it easily, then sat out in his car for a moment, bracing himself for what he might discover inside. Was there an abandoned child who needed her?

He went inside and found the children all lying on little cots and in their baby beds. It was naptime, and soft lullaby music played over the intercom.

One of the teachers got up and started toward him. "May I help you?" she asked in a voice just above a whisper.

"Yes," he said, flashing his badge. "Is there someplace we can talk?"

She nodded to an office and led him inside. He closed the door quietly, hoping not to wake the children. These teachers probably needed this break.

"I'm Matthew Cade from the police department," he said, not bothering to clarify that he was from Cape Refuge, not Atlanta. If Sadie was in trouble, he didn't want to lead a trail to her.

"Yes, officer, what can I do for you?"

"I understand you have a child here by the name of Caruso. Caleb, I think it is?"

"Yes," she said. "I wondered if something was up—with his mother in jail and all those calls from his sister."

Cade leaned forward. "His *sister*?"

"Yes," she said. "Sadie keeps calling to make sure he's all right."

"So—who does the baby live with?"

"His father, poor child. The rumor is that Sadie ran away. Is that why you're here?"

"No one's reported her missing," he evaded. "How can I reach her father?"

"Oh, he's not *her* father. He's her mother's boyfriend—or he *was* before she went to jail. A real scary guy, if you ask me. No wonder Sadie ran away."

He let those words sink in for a moment. Her broken arm and the bruises on her face bore witness to that fact. "Do you know how old Sadie is?"

"Sixteen. Sweetest kid in the world. I hope nothing happened to her. On the other hand, she's probably better off now. I feared for her, living with that man. Poor little Caleb. Shame she didn't take him with her."

Cade took his pad out of his pocket. "Could you tell me his name?"

"I don't know his first name. Last name is Dent. I can give you an address, since you're the police. Caleb's mama registered him, but it's the same address."

Cade wrote the address down, then looked up at the woman again. "Why is his mother in jail?"

"Some kind of drug charge. And she seemed like such a nice person. Nearly broke Sadie's heart. I know, because Sadie used to pick Caleb up every day." She looked down at her desk. "Caleb. That's a Bible name, you know."

Cade nodded.

"It's a good name for that baby. As scary as the father is, I'd say he's going to have to be very strong and courageous."

Cade got to his feet. "Can I see the baby?"

"Oh, he's not here today. Sick, I guess. Didn't come in."

Cade had a lot to think about as he made his way back to the nursing home and checked at the front desk to see if Rick had been by. He hadn't.

He went by the Atlanta Police Department to see if a missing-persons report had been filed on Sadie. Either no one had noticed her missing or no one cared.

Then he found the street where Dent lived and counted off the house numbers until he was sure he had the right one. He pulled into the driveway of the old house with peeling paint and a leaning foundation. As he walked up the cracked sidewalk, he saw that the second step on the porch had caved in. Carefully, he stepped over it.

He heard a baby crying through the door and something crashed. The baby's cries hit a higher octave.

He knocked. When no one answered, he rang the bell and knocked again, harder this time. Finally, he heard footsteps bounding across the floor, and the door jerked open.

Through the screen he smelled the alcohol breath of the man standing before him with a week-old growth of beard and a base-ball cap on backwards. Scraggly, dirty auburn hair stuck out beneath it.

"Yeah?" the man barked.

Cade knew better than to tip his hand about Sadie's where-abouts. "I was looking for Mrs. Caruso," he said. "I'm with the school board."

"Sheila ain't here," he said, talking loud over the sound of the baby's cries. "She's in jail."

"Oh," Cade said. "And where is she being held?"

He gave him the name of the prison. "So is this about Sadie?"

"Yes. We're checking on her truancy," he said.

"I didn't know they came after tenth graders. I thought you could drop out any time you wanted to."

"We like to have our paperwork in order," Cade said.

The man stepped out on the porch and spat. He wasn't wearing a shirt, and his hairy chest covered a tattoo that was indiscernible. "Well, I ain't signing nothing," he said. "That girl's nothing but trouble. I ain't even related to her except through that kid in there." He nodded toward the door.

The baby kept screaming, anguished, gut-wrenching cries. "Do you need to go get the baby?"

"Naw, he squawks whether I'm holding him or not," he said.

"Where is Sadie?" he asked. "I need to talk to her."

"She ain't here right now," he said. "Girl runs wild."

"Do you know when she'll be back?"

"Got me."

"When's the last time you saw her?"

The man squinted at him, as if he'd asked one question too many. "What difference does that make to you?"

"Just trying to get a clue where I might find her."

The man studied him through his bloodshot eyes for a moment, then shook his head. "I got a baby to tend to," he said.

Before Cade could answer, the man slammed the door. He heard him bounding back across the house as the baby continued to scream.

Cade's heart was heavy as he headed back out to his car. Something had to be done about that child. It wouldn't take a rocket scientist to see that the man was an unfit parent. But first he needed to talk to the mother.

That would shed a lot of light on Sadie's and Caleb's situations.

CHAPTER

67

*S*adie's mother, Sheila Caruso, was in the jail in downtown Atlanta. Cade found it easily.

She came to the visiting room wearing a baggy brown jumpsuit. Her brownish-blonde hair was pulled back in a rubber band. He could see Sadie in her face and knew she had once been pretty.

She eyed him suspiciously through the glass, then picked up the telephone that opened their communication.

"Who are you?" she asked.

"Mrs. Caruso, I'm Matthew Cade," he said. "I'm police chief in Cape Refuge, and I wanted to ask you some questions about your daughter, Sadie."

The woman burst into tears and leaned forward, her eyes fixed on his. "Leave her alone, won't you?" she said. "I know she's run away, but please let her go. Wherever she is, she's better off."

Cade hadn't expected that. He waited for more.

"She wasn't safe in Atlanta," she cried. "And neither is Caleb. If you're concerned about any laws being broken, then go get my baby out of that house, get him away from Jack. He'd be better off with almost anybody. Just, please, don't leave him with him."

"Mrs. Caruso, if he's his father, then—"

Her eyes grew hard, more determined. Though she looked young—no more than thirty-five, perhaps—her skin was lined and tired. "You take children away from parents all the time. You can do this. I'm telling you, he'll hurt the baby. He may even kill him like he tried to kill Sadie."

"Mrs. Caruso, if he's abusive, why hasn't anyone reported him to Human Services?"

"I have, but nothing's been done," she said. "They think I'm saying it for spite, but I told them Sadie'd had a broken jaw and a concussion and two broken ribs. There are doctors who can vouch for it, X-rays, but they won't do anything. Sadie came here with her arm all bashed in and her face swollen, and I told her to get on a bus and go as far as it would take her. That's why she left. So you might as well not be looking for her. She's going to be all right. She's got a good head on her shoulders and she's been through tough times. She practically raised herself, when I was doing drugs, and she took care of me—"

She collapsed in sobs, and Cade felt as though he had intruded on her private sorrow. All he could do was hold that phone and avert his eyes. He looked at a spot on the ledge of the glass until she could speak again.

"She's run away before, but he goes after her, chases her down, and drags her back. I'm going to be in here for five years, at least. I want both my kids in one piece when I get out. 'Til then, there's nothing I can do except beg. Please, I don't know why you're here, but please get my baby out of that house."

"I'll do what I can," he said. "Meanwhile, I can tell you that Sadie's safe, her arm's in a cast, and she just started a new job. She has a nice place to live and people watching over her.

Her face twisted, and she touched the glass. "Thank you," she said.

Cade could only nod, for his throat was too tight to say another word.

The best Cade could do was report possible abuses to Human Services before he left Atlanta. It was clear that they were overworked and understaffed and had a long list of abuses to look into. He tried to convince them to move little Caleb to the top of their list, but he wasn't sure that they would.

As he drove back to Cape Refuge, everything kept running through his mind. He hoped the baby would survive the father's abuse, and he didn't know what to do about Sadie. No missing-persons report had ever been filed, and technically, she wasn't a runaway since her mother had sent her away. He needed to pray over this a while before he took any action. And while he was at it, he would pray for little Caleb, and for the mother who seemed so remorseful and helpless as she sat in prison.

CHAPTER

Cade went straight to Hanover House as soon as he got back to Cape Refuge. He found Morgan, Jonathan, and Blair in their parents' office, trying to figure out how they could hold onto the house if the city forced them to evict their tenants.

Blair noticed the somber look on Cade's face. "Cade, what's wrong? Has something happened?"

He shook his head. "No, I was just in Atlanta for the past couple of days trying to find some leads on Rick."

"And?" she asked.

"Didn't find anything. But I came here to talk to Sadie. She home?"

Morgan looked up at him. "Upstairs. Want me to get her?"

"If you don't mind."

Blair got up and came closer, searching his face. "Cade, what is it? Has she done something wrong?"

"No. I just . . . I found out where she's from." As Sadie came down the stairs, he stepped out of the office into the living room. Blair followed.

Sadie stopped at the bottom and stared at him with big, worried eyes. It was clear she thought she had been found out, that she would be arrested and sent back to Jack.

"It's okay, Sadie," Morgan said. She took her hand and pulled her down to the couch, sat next to her with her arm around her. Blair sat on the other side, staring at Cade as she waited. Jonathan kept standing.

Cade sat down and fixed his eyes on the girl. "I was in Atlanta today, Sadie."

She leaned back hard on the couch, as if she knew what was coming.

"I met your stepfather."

"He's *not* my stepfather," she said. "He was my mother's boyfriend. That's all." Her face twisted as she started to cry. "Why'd you go there? I haven't done anything wrong. I've been getting along with people, and I've got a job. I'm earning money. I'm going to be able to support myself and take care of everything."

"Sadie, you're sixteen," Cade said.

Morgan didn't look surprised.

"You don't understand," Sadie said.

"I understand more than you think," Cade cut in. "I told you, I met Jack. I saw what kind of man he is, and I can see what drove you away."

She sprang up off of the couch and cut across the room. "He's the devil himself, that's what kind of man he is," she said. "My mama let him move in because she was lonely and he gave her drugs. That's not the first dumb thing she's ever done."

Morgan went to her. "But isn't she worried about you?" she asked. "I mean, your mother must be crazy wondering where you are."

"My mother's in jail."

Morgan caught her breath and looked at Cade.

"I met her too," Cade said.

Sadie's face changed, and she stepped toward him. "You met my mom? You went to the jail?"

"Yes," he said, "and the fact is, she begged me not to tell where you are. She said to let you stay here, that you were better off."

"She's right," Sadie said. "I may be sixteen, but I'm old enough to know when I'm in danger." She took another step toward him and breathed in a sob. "Did you see Caleb, my baby brother? Is he all right?"

"I talked to his day-care teacher," Cade said. "She said he seemed all right."

"But did you *see* him?"

"No," he said. "I heard him crying in the house, though."

"I've got to get him out of there," Sadie said. "He won't be safe. Jack's a crazy man. He has a methamphetamine lab, and he's a drug dealer. He gets high and comes home with all these lunatics for friends. And when Caleb cries, he just goes berserk."

She knelt beside Cade's chair, looking up at him with beseeching eyes. "Please. Isn't there something you can do to get him out of there?"

"Your mother asked me the same thing." He touched her shoulder and looked into those big eyes. "I'll do what I can, Sadie," he said. "I can't promise anything. This is way out of my jurisdiction. But I do think you're all right staying here. No missing-persons report has been filed. Your mother knows where you are, and she gave her permission—so technically, you're not a runaway."

Her face twisted. "You didn't tell *him* where I am, did you?"

"No," he said. "You don't have to worry about that."

"He's smart. A lot smarter than he looks. Every other time I've run away, he's found me."

"You don't have to worry," Cade said.

Sadie stood back up, and Morgan touched her face. "Honey, is he the one who beat you up?"

She nodded. "I should have brought Caleb with me. He beat me and threw me out of the house, and I slept in a car that night. The next morning I hitchhiked to visit my mom, and she told me to get on a bus, not to go back home for anything. But I shouldn't have left Caleb that way. He doesn't have anybody to protect him."

"How old is he?" Blair asked.

"Nine months. That's all. He's so little, so helpless. He cries all the time unless I'm there. He misses Mom. And now he misses me."

"We'll get him out of there, won't we, Cade?" Blair asked.

Cade nodded. "I reported him to HRS before I left town. Hopefully, they'll remove the child." He looked at the broken girl. "I'll follow up on it, Sadie. I won't let you or your brother fall through the cracks."

"Thank you," she whispered.

As he left the house, his heart broke for the desperate girl and for the baby whose cries would haunt him tonight.

CHAPTER

*T*hat night, Morgan lay curled up next to Jonathan, her head on his chest. She could tell he had something on his mind, but these days so many things weighed both of them down. "What's wrong, Jonathan?" she asked quietly.

"Nothing," he said. "I was just thinking." His voice was a deep, thoughtful rumble. "The other day when I went to the dock to check my rig, I went into the warehouse. I just sat there and thought what a shame to let the church fold, and all those people who would have to go somewhere else to worship."

"I know," Morgan said. "It seems like all of Mama and Pop's work was for nothing. It's all just disappearing."

"It doesn't have to be that way," Jonathan said.

"What do you mean?"

He sat up. "Morgan, I sat there, looking at that pulpit, and had this overwhelming sense that we need to keep the church going, and that you and I are the ones who are going to do that. And since then, I've been praying and thinking and planning . . . and I'm just wondering how you would feel . . . about us having services starting Sunday."

She thought about going back into that building, trying to forget the sight of her parents lying there in their own blood. . . . "I don't know," she whispered. "Who would preach?"

"At first I thought we should try to get a guest preacher, but I realized our members need someone familiar, someone who suffers with them, someone who grieves as they grieve. And all of a sudden, I felt as if I had a whole lot to say to them. I thought I could speak the first Sunday. After that, we could get guest preachers until we found the right person."

She sat up and hugged her knees. "I could play piano just like Mama did. I never had the confidence to do it before, but I think I could do it now."

"If we got the word out, let the congregation know, we could open up this Sunday," he said. "I think I could be ready. Being in jail gave me a lot of time to think. I could make it a memorial service for your folks. I think a lot of people would come, and then I could tell them about Jesus and why Thelma and Wayne are the only ones not grieving over their deaths. I could tell them what death looks like from the other side. The celebration, the joy, the rewards . . ."

That pain that had hidden in her chest for the past several days swelled and blocked her throat. She couldn't speak.

"They'll come if they don't think of me as a killer," he said.

She swallowed back her pain. "That's their problem. Our job is to carry on and trust God with the hearts of the people. Just like Mama and Pop always did."

He drew her into a tight hug, and she clung to him with all her might. Those she loved were so easily snatched away.

"I've felt so frustrated lately," she whispered. "About the unsolved murders, about the things I found out about Mama and Pop's past, about Blair's scars, about you and Gus and Rick. And Sadie's constantly on my mind. She's just so young. She needs an anchor. A family. People she can count on."

"I think she's found it," Jonathan said. He stroked his wife's cheek with gentle fingertips. "I see so much of your mother in you. The way you've taken over the care of this house. The way you've mothered Sadie."

"She's a good kid," she whispered. "I wish I knew how to keep her from ever going back to that man."

Jonathan stared at the air for a long moment, then finally whispered, "Maybe there is."

"What?" Morgan asked.

"If her mother's so adamant about her not going back there, maybe she'd sign papers to let us have legal custody."

Morgan got up and looked down at him. "Jonathan, do you mean it?"

"Well, sure. That way, when the tenants have to move out, she won't have to go."

"It'd solve so many problems for her. But let's not tell her until we know it'll work out. She's had enough disappointment." She reached up to kiss him. "It's so good to have you home," she said. "You're the problem solver around here."

"Yeah," he said. "If only I could solve the murders."

CHAPTER

70

Jonathan answered when East Coast Properties called the next morning. They demanded to know if Blair and Morgan had made a decision yet. "We're keeping the place," he said. "But we appreciate the offer."

"Mr. Cleary, perhaps your wife didn't convey our generous offer to you. It's cash, full market value. We're prepared to offer more if necessary. . . ."

"Sorry," he said. "We're not interested."

The man sounded stunned. "Mr. Cleary, it's come to our attention that you're being ordered to close the place down. How do you suppose that you can afford to hold onto the house and pay the substantial taxes on the property, when you can no longer accept the donations and rents that keep it afloat?"

"That would be our problem, not yours," Jonathan said. "Please don't call here again."

He took great pleasure in hanging up in the man's ear!

A few hours later Morgan was served with papers from the city's legal department. She scanned the document and handed it to Jonathan.

He quickly read over it. "Another threat to close us down in . . . twenty-seven days."

"It's not a threat, Jonathan. They're going to do it."

"They can't take our property," he said. "All they can do is tell us we can't do business, and even that's debatable. We're going to see a lawyer as soon as we can get an appointment."

Morgan grabbed the phone. "I'm calling Blair."

When she had told her sister what had just happened, Blair wasn't surprised that the papers had been served. "I've got an idea," she said. "We're about to start a propaganda war. We're going to change the tide of public opinion. Just leave it to me."

Sadie had a hard time concentrating on work that day. Her conversation with Chief Cade played through her mind. He had made promises, but she didn't know if she could trust him. He seemed kind, but others had seemed kind before. They hadn't been able to help her or her little brother.

She sat at the computer on her desk, searching the Net for some statistics Nancy needed, when Blair burst through the door.

"Sadie, where's Nancy?"

"Back in her office." She got up. "I'll get her."

"No, I'll get her myself." Blair whizzed past her and reached the door before Sadie did. Nancy looked up, surprised. "I need your help, Nancy," she said.

The woman sat at her cluttered desk, digging through a pile as if searching for something. "Blair, you've got a lot of nerve. After what you said about me at the city council meeting, you have the gall to ask for my help?"

Blair sighed. "Nancy, after all the things you've written in the past few months about Hanover House, you have a lot of nerve being insulted."

Nancy set her chin on her palm. "What do you want?"

"I want to give you a story. News, Nancy. The real kind. The city council just served us papers. I need some publicity. You could do an article on this. You know it's big news and the townspeople would want to know."

"Of course," she said, pulling a pencil from behind her ear. "Sit down."

Blair looked suspicious, as if she knew better than to think Nancy could turn on a dime.

"I could write it!" Sadie said from the doorway. "I mean, living there and all, I could do a good job."

"Sure you could," Nancy said. "Come on in and sit down, Sadie." She pulled a legal pad out from one of the stacks. "Here, take notes."

Pride swelled in Sadie's heart, but her stomach tightened. She hadn't expected it to be quite that easy.

Blair wasn't buying it, either. "Come on, Nancy. I was thinking you could probably devote a whole issue to it. Think of it. You could interview people who've stayed there over the years, do a piece about Joe and Miranda Hanover, interview people in the community about their feelings about the House. . . . No offense, Sadie, but I had a substantial article in mind."

"I can't give it a whole issue," Nancy said. "Sadie can write it up, and if it's any good, I'll run it."

Her noncommittal attitude worried Sadie as she followed Blair back to the front. "Do a good job, Sadie. Hanover House depends on it, and we're not gonna get a lot of help from Nancy. Fax me the article when you're finished with it, and I'll proof it for you."

Sadie felt as if the fate of the beloved home rested on her shoulders. She hoped they were strong enough to carry it.

She spent the rest of the day in a nervous flurry. She went to Hanover House and listened as Morgan gave her a quick rundown of the history of the house, complete with newspaper clippings and pictures of Joe and Miranda Hanover. She had Blair explain in detail what the city council was doing, then she rushed to Crickets and interviewed the few midday diners about their thoughts on the home.

She went back to the office and typed up the article, then faxed it to Blair at the library.

When Blair called five minutes later to say, "It looks great, Sadie. You got talent, kid," Sadie wanted to dance and leap and let out a loud cheerleader whoop, but she had to act old enough to be a newspaper reporter. She took the article in to Nancy's office.

Nancy was laying out the day's edition, and Sadie saw with disappointment that the front page was already full.

"I finished the article," she said. "I hope you like it. I can make any changes you want."

Nancy took it and devoted three seconds to reading it over. Then she tossed it down. "Good job, Sadie, but I'm not going to put it in."

"What? Why not?" Sadie picked it back up, feeling like a failure. "I can redo it. Maybe I just rushed too much. . . ."

"No," Nancy said. "I've just given it more thought today, and I've decided it's not newsworthy."

"But . . . it's Hanover House. People had nice things to say about it. I got a lot of good quotes. . . ." Her voice trailed off. Nancy wasn't even listening.

"Maybe tomorrow's issue, then?" Sadie asked.

"No, not tomorrow either," Nancy said. "The community's tired of hearing about Hanover House."

Blair was waiting at Hanover House when Sadie got home from work that day. The girl came in, a sheen of perspiration on her face. She was flushed, angry, and shaken.

"How'd it go, Sadie? What page did she give the article?"

"She isn't putting it in. She has no intentions of publishing it."

"What?" Blair asked. "Are you sure?"

"She said it wasn't newsworthy."

Blair slammed her hand down on the counter. "Not news-worthy? And the article on the pros and cons of the post office being closed on Wednesday afternoons *is*? She ran a whole series on whether World's Finest Chocolate was a better school fund-raiser than popcorn! Last week there was a front-page article about that thirteen-year-old who got her hair cut for the first time. Give me a break!"

"Did you ask her why she didn't think it was newsworthy?" Morgan asked.

"I tried, but she told me the community is just sick of hear-ing about it."

Blair shot Morgan a look. "That's the most absurd thing I've ever heard. If this isn't news, I don't know what is. Has the whole world gone crazy?"

"Not the whole world," Morgan said. "Just Cape Refuge." She crossed her arms, and looked at the girl. "Sadie, do you think you can get that article back tomorrow?"

"Sure," she said. "I kept a copy."

"We could buy an ad for the paper and put it in that."

"Contribute money to that rag?" Blair asked. "I don't think so. Let's just print it up ourselves and pass it out all over town."

"We can send a copy to East Coast Properties," Morgan said. "Just a few hours before we got served yesterday, they called and demanded an answer. Even raised the offer. Jonathan told them no."

"What did they do?" Blair asked. "Call the mayor and get him to serve us so we'd change our minds?"

"Do you think someone pressured Nancy into not publish-ing the article?" Morgan asked.

"Could be. But if that's the case, we're about to show them that it didn't keep us quiet. Before the end of the week, we'll make sure everyone on the island knows what's happening to Hanover House."

CHAPTER

71

*T*he more she thought about it, the more suspicious Blair became. Things seemed too coincidental. First, the call from East Coast Properties, then the serving of the papers just hours later, and now Nancy's refusal to run an article about the closing of the island's most revered landmark. . . .

She went back to the library and turned on her computer. Her fingernails drummed on the table as she waited for it to boot up. She clicked in "Copernic," the search engine that had access to eighty databases. She typed in "East Coast Properties, Inc.," and watched as the bars traveled across the screen.

The search didn't come up with anything she could use, so she logged onto the public-records database she was able to access.

While the database searched for East Coast Properties, she went to the bathroom for a glass of water. She turned on the faucet and stuck the glass under it, but her mind drifted back to the company, to those papers, to Sadie's article, to Nancy's refusal.

Something wasn't right.

The water ran over the glass, wetting her arm, and she pulled it back and dried off her hand.

Her computer bell rang, so she rushed back into her tiny office. A few things had come up, so she quickly clicked the first.

East Coast Properties was owned by another company called Georgia Estates. She did a quick search to see who owned Georgia Estates.

Her heart jolted when she realized it was owned by Savannah Enterprises. She saw the pattern forming as she did the search on Savannah Enterprises. It was the classic modus operandi of dummy corporations set up for tax shelters or money laundering.

One company owned by another and another and another in a never ending trail that led nowhere.

But Savannah Enterprises did own quite a bit of property on Cape Refuge—three souvenir shops down by the beach and the Green Eggs and Ham Breakfast Nook near the Pier. They also owned three hotels along Ocean Boulevard, some condominiums on the north side of the island, and various houses and convenience stores that she knew had been bulldozed for parking lots. So what did they want with Hanover House?

She sat back in her chair and stared at the screen.

Who was really behind East Coast Properties, and what did they want with her family home? Did they want to tear it down to build a parking lot, or did they plan to turn it into condos? Or did they hope to remodel it and turn it into a high-priced bed-and-breakfast that only wealthy tourists could afford?

And was it a coincidence that the city council's harassment and the offer had come at roughly the same time?

She couldn't say for sure. Not yet. But she was determined to find out.

CHAPTER

72

*C*ade leaned against the wall in the back corridor of the Municipal Court building, waiting for the judge to come out of the courtroom. He had timed it so that he wouldn't have long to wait—Randy Simmons never held court after three o'clock.

Randy was already unzipping his robe as he burst out the door. He wore a pair of baggy shorts underneath. "How's it going, Cade?" Randy asked him.

"Pretty good. Can I talk to you in private?"

"Sure." The judge led him back to his chambers, which consisted of a small office just barely big enough to hold a desk and a couple of chairs. Since Cape Refuge wasn't big enough to have court every day, he did most of his work at his law firm.

He took off his robe, tossed it over a chair.

Cade chuckled. "I see you're still taking the office of judge as reverently as always."

Randy sat down behind his desk and propped his flip-flopped feet on it. "If you had to listen to a hundred people whining about speeding tickets and bad checks, you'd want to be comfortable too."

"I guess you're right."

"So, what's on your mind?" the judge asked. "Have you found that Rick Dugan character?"

"No, not yet," he said. "We're still looking for him. It's strange that we haven't found him. I have APBs in every county in Georgia and most of Alabama and Mississippi too. But that's not why I'm here."

Cade got up and slid his hands into his pockets. "Sadie ... the girl who's working for your wife—I found out she's a teen runaway, but when I went to check on her family, I learned that her mother's in jail, and she's been living with the mother's boyfriend. Name's Jack Dent. He's a drug dealer and abusive— which is why she came here so beaten up. She begged me not to send her back to him, and her mother did too. Morgan and Jonathan Cleary want to take temporary custody of her, with the mother's permission."

The judge dropped his feet and scooted his chair closer to the desk. "You'd have to get the proper papers drawn up, then have the mother sign them. It's no hill for a climber. I could draw the papers up in my lawyer hat if you want me to."

Cade nodded. "I would like to get this taken care of as soon as possible."

"Tell Morgan to call me, and we'll get the papers drawn up this week."

"Meanwhile," Cade said, "can you give me some kind of court order to keep her here?"

"I can't do that," Randy said. "It's not my beat. But drawing up the papers and getting the mama to sign them should be enough."

Cade had to be satisfied with that. He shook the man's hand. "Well, thanks. I appreciate it. I'll get details to you so you can draw them up. I'll take them to the mother myself."

Randy dropped his feet. "Sounds good. So how are Morgan and Blair? I heard Hanover House is being shut down. Any word on where they'll go?"

Cade frowned. "They're not going anywhere, and they plan to fight this."

Randy breathed a laugh. "That's crazy. They ought to just sell the thing and get it behind them."

"I understand they've had offers," Cade told him, "but I don't think they want to sell. Looks like they're going to dig in—and Sadie's one of the big reasons."

"What's she got to do with it?" Randy asked.

"Well, if Hanover House is closed down, they have to ask all their tenants to leave."

"They could get another place, take her with them."

"But they're real attached to that place, you know. They grew up there. Their parents were so invested in it. All this has happened kind of fast, and they're just not ready." Cade moved his chair out of the way so he could get to the door. "Thanks a lot, Randy. I'll get in touch with you."

"Yeah," Randy said, behind him.

Cade was hopeful that they had an answer for Sadie as he went back to the station.

CHAPTER

*J*onathan couldn't help being amazed at the number of people who turned out for the memorial service for Thelma and Wayne Owens. Many had come to the funeral, he understood, but now that their grief had taken root, they needed more of a good-bye to their friends. Some were gawkers, and others just came for the gossip value. But most came because they had loved the vibrant couple who had been such a part of the island's life.

Jonathan was nervous and found himself perspiring more than he had ever done when he had come to this church before. He had them open all the doors, and as they began to sing the praise songs that Thelma and Wayne would have led, he felt a calm wash over him, reminding him that it wasn't about how good he was as a preacher or how well he filled Wayne's shoes. It was about reaching people, changing hearts for Christ just as they had always done. That is what Wayne would have wanted.

As their songs rose to the sky and spread out to the street, stragglers began coming in from the dock, seamen who had just come to shore, and customers from Cricket's who heard the sound of praise. They all stood at the doorways, peeking inside. Morgan smiled as her mother would have done and played the chords of the praise songs that Jonathan led.

When they stopped singing, Jonathan began to preach about the two lives that had been so beautifully dedicated to the Lord, about the work and the place where they had invested their lives, and he told where they were and what their legacy was to the people of this community. And then he told why. As he did, he realized that the inadequacies of his own speech were overshadowed by the Holy Spirit as it worked in the hearts of those who listened.

Blair sipped her coffee at the picnic-style table in Cricket's, watching through the screen window as people crowded into the doorways of the warehouse. She had not been able to make herself go. She didn't want to hear testimonies about her parents and their life's work for the God who had allowed them to be murdered.

She could hear the singing, the sweet peaceful sounds of praise for a God that so many seemed to believe in. She watched as people from the restaurant got up and gravitated toward the music. Whether it was curiosity or religion that drew them, she wasn't sure. All she knew was that it wasn't for her. She knew her sister would be disappointed, that others would wonder where she was. But they would just have to understand.

"Gonna miss the service," Charlie said from behind the bar as he wiped the counter.

Blair stared into her cup. "I was at the funeral service," she said. "I don't need to say good-bye again."

The screen door to Cricket's bounced, and Cade walked in, looked around, and caught her eyes. He was wearing a sport coat and khaki pants, a white shirt that contrasted nicely with his tan. She propped her chin on her fist and looked out at the water.

She heard his footsteps approaching on the wooden floor.

"Mind if I sit with you?" he asked.

"Sure."

He slid across from her, his eyes silently resting on her. "I thought I'd see you there," he said finally. "Somebody said you were over here. Thought I'd see if you're okay."

"I'm fine," she said. "I'm just not into church. Never was. You know that."

"It's no big surprise, but this *is* a memorial service for your folks."

"As I was telling Charlie, I've been there and done that."

"And then there's that minute possibility that you might learn something."

"Doubt it." She brought her cup to her mouth.

He just gazed at her, those eyes seeing far too much. She turned her face again, hiding the scars.

"So tell me what you're thinking about while you watch those people fill that little building."

"I'm thinking that I'm tired of this town, Cade," she whispered. "That I don't know why I stayed here all these years."

"I sometimes ask myself the same thing," he said, "but I think the island gets under your skin, in your blood. We couldn't leave if we wanted to." He shifted his body and looked back toward the warehouse. "Look at that, Blair. Those are your friends. Your parents' friends. They love your family and what it represents. Those are the ones who make up the real Cape Refuge. Not that city council. That's why you can't ever leave."

"Think again," Blair said. "I'm thinking about doing just that." She met his eyes and saw the concern on his face.

"You'd miss the ocean," he said, "the sound and the smell. You'd miss the sand and the sunshine."

"There are other beach towns," she said, "but I was thinking of going to the mountains. Colorado, maybe. I want to live where there's snow."

His eyes were as serious as she had ever seen them. "There are people here who'd miss you, Blair."

She smiled. "Who? My sister has Jonathan, and all those people she hovers over. They probably wouldn't even notice I was gone."

"You'd miss her."

"Yeah, well, everything's a trade-off."

He reached across the table, took her cup out of her hands, sipped it. There was something strangely intimate about that, and Blair questioned the warm feeling it gave her.

He set the cup down and put her hands around it, pressed his over them. "And then there's me. I would miss you, Blair."

She knew her scars were probably blood red again, so she turned back to the window. "That's nice, Cade. But soon enough you're going to meet one of these blonde tourists breezing through town, fall in love, marry her, and have tanned little children running around crabbing on the beach."

He grinned. "Or you could," he said. "There are plenty of tanned *men* breezing through town."

She smiled a sad smile. "Not going to happen," she said, "not to me."

She dug into her purse, pulled out two dollars, and set them on the table. "You better get back to the service, before somebody misses you and turns you in to the spiritual police."

He smiled and slid out of the booth. "You won't run off to Colorado without letting me know, will you?"

She sighed. "Don't worry. I'm not planning to leave in the next few days. Too much is unsettled. I fight to win."

She started past him to the door, but he caught her arm and stopped her. She turned around and looked up at him. "Are you okay?" he asked in a low voice. "I mean, really okay?"

She felt exposed, and she didn't like it. "I'm fine," she said. Then before he could say anything else, she pulled out of his grasp and headed back to Hanover House.

CHAPTER

74

$\mathcal{M}$organ found Blair lying in their parents' bedroom at Hanover House, curled up on the bed, clutching both of her parents' pillows.

"We missed you at the service," she said.

Blair sat up as if she didn't want to be seen that way. "I saw that it was a big crowd. I'm glad it went well."

Morgan came in and closed the door behind her. "Jonathan was wonderful," she said. "He did a good job. And Wilson Riley offered to preach next Sunday. He's a retired preacher, you know. He wants to do it."

Blair breathed a laugh. "No one can fill Pop's shoes. You know that."

Morgan sat on the bed and pulled her feet up beneath her. "What's the matter, Blair?"

"Nothing. I'm just a little amazed at how easy it is for you."

"What's easy?"

"Just moving on," Blair said, "picking up and filling Pop's shoes. Mama's too."

"All I did was go to a church service," Morgan said.

Blair pulled herself off the bed. "I'm sorry. I didn't mean to snap." She fiddled with something on the bed table, then turned around and looked at her sister. "I think I've changed my mind about selling Hanover House."

Morgan grunted. "Why? I thought we had decided that we wouldn't. I thought we were going to fight it, stand firm, and not let the city council intimidate us."

Blair's eyes were misty as she turned back around. "But I'm tired, Morgan," she said, and the weariness was apparent in every word. "I need help moving on."

"How would it help?" Morgan asked. "Selling our home and everything that belonged to Mama and Pop—how in the world could that help?"

"I could use the money," Blair said.

Morgan's mouth fell open. "For what?"

"To move out of this place, to start over someplace else where no one knows me."

"How'll that help?" Morgan cried. "Why would anybody want to go where no one knows them?"

"Because they could start over," Blair said. "There'd be hope for a future."

"You have hope here. You were happy before all this. You never wanted to move before."

"I've always wanted to move," Blair said, "but I never did because they were here, and it would have broken their hearts. But now it's easier. I want to do it, Morgan. I want to sell this house."

"Well, I don't! Mama and Pop would have wanted us to keep going. The church service, Hanover House, they were all tools to Mama and Pop to help them reach people, and I want to do that too. I have it in me and so does Jonathan. We can do it. It can be my mission field just like it was theirs."

Blair ground her teeth together. "Don't you tell me you feel called."

"That's exactly what I feel."

"Oh, please!" Blair shouted. "You make me want to throw up. Why is it that every time a Christian gets a bee in his bonnet they say they feel 'called'?"

"Because it's true."

"It's not true," Blair said. "It's just another manipulative technique that ends the conversation. If you feel 'called,' then nobody can argue with it. But you know what? I don't believe, so it doesn't work with me."

"So you don't believe," Morgan said, smearing a tear across her face. "Mama and Pop couldn't change that, and I haven't been able to change that. But you don't have to mock my beliefs. I do feel a calling and so did Mama and Pop."

"That's right," Blair shouted. "They felt that calling to serve God. They gave him their lives. They served him night and day. And look how protected they were! Look how blessed! They were *murdered*, Morgan! Where was he when they were screaming for their lives? Where is he now, when that killer is still out there, walking around free and laughing because he got away with it?"

Morgan sank back down. "There'll come a time when God's wrath will come down on the person who did this, Blair. When God's anger over Mama and Pop's deaths is avenged."

"How do you know that?"

"Because it says so in the Bible, and I believe it." She wiped her tears and tried to find the words. "Blair, we live in a violent, dark world. It wasn't the way God wanted it in the beginning."

"Oh, right," Blair said. "The fallen nature. Adam and Eve sinned, so our parents had to be murdered. Makes sense to me."

Morgan looked helpless. "Blair, I ask the same questions. Where was God? Why did he let this happen? And I don't know the answers. But I know that our parents are in heaven because Jesus shed his blood so that this world wouldn't be imprisoned to sin anymore. The person who did this will have to face God one day. His knees will bow and his tongue will confess that Jesus Christ is Lord. And he's going to pay for what he did."

"By going to hell? So let me get this straight," Blair said. "Because I don't believe, I'll be in hell with the same person who killed our parents?"

Morgan slammed her fist into the mattress. "Oh, Blair, God never wanted you to go to hell. We were all headed there, anyway. Jesus died on the cross to save us from that. He died to save you too. He probably mourns every day because you haven't reached out and taken the life preserver he's thrown out to you. You'd rather drown in your confusion, in all your unanswered questions, in all the pain you carry around."

"And *you'd* rather drown in your faith."

"Faith doesn't make you drown, Blair. It makes you walk on the water. It makes you go on when life doesn't make sense, when it isn't fair, when horrible things happen. It reminds you that you're not alone. That Someone is there with you, carrying that burden that's so crushing that you can't even stand up straight."

Blair only shook her head and wiped the tears on her face. "I can carry my own burdens."

Then she left the room, ran down the stairs, and out the front door. Morgan just curled up in the same place her sister had been, and wept into her father's pillow.

CHAPTER

*B*lair crossed the street and headed along the beach, her feet digging into the powdery sand. She tried to flee from her rage at the God she didn't believe in, tried to escape the cares that crushed her, just as Morgan had described. But there was no escape. They went with her, wrapping around her throat and constricting it, keeping her from being able to swallow or breathe. Where had they come from, these tears? They came in a torrent streaming down her face, stinging her eyes, dripping from the bottom of her chin. She walked faster and faster as that anguish poured out of her.

She passed the South Beach Pier, where tourists lay as limp as the towels beneath them. She glanced up to the pier, hoping no one she knew would see her in this condition. No one even noticed her.

She walked faster, the angry wind whipping through her hair. Black clouds blew up from the east, threatening furious storms that would slow the island down. She welcomed that storm, longed for the lightning and the claps of thunder, the sound of pouring rain on her roof. It would feel like justice.

She kept walking until she ran out of beach; then she took to the grass and the occasional sidewalk and the packed dirt, walking from pier to pier around the cape.

She had meant what she said about leaving Cape Refuge. Somehow, she would make it happen. She could sell her half of Hanover House to Morgan and take off to Colorado. She could find a research job or a librarian's position there, rent a little apartment overlooking the mountains, soak up the peace and the newness of the place, and put the past, with all its questions and maddening answers, behind her.

She trudged along the river wall, through backyards, and around boathouses. A few residents waved at her and asked how she was doing, but she just waved and walked on.

She rounded the northern tip of the island, only a mile across the river from Tybee Island. The back of the Simmons's house came into view, and she saw the judge and Nancy sitting out beside their pool. A red-haired man, dressed in a Miller Light T-shirt and jeans, sat with them, deep in conversation.

She didn't want Nancy to catch her with tears on her face and drill her with a million insincere questions, and she wasn't up for a fight about the article Nancy hadn't printed. So Blair chose, instead, to turn around and head back the way she had come, before they even saw her.

She'd be glad to put people like Nancy in her rearview mirror, she thought—along with their arrogant opinions and lethal tongues and complete lack of regard for the things that made this island great.

Her house would sell quickly, as property on Cape Refuge always did. She would make enough to get started. She'd call a realtor tomorrow, she thought. She wouldn't let Morgan convince her to stay. And she wouldn't let Cade's soft, knowing gaze change her mind either.

Her mind was made up, but as she walked the perimeter of the island, she realized that, no matter how fast she walked or how far she went, Cape Refuge was still with her.

She wondered if she could ever really escape it.

CHAPTER

76

*S*adie's first paycheck came the next day. It was such a thrill that she didn't know what to do first. When she left the office that afternoon she hurried through the rain down to the bank a block away and cashed the check. With her money tucked into her pocket, she hurried back to Hanover House, anxious to pay the rent and show them that she could indeed earn her keep.

Soaking wet and almost running by the time she got to the front yard, like a child with a straight-A report card, she bounced up the steps and across the porch.

"Morgan, you won't believe it!" she cried as she burst into the kitchen. It was empty. She went through the rest of the downstairs rooms, searching for someone to tell, then looked outside and realized that Morgan's car was gone. She would have to wait.

She heard movement upstairs, a door closing, footsteps across the floor . . .

She ran up the stairs, turned the corner—and stopped cold.

It was Jack.

The man who had beaten her leaned against the wall, smoking a cigarette and watching the shock on her face.

"Surprise," he said in that voice heavy with evil.

She screamed and started to run down the stairs, but he was on her in seconds. He knocked her legs out from under her, and she tumbled down, her cast breaking as it hit against the stairs.

She managed to get up before he was on her again, but he grabbed her and knocked her to the ground. His fist cracked across her cheek, producing a bloody gash, but she got her feet under her again and ran. She stumbled out the back door and took off into the trees, knowing he was behind her. She could hear him panting and calling her name.

"Thought you could hide, did you?" he was saying. "Thought you could report me to HRS and get away with it? You can't hide from me, Sadie. You ain't smart enough."

But she *was* smart enough to get away. She had walked this way too many times and she knew which routes might lose him. She ran for her life, through yards and behind houses, into the heart of Cape Refuge, running, running until she thought she had lost him. Because if he ever did catch her, she knew this time he would kill her. There was no mistaking it.

Her breath sounded amplified in her ears, and her heart beat rudderlike against her chest. She stopped and hid in a cluster of wet bushes in someone's yard and waited there as rain drizzled down and the moments ticked by. She listened for him, smelled for him, but when he never made a move, she knew she had lost him. Finally, she made her way to a convenience store with a pay phone. She thought of calling the police, but she'd never had good luck with them before. Morgan wasn't home. So she called information, got Blair's number, dropped in some more coins, and dialed.

Lightning shocked overhead, making her jump, and she put her back to the wall and clutched the phone tight as she waited, watching for him to come upon her and finish the job. Blair's phone rang once, twice, a third time.

"Please answer!" she whispered.

The voice mail picked up.

"I'm not home right now," Blair's voice said, "but if you'd like to leave a message, wait for the beep."

She waited for the beep, then in a breathless, panicked, high-pitched voice said, "Blair, I went home, and Jack was there waiting for me, trying to kill me, and he chased me, and I got away, but he'll find me." She stopped on a shivery sob and brushed her wet hair back from her eyes. "I don't know where Morgan is, so I'm going to Nancy's to see if I can hide there so he can't find me. Please, when you get this, come get me there. I'm so scared."

She hung up the phone, then took off walking to the judge's house, praying that Nancy would take her in.

The light on Blair's machine was blinking when Blair got home from the library. She didn't want to talk to anybody. She had spent the day secluded in the back room. Because of the storm, hardly anyone had come in, and those who had were not interested in conversation.

Still, she pushed the button and went into the kitchen as she listened.

The tape beeped. "Blair, it's Morgan. Call me, please."

Blair got a can of Diet Coke from the refrigerator and poured it into a glass. The tape beeped again. Sadie's high-pitched, panicked voice fired across the line: *"Blair, I went home, and Jack was there waiting for me, trying to kill me, and he chased me, and I got away, but he'll find me ..."*

The glass slipped from Blair's hand and shattered on the tile.

"I don't know where Morgan is, so I'm going to Nancy's to see if I can hide there so he can't find me. Please, when you get this, come get me there. I'm so scared."

Blair crunched the glass under her shoes and reached the phone. She dialed the police station and waited as the call was routed to Cade. "Cade, Sadie's in trouble," she blurted. "She left me a hysterical message that Jack is in town, that he broke into Hanover House and was waiting for her. She's hurt."

"Jack? The mother's boyfriend?"

"Yes. Cade, you've got to catch him before he kills her. She said she was going to Nancy's because he wouldn't look for her there."

"I'm on it, Blair," he said. "I'll get back to you."

77

Limping and clutching her broken arm against her body, Sadie made her way to the northern tip of the island where the Simmons lived. She rang the bell, then banged urgently on the front door. After a moment, Nancy opened it. "Sadie, what happened?"

"He's here," Sadie cried, stumbling in. "Jack's after me." She closed the door behind her, and looked out the window.

"Jack who?" Nancy's voice was laced with irritation.

"*Jack!* My mother's boyfriend. He tracked me down. I can't ever get away from him! Please, can I stay here, just until they catch him?"

"Of course you can," Nancy said.

"We have to call the police," Sadie cried, running from window to window to check the locks.

"Sadie, calm down," Nancy said. "Let's clean that cut—"

Sadie was wet and cold, shivering so badly that she could hardly stand. "They have to find him before he tracks me here. They have to catch him . . ."

"Sadie, stop!" Nancy turned her from the window and looked her in the face. "You're bleeding, and your cast is messed up. One thing at a time."

"The police," Sadie cried. "Please, the police . . ."

Nancy walked her into the bathroom and made her sit down. Sadie hugged herself and wished for a blanket. Her clothes were wet, and she couldn't stop shaking.

Her eyes shot to the window, and she wondered if it was locked. He could break the glass and come in after her.

"Here," Nancy said, pouring two pills into her hand. "It'll help."

"No!" Sadie squealed. "The police—"

"Take these, Sadie," Nancy insisted, filling a glass with water. She thrust the pills into her trembling hands. "They'll help the pain and calm you down."

Sadie took the pills, and Nancy came at her with a cotton ball and alcohol.

"You need stitches," she said. "And your arm—we need to get you to the hospital."

"No," Sadie cried. "I can't go out. He's waiting for me. He wants to kill me."

"Okay," Nancy said. "Let's just stop the bleeding, and we'll call the police."

Sadie felt the fight draining out of her. "Yes," she whispered. "Tell them . . . he's after me . . . little Caleb . . ."

Nancy walked her to the guest room and turned on a lamp. There were family pictures, plants, a clock that ticked too loudly . . . and windows. "Lie down and rest now," Nancy said, "and I'll call the police. Just keep this towel pressed against your face to stop the bleeding."

"The window," Sadie said. Her voice was weak. Her body felt as if she had strapped weights to her limbs.

"It's locked," Nancy assured her. "Now you just rest here. I'll get the police."

Sadie lay down and pulled her knees to her chest, pressing the towel to her face. She was still wet and so cold but too tired

to pull the blanket over her. . . . She thought of little Caleb, screaming out his pain and anguish with no one there to help him. Where
was he? What had Jack done with Caleb?

The rain's patter against the panes of glass soothed her,
lulling her mercifully into sleep. She felt as though she had fallen
into a deep pool, her limbs moving slowly around her. She floated
that way as her fear lifted and her body warmed. . . .

The door to the room opened so hard that it banged against the
wall, shocking her out of that warm pool. She sat up, her body
still heavy, her eyes trying to focus.

Jack stood in the doorway. "I told you you can't hide from me."

She opened her mouth to scream, but he slapped his hand
across it. She tried to fight as he lifted her, but she was so tired.
Nancy would stop him, she thought, the police would come. . . .
But no one was there as he carried her through the house.

He got her out into the closed garage, and she saw that his
car was sitting there, sheltered from the view of neighbors. He
threw her in and got in behind her, forcing her down to the floorboard. She tried to get up, but the debilitating fatigue kept her
down. Somehow, he had gotten the remote that opened the
garage, and the door slid open.

He pulled out of the garage, and Sadie wondered where
Nancy and the judge were and why they weren't helping . . . how
Jack had gotten into their garage and their house . . . whether they
were all right . . .

Something hard whacked across her skull . . .

. . . and everything went black.

CHAPTER

*N*ancy was waiting when Cade and Cald-well arrived. Randy rushed home as well, with his baseball cap on backwards and a Dr Pepper in his hand.

"Where is she?" Cade asked as Nancy let them in.

"Asleep in the back. She was hysterical, so I gave her some codeine to calm her and help with the pain." She started leading them up the hall.

"She all right?"

"She's got a cut on her cheek. Bruised and limping. And he may have rebroken her arm." She got to the guest room and knocked lightly.

"Sadie," she said as she opened the door.

The room was empty.

"She's not here," Cade said. He met Nancy's eyes.

Nancy rushed out and went up the hall. "Maybe she's in the bathroom."

Cade followed her but Sadie wasn't there. "Cade, she was right here. I cleaned her cut myself. She was panicked and dripping wet."

Randy stood at the end of the hall, looking irritated, as if they were making him late for soccer practice.

There was a scuff mark on the wall, like a foot might have kicked it. "Randy, was this here before?"

He gave it a cursory glance. "Before what?"

"Before Sadie got here."

He studied the scuff mark, shrugged. "I couldn't really say."

Cade knew better than that. He had been in this house before for some of the parties that Nancy and Randy threw, and he knew that it was always immaculate and perfectly decorated. Nancy was known for being obsessive about her home, even though her office was cluttered beyond reason. Once he had been at a Christmas party here when a candle had caught a wall hanging on fire. Nancy had put it out and repainted the wall while the party went on around her.

"She probably just took off again," Randy said. "Who can understand a teenager?"

"Have you both been here the whole time?" Cade asked.

"No," Randy said. "I was at the office late. She was already here when I got home."

"Did you leave the house at any time?"

"We were sitting on the covered patio, watching the rain," Nancy said.

Cade gaped at him. "While you were supposed to be guarding Sadie? Why would you leave her alone when she told you someone was trying to kill her?"

"Well, we didn't think he knew where she was," Nancy said. "We thought—"

Cade threw the door open and headed outside. "I'm going to talk to the neighbors."

It didn't take him long to find a witness who had seen Jack's car pull into the judge's garage. It didn't make sense, he thought. The judge had the best security system money could buy. Why hadn't it kept Jack from getting to Sadie, and why hadn't Nancy and Randy heard her fighting?

And how had Jack figured out where Sadie was? Here he was, new to the island, not knowing anybody, and yet he was able to find the house where Sadie just happened to be hiding?

When he got back to the squad car, he called in an all-points bulletin for Jack and Sadie. When he got back to the station, he called Blair to warn her that Sadie was missing and the man was still at large. He told her about the scuff on the wall and the judge's nonchalance.

"This guy Jack's dangerous," he said. "He's about six feet tall, has long red hair, a goatee . . ."

"Cade!" she cut in. "I saw him yesterday. I was walking around the island, and he was sitting in the judge's backyard, talking to him and Nancy!"

Cade just stared at a spot on his desk as the words sank in. "If Randy Simmons has been in contact with Jack. . . ." His voice trailed off as he tried to process the thoughts whirling through his mind.

"Why?" she asked. "How would he know about Jack, and what would he have to gain?"

Cade closed his eyes. "I told him about Jack, when I asked him to do the paperwork for Sadie. I also told him that Sadie was one of the reasons you wouldn't let go of Hanover House."

His heart ticked off milliseconds as Blair sat silent. "Cade, you don't think he's the one who—?"

"I'll call you back, Blair," he said, and cut her off.

His mind reeled with the disconnected facts, the fragmented hunches, the threads that ran through every part of these crimes. He needed more to go on, something substantial, before he could pick up the judge. And if he was involved, what about Nancy?

What would have motivated them?

He bolted out of his office. McCormick was on the phone, a look of disbelief on his face. At the sight of Cade, he put his hand over the phone. "You'll never believe what just washed up on the shore over by the South Beach Pier."

Cade braced himself. "Tell me."

"Rick Dugan," he said.

CHAPTER

Morgan mothered Sadie's room, smearing her tears with trembling hands. "When's it going to end?" she muttered. "So much violence."

Jonathan tried to calm her with a hug, but she slipped away and straightened the comforter on the girl's bed. "She'll be okay, honey. They'll find her."

"Like they found Rick?" Her voice choked off, and she went to the mirror, where Sadie had a picture of Caleb wedged in the wood frame. What would become of the baby?

Blair stood dry-eyed in the doorway. Morgan could tell her wheels were turning, working through scenarios, solving the crime. "I know the judge is involved," she said.

Morgan took Sadie's pillow off the bed and pulled the loose sham over it. Her gaze drifted out the window, and she searched the street, silently praying that it wasn't too late. . . .

"That article came out in the paper," Blair went on, "full of lies, yet Nancy wouldn't print a retraction, then Rick disappeared, making him look doubly guilty, only to show up dead. Meanwhile, Jack shows up out of nowhere after Cade told Randy about him, and he comes straight to where Sadie's staying, finds her where she's hiding—"

Morgan turned from the window. "Why haven't they found her yet? It's a tiny island. How hard could it be?"

Jonathan put his hands on her shoulders. "Maybe they're not on the island," he said. "Maybe they got out before anyone knew to start looking."

Blair slid her fingers through the roots of her hair. "And that delay is, once again, traced back to our judge."

"Then what're they waiting for? Why don't they arrest him and force him to tell them where she is?"

"Cade's working on it. I'm sure he'll get him soon. But he's also trying to catch up with Jack and Sadie and figure out what happened to Rick." Blair walked to the window, and she too looked out. It was still raining. Dark clouds hovered over the water.

She imagined Sadie, soaked and beaten up, terrorized by the man she feared the most. She wished she believed in prayer. Instead, she believed in the gun she had in her pocket.

"I need to go home," she said. "I need to use the computer at the library. I was getting to the bottom of this dummy corporation thing, all these businesses that owned East Coast Properties, Incorporated. Maybe with a little more searching, I can find out who owns what."

"What difference does it make now?" Morgan asked her. "I don't really care who owns East Coast Properties."

"But it could tie in," Blair said. "I have a hunch."

"You can't go alone," Jonathan said. "It's too dangerous."

"Then come with me," she said. "Please. It's something I really need to do. Maybe it'll shed some light on all of this."

"All right," Morgan said. "But we have to tell Cade where we're going in case he finds Sadie."

Within half an hour after getting to the library, Blair had found what she was looking for—the owners of each of the dummy corporations.

"Just what I thought," she said. "Randall and Nancy Simmons . . . and look—Fred Hutchins."

"The mayor?" Jonathan asked. "You've got to be kidding."

"So this is why he was so gung ho about closing us down. Between him and Nancy, they got the whole city council inflamed against us."

"Boy, this smells bad," Blair said. "The mayor convincing the City Council to close us down, the judge casting doubt on Gus and Jonathan by keeping them locked up. Rick Dugan dead after Nancy publishes a bunch of lies about him, Sadie kidnapped from their very house—"

"I think I'm gonna be sick," Morgan said through tight lips. "To think that Mama and Pop might have been—murdered over money."

"I bet they knew about all these dummy corporations," Blair whispered. She turned around in her chair. "Morgan, remember that day—how confident they were about the City Council meeting? When I talked to Pop that afternoon, he told me not to worry, that there had been some new developments. Maybe they'd discovered who was behind East Coast Properties and that the city's threat to close them down was only to force them into selling, so the mayor and the judge could get their hands on the property and turn it into some kind of tourist trap. Maybe the judge knew it and wanted to shut them up."

"But what about Jack? Where does he fit into the whole thing?"

"Maybe he's just a pawn."

Jonathan grabbed his keys. "Come on. We're going to find Cade and tell him what we know."

CHAPTER

80

*T*hey found Cade at the South Beach Pier, where Rick's body had washed up. The rain hammered down as they approached the yellow crime scene tape and asked for Bruce, the police sergeant, to get the chief. Rick's body wasn't visible from where they stood, for a crowd of police blocked the view. If it had been, Blair would have had to turn away. She couldn't bear the sight of another dead body.

Cade's eyes were alive with fire and fury as he crossed the sand toward them.

"What happened to him?" Blair asked.

"He was murdered," Cade whispered. "Neck was broken. He was probably dead before he hit the water."

"Cade, we need to talk," Blair whispered. "I just finished tracing the companies that own East Coast Properties. You'll never guess who's on the list of owners."

"Who?"

"Judge Randy Simmons, his wife, Nancy—and the dear mayor of our town."

"*My uncle?*" Cade asked. He took a step back, turned around to the crowd of cops working the scene, then settled his eyes back on Blair. "It's not possible," he whispered. "My uncle's not a killer."

"They were trying to force the sale through," Blair said. "He was in on it, Cade. I think our parents knew. I think they'd found out and were going to expose them. That's why they wound up dead."

"Blair, it's one thing to carry out a shady business deal, but to kill over it . . . ?"

"Think about it. If it came out that Randy and Nancy Simmons and Fred Hutchins were part owners in the company, people all over the island would put two and two together. They own dozens of places around town, and a lot of them were sold when the owners were at the end of their ropes financially, sometimes due to hassles from the city council. East Coast Properties happens to extend an offer at the right time, and people are so fed up they sell. The judge would lose his bench and be disbarred, no one would ever trust Nancy's paper again, and the mayor would be forced to resign. Not to mention the fact that they'd probably be in trouble with the IRS once all their holdings were exposed."

Cade looked back to the place where Rick's body lay. "So the article about Rick and his subsequent death . . . were just to make Hanover House look even more dangerous. . . ." He closed his eyes. "And I told Randy about Sadie hiding from Jack. I even mentioned that she was one of the reasons you probably wouldn't let go of Hanover House."

"He called him," Morgan said, her face twisting at the danger they had brought upon Sadie. "Randy helped Jack get to her. So help me, if anything happens to her—"

"Can't you just go and arrest Randy?" Jonathan asked. "Right now. Handcuff him and parade him out like you did me?"

"The problem," Cade said, "is he's the one who issues the arrest warrants."

"But there must be somebody you can go to."

"There is," Cade said. "The supervising judge in the county. I can get a warrant from him. But I have to be able to convince him, and right now all we've got is circumstantial evidence and hunches. It's going to take some heavy persuading ... and some time."

"We may not *have* time," Morgan cried. "Cade, you've got to hurry before they kill again."

Cade swallowed and looked back toward the body. When he turned back to them, that fire in his eyes burned brighter. "Okay, you've got to keep this quiet," he said. "If word gets out, it could all slip through our fingers."

"Not a word from us," Blair said. "Just please hurry. Randy may know where Jack went with Sadie. If you can get him to talk, it could save Sadie's life."

CHAPTER

81

*A*s Blair, Morgan, and Jonathan drove
back toward Hanover House, Blair scanned the woods
through one car window and the water through the
other. They drove past the Crab Shack tourist trap, carefully hidden in the woods on the north side of the island,
where the boats made their way up and down the Bull
River. They drove past Chutney Creek, where Toothless
Joe started his dolphin tours. And they drove past the
gate to their own boathouse.

It was open and there were tire tracks in the mud.
Blair caught her breath.

"Jonathan, were you at the boathouse today?"

"Not in this rain."

"Then why's the gate open?"

Jonathan met her eyes in the rearview mirror. "You
don't think . . ."

"Turn the car around!" Morgan cried.

He made a U-turn on the road, then pulled into the
muddy driveway. The boathouse couldn't be seen from the

entrance. He stopped the car. "There are clear tracks going in, but it doesn't look like they came back out."

Morgan's face lost all color, and she grabbed her husband's arm. "Jonathan, we've got to get to a phone. We have to call Cade."

"How would Jack know about the boathouse?" Jonathan asked. "Sadie wouldn't tell him."

Blair clutched the gun in her pocket and opened the car door. "Maybe Randy did, as a way to help him stay low until he could get out of town. I'm going down there to find out. Cade said he's driving an old gray Malibu. If it's his car, I'll signal you, and you can go call the police."

"No, Blair!" Jonathan said. "If anybody's going, I am. Get back in the car."

But Blair's mind was made up. She jumped out of the car and took off into the trees before anyone could stop her.

CHAPTER

$\mathcal{B}$lair's feet slipped on the mud. She fell to her knees, got up, and steadied herself on a tree. She searched for footholds, rocks or tree roots or grass.... The storm roared overhead, dripping through the trees.

She trudged on, stepping carefully, her feet sliding and sucking. She pushed through the brush, stepping over decayed logs and straining to see the boathouse through the trees. As the small structure came into view, she saw the Malibu parked in front.

Just as she started to turn back and tell Jonathan and Morgan, a scream ripped through the air—

Sadie!

Something erupted inside her, hot and volcanic. Another murder was taking place, and she was close enough to stop it.

She launched forward, tripping and skidding in the mud. She reached the door and threw it open. Jack stood over Sadie, who was crumpled in a heap at his feet.

He swung around, training his rifle on Blair. She raised her .22.

Sadie raised herself up behind him and flung her body at him as his gun went off. The bullet missed as Blair hit the floor. She kept the gun aimed at him, but she knew she couldn't fire. Sadie was too close . . .

Suddenly, Jack dove for Blair, knocking the breath out of her and grabbing her pistol.

Sadie's screams shrieked through the air, and she got into the boat and hunkered down. Jack put his muddy boot on the scarred side of Blair's neck, holding her down with the barrel of his rifle on her temple.

Blair's mind raced with hot, dizzying images: her parents' bodies on the warehouse floor, Rick dead on the beach, Morgan terrorized in Blair's own home, Sadie on the floor of the boat, abused and beaten . . .

Adrenaline burst through her head, and she told herself she would not die here . . . not like this . . .

She twisted her body, knocking him off balance. The gun fired again as she scrambled into the boat. Sadie grabbed her, trembling. Blair groped around. There were things she could use for a weapon. The anchor . . . where did they keep the anchor . . . ?

But there was no time.

He brought her .22 up . . . aimed . . .

Blair grabbed Sadie, threw her off the end of the boat, and dove in after her. Her face slapped the cold water, but she pulled deep into the emerald darkness, her eyes open and searching for the girl . . .

Sadie's eyes were panicked as she groped toward the top for air, weakly fighting the current. Blair followed her up toward the angry, rain-rocked surface and drew in a deep breath as she came out of the water.

She heard a crack like thunder, and pain shattered through her, thrusting her back under, ripping through her side. She gurgled water, and blood floated up around her as she sank deeper, deeper . . .

She was dying, she thought. Bleeding to death at the hand of a maniac . . .

She sputtered in the water and tried to pull herself up, but the current was too strong, and the strength had been blown out of her . . .

Darkness closed over her as the water marked its claim.

Sadie gasped for air, sputtered to stay at the top, and searched frantically around her for Blair. Jack stood in the bobbing boat, holding that rifle.

She tried to swim, but pain ratcheted through her arm, rendering it useless. Where was Blair? She had to find her.

She went under again, her face stinging in the salt water, and saw the cloud of blood.

She shot out of the water and sucked in air.

The gun fired, and she screamed wretchedly, desperately . . .

Jack splashed into the water.

Sadie blinked the water from her eyes and tried to find him. She saw the blood rippling out from where he'd fallen.

Confusion played in tandem with her fear, and she found it hard to focus, hard to think, hard to tread water—

Then she saw Randy Simmons, standing on the opposite bank with a gun in his hand. The world slowly shifted into clear focus. The judge had shot Jack. He had come to rescue her. He could save Blair, and pull Sadie from the water. It was over, she thought. All over.

She started to swim toward him, her rescuer, her salvation . . .

But he slowly raised his gun again.

CHAPTER

*A*fter receiving Morgan's frantic phone call, Cade arrived at the boathouse entrance in moments. Morgan was there, standing in the rain near the gate and crying for help.

Jonathan had gone down after Blair, and as Cade, McCormick, and J.J. Clyde fanned out to make their way down to the building, they heard the gunshot rack the air like a thunderclap through the sky.

Cade's world seemed to retreat into slow motion, while his body lunged fast-forward toward the sound of water splashing, someone gasping for breath, a woman crying . . .

He reached the door and went in barrel first. Competing images slammed through Cade's brain: Jack in the boat, his rifle aiming, a blood cloud in the water, Sadie sputtering and splashing . . .

He raised his gun, but before his finger closed over the trigger, another shot fired, and Jack doubled and splashed into the water.

Again, the world moved slowly, seconds like hours, as Cade sought the source of the bullet. He saw Sadie calling for Blair, jerking in a circle in the angry water, seeing someone on the other side of the river.

His eyes moved up, to the lone figure standing in the trees, the man's gun following Sadie's progress as she swam toward him.

Cade raised his gun with both hands, and muttered a silent, pleading prayer . . .

He fired.

The municipal judge of Cape Refuge dropped to the ground.

Sadie went under, then bobbed back up, screaming out her terror at the horrors unfolding around her, closing in on her, floating near her—

But Cade couldn't see Blair.

"Blair!" he shouted, but he knew without waiting for an answer that one of the circles of blood at the top of the water was hers.

He dove in and swam out past Sadie, came up for a gasp of air, and looked around. Seeing nothing, he dove down again, searching for her, swimming, searching, swimming—

He came up again, and as he did, he saw Jonathan breaking up out of the water, pulling Blair with him.

She didn't gasp for air, didn't fight for release. Her face was white, and even her scars were void of color.

"She's shot," Jonathan yelled.

Cade took her from Jonathan's arms and carried her to the river wall. Sirens blared and horns bleated, but Blair couldn't wait for help.

He laid her down, his heart wildly beating, ticking out escaping seconds. Cade bent over her and pressed his mouth against hers, began pumping air into her lungs. As he did he sent a soul-deep cry up to heaven, pleading with God not to take her yet.

CHAPTER

*B*lair woke to a blur of voices and faces. She began to cough and sputter; then she vomited on the dirt. Her lungs rebelled with a fit of coughing, and a sharp pain webbed out from her side.

"She was shot in the back," someone shouted. "She's lost a lot of blood."

Hands poked and prodded, needles pierced, voices yelled in sounds she couldn't understand.

She felt herself being lifted, rolled, loaded ...

And numbing fatigue removed her from it all.

Hours later, Blair woke, groggy in the aftermath of anesthesia. She recognized that she was in a hospital bed with an IV in her arm. Morgan lay in the small space next to her.

"Couldn't you afford a bed of your own?"

Morgan sucked in a breath and lifted her head. Tears filled her eyes, but she started to laugh. "You're awake."

"What'd they do to me?"

"They repaired the hole in your side. Jack almost killed you."

"Is he dead or alive?"

"Dead. The Honorable Judge Randy Simmons shot him. Then Cade shot Randy."

"Randy? Where was he?"

"Across the river," Morgan said. "It was all a setup. He told Jack to hide there with Sadie until he came. He was going to kill them both to get Sadie out of the way because Cade told him we wouldn't sell the house because of her. Jack was his pawn; someone to blame when Sadie wound up dead. He didn't count on you showing up before he could silence both of them."

Blair just stared at Morgan for a moment, taking it all in.

Morgan tipped her head, and grief reddened her face. "He killed Mama and Pop, Blair. Just like you thought."

Blair swallowed. "I hope he's dead, too."

"No. He's alive. Just barely. He's in intensive care, unconscious. They don't know if he'll make it through the night. Cade arrested Nancy and Fred Hutchins a few hours ago. Nancy's confessed to her part as an accessory in exchange for some kind of plea bargain. Fred caved pretty quickly too and spilled his guts to get out of a murder-one charge. Said Randy killed Mama and Pop because they were going to expose him at the city council meeting. Randy broke into the shed and stole the speargun the night before, to set Jonathan up. It almost worked. Jonathan's fight with Mama and Pop that morning only helped Randy's plan along."

Blair closed her eyes as the pain of that information cut through her. As much as she had wanted to know, as hard as she had struggled to solve this crushing mystery, the truth only made her grief twist into bitter, burning anger. "How did he do it?" she asked. "How did he get in and out of the church in broad daylight, without being seen?"

"Came through the water, went in the side door. Fred said that Randy told him he shot Pop first. Mama fell to his side, and Randy had time to reload and shoot her too."

Tears rolled down Blair's face, and Morgan wiped them away. "Unbelievable," Blair said. "The good guys die, and the bad guys live to cheat justice and move on."

"They won't cheat justice," Morgan said. "And Randy may not cheat death. Besides, good guys don't always die." She touched Blair's face and tilted her head as tears rolled down her cheeks. "Sometimes the bullet misses all of the major organs, and the good guy lives to see justice done."

"That a fact?" Blair asked in a weak whisper. "I could've sworn this was going to be that conversation you'd always remember. My last words."

Morgan smiled and wiped another tear. "Well, I have no doubt that you *will* have the last word, in this and almost every other conversation we have. Or you'll try. But I guess I have to remind you that I'm older than you, so according to nature, and probably God, I'm supposed to go first. Sorry, Sis, but that's just the way it's got to be."

"We'll see about that." Blair lay still, looking up at the sister and friend who had always been there for her. She reached for Morgan's hand and squeezed it hard. Morgan leaned down and hugged her, and the two sisters clung together, as grief and relief battled for places in their hearts.

Blair slept for a while, then woke to find her sister, sitting in a chair beside her bed, her Bible open in her lap. "You haven't been quoting scripture to me in my sleep, have you?" she asked weakly. "Trying to give me some kind of subliminal conversion experience?"

Morgan smiled and closed the Bible. "How do you feel?"

"Like I've been drawn and quartered. But hey, I'm tough."

"God was with you in that water, Blair. I know you don't want to admit it, but he was. And he was with Sadie."

"Good," Blair whispered. "I mean, that she's all right. She sure had the deck stacked against her."

"There was no deck, Blair. God was on his throne the whole time." Morgan leaned over her, her eyes wet and sad. "Blair, after you came out of surgery, I was sitting beside you, waiting for you to wake up, wondering if you would. And I thought a lot about what you asked the other day. About where God was when Mama and Pop were screaming for their lives."

Blair closed her eyes. "I don't want to talk about it, Morgan."

"Well, I do," Morgan said. "And since you're too weak to fight me, I'm going to have my say. Earlier today I read again in Genesis about Joseph. His brothers threw him into a pit—"

"I know the story, Morgan," Blair said wearily. "I grew up hearing it just like you. His brothers were jealous, sold him to slave-traders."

"But think about it," Morgan said. "You want to know where God was when tragedy struck our family. He was on the same throne as he was when Joseph was in that pit, screaming and begging for his brothers to let him out. When he was bound and dragged off to Egypt. When he was thrown into jail for something he hadn't done—"

"You're making my point for me, Morgan. Either he's a helpless god watching a world spin out of control, or he's a mean god orchestrating the cruelest kind of pain. If you want to believe in a god like that, Morgan, be my guest."

"You're not thinking, Blair. Think about the suffering Joseph went through. The injustice. The tragedy and loss and heartache. But it was for a purpose. He had to be there, to save his family when there was a famine. He saved a nation, Blair. God put him there for a reason. And he told his brothers that what they had intended for evil, God meant for good."

Blair was getting angry. "So—what? God murdered my parents so I could save a nation? I don't think so, Blair, not from Cape Refuge, Georgia. Tell me what good can come of that."

"Blair, when things looked dark and grim for those first people of Israel, God gave them a savior. When things were dark and grim for Mama and Pop, there was a savior."

"No, there wasn't!" Blair shouted. "He didn't save them!"

Morgan's answer came on a tearful whisper. "Oh, yes, he did, Blair. He saved them, all right. Took them right to heaven. Salvation was there, when evil tried to take them out. Our parents probably died with the name of Jesus on their lips, and when they called him, he came for them. They're with him now."

Blair was too tired to fight. She just let out a long, loud sigh. "It's a comforting thought, Morgan. I'm glad you believe it."

When Cade and Jonathan came in, the conversation ended, but Blair played it through her mind for the rest of the night, dreaming of her parents in heaven, laughing and young, standing at a sea of glass, full of some nameless wonder that no mortal could ever describe.

She woke up angry—at her parents, at her sister, at Matthew Cade, at the mayor, and at Nancy and the judge who had instigated the greatest injustices in her life.

And most especially at the Honorable Judge Randy Simmons, who lay in a hospital bed one floor beneath her . . . probably plotting his defense.

She had sworn that when she learned who had killed her parents, she would kill him herself. She owed that to her parents, she thought. She owed it to herself.

Morgan lay sleeping on the small sofa by the window. Blair sat up, waited to get her balance, then tested her legs. Though pain shot through her side, she was able to stand. Shaking, she pulled off the tape covering her IV needle. Then she pulled the needle out.

She walked barefoot to the door, peered out, and saw that the hall was quiet. Slowly, she walked toward the elevators. She pressed the button for the fourth floor and got off at the intensive care waiting room. People slept in plastic recliners with blankets too short to cover them completely. She wondered if anyone was there waiting for word on Randy.

The double doors of intensive care required a security code, so she waited in the hall until a nurse came out. She caught the door before it swung shut, and she slipped inside. She made her way from one care cubicle to another, careful to avoid the nurses in the center station.

Finally, she saw him. She could see the long gray hair and his tanned face, though the dark circles under his eyes spoke of his battle with death. The floor was cold beneath her bare feet as she went into the room and stood over his bed. Hatred tore at her like a hungry animal as she gazed down at him. He was hooked up to several monitors and had a respirator mask over his mouth. She thought of unplugging it, watching him choke and struggle until the life smothered right out of him.

But she didn't move. She just stood there ... staring down at the man who had killed her parents ... hating herself for not grabbing that plug.

"What are you doing here?" The nurse's bold voice startled her, and she swung around.

"I just wanted to talk to him."

"He can't talk to you. He's in a coma," she said.

She let the nurse usher her out of the intensive care unit. Then she stood in the hall, feeling weak and tired and helpless. He would probably die anyway, but her parents would still be gone, and Rick Dugan's death would still be senseless and without purpose.

It was all out of her hands.

She just didn't know whose hands it was in. A benevolent, gentle god with some great purpose, or a cruel, unfeeling god who saw them all as toys to be shuffled around.

But her troubled mind wanted her life to be in someone's hands. The thought of it all being random, hopeless, was more distressing than anything else she had suffered.

Slowly, she made her way back to her room, but any kind of peaceful rest was out of her reach.

CHAPTER

85

*O*n the day Blair was to be released from the hospital, Sadie and Morgan fussed over her, driving her nuts. Sadie looked worse than she had when she had come to Cape Refuge, but her arm had been re-set and her wounds were healing. She and Morgan chattered like kids as they packed Blair's things. Then the room got quiet as five members of the City Council filed in.

Awkwardly, Sarah Williford said, "Blair, we wanted to come together today to tell you how sorry we are about all that happened ... with us closing down Hanover House and everything. We were taken in just like you were. Fred was working us hard, trying to convince us it was the right thing to do. And with the murders and the articles coming out in the paper ..." Her voice trailed off.

"We were caught up in the emotion and fear," one of the others said. "We hope you'll forgive us."

"Truth is," Sarah said, "our phones have been ringing off the hook. Half the town has called us to tell us not to close Hanover House. Folks are fed up with change on this island. That's one change they especially don't want."

Blair met Morgan's eyes, then looked at Sarah again. "I'm a little fuzzy with all the medication and stuff. You'll have to make this real clear for me. Are you saying . . . ?"

"We've rescinded the order to close Hanover House."

As she and Morgan embraced with the thrill of victory, Blair began to wonder if miracles did happen, after all.

That night they got Blair home from the hospital, and Morgan smiled as she apologized to Gus for suspecting him. He wrote her a song on the spot and played it with a reggae beat on his guitar. It actually made Blair smile. Sadie laughed out loud, the first time they had ever heard that, and Gus promised to write her one next.

Later that night, as Morgan lay next to Jonathan in bed, he brought up something that had been on his mind. "Something's got to be done about that baby," he said. "Little Caleb, Sadie's brother."

"I know," she whispered. "They're not going to let Sadie have him. And he can't spend those crucial years going from one foster home to another."

"Unless it was this one."

Morgan sat up in bed and smiled down at him. "Do you really think we could take him?"

"I can't imagine leaving him there."

"But what about his mother? We'd get attached to him, and then she'd get out of prison and want him back."

"She'll need a place to stay when she gets out," Jonathan said. "We could take her too."

Morgan began to laugh and threw her hand over her mouth. "Jonathan, I love you. I really, really love you!"

He grinned and pulled her back down. "This doesn't mean we'll quit trying to have one of our own."

"Of course not," she whispered, and melted into a kiss that tasted like joy.

She knew the dark hours of her suffering had passed and light shone over her now. And in the rays of that sunshine, she thanked God for redeeming the pain and filling her with new hope.

CHAPTER

*C*aleb was not in a foster home. The HRS had no idea where he was. When Jonathan questioned them about reports of child abuse, he learned that they had only interviewed Jack Dent but had never actually removed the baby from the home.

After Sadie thought of several names of people with whom Jack might have left the baby, she, Jonathan, and Morgan took off for Atlanta.

They found Caleb at the home of one of Jack's girl-friends who lived in a trailer park with mounds of garbage festering in a ditch outside. She answered the door with a glazed look in her eyes.

"Stacy, did Jack leave Caleb with you?" Sadie asked.

"You bet he did," the woman said, letting them in. "It's about time somebody got here."

They heard Caleb crying in a back room. Sadie ran through the house and snatched him out of a playpen. The child was dirty, with thick caked snot crusting his nose. "Sadie's here, sweetie," she said, crying as she pressed her face close to his. "Oh, honey, Sadie's here."

His sobs faded into hiccups, and he looked up at her with mournful eyes. She held him tight as he laid his head against her chest.

"Jack said two days," the woman shouted. "Two days, and here it's going on a week. I thought that kid'd never shut up."

She ran and got his diaper bag and the things she had in the refrigerator, threw them into the bag, and thrust them at Morgan. "Take him. Good riddance. And tell Jack Dent that he owes me big for this."

"I'm sorry, Stacy," Morgan said. "But Jack's dead."

The woman gaped up at her, then turned to look at Sadie. "Is that true?"

Sadie nodded. "He was shot . . . trying to kill me."

Stacy was quiet as they gathered the rest of Caleb's things and loaded them into the car.

As Sadie hooked him into the car seat they had brought with them, the child put his thumb in his mouth and looked up at his sister.

"I missed you," Sadie cried softly. "Big time. I'm sorry I left you. I'll never do it again."

He hiccuped another sigh, and she kissed his wet cheek. Morgan leaned over him with tears in her eyes as she saw what a beautiful child he was. "We're so blessed, Sadie," she whispered. "Jesus is watching over us."

"I know," Sadie said. "He's answered my prayers. He saved me from death . . . and from Jack. And he saved Caleb too."

Before they left Atlanta they went by the jail, where Sadie had a brief reunion with her mother. Morgan and Jonathan got to know Caleb in the car, keeping him out of the jail so as not to traumatize him further with the confusing sight of a mother he couldn't touch. Sheila Caruso signed the papers allowing Morgan and Jonathan to take temporary custody until she was out of jail.

She was neither surprised nor saddened to hear of Jack's death.

In fact, no one mourned Jack's death.

No one at all.

CHAPTER

*B*ut Rick was mourned for. On the day of his funeral, Blair, Morgan, Cade, Sadie, Gus, and Mrs. Hern were the only ones who attended. As it turned out, he was all that he said he was. He had never killed anyone, and there really was a wife and baby who had died. It seemed that Randy Simmons had set him up because he was convenient, having the most mysterious background of all the tenants at Hanover House.

Cleaning out Rick's room after he was found, Morgan had found Rick's journal. Jonathan read an entry from it as he stood at the pulpit in their warehouse church. It was written on the day that Thelma and Wayne had given him the check for ten thousand dollars.

"'Thelma and Wayne discovered the money,'" Jonathan read. "'And I felt more shame than I'd ever felt in my life. I finally decided I would take the money back, put it right back where I'd found it, and Gerald Madison would never know it was gone. I thought Thelma and Wayne were going to turn me in, anyway, have me arrested, and I figured I deserved it.

"'Instead, they told me they knew about the money, and they handed me a check for ten thousand dollars. Said it would pay my debts in the same way that Christ had paid my spiritual debt. They were more concerned about my soul than they were about justice. It moved me to tears. It moved me to Christ.'"

Jonathan's voice cracked as he read those last words, and he looked up across the meager congregation, saw the tears on his wife's face . . .

. . . and on Blair's.

After the burial, Blair and Morgan sat quietly on a bench at the grave site, staring at the mound of dirt with flowers laid over it. "He's with his family now," Morgan said. "His wife and his daughter. And with Jesus."

"I wish I could believe that," Blair whispered.

"You can," Morgan said. "You know in your heart that it's true."

She struggled with the thought. "Morgan, why did Mama and Pop do the things they did for people? Like giving Rick ten thousand dollars? That was probably their life's savings. There sure wasn't much left in the bank. Why did they feel such a need to provide refuge for the lost and the weak and the despairing? Why did they give people so many chances?"

"Because it had been done for them."

Blair tried to get her mind around the thought of grace being dispensed because grace had redeemed them. But grace was a concept that couldn't be seen or smelled or tasted . . . and as much as she wanted to stand on ground as solid as that beneath Morgan, she still couldn't quite believe.

Morgan hugged her, kissed her on the cheek, then got up and left her alone there to think.

Cade had been watching from the street, hoping for a chance to talk to Blair, but when Morgan had joined her on the bench, he hadn't wanted to intrude on a private moment.

When Morgan left Blair alone, Cade got out of his car. Blair was alone at last. He started down the hill toward her.

She looked up at him.

"Mind if I sit down?" he asked.

She shrugged and nodded, and he took the seat that Morgan had just left. Quiet settled between them. Blair looked past the gravestones to the water beyond, to the sailboats lined up in the harbor. "I'm thinking of leaving Cape Refuge soon," she said. "As soon as I'm well enough."

"I've been thinking about that too," Cade said. "About what it would be like here without you."

She looked over at him, surprised that he had given it any thought at all.

His eyes were misty, serious, as he held her gaze. "I really wish you wouldn't go, Blair."

She swallowed and looked back at the harbor. Something about those words changed things in her mind. She didn't even know why. She couldn't think of a thing to say, so she just sat there staring, and he sat there with her, quietly content in her presence.

For the first time in her life, she didn't analyze the peace that he seemed to radiate like a warm wind. She just borrowed from it—astonished at the way he seemed to fill in the loneliness.

And she wondered if there was really any hurry to leave Cape Refuge. Maybe she would stay for just a while longer.

T H E   E N D

AFTERWORD

I don't understand suffering. This past year has been a time of grief for my family and many of my friends, and if I could, I would lift it off us and make it go away. But I can't.

At this writing, I'm grieving over the death of Landon Von Kanel, my daughter's eighteen-year-old friend, who was taken unexpectedly in a car accident. Just two years ago, we buried another of her friends, Anthony Shams, sixteen. Both of these young men had circles of influence that reached far across the globe. Their unique and vibrant personalities, their colorful wit, their big dreams, made them unforgettable and irreplaceable. I daresay that thousands have been impacted by their deaths, many for eternity. But I don't understand why Randy and Cindy, or Deborah and Al had to bury their children.

My friend Rick McMahan died a year ago. He was a mentor and friend to my husband and me. He and his wife, Lynda, were a true brother and sister. I miss seeing him on Wednesday nights after church, leaning on the visitor's booth as he waited for his wife and daughter to come down from youth group. He was the one I always gravitated to, to air my latest complaints about children or parenthood or life. He always seemed so in tune with God, and his wisdom always challenged me. I miss him on Sunday mornings. He and his family used to sit behind us, worshiping the Lord and shedding tears over his goodness and his awesome sovereignty. I miss him on Sunday nights, when we would sit together and worship again, and share stories and laughter and praises afterward. I miss his sense of humor, and his hugs, and the peace that he radiated. I miss the fact that my youngest child will not get to go through his Sunday school class and experience the love he had for the kids to whom he ministered. I miss the way his marriage set an example for the rest of us, of love and protection and nurturing and endurance.

I don't know why God chose to take Rick so early, or why he allowed him to suffer as cancer ravaged his body. I don't know why Lynda and his children, Kerry and Brad, had to say good-bye to their husband and father.

I have also grieved for Stephanie Whitson, another Christian writer, who said good-bye to her husband, Bob, after a long, exhausting struggle with cancer. In his last days, when he could barely sit up, Bob searched through his Bible for reasons that we suffer and wrote it all down. This long list of God's reasons for putting us through adversity has blessed my friend Lynda as she has grieved and suffered over Rick's death. It has also blessed many, many others. And his love and urgency to make others understand the Lord will live on long after him. Bob's teaching and his wisdom will continue to work in the lives of all those he touched. Yet Stephanie has a hole in her life, and she and their children miss him terribly.

And I have grieved for a friend, Patricia Hickman, another Christian writer who is completely sold out to the Lord. She and her husband, Randy, have devoted their lives to planting churches and drawing people into a knowledge of Jesus Christ. Why, then, did God choose to take their beautiful twenty-year-old daughter, Jessi, in another terrible car accident? I have so many questions for the Lord, so many whys as I weep for that loss that can never be replaced. With a daughter almost the same age, who has the same goals and interests as Jessi, I find myself shaken and humbled and slightly frightened by the suddenness of death. And my heart is broken for this dear family.

But I see so much fruit that has sprung up from these deaths and know that entire crops are yet to come. And I can't help remembering that my own salvation was the result of the death of a boy in my school, Ricky Bogan, a fifteen-year-old who died in an accident on the way home from school. Whatever fruit I bear is his fruit too. And despite the sorrow his death produced in me as a fourteen-year-old seeker, I am glad that God used it to bring me to him. I know the Lord well enough to trust that he is doing the same to many others as the result of these deaths.

Psalm 116:15 says, "Precious in the sight of the LORD is the death of his saints." I know this is true, and I also know that Jesus weeps over our losses, and he shares our grief. But he also sees the future, and he sees the whole picture. He knows his purpose in taking Landon and Anthony and Rick and Jessi and Bob. And he's already seen the reunions that are yet to come. Joyful, over-whelming, celebratory reunions.

We cannot control God, and we cannot second-guess him, as much as we'd like to try. Our God has plans and purposes that are far beyond our understanding.

Sometimes those plans and purposes break our hearts.

Sometimes they require sacrifices we never agreed to make.

Sometimes they stop us dead in our tracks, turn us upside down, inside out, and paralyze us with pain.

But his comfort is not far behind. And as we climb up into his lap and weep into his chest, he whispers in our ear, "Shhh. It's okay. I did it for a reason, and some day I'll tell you what it is." He strokes our hair and hugs us tight, and cries with us. "Shhh. Just hang on. It's not that long before you'll see them again. And then you'll be with them for eternity. I promise to see you through this."

Our whys are not answered, but we trust that there is a reason. God is in control, and he loves us through our pain.

As the song says, "Life is hard, but God is good." How precious is that goodness, and how sufficient is his comfort. And how thrilling are his promises of what will happen when he returns for us.

Come quickly, Lord Jesus!

ABOUT THE AUTHOR

Terri Blackstock is an award-winning novelist who has written for several major publishers including HarperCollins, Dell, Harlequin, and Silhouette. Published under two pseudonyms, her books have sold over 5 million copies worldwide.

With her success in secular publishing at its peak, Blackstock had what she calls "a spiritual awakening." A Christian since the age of fourteen, she realized she had not been using her gift as God intended. It was at that point that she recommitted her life to Christ, gave up her secular career, and made the decision to write only books that would point her readers to him.

"I wanted to be able to tell the truth in my stories," she said, "and not just be politically correct. It doesn't matter how many readers I have if I can't tell them what I know about the roots of their problems and the solutions that have literally saved my own life."

Her books are about flawed Christians in crisis and God's provisions for their mistakes and wrong choices. She claims to be extremely qualified to write such books, since she's had years of personal experience.

A native of nowhere, since she was raised in the Air Force, Blackstock makes Mississippi her home. She and her husband are the parents of three children — a blended family which she considers one more of God's provisions.

Terri Blackstock (www.terriblackstock.com) is the #1 bestselling author of the Cape Refuge, Sun Coast Chronicles, Second Chances, and Newpointe 911 suspense series, and other books.
With Beverly LaHaye, she wrote *Seasons Under Heaven*, *Times and Seasons*, *Showers in Season*, and *Season of Blessing*.

The Highly Anticipated
Sequel to *Cape Refuge*!

Southern Storm
Cape Refuge Series

Terri Blackstock

Police Chief Cade disappears after
hitting and killing a man with his car.
Without a trace, without a note, without taking clothes or his car
or money, he is gone. When a witness says she saw Cade getting
into a blue Buick with a woman before his disappearance, the
newspapers report that Cade left town to be with her. Blair knows
it doesn't make sense for Cade to leave without word for any reason. The dead man is identified, and it soon becomes clear that
the woman Cade was seen with was the wife of the dead man.
Newspapers begin to ask hard questions. Was the Cape Refuge
Chief of Police having an affair with this woman? Did he deliberately kill her husband and then make it look like an accident?
When the police department receives a handwritten note from
Cade that he has run off to get married to a woman he's kept
secret, everyone breathes a sigh of relief. But Blair notices his
unusual signature: Matt Cade. Cade never goes by his first name,
and he especially never calls himself "Matt." She thinks it's a signal from him that the contents of the note are false.

Meanwhile, around the south, there are news reports about
babies being kidnapped from area hospitals. When a ransom call
comes to Hanover House from the baby's kidnapper, they are all
shocked to see that the phone it is traced to is Cade's cell phone.
Is he involved in the baby's disappearance? Is that why he's disappeared?

Softcover: 978-0-310-23593-4

CHAPTER

1

The Georgia Weather Bureau's prophecy of fifty-mile-per-hour winds had been fulfilled and surpassed, much to Matthew Cade's chagrin. As chief of the small Cape Refuge police force, Cade could do little about the ravages of the storm as it beat across the island toward Savannah. But the safety of the residents was always his concern.

Though it was two in the afternoon, the sky looked as dark as nightfall.

Lightning bolted overhead in a panoramic display of white-hot fingers, grounding on the island and splaying across the angry Atlantic. The thunder cracked in rapid crashes, and rain slatted down at an angle that made umbrellas useless and flooded some of the streets.

Cade strained to see through the windshield of his squad car. The rain pounding on his roof and his wipers slashing across his windshield made it difficult for him to hear the radio crackling on his dashboard. He turned it up.

Fender benders had been reported at three locations on Cape Refuge, and a power line was down near the condos lining the north beach.

If everyone would just stay inside, maybe they could avoid any more problems. But that never happened. On days like this, residents insisted on driving through the storm at the same speeds they used on dry, sunny days. Tornado watchers stood out on their front porches, watching the sky for funnel clouds. And the most reckless among the residents would brave the lightning and drag their surfboards out to the waves, hoping to catch a thrill in the tempest.

Cade and his police force were left to clean up the messes and head off new disasters.

The dispatcher's voice crackled across the radio, and he picked up the mike. "Go ahead, Sal."

"Chief, there's another power line down on a road over at the dock. Somebody's going to get hurt unless you detour that traffic."

Cade sighed. "All right, I'm on my way."

He set the mike back in its holder and turned on his blue lights. Making a U-turn, he headed back around the southern tip of the island, then northbound toward the dock. He couldn't have residents driving over live power lines. He hoped the power company would hurry up and get its trucks out here.

The wipers swiped across his windshield, but the rain pounded too hard to give him much visibility. He strained to see.

Most cars pulled to the side of the road to let him pass. He turned on his siren to alert the others, but three or four kept their course in the lane in front of him.

"Get out of the way!" he yelled, pulling so close to the car in front of him that he knew one touch of its brakes would put him in the front seat with the driver.

Fortunately, the man pulled over. The other cars ahead of him still hadn't heard or seen him, so he moved up behind the next one, his siren still blaring. A block ahead, Cade saw a man standing on the opposite side of the road, seemingly oblivious to the rain pounding down on him. Passing traffic sprayed walls of water up over him, but he just stood there, watching the traffic pass.

The car in front of Cade still didn't move, so he punched his horn. The southbound lane with traffic coming toward him had cleared as drivers pulled off to the shoulder of Ocean Boulevard. He pulled around the car in front of him into the southbound lane and gently accelerated.

The man on the side of the road still stood there, drenched and undaunted. Cade knew that, as he passed, his tires in the water would spray him. Why didn't the man move?

He kept his siren blaring and pushed his horn again as he drove northbound in the southbound lane. He pulled even with the car that had refused to move out of the way and looked across at the driver. The driver looked back, panic evident on his face—a teenager, probably a new driver with no idea how to react. The kid slammed on his brakes.

Cade stepped on his accelerator and turned his eyes ahead again—just in time to see the pedestrian step out in front of him.

Cade yelled and slammed on his brakes. His car slid straight toward the man. . . .

Thunder cracked at the same instant as the impact. The man flew up over the hood and smashed into Cade's windshield, shattering it . . . then, as if he'd bounced, he flew out in front of the car and landed in a heap in the middle of the road. Cade couldn't move for a few seconds, then fumbled for the door handle and managed to get out. The rain flooded over him, and the wind almost knocked him back into the car. He rushed toward the man.

Oh, dear God, what have I done?

He heard yelling and doors slamming as other drivers got out and splashed toward him.

Reaching the man first, Cade knelt in three inches of water. The victim's eyes fluttered open, and his lips moved without sound. Cade grabbed the radio on his shoulder. "Sal, I need an ambulance just half a mile north of the Pier!" He yelled the words to make sure he was heard. "I need it right now! I just ran over a pedestrian!"

"Right away, Chief."

Cade touched the man's head, careful not to move it. Warm blood soaked his hand, but the pelting rain quickly washed it away.

"Can you hear me, buddy?"

The man tried to speak, but Cade couldn't hear him. Thunder crashed again.

He touched the man's throat; his pulse was weak, erratic.

"Hang on! You're gonna be all right. Just hang on." He had to stop the bleeding, so he pressed against the wound at the back of the man's head. But there was so much blood . . . too much . . .

The man tried to rise up, and this time Cade heard his raspy voice. "You have to . . . please . . . out of control . . ."

"Don't move!" What did one do for an open head wound?

He heard sirens blaring, voices calling. Someone opened an umbrella over them in a feeble attempt to shelter the victim from the storm, but the wind turned it inside out. Someone else threw a raincoat over the man. . . .

Lightning flashed, thunder bolted. . . .

"Cade," someone said, "he just ran right out in front of you!"

The blood was coming so fast. The man's pulse weakened. Where was that ambulance?

"I saw him. It was like he was in a trance or something."

"Is he dead, Cade?"

The siren grew closer, and he prayed that people would stay off the road and leave the ambulance a path. It stopped short, and he heard feet running toward him. Paramedics knelt beside the body, and Cade moved back. "Head injury," he yelled over the storm. "He bounced off my windshield."

As the medics worked, Cade backed farther away, his mind racing with the facts.

I've hit a man . . . an innocent man. . . .

He started to whisper rapid-fire prayers for a miracle. The man couldn't die. That was all there was to it. Police cars were meant to keep people from danger, not kill them.

"Call for a Medi-Vac, Cade!" one of the medics cried. "And
clear us a path. He's running out of time."

"The helicopter can't fly in this! You'll have to drive him."
He helped the paramedics get the man into the ambulance and
then directed traffic as the ambulance headed out.

He shook his head, trying to pull himself together. Somebody
had to be in charge here. But what did the chief of police do when
he was the one who had almost killed a man?

He turned and saw some of his uniformed officers coming
toward him.

"J.J., detour traffic," he yelled. "Keep it off of this block until
we finish here. Jim, get over to the downed power lines out in
front of the dock and divert traffic there. Alex, you take pictures
and work the accident...."

"But Cade, are you sure you don't want to work it?"

"I've got to get to the hospital and see if he's all right." His
voice broke. "Just write the report and treat me like any other
driver who hit a pedestrian. Call my cell phone if you have questions. It should get a signal by the time I reach Savannah." He
walked back to his car and got in.

Through the shattered windshield, he saw Alex looking back
at him as if he wasn't sure what to do. Then he turned away and
began questioning witnesses.

Cade closed his eyes and lowered his head to the steering
wheel. *That man could die.*

Why had he stepped out into traffic? He must have seen
Cade coming. The squad car lights had been flashing and his siren
was on. Even people in cars with radios blaring and air condi-
tioners humming had heard him and gotten out of the way. How
could this man have stepped into the path of a speeding police
car?

He felt as if a fist had punched a hole in his lungs. He found
it hard to breathe, and his head had begun to throb.

He reached for the keys hanging in the ignition, then realized that he couldn't move this car until they'd finished working
the scene. Besides, he couldn't drive with a busted windshield.

He got out of the car and started walking through the rain.

"Where are you going, Chief?" Alex asked him.

"To find a ride back to the station so I can get my truck."

"I'll take you, Cade!" Melba Jefferson, a little round woman who attended his church and made it her business to comfort those in need, stood nearby, fighting her umbrella with a distraught look on her face.

"Okay, Melba," he said. "Let's go."

She led him to her car parked on the side of the road. He got into it, and she slid her round body into the driver's side. "Honey, are you all right?"

He shook his head. "It's not about me, Melba. There's a man dying."

She reached into the backseat and got a box of tissue. "Sweetie, your hand's all bloody."

Cade looked at it. The man's blood had stained it, though the rain had begun to wash it away. He pulled out several tissues and wiped the rest of it off.

Melba pulled out onto the street, and Alex directed her so that she could turn around and head back to the station. When they were on their way, she stayed quiet, which Cade appreciated. Clearly, Melba knew when words were appropriate and when they weren't.

She drove him up to the station, pulled into the parking lot. "I'll get some people praying, Cade," she said.

He nodded. "You do that. Thanks for the ride, Melba."

Cade jogged across the gravel parking lot to his truck, jumped inside, and was pulling out onto the street before Melba could get her car turned around.

Other great books from Terri Blackstock

NEWPOINTE 911 SERIES

Softcover: 978-0-310-25767-2   Softcover: 978-0-310-25768-6

Softcover: 978-0-310-25769-9   Softcover: 978-0-310-25769-2   Softcover: 978-0-310-25770-7

Pick up a copy today at your favorite bookstore!

Other great books from Terri Blackstock

SECOND CHANCES SERIES

Softcover: 978-0-310-20710-8

Softcover: 978-0-310-20707-8

Softcover: 978-0-310-20708-5

Softcover: 978-0-310-20709-2

Pick up a copy today at your favorite bookstore!

Other great books from Terri Blackstock

A Restoration Novel Series

Softcover: 978-0-310-25767-7

Softcover: 978-0-310-25768-4

Softcover: 978-0-310-25769-1

Softcover: 978-0-310-25770-7

Pick up a copy today at your favorite bookstore!

ZONDERVAN®
.com

Share Your Thoughts

With the Author: Your comments will be forwarded to the author when you send them to *zauthor@zondervan.com*.

With Zondervan: Submit your review of this book by writing to *zreview@zondervan.com*.

Free Online Resources at
www.zondervan.com

Zondervan AuthorTracker: Be notified whenever your favorite authors publish new books, go on tour, or post an update about what's happening in their lives at www.zondervan.com/authortracker.

Daily Bible Verses and Devotions: Enrich your life with daily Bible verses or devotions that help you start every morning focused on God. Visit www.zondervan.com/newsletters.

Free Email Publications: Sign up for newsletters on Christian living, academic resources, church ministry, fiction, children's resources, and more. Visit www.zondervan.com/newsletters.

Zondervan Bible Search: Find and compare Bible passages in a variety of translations at www.zondervanbiblesearch.com.

Other Benefits: Register yourself to receive online benefits like coupons and special offers, or to participate in research.